A Pebble To Polish

A Pebble To Polish

Janet Lord Leszl

2007

A Pebble To Polish

To all who polish the pebbles they encounter throughout life's journey.

Also, a special note of thanks: to earthly angels who earned their wings after our devastating fire.

Life Lotteries

Chapter 1.

"This is going to be the most important day of my life. I can just feel it. If only I didn't have to spend most of it in classes," Cassie pouted to herself. "My twenty-first birthday would have to fall on a Thursday!"

In the distance Professor Stimmer droned on and on about a topic that held little interest for this bright, attractive blond. Unfortunately, if she ever wanted to graduate this was a must have class she couldn't afford to skip. The former honor student should have been acing all her courses; instead, she was just squeaking by. There were just too many distractions. College was such a bustling adventure full of friends, parties, and, oh yes, these damn classes. Cassandra Delaine had changed her major twice already; she had absolutely no idea what she wanted to do with her life. None of the required courses seemed to have any possible relevance in the real world. How was she to determine what her life's passion should be with boring classes like this one?

What little could be seen of the instructor's pudgy face was comical. Were there two eyebrows or one mass of gray cactus thorns shrouding his eyes? The lecturing figure resembled a walrus as he waddled slowly back and forth presenting tedious data. Cassie suppressed a giggle. Long bristles of his tusk-like mustache camouflaged his mouth moving forcefully up and down as if he were chewing a tremendous wad of bubble gum. Surely he was spouting important information, but his words failed to penetrate her hopelessly wandering thoughts.

Shifting the weight of her light frame, she uncrossed her shapely legs then re-crossed them again; the worn padded seat cushions provided little comfort at this late hour. Rapidly fading daylight tempted escape from the cavernous lecture hall. With nervous impatience, Cassie was driven to drum her fingers along a massive textbook.

Her attention shifted to the clock on the wall. Invisibly the minute hand pounded like a kettledrum for all to hear. Yet somehow the other students were oblivious to the thundering tic and tock as they furiously scribbled answers to potential exam questions.

Abruptly the walrus stopped in mid-stride to face his captive audience. Again a metamorphosis occurred as the massive sea lion transformed into a symphony conductor. Books slammed shut in one synchronized, grand crescendo under his direction; finally the lecture was finished.

Cassie gathered her belongings to eagerly join the departing chorus. She couldn't remember why Professor Stimmer had insisted they bring their textbooks to class this day. Even he had seemed to have forgotten the reason. Still, at last she was released from this final obligation of *her* day.

She reveled in Indian summer warmth as she strode back to the dormitory. Brilliant rust, gold, and crimson leaves clung tenaciously to ancient limbs lining the commons. The defiant foliage commanded winter to wait just a little longer. A leaf or two dared descend only to be prodded back into the air by a gentle breeze. In less then a month nature would win out: bare maples and half-naked oaks would starkly punctuate the campus. But on this glorious day the impending dreariness of winter seemed a long way off.

As Cassie walked, the Colonial-era buildings of this religious university evoked a fanciful image in her mind. She envisioned dozens of ladies in hoop-skirted gowns. Horse-drawn carriages would cart guests to a grand ball for her birthday.

This romanticized view of history made her wistful for a time women were not pressured to have a career. She chose to forget that women had no rights then; only the relatively few wives and daughters of the wealthy enjoyed such a grand lifestyle. Her visions of sweeping ball gowns certainly did not include the notion of uncomfortable laced bodices, nor did she consider the era's lack of creature comforts such as indoor plumbing or air-conditioning. Instead, she wished reality could mimic dress-up events from her past.

Smiling, she recalled a visit to colonial Williamsburg with her church's youth group. Next, her thoughts wandered to a princess-theme party where every guest had dressed in flouncy gowns. For the occasion, her father had constructed a set in the basement, complete with throne and pleated fabric tacked to the walls. Then there was the Renaissance fair. Her mother had sewn for days producing elegant costumes for their family to wear.

Her daydreams were abruptly swept aside as she arrived at her dormitory and her thoughts shifted to the present era. After all, today was her special day; it was time to do some serious partying. But there hadn't been time to discuss any plans with her friends earlier because everyone had a full day of classes.

Ignoring the musty odor of Fulton Hall, she climbed the stairs. It would be a relief to shelve her hefty textbooks for the evening. That is, if she could push the door open to her cramped room. Whoever had designed these dormitories likely never had teenage daughters. Thankfully, though, someone had the foresight to install a mirror, sink, and towel bar in each room; otherwise mornings with a whole floor full of females in the common bathroom would be a nightmare.

The message board by her doorway was empty of birthday greetings. *Strange*, she thought. Maybe there were some cards slid under the door. Aware that most of her friends had little money for gifts, she certainly expected they would at least spend a couple of dollars for a birthday card. After all, whenever one of her friends had a birthday, Cassie happily labored over racks of cards in the stationary store for just the right one. Undoubtedly, there would be a pile waiting for her to open.

She pushed the door open to find her roommate straining over the sink to get a better view of her reflection in the mirror above it. A contact lens was poised on her forefinger an inch away from her right eye.

"Jeez, Cassie, you startled me! I nearly poked my eye out." Contact lens now in place, Angela Corletti quickly ran a comb through her short, curly black hair, then casually tied a lightweight sweatshirt around her shoulders. "Oh, by the way, happy birthday."

A quick glance around the room revealed no waiting stack of greetings to be read.

Angela continued. "Cassie, I've got an early class tomorrow. I can't stay up too late, so I'll tell Beth and Cindy to bring some champagne to our room tonight for a toast. We'll have to wait and go out tomorrow night to really celebrate. Come on; let's go get some grub from the dinning hall. I'll round up the girls when we're through."

Normally Cassie enjoyed her roommate's bubbly, take-charge personality. But this evening she was disappointed that her momentous birthday failed to generate a more enthusiastic response in such a close friend. The girls had met near the end of their freshman year and quickly grew to be more like sisters; the following semester they requested to room together.

Angela's persona was stereotypical of her Italian ancestry. She was gregarious, quick to anger, and just as quick to resume an affable temperament. Striking up a conversation with a complete stranger and getting them to like her was as easy as breathing for Angela. In fact, she probably could have a pleasant discussion with a brick wall if she wanted to.

But none of this cheered Cassie now. Hoping to raise her falling spirits she asked, "Do you think maybe Greg will be at Belmont Dining Hall?"

"Greg? I thought you had given up on him." Angela scowled. "He's only interested in you for one thing, you know. He'll dump you as soon as he gets it. Trust me; I've been burned by guys like him before. They're handsome, they know it, and they use their looks for a trophy night to brag to their friends about—that's all. You're better than that, Cassie. Come on, forget about Greg and let's go eat."

Another glance around the room revealed no evidence her friends had given any forethought at all to commemorate her significant birthday. At least her parents had called bright and early that morning. Unfortunately her gift was too large and heavy to mail so it was waiting to be opened on her next trip home.

Dejected, Cassie dumped her books on the bed. Apparently there would be plenty of time to properly put belongings away when they returned from dinner. Resigned to Angela's lead, Cassie followed down the stairs and back across the commons.

On the way to Belmont, they spotted Cindy Lee next to a statue of some obscure Revolutionary War hero. Her left foot was propped up on a park bench as she adjusted the strap of the latest addition to her footwear. Cindy's perpetual smile and careful attention to the latest fashions made her easy to pick out even in a crowd. Also, perhaps the fact that there had not been any Asian girls in the rural town where Cassie grew up made her notice this friend all the more.

Angela called out, "Hey, Cindy, where's Beth?"

"Oh, hi, guys. Beth went over to the mall to buy some shoes." Cindy straightened up and combed her fingers through her long, jet-black hair. "I'm going to meet her there for dinner. Why don't you two come with me? I already checked out the dining halls; the food looks pretty gross tonight." She wriggled her nose in disgust just thinking about it.

"Hey, that's not a bad idea. I could really use a change from what this place considers to be edible food." Angela grimaced. "I used to think my mom was a bad cook until I moved on campus. She wasn't bad though, just boring—spaghetti on Tuesdays, rigatoni on Thursdays."

Angela and Cindy continued twittering back and forth like birds while Cassie followed behind. Secretly she was offended that Angela hadn't even mentioned her birthday to Cindy. Did she have to fish for birthday wishes from her closest friends? Surely Cindy hadn't forgotten! She was probably waiting to bring it up at dinner.

At the student parking lot, Cassie recognized Cindy's second-hand car by its crumpled rear bumper.

Angela yanked open the rusting, front-passenger door. Relegated to the back seat, Cassie climbed in for the brief drive.

Although conveniently situated close to the college, Oakwood Mall had been built some forty years ago. Dated neon signs still flickered above the doorways of several shops in the one-story shopping center. Renovation was desperately needed throughout, but despite the lack of pizzazz that more modern malls possessed, pretty much everything the local students wanted could be found there. There was even a movie theatre by the food court at the east end where Cassie had met Greg for a matinee showing last Saturday. Their few dates had been kept a secret to avoid disapproving lectures from her roommate.

Cindy parked her clunker and struggled with the emergency brake. While slamming the stiff car door shut as she exited, she inadvertently bumped into a convertible parked next to them. Blaring staccato honks screamed from the car's alarm, shattering the quiet peace of early evening. Giggling as they ran through the parking lot, the trio darted toward the mall entrance.

Embarrassed by the glares of a few other patrons outside the mall, Cindy mocked, "Stupid car alarm. Who would want to steal that piece of shit convertible anyway?"

Angela feigned shock. "Oooh, Cindy! I can't believe *you* cursed!"

"Well, maybe there's a lot about me that you don't know after all." Cindy pushed open the door at the mall's north entrance.

"Right, Cindy. Sure! As if you curse like a drunken sailor when we're not around. The only reason you chose our university is because the pastor of your church recommended it. The only thing more annoying than your being the world's biggest goodie two-shoes in the world is the way you know absolutely everything about everybody else."

Coming from someone else those words might have been hurtful, but Cindy knew Angela was only joking. Instead of being insulted, she bantered back, "You never know. Maybe I'm really an undercover agent infiltrating our college campus to discover secrets for the CIA, and when I talk to my colleagues I've got a really filthy mouth. But wait, maybe I'm really a double agent and..."

Angela interrupted, "Oh, please! Christ, Cindy, you sure have a fantastic imagination. You should go into the movie business dreaming up stuff like that. It sure was funny hearing *you* say 'shit' though. You're one to talk about shitty cars."

Cindy's dilapidated car was notorious, but its owner feigned a hurt look. "Don't make fun of my baby! She gets me around where I need to go. I don't see you complaining about getting a lift when you want to go shopping, do I?"

"Speaking of shopping, it looks like Beth found what she wanted at Kingston's," Cassie interjected, feeling slightly left out of the conversation.

Slightly plump, red-headed Beth Franklin stood window-shopping outside Freda's Fashions, a Kingston shopping bag dangling from her right hand. She spotted her friends as they approached. "Hey guys! I can't wait to tell you what happened in Professor Cromwell's chemistry class today, but I'm starving. You know how grouchy I get when I'm hungry. Let's go to Antonio's. If we hurry maybe we can get a table right away."

Now Cassie was really feeling depressed; neither Beth nor Cindy had even wished her a happy birthday yet. Perhaps they *had* forgotten. It was turning out to be one huge disappointment instead of a special fireworks sort of birthday. If she had been home, her mother would have rented out the fire hall and invited the whole town to celebrate. Instead she was stuck at college with friends that seemingly didn't even care.

Out of the corner of her eye, Cassie spotted a brightly colored sign in Virginia's Best Tobacco Shop. Fishing for some kind of acknowledgement was not normally her style, but she desperately wanted to draw attention to herself. "Wait a second," she called out. "Powerball Lottery is up to forty-two million. I'm twenty-one now so I think I'll take a chance."

"What's twenty-one got to do with it?" Angela impatiently asked. "I thought you only had to be eighteen in order to play the lottery."

"Well, since I'm twenty-one and finally able to legally drink, I may as well get all my vices in at once. After all, maybe my birthday will give me some added luck."

"Oh, yeah, that's right. Happy birthday, Cassie," Beth casually replied. "Well, go ahead in; we'll just wait here. But hurry; I'll pass out if I don't get something to eat soon!"

Her ploy hadn't worked. But Cassie didn't want her attempt to be too obvious, so she reluctantly entered the tiny tobacco shop. Only a stocky construction worker, a sales clerk from Steiner's dress department, and a young mother with a toddler in tow preceded her. Noisily the lottery machine churned out tickets and the line moved up. As Cassie waited her turn, she glanced back through the doorway. Angela tapped her foot anxiously checking her watch. Her friends were obviously impatient as they waited for her. *Well, let them wait, damn it, it's my birthday!* she thought.

"Next," the middle-aged balding man behind the counter called out.

"I've never purchased a Powerball lottery ticket before," Cassie explained nervously. "What do I do?"

With mild annoyance the man responded, "Fill out this card with the numbers you want, or you can get a computer pick." His attitude screamed, *How could you be so stupid as to not know what to do?*

Since Cassie had not really given it any thought, she didn't have any special numbers in mind. Behind her the line began getting longer with regular lottery players on their way home from work.

A short, frail, elderly woman with thick spectacles gently tapped Cassie on the shoulder. Kindly she whispered, "You're a college student, aren't you? I've got fifteen grandchildren and one more due any day now. I'm hoping to win so they'll all be able to go to college. I play their birth dates. But honestly, sweetie, your chances are really just as good with the computer picks, or at least that's what they say."

The waiting clerk impatiently tapped his fingers.

Cassie had begun to regret this idea. "I'll take the computer pick, please."

Relieved to dispense with the novice player the clerk punched a button bringing the machine to life. Piercing screeches whirred from the contraption as numbers were randomly assigned and then spat out onto a stubby card.

A shiver traveled down her spine. Once again Cassie had the overwhelming feeling a life-changing event would take place this evening. Tossing the ticket into her purse, she dismissed the silly notion and rejoined her friends.

At Antonio's, Angela characteristically took the lead, requesting a table in the back room. While waiting for the costumed hostess to check on the availability of the request, Cassie took note of the restaurant's décor. Candle wax dripped down the sides of raffia-wrapped wine bottles centered on red and white-checkered tablecloths. Lamps suspended from the ceiling provided additional soft lighting. Accordion music softly played Italian love songs from hidden speakers while waitresses in white peasant blouses and flowing red skirts took orders from diners in cozy booths.

Clearing a table to Cassie's right, a young bus boy appeared to be embarrassed at having to wear the required half-open, billowing white shirt, black knickers, and a wide red sash tied around his waist.

"So, Cassie, what numbers did you play?" Beth asked.

"Huh? Oh, I just got the computer picks."

"What? You mean you didn't play any special numbers like your street address, your telephone number or say maybe...your age?"

"No, but I..."

Before Cassie had a chance to complete her sentence, the hostess returned. "Follow me please," she instructed, ushering them through a dark stone archway into a small separate room.

As soon as Cassie entered she heard a resounding yell of "Surprise!" Immediately her fellow college students crowded around her laughing and patting her on the back.

Beth shouted above the din. "Cassie, did you really think we would forget your birthday? I thought I was going to burst keeping this a secret. Angela plotted the whole elaborate ruse to get you here with the precision of a general. So many of your friends wanted to come we weren't sure there would be enough room!"

"I got so tired waiting by that statue so that you could 'accidentally' on purpose run into me," Cindy laughed. "I was afraid it would look too contrived if I just stood there. So I propped my foot on the bench pretending to fix my shoe for the longest time. My back was killing me!"

Angela teasingly admonished, "You threw my timetable off a bit with your Powerball purchase. I was afraid you were going to want to keep shopping and I knew everyone was waiting. Really, Cassie, you should know I wouldn't let this day pass without a big bash." Angela gave her roommate a big hug. "Happy birthday! Now come on, let's party!"

In short order, waitresses served the spirited crowd with a prearranged meal of lasagna layered with gooey cheeses and a tangy marinara sauce. Complementing the pasta was a house salad and warm crusty Italian bread. The intoxicating aromas added to Cassie's enjoyment as she savored every morsel. She welled up with genuine appreciation at the thought of so many friends showing up on a Thursday night to celebrate with her.

Angela stood, called for the room to quiet, and then said, "Everyone here chipped in to get this for you, Cassie. Happy birthday."

She deposited a large, brightly wrapped package on Cassie's lap. Cassie tore through the paper to find an elegantly carved wooden jewelry box. Delicate hand painted flowers on the lid surrounded the word *Dreams*. Two weeks ago the roommates had visited a local craft fair where Cassie had spotted this beautiful box and raved about how she would love to have it. But it was out of her price range.

Angela reached over and lifted the lid revealing an envelope tucked inside. Witty sayings accompanied the numerous signatures on her card. Last but not least was a gift certificate for Steiner's department store.

Glasses clinked in toast wishing many happy returns. The next few hours were filled with boisterous laughter mingled with the latest campus gossip.

"Hey, you guys. Earlier I was dying to tell you what happened during Professor Cromwell's lecture." Beth giggled. "Jim Harrison dozed off in class. No one would have noticed if he hadn't started snoring. Professor Cromwell stormed up the aisle and slammed a book on the desk in front of him." Beth put both hands on her hips and deepened her voice, mimicking the angry instructor. "Well, Mr. Harrison, since you are so knowledgeable that you can sleep during my class, you'll have no trouble enlightening us all with a complete review of chapter eight tomorrow."

"Oh God, how embarrassing," Cindy commented over giggles and guffaws from the room full of college students.

"You think that's embarrassing?" Amber chimed in. "Last night a mouse ran out from under Helene's bed. Frank Blair was in the hallway when she tore out of her room half naked."

"Frank?" Rachel gossiped excitedly. "I heard he got kicked off the football team for using drugs."

Larry shook his head. "I heard it was just a little weed. I don't see what the big deal is." He took another gulp of beer. His voice slurred as he continued. "But, I bet we don't win another game without him as quarterback."

Cindy leaned closer to Angela and gleefully whispered, "What do you think? Will Courtney dump him now? She's so superficial."

Angela snipped, "It would serve him right if she did." An air of superiority accompanied her loud response. "Spoiled rich kids like him get into trouble all the time because they're bored and never have to work for anything. I know one thing for sure, if I ever get rich, I'm not going to spoil my kids." Pointing an inebriated finger at her roommate, she said, "Hey, Cassie, when you win that Powerball, don't spoil any kids you have. It'll only lead to trouble."

Cassie laughed. "Don't worry. No chance of that. From the time I was born, every time I got a spare dime, my parents lectured, 'Put it in the bank, don't spend it; you never know when there will be a rainy day.' I don't think I'd be able to shake that programming for very long if I ever did come into any money."

Conversation splintered off into several directions at that point. As the hour grew late, Antonio's slowly emptied, and one by one the guests headed back to their dorms. Cassie grabbed her present and her purse and headed for the door with her chums. Just then, a strikingly handsome young man with wavy brown locks and piercing blue eyes approached Cassie at the restaurant's entrance.

"I'm sorry I couldn't make it to your party, Cassie," Greg said. "I got tied up with my study group. Can I give you a lift back to the dorm? I've got a little something special for you."

Angela glared at Greg. "Oh, please, Cassie, how predictably contrived is this?" she muttered under her breath.

Ignoring Angela's remark Cassie profusely thanked her friends for a fabulous party and said she would see them later.

Greg gently wrapped his arm around Cassie's shoulder as they walked to his car.

"Your roommate doesn't trust me, does she, Cassie? I know we've only gone out a short time but you're very special to me. I have a gift for your birthday...but somehow the parking lot of Oakwood Mall seems a bit cold. Let's drive over to Jefferson Park's lookout point. We can count the stars together."

Greg steered the car to a secluded section of the park. Many a young couple in love came here on the weekends, but this being a Thursday night they had plenty of privacy. Greg retrieved a blanket from the trunk and they walked a short distance to where a curtain of pines parted to reveal the valley below. Twinkling lights from distant homes met the starry sky at the horizon.

The two sat on the blanket in silence for a few moments. The fiery sky matched the emotions welling up within Cassie. She definitely was falling in love with Greg, and it appeared he felt the same way about her. All thoughts of boring classes, disapproving friends, and uncertainties about the future were left to rest on some distant galaxy. Now all that existed was this moment, this place.

Gently, Greg turned her face to his. A caress of her cheek followed by tender strokes across the back of her neck sent shivers down her spine. "Cassie, I don't know how I got so lucky to have you come into my life. You're the most beautiful girl I've ever known. I can't believe I've fallen for you so quickly. I hope you feel the same way, too. Happy birthday." He reached into his jacket pocket, retrieving a small royal blue jewelry box.

Cassie instantly knew it was from Branscome's, the jewelry store on Main Street.

Timidly she opened the elegant box. Nestled in the pale blue satin lining was a 24-carat gold heart. Several small diamond chips sparkled beneath the raised rim on the left side. Engraved in ornate script lettering was Greg's name.

"In such a short time your spirit has touched mine," he whispered as he lifted the necklace out of its presentation box and delicately fastened it around her neck. "This is so you can keep me close to your heart." He unbuttoned the top two buttons of his shirt to reveal a matching heart inscribed with *her* name resting on his chest.

Cassie felt her pulse quicken as he brushed the hair back from her face and gently pressed his lips to hers. If she had her wits about her, she would have surmised this was a carefully crafted romantic ploy by someone unconcerned with money. It seemed a bit too corny. Angela's warning tried to push into her consciousness. But Greg's words, his touch, his eyes dissolved any sense of reason. She was enveloped in his firm embrace.

Slowly his hands skimmed the surface of her skin under her blouse. The fabric melted away as if by magic. Passionate kisses quelled any idea she had to resist the light touch that slid under her skirt and between her thighs. Caressingly gentle hands released the remaining garment impediments. A gentle breeze tickled her naked body causing every cell of her being to tingle as Greg's muscular frame cocooned her. They entwined, forming one being until they could breathe no more. Stars swirled millions of miles away and under her skin, and spider web clouds whispered across the moon, washing away all awareness of where she was in time or space.

Chapter 2.

How did she get home? When? It was all a blur of tender passion. Cassie awoke the next morning snug in her bed. She fingered the gold chain around her slender neck, convinced that it had been a life-altering evening. Slowly she opened her eyes, nagged by the persistent radio alarm. Her schedule was thankfully light on Fridays with only one early afternoon chemistry lab, but she had forgotten to reset her clock the night before.

Looking around the room she found she was alone. Apparently her considerate roommate had quietly dressed for an earlier class. Cassie particularly appreciated Angela's absence this morning. The ecstasy of the preceding evening still resonated within her; she didn't want her mood spoiled by a confrontation with her best friend.

It wasn't until that evening that the girls ran into each other.

"Prince Charming left this for you tacked to the cork board," her roommate informed her disapprovingly.

Cassie's heart sank. Was Angela right? Was it all a façade to elicit a trophy night? It wasn't possible that he was dumping her already. Was it? She tore open the envelope. Greg's hasty scrawl apologized, writing that a family emergency had arisen. He'd be gone for a few weeks and would call when he got back. Relief flooded through her veins. She was sure they had a real connection.

Cassie glanced up from the letter to catch Angela's wary countenance mixed with curiosity. She informed Angela of the emergency lightheartedly, determined to cling to the rapture of the previous evening, and shook off her own disappointment at the prospect of his long absence. "It looks like I'm free tomorrow and it's supposed to be another gorgeous day. Let's plan a picnic and go on a scenic drive with Beth and Cindy."

The next day the four friends got a late morning start. After all, Saturdays were for sleeping in when you were in college. But the prospect of viewing an inspiring autumn show was enough to eventually drag them out of bed. Somehow it felt strange to be wearing shorts and going for a drive to see fall foliage. Strange or not, they intended to enjoy every moment before the cold winds blew in.

Cindy made Angela promise not to insult her chariot as the quartet piled in for a long drive. Sure, her car was a bit beaten up from many years of use and abuse, but it was still more dependable than any boyfriend she'd ever had. After patting the dashboard as if to reassure a family pet, she turned the key in the ignition and begged it to be faithful once more.

Breathtaking foliage drew them onward, promising to be even more spectacular around each bend in the highway. Yet finally Beth could no longer ignore a gnawing rumble. "Pretty leaves or not, I'm hungry. Let's pull over somewhere and eat!"

A few minutes later Cindy slowed the aging sedan onto the graveled shoulder of the road. She popped open the trunk and retrieved a tattered bedspread stuffed in an oversized backpack. Beth grabbed plastic bags laden with picnic fare that she and Cindy had purchased from the campus supermarket before their drive, while Angela lugged bags of bottled water and juice out of the trunk.

"Here, Angela, give me something to carry," Cassie offered.

Warm breezes playfully tossed their hair around their faces as the foursome carefully picked their way to a small clearing. The girls spread the picnic blanket on the grass and placed their containers of fried chicken and pre-cut veggies in the center of the blanket. Beth had wanted potato salad but feared it might spoil, so she had purchased chips and cheese curls instead.

Bowman's famous pound cake would make a fine dessert. They all settled on the old bedspread in a circle around their feast.

"Where are the paper plates and napkins?" Angela asked.

"Damn it. I knew I forgot something," Beth responded. "I guess we'll just have to pass the containers around. Wipe your fingers on the blanket; I'll wash it when we get back."

"I've got some tissues in my backpack we can use," Cindy offered. "Anyway, if Cassie wins the lottery our next picnic will be catered with linen tablecloths, sterling silverware, and a butler to boot!"

Angela mumbled through a mouthful of chicken, "What would you do if you won all that money?"

"Oh God, my chances of winning are so small I hadn't really given it any thought." Cassie had forgotten all about the Powerball ticket.

"Still, somebody has got to win. What would you do if it was you?" Cindy persisted, passing the veggies.

"Hmm, a huge mansion, a fancy car, and trips around the world would be nice." Cassie laughed offhandedly as she crunched a carrot. She thought a moment more then added, "I'd probably give something to Amberville Manor too."

"What's that?" Angela asked.

"Oh it's a retirement home. When I was in Girl Scouts, our troop volunteered there a lot. On Wednesdays, I used to help Mrs. Salerno find her bingo numbers. We planted and weeded a flower garden for the residents, too. I got to really enjoy helping out there. It was sad when Mr. Richardson passed away, though." Sensing that her last comment was a bit too serious for their casual daydreams, she playfully tossed the bag of chips to her right. "What about you, Beth? Do you have any fantasies about what you would do with a fortune?"

"You know me and my love of food," Beth giggled. "I'd open a gourmet restaurant." She grabbed a handful of chips and passed the bag to Angela.

"I hear some people who win huge lotteries blow it all within a few years with extravagant spending like that," Angela cautioned. "Others wind up with friends, relatives, and every charity in the book holding their hands out expecting to be taken care of. There are so many scam artists out there. Lottery winners are easy pickings. We're fortunate that we live in a state that the winner doesn't have to be made public if they want to keep it a secret."

"How on earth do you keep winning that much money a secret?" Cindy asked incredulously.

Angela took a swig of water then wiped her mouth with a tissue. "Damned if I know all the details of how I'd do it, but if I won the Powerball, I wouldn't tell a soul. Not even you guys!"

"Gee, thanks a lot. Some friend you are." Cindy feigned hurt as she spoke.

Confused, Beth asked, "Why wouldn't you tell us?"

"Beth, you know what a hard time you had keeping Cassie's party a secret. There are three things a woman should never willingly divulge: her age, her weight, and her financial status. There's just too much chance of inviting gossip or having someone else use that information against her somehow. Anyway, if I won a huge amount of money like that, I'd get some expert advice before I did anything." Angela again wiped her mouth with a tissue. "It doesn't matter, though. I'm not going to win because I'm not going to stupidly waste my money on something that I don't have a ghost of a chance of winning."

"Well, maybe Cassie will win. Are you going to stay up and watch the drawing on TV tonight?" Cindy prodded.

"Oh, I don't know, maybe." Cassie shrugged.

Numbered ping-pong balls danced wildly, blown through a huge acrylic globe. A sequined model flashed a frozen plastic smile to the camera. One by one she released doors to five individual chutes. The announcer's voice dramatically boomed each number as it landed in place. "The winning numbers are 16...4...25...41...and 36." Another sphere whirled with red balls until one collided into place. "And the Powerball number is...5."

Cassie tore her ticket into shreds and watched the pieces flutter into the wastebasket. It wasn't meant to be. *Hopefully the winner will put the money to good use*, she thought.

Sunday morning found most of the dorm still hibernating after the previous evening's various escapes from studying. A gentle rain tapped against the windowpane. Slowly, a quiet but anxious knocking crept into her awareness. Cassie gradually became aware that the rain was not the only tapping she heard.

"Are you guys awake yet?" Cindy's voice whispered from outside the door.

Angela stumbled over grumpily to let her in. "What's got you up so early?"

"It's half past nine. It's not that early," Cindy sheepishly defended herself.

"It is to me," Angela growled back, still half asleep. "Like I said, what's up?"

"It's official, I've caught the fever!" Cindy excitedly gushed.

"What the hell? What on earth are you talking about? Are you sick?"

"Of course not, I've got Powerball fever!" Cindy laughingly explained. "Didn't you hear?"

"Hear what? We just woke up, remember? A certain someone just roused me out of a sound sleep!" Angela dropped back on her bed, pulled the covers up to her chin and squeezed her eyes shut.

Cassie sat up in bed as Cindy bounded over to her. "Nobody won last night! The lottery is up to fifty-six million and rising fast. I heard it on WTBA radio this morning. The next drawing is Wednesday night. The DJ said he's tired of the winners always being from another state. He said we should all *catch the fever* and make the next winner be one of us. I'm old enough to play; it might as well be me, right? Just think of the possibilities with that much money. Do you want to come with me to buy some tickets?"

In one motion Angela threw the blanket back and sat up again. "Are you crazy? You woke me up for that?" she snapped. "Cindy, be realistic. Your chances are greater of being hit by lightening than of winning that thing. Even if you did win the government would take half of it in taxes."

"Oh Angela, you're such a pessimist! Come with me, Cassie. Please. I don't want to stand in line all by myself. I'm sure you want to try again."

Not wanting to admit that it was just a ploy for attention, Cassie wiped the sleep from her eyes. "Okay," she replied. "Just let me throw something on. But I don't think the mall is even open yet. Let's grab a bite to eat at the diner first."

At eleven o'clock Cassie and Cindy found themselves waiting behind a dozen other lottery hopefuls as an employee of the tobacco shop unlocked the door. Apparently the radio announcer's plea had resounded with the locals.

"I don't know why the mall opens so late on Sundays," grumbled a portly man in a suit and tie. "That kind of thinking is archaic nowadays."

"He's probably supposed to meet his family at church and his wife will be mad at him for being late," Cindy giggled to Cassie. "I'm glad we went last night."

Cassie eyed the microcosm of society before her and contemplated their reasons for being in line. Young adults eagerly anticipating the future were mixed with the elderly hoping to pass dreams onto their progeny. Tailored suits reaching for another rung on the ladder mixed with raggedy jeans hoping to never have to wear a suit. Black and white, fat and thin, short and tall stood together. Each looked optimistic that an overflowing bank account would right all the wrongs in their world.

Cindy brought her back to the moment. "If you win, where do you see yourself in ten years? Do you think you will change, will we still be friends?"

Cassie shook her head. "First of all, I don't think we have to worry about me winning. I'm more likely to have a piano fall on my head than win the lottery. It just won't happen." She paused for the first time to actually consider what it would be like. "It sure would be nice, though. If it did happen, which of course it won't, I think I'd be married with a child or two living in a grand house. And of course we'll still be friends. Nothing could change that. Hey Cindy, this is the second time you asked *me* what I would do if I won. What would *you* do with that much money?"

Cindy smiled even wider than her normal cheerful grin. "Oh, I think I'd like to go out to Hollywood and rub elbows with all the celebrities. Maybe I'd even finance a film. Wouldn't it be fabulous to see your name in the credits of a movie? Then I would go to the Hollywood premiere and sit next to some big star. Everyone would wonder who I was."

"Boy, when you dream, you dream big!" Still rubbing the final remnants of sleep from her eyes Cassie asked, "Do you have any special lucky numbers to get you this fantasy?"

"Naw, I think I'll just go with the computer picks. They're random and when you think of it, the chance of being the winner is random, too. Come to think of it, so is most of life," Cindy observed.

"Aren't we philosophical all of the sudden?" Cassie teased as she moved forward with the line. "What brought that on?"

Cindy shrugged. "Oh, I don't know. I've been thinking a lot about luck and chance lately. I've been wondering what roll of the dice made us wind up born in this country to middle-class families. Somehow fortune gives some people a lot of benefits that others don't have. I mean, how do celebrities get to be famous? Are they better than everybody else or just plain lucky?"

"I don't know, maybe a little of both." Cassie gave a bit of a laugh. "You surprise me, Cindy. I wouldn't have thought of you as given to contemplating the roles of chance versus fate. Anyway, let's just hope that it's *our* turn to be lucky!"

"You know, I'm not the total airhead some people think I am," Cindy said with surprising seriousness. "Even my parents don't give me enough credit for having half a brain. They think that just because I'm not in pre-med I must be a dunce. My father is a doctor, my mother is a doctor, my aunt is a doctor, and even my brother is a doctor. Talk about pressure! Medicine is just not my thing. I don't have that in me. But I'm not stupid!"

Cassie was taken aback. "Hey, I'm sorry. I didn't mean to offend you. It's just I never heard you talk like that before."

"Well, I've been thinking about it a lot lately, Cassie. Come to think of it, I guess it started after I finished watching a movie the other night in my room."

"Now that sounds like you." Cassie laughed. "Which one was it?"

"*Titanic*." Cindy sighed. "I just love that movie. Sure, it probably romanticized the idea of the rich girl falling in love with the poor guy. But there really was so much going on in that film to think about. Throughout history there have always been wealthy aristocrats and poor working stiffs. What determines whether you are born rich or struggle just to get by? And what about the whole tragedy of all those people dying? Was there a reason the ship hit an iceberg and sank? Was it fate or was it purely chance that those people were the ones on that particular ocean liner? I can only imagine the horror. It must be horrible to know you are about to die and not be able to do a thing about it."

"Move up, honey," barked an impatient man with a scruffy beard.

The girls had been so engrossed in their conversation they hadn't noticed it was their turn. Cindy quickly paid for her computer picks and Cassie for hers. The lottery machine screeched as it spit their numbers onto tiny cards.

The friends then poked around Oakwood mall for a while. They sauntered into Freda's Fashions where racks of trendy garments tempted payment with plastic.

Cindy fingered a lilac blouse and hesitantly asked, "Cassie, can I ask something without you getting mad?"

"Sure, what's the problem?"

"I know it's not my business, but are you and Greg serious? You left with him after your party and I heard you two have been seen together a couple of times over here at Oakwood. Angela thinks he just wants to use you."

Cassie snapped, "It is not up to Angela who I see!"

"I know but she only interferes because she cares about you like a sister...and so do I. If you don't want to tell me, that's okay, but I was just curious. Are you and Greg serious?"

Cassandra calmed down. "It's too soon to tell for sure, but I really think he loves me. I think I love him, too. My pulse races every time I think about him. I wish he were here now but he had to go home for some sort of a family emergency."

"I know. My friend Steve said Greg's father had a heart attack and he's going to be gone for a couple of weeks to help his mother out."

"Jeez, Cindy, you're such a social butterfly! Is there anything about anyone that you don't know?"

Cindy laughed. Conversation drifted away from serious matters to more gossip about fellow students. They continued shopping and for a few hours Cassie's attention was distracted away from obsessing about Greg.

The next few days were centuries. Classes were endless. There was no phone call from Greg, and the empty hours on Wednesday were accentuated by Angela's absence. Her roommate's evening study group was keeping her out late as they crammed for a major exam.

Twirling a strand of hair around her forefinger, Cassie sat at her desk staring out the window, completely unable to concentrate on her paper. Short on a social-science course for graduation requirements, she had chosen psychology. It had sounded like an interesting class and she had hoped it would be easy. Boy, was she wrong! Trying to decipher the meaning of the last chapter was like trying to separate mashed bananas from oatmeal. Vainly she attempted to concentrate on the task at hand, but even drumming her pencil on the desk didn't drown out the dull hum emanating from her computer.

Pointless! she thought as she slammed her notebook shut. After turning off the computer, she set the alarm intending to resume work early in the morning with a clearer head.

Flicking the television on for some company before crawling into bed, Cassie paused as an overly cheerful news anchor gushed on and on about the multi-state Powerball fever that had struck the surrounding area.

Just goes to show what a boring news day it must have been, Cassandra thought. She wasn't surprised, though, observing that local stations magnified what she considered to be minor stories. Every time more than a quarter inch of snow was predicted for the campus town, they preempted regular programming for non-stop weather reports.

Local coverage switched to the live broadcast of the drawing. Cassie retrieved her purse and fumbled through it for the forgotten ticket stub. Just as the first number was being drawn, she found it. Wow, what a coincidence, she had the first number. The second number drawn was on her ticket as well. Three numbers? At least her winnings would pay for this ticket and Sunday's breakfast with Cindy. Four numbers, five...?

Oh God, all she needed now was the red Powerball. Excited anticipation bubbled within her as she watched the magical red ping-pong ball rocket into place.

The impossible happened.

Cassie let out a startled, exuberant screech. Jumping up and down she grabbed a pillow from the bed, hugging it so close that had it been alive, it would have gasped for air. Just as quickly, she felt panic. Quickly she cupped a hand over her mouth. Nervously her gaze darted around the room as Angela's caution regarding secrecy buzzed in her brain. Still her tingling excitement battled with sober reason. Who could give her good counsel?

Mom and Dad will know what to do, she thought. *I'll go home on the weekend. They'll help me figure it out.*

Cassie tossed the pillow back onto her bed, stowed the ticket into the back of her wallet, buried it in her purse, and shoved the treasure into the back of her closet.

Footsteps pounded down the hallway. Beth burst into the room, one arm through the sleeve of her bathrobe, the other sleeve trailing behind in her haste. Puffing for breath she asked, "Cassie, are you all right? I heard you scream."

Displaying her best acting talents, Cassandra hobbled over and dropped onto the corner of her bed, grabbing her foot. "I stubbed my toe getting up to turn off the TV. I hope I didn't wake you."

"No, I was just about to fall asleep, though. Jesus, Cassie! It sounded like you were being killed. Are you sure you're all right?"

"I'm sorry I startled you. Go on back to bed, I'll be fine. It just hurt like hell, that's all." Cassie rubbed her toes to maintain the charade. "See you in the morning, Beth."

"Okay, if you're sure." Beth yawned and reluctantly stumbled, bleary-eyed, back to her own room.

A violent tornado of thoughts and emotions whirled through Cassie's consciousness until several hours later when fatigue finally overtook the newest Powerball winner.

Chapter 3.

Cassie spent the next two days about ready to burst through her skin. She tried to keep her routine normal so no one would suspect. But it was nearly impossible to retain a calm exterior while extraordinary news tickled just under the surface, begging to break free. Throughout campus, conversations were electrified as word spread that one of the two winning tickets was sold at *their* mall. Everyone wondered if a lottery winner walked among them. While eating lunch at the student center, Cassie desperately wanted to shout the news to her friends, but a cautious inner voice that sounded a lot like a combination of Angela and Cassie's mother reminded her to be still.

Cindy squealed with excitement. "Cassie, remember the old lady that was in front of us? Do you think she's the winner? Oh, oh, I know, maybe it was the man who was late for church. I'll bet his wife has forgiven him by now."

"Maybe it was a student," Beth suggested. "Did you recognize anyone else in line?"

"No, I don't think so," Cassie replied nervously.

Cindy perked up. "Wait a minute. I think I remember Grace saying that Amber bought a ticket; maybe it was her. Can you imagine? Wow, that would be so cool to have all your student loans paid off. I only wish it were me. Not having to worry about money would sure take the pressure off of studying."

"Who are you kidding?" Angela said. "If you had won, you would have been on the first plane out of here to the West Coast! I know you; finishing your degree would be the last thing on your mind." Before finishing the last bite of her burger, Angela looked over at Cassie's tray. "What's the matter with you? You hardly touched your sandwich."

"I don't know; I think I'm coming down with something. Maybe I'll just skip chem lab and head on home to see my folks. I'm sure Mom's chicken soup will fix me right up." Tossing her purse over her shoulder, she dumped her remaining lunch in the trash before she left.

Her excitement begging for an outlet, Cassandra Delaine kept a wary eye on the speedometer as she steered her rundown puddle jumper along the interstate. Despite the straining engine, her secondhand Civic had managed to travel this route many times before, as if magnetically drawn by home-cooked meals.

Sunlight seeped through the gold and rust leaves lining a winding narrow pass.

A sudden gust fluttered a storm of spent foliage to the blacktop and fond memories of autumns with her grandparents came flooding back. Long walks during her pre-school years were spent collecting leaves to make collages and tracings. Many afternoons Mom-Mom and Pop-Pop helped her gather piles of acorns for squirrels before going home for an elaborate tea party. How she wished they were still alive to share in her good news.

As the miles ticked slowly by, Cassie began to feel a little nauseous. The stress of bottling up such a tremendous secret awakened road sickness that she hadn't experienced since childhood. Her racing thoughts and queasy stomach caused Cassie to nearly miss the exit for Amberville. A few more turns and then she was home.

Just stepping out of the vehicle and stretching her legs began to ease her tension headache. Hoping to relieve the dull throb low in her back, she decided to walk around a bit before going in. Greeted by familiar visions, a wave of comfort washed over her like a warm hug. Cheerful chrysanthemums purchased several years ago managed to bloom here each year just in time for her mother's birthday. Amanda Delaine loved to garden, but she especially treasured these autumn beauties running the length of her front flowerbed.

Cassie strolled past the maple tree planted when she was born then climbed the front porch. Suddenly a shiver shot down her spine. With any luck, she thought, her dad would have laid a fire on the hearth in anticipation of approaching evening chills.

A few short years ago, Cassie had scorned any and all parental advice, as teenagers often do. But now she was eager to seek her loving parents' guidance regarding her miraculous fortune. Gingerly, she opened the front door. In some ways it was a little awkward whenever she returned for visits home. She teetered back and forth between being an independent young woman and a tentative little girl with her parents.

As the door creaked open, an orange ball of fur peeked out from behind a living room chair.

"Burt, it's just me. Don't be afraid," Cassie cooed. She stooped to pet the panicky feline. Burt was named for the actor who played the cowardly lion in the Wizard of Oz. "Come here, you old scaredy cat."

Slinking low to the ground Burt ventured from the perceived safety of the wingback chair to twine himself around her legs and nudge her hand to scratch his ear. In the distance, the sound of dishes clinking together announced dinner was nearly ready. Cassie scooped the fuzzy creature into her arms and proceeded to the kitchen.

"Hi, Mom."

Her mother dropped the flatware she was setting the table with and jumped back from the table. "Oh, Cassie my dear, you startled me. I didn't know you were coming home. Why didn't you call?" Dismissively she waved her hand. "No matter. I'm sure I made enough. I still think I'm cooking for an army the way I did when you had friends over all the time from Trinity High. Go ahead and set a place for yourself. You timed it just right; we're just about to eat."

Barely pausing for a breath, Amanda Delaine called out "Carl! Carl, it's dinnertime. Look what the wind blew in!" Her mother gave her a quick kiss before returning to the stove.

The stairs creaked as a loose floorboard complained. Her father beamed with pride as he rounded the corner to the sight of Cassie still cradling Burt. "M'lady fair," he bellowed, grandly bowing in reminiscence of a game they played when she was a child. "To what do we owe the unexpected pleasure of your company, m'lady?"

Before there was an opportunity to respond, Amanda commanded, "Cassandra, put down that cat and wash your hands. Dinner is getting cold."

No one dared defy the loving general, so conversation waited a few minutes more. Cassie's mother wiped perspiration and a loose strand of graying hair from her face with the back of her forearm, then carried to the table a large casserole dish filled to the brim with savory beef stew. Carl cut a loaf of crusty warm Italian bread and laid the slices in a basket.

Amanda resumed chattering as she ladled out servings onto each plate. "So, Cassie dear, what do you think about the local news in your neck of the woods? Can you imagine! Someone actually bought the winning Powerball ticket at the mall near your college. Well, there were two winners, I heard, but one of them was in another state. But still, one of the winners got their ticket at that Oakwood Mall. We read all about it in the paper, didn't we, Carl? What on earth do you suppose they will do with all that money? I certainly would want to keep my business to myself if it was me."

Exasperated at trying to slip a word in edge-wise, Cassie yelled "Mom! It was *me*!"

Amanda dropped the ladle in mid-serving. Bits of peas, carrots, and potatoes in brown gravy splattered across the table. Cassie's mother stood, eyes wide and mouth open like a deer caught in headlights, silent for the first time since her daughter's arrival.

Dazed, her father exclaimed, "My God, Cassie. Is this true?"

"I've been dying to tell someone ever since the drawing Wednesday night. I figured I didn't want to go public with the news so I've been trying desperately to keep my routine as normal as possible until I could get home to talk with you. I didn't call to tell you I was coming home because I wanted to tell you in person. I was afraid if I phoned I wouldn't be able to keep it in. I really need some advice so I don't screw up."

Carl gently grasped his daughter's hand from across the table. "Cassie dear, this is amazing! Of course we're thrilled for you, honey. This is fantastic news. I'm sure everything will work out just fine. You know, just realizing the need for guidance is a very mature step." Thinking out loud, he continued with fatherly advice. "Hmm, let's see, the first thing to decide is whether you want the annuity or take the cash lump sum to invest on your own. Cash. Yes, that might be the best bet. But if you take the cash up front you'll have to be very disciplined not to go hog wild and blow it all in a couple of years. If you're smart about it, you could be set for life, sweetie."

Pausing to survey the mess before him, he continued, "How about we see if we can scrape some of this dinner off the table and eat while we talk it over? Multi-millionaire or not, I'm hungry."

Amanda finished serving the stew then passed the breadbasket to Cassie. She said, "Cecelia would be so green with envy if she knew. My sister plays the lottery twice a week religiously. If she had won, she'd live out her fantasy of one endless shopping spree."

Carl snapped, "Don't you dare tell your sister! First of all, you know Cecelia couldn't keep a secret if her life depended on it. And another thing, if she knew about Cassie's fortune she would find some way to leech every last penny out of her to spend it on one damn frivolous thing after another."

"Oh, don't worry. Of course I won't say anything. I was only commenting that if—"

"I mean it, Amanda," Carl interrupted. "I know it drives you crazy the way she always has to do you one better. She has to be queen bee all the time. But don't let it get to you. This is for Cassie's protection."

Cassie's mother put her hands on her hips. "For God's sakes! No need to lecture me. I know better than to let my sister get anywhere near our daughter's money. Frankly, Cassie needs to be protected from people like Cecelia. Cassandra has to safeguard her future happiness by investing wisely."

Carl swallowed a mouthful of stew. "Your mother's right, but the stock market can be very fickle, honey," he warned. "You need to diversify the kinds of stocks you get. It's probably a good idea to get a financial advisor to help you set up a good portfolio. Put some of your money in bonds, and of course real estate is always a good investment," he advised. "But be sure to be careful. You hear about real estate swindlers all the time."

Cassie rolled her eyes, softening it with a smile. "Okay, Dad. I get the picture. I'll be careful, I'll be very careful. And I promise I'll keep it a secret for my own protection like you said."

"Good." Carl sopped up some gravy with a crust of bread. "What little of this stew made it to my plate is actually pretty good, Amanda." Turning again to his daughter he said, "As long as you keep an eye on the big picture and don't go overboard, you may as well have some fun, too. Have you given it any thought?"

Cassie smiled mischievously. "Actually, yes I have. I thought about some traveling. What do you think about Europe, a cruise or maybe Hawaii?"

Not picking up on her daughter's hint, Amanda interjected, "Those ideas sound like good choices. But you'd have to get a passport, Cass."

"So would you," Cassie responded.

"What do you mean?"

"What good is having all this money if I can't share it with the ones I love? Let's take a nice long vacation together. You've been the best parents anyone could possibly hope for. I know you gave up lots of things over the years for me. Now I can do something for you."

"Cass, hon, you don't have to do this," her father objected.

"I know I don't have to; I want to. So, where do you guys want to go?"

Amanda sighed dreamily. "I always wanted to go to Hawaii. Claire Preston down the street went to Maui to celebrate her fortieth birthday with her husband. She raved about how beautiful it was for weeks when she got back."

"And you complained every day to me about her bragging," Carl laughed. "Now I guess we'll be the ones showing off pictures all around town when we get back."

"Then it's settled." Cassie beamed at having made the first decision on what to spend some of her lottery winnings on. "First thing tomorrow morning we'll go to the travel agency. We'll pick up all their brochures to choose the best hotel in the Hawaiian Islands. Then you can help me pick out a new car at Supreme Motors. The Civic has been good to me but it is on its last legs."

Amanda frowned. "I know you need a new car, but it wouldn't be wise to flaunt your newfound wealth," she chided. "It's one thing to take a nice vacation together. We could do that without raising too many eyebrows. But if you get too expensive a car, people will be suspicious around here. Besides, you're an attractive young woman. You'll surely want to find a young man to spend your life with. I heard this story about a wealthy woman over in Paradise Valley who didn't get a prenuptial agreement when she got married. He divorced her just a couple of years later after gambling away most of her money. Then he moved on to some other unsuspecting rich woman. Men marry for money the same way some women do. If you're not careful you could attract the wrong sort. You better keep your money a secret until there is a ring on your finger. Perhaps even then you should keep it to yourself."

Cassie absentmindedly touched the chain around her neck. Its gold heart was hidden by the neckline of her blouse. There had seemed to be a real connection with Greg even though she knew relatively little about him. Perhaps he was the one for her, but it might be wise to hold off on sharing her financial situation until she was absolutely certain.

"Enough of this serious talk; this is a night for celebrating!" Carl bellowed with a jovial laugh. "Let's go in town for a bottle of champagne and have dessert at the Bavaria Haus!"

"Okay. But if anyone asks, we're belatedly celebrating Cassie's twenty-first birthday," Amanda cautioned as she grabbed a light jacket. "It's getting a little chilly. At least put on a sweater, Carl. I'll clean up the dishes and Cassie can open her birthday present when we get back."

There weren't many places to go out for a celebration in Amberville. Bavaria Haus was a simple German restaurant, but even so, the locals liked to frequent this establishment for its hearty dark beer, jovial atmosphere, and the camaraderie it engendered. The dark paneling and friendly service gave it a warm, cozy feeling. This was one of Cassie's favorite restaurants from early childhood. Dinners were filling, but she always saved room for plum cake, apple strudel, or Black Forest cake.

Flirtatious laughter cut through the lively establishment as the Delaines entered to find three of Cassie's high school friends seated at the bar. Allison King and Valerie Harris flanked Jordan Davis, a cuddly bear who always had the honeys swarming to him. He proudly sported the newest addition to his attraction—a police uniform.

"I'm gone for a little while and the whole world turns upside down," Cassie ribbed as she approached Jordan. "This county is in trouble now if we have to trust our safety to you. Drinking on the job! Shame on you!"

"Cassie! It's great to see you." Jordan held up his glass. "I assure you, it's only ginger ale. I'd love to stay and chat, kitten, but I go on duty in fifteen minutes. I have to get over to the station. It wouldn't do for a rookie to get caught speeding on the way to work, now would it?" He downed the remainder of his beverage then gave Cassie a peck on the cheek. "Catch you later."

"Just you try!" Cassie laughed back.

Carl Delaine smiled widely. "Ladies, we're belatedly celebrating Cassie's twenty-first birthday. Would you care to join us?"

Allison and Valerie eagerly agreed. Cassie appreciated that her father recognized her desire to socialize with her high school chums. A waiter seated the group at a table by the window. Promptly glasses were filled with champagne and Mr. Delaine rose to toast his daughter. "To a wonderful daughter on a very special evening on the verge of a miraculous future."

Her friends exchanged confused looks, obviously unaware of the toast's full significance. They said nothing though, as Cassie's father was known to lavishly embellish anything to do with her. He often remarked that she put the sparkle in his eyes.

Hours melted away with the warmth of conversation. Yet, Amanda Delaine was unusually reserved for such a verbose woman. Whatever the cause, she finally spoke up. "Cassandra, your father and I should be getting back. I'm not as young as I once was. We have much to discuss in the morning and I need my sleep." She turned to Cassie's friends. "Do you suppose one of you could be a dear and give Cassie a ride home when she's ready? There's no need for her to leave now if she doesn't want to."

"Of course, Mrs. Delaine," Allison replied. "Thanks for including us in the celebration. It's been so much fun, but we still have a lot of catching up to do."

"Don't stay out too late, dear," Carl gently admonished "Love ya, honey."

Cassie's parents glanced back as they approached the door and Amanda blew a kiss to her daughter. Emotion welled up as Cassandra Delaine realized how lucky she was to have such loving parents. Their advice would be so valuable in the coming days.

But quickly her attention was drawn back to her friends; the girls continued to giggle about the latest gossip circulating about former schoolmates. One story led into another until it was unclear what the original topic was.

Slowly in the distance the screeching of sirens magnified. At first there was just barely a dull annoyance in the background of conversation like a pesky bee. Then as if someone was holding their finger on a remote control, the volume increased. Suddenly, the stinging sound stopped.

"Jordan must be trying to fill his quota of speeding tickets tonight." Valerie blushed, vainly trying to conceal her crush. "Who do you think has a better chance with him, Cassie: Allison or me?"

Cassie's eyes widened. "Come on. It's not fair to put me in the middle. Anyway, you're putting your friendship in danger competing for the same guy. Why don't you check out our waiter? He's been keeping an eye on us the whole evening."

The girls giggled while surreptitiously shooting glances in his direction, and conversation continued about the appalling lack of suitable young men in Amberville.

As the hour grew late, slowly the establishment emptied out until the three young ladies were the last remaining customers of the evening. Headlights glared through the window as a vehicle rapidly pulled into the parking lot. Suddenly an ashen-faced Jordan Davis emerged through the front door with his partner steadying him.

"Jordan, are you off duty already?" Valerie joked. Then she noticed his expression. "Jordan! What's wrong?"

The young rookie and his mentor approached the group. Jordan lowered himself into the seat next to Cassie and gently placed his hand over hers. "Kitten," he began, "I don't know how to break this to you, but I have some very bad news. There has been an accident." He paused and drew a deep breath.

Cassie's eyes widened and began to fill with tears as she realized what she was about to hear. She felt as though gravity suddenly increased tenfold, suctioning her to the chair. Simultaneously her spirit retreated miles away, vainly hoping to postpone the impending news.

"A drunk driver careened around the construction barrels on Route 42. He was in the wrong lane as he rounded the bend near Greenhouse Lane. The vehicles collided head-on. There was nothing the paramedics could do." Though visibly shaken himself, Jordan attempted to remain professional. "Your parents were killed instantly; at least they didn't suffer. The drunk driver was taken to Saint Agnes Hospital but died en-route." He took a deep breath. "Cassie, I'm so sorry. I can't believe this either. I knew and liked your parents a lot. I can't believe I just saw them tonight when you guys came in here."

As Jordan started to lose what little composure he had left his partner took over. "Miss Delaine, I know this is difficult but there are some details we need to take care of. We will drive you home and discuss them. The coroner will need to know which funeral home you would like your parents released to."

Cassandra rose to her feet as if levitated. She no longer heard what was being said. Trance-like she was led to the squad car. A short time later the officers deposited her on the sofa in her parents' living room, where she answered their questions and assured them she was fine, although later she could not remember doing so.

Alone. The only sounds in the solitude were the tick of the clock and the refrigerator's hum in the kitchen. Alone, she was no longer capable of containing her anguish. She released a gut-wrenching wail. Burt sensed her distress and leapt to her lap in an effort to console her. Cassie clutched him in her arms and sobbed uncontrollably until exhausted sleep rescued her from consciousness.

Chapter 4.

Baines Funeral Home stood guard stoically at the end of Trimble Lane. In Cassie's eyes the edifice itself wore an aura of death. The façade was constructed of pale gray stones reminiscent of tombstone rows, and each window stared blankly, soulless eyes framed by ribbed shutters resembling stark white skeletons. Once inside, sparse, severe furnishings did little to dispel the ominous feeling of aloneness. Against heavy folds of drapery, her parents' caskets were surrounded by an ostentatious display of huge floral arrangements.

Despite wishing she could flee this obligatory ritual, Cassie was grateful the mortician had been a close friend of her father. Several years earlier, Virgil Baines had convinced the Delaines to make pre-need funeral arrangements. Cassie was not sure how she could have managed to make the necessary decisions otherwise. She moved as if on autopilot. Each time awareness intruded into her tormented psyche, nausea overtook her. The overpowering perfume of all the flowers did not help.

She stood rigid to the left of the caskets. Dozens of strangers mingled among acquaintances in the unending line of mourners prepared to pay their respects. Cassie was amazed by how many people knew the Delaines. One by one, they solemnly tiptoed forward to present condolences to the grief-stricken daughter, engaging her in rote and meaningless conversations. But saying anything was preferable to awkward silence.

Mrs. Brandt, her parents' neighbor, croaked in the same gravelly voice that had scared her as a child. "Our sympathies are with you, dearie." With a mute nod, her husband shook Cassie's hand then led his wife over to a vacant seat.

Cassie's old Sunday school teacher told her, "They're in a better place now. God will look after them."

"How tragic," Mrs. Rothman sobbed.

Emma Farrell added, "At least they didn't suffer. My mother suffered in agony for months with her cancer before she passed."

Uncle Fred dutifully followed at Aunt Cecelia's elbow. She grasped Cassie's hand with both of hers, looking intently into her eyes. "Honey, we know you're going through a tremendous amount of pain, but the sooner you can get through the ordeal of going through their things, the sooner you can move on with your life. I'll give you a call and let you know when I can come over to help you. Most of it should probably go to charity but there are a few things I would like to have to remember my sister by." She released Cassie's hand then embraced her with a hug stronger than any she had ever offered before. Grabbing her husband's hand, Cecelia dragged him over to stand in front of Amanda's casket.

A stranger approached Cassie next, explaining his connection to her parents and expressing sadness at their passing. The line thinned as mourners took their places to await the funeral service. Cassandra glanced over the rows of waiting chairs and saw several familiar faces enter the back of the room. Someone must have notified the college. Tastefully dressed in dark suits, Angela, Beth, and Cindy had driven hours to show their support for her.

When they reached her, Angela began to speak, but before she could say a word, Cassie broke into a flood of tears. Her legs began to give out beneath her. Angela embraced her and guided her to an empty seat. Beth and Cindy hovered behind the chair as Angela knelt facing her roommate. Words were unnecessary; their mere presence spoke volumes. But as always, Angela managed to speak first.

"Cassie, I...I mean, we don't know what to say. We're so sorry for you. You have to know that we're here for you. We're skipping classes for the next few days to be here with you. Whatever we can do to help you, please tell us."

Cassie dabbed the tears from her eyes with one of her mother's old lace hankies. "I can't tell you what this means to me, having you guys coming all this way. Will you stay with me at my parents' home? It's so unbearably quiet at night."

"Of course," Beth and Cindy replied.

Before they could say anything else, the preacher approached. "Dear Cassandra, my deepest condolences." Reverend Simonson gently grasped her hands in his. "If you are ready we'll begin the service now."

The white-haired cleric deftly skirted the senselessness of the accident as he spoke a message of hope. Many were moved to tears at his eloquence promising reunion in the hereafter, but Cassie was only vaguely aware of what he said as she prayed for these rituals to end.

Neighbors had graciously prepared mountains of food, and when the horde of mourners was satiated and felt their somber duty fulfilled, they faded away. At long last the house was emptied of all but her college friends. Exhausted, Cassie slumped into a kitchen chair. She had tried to eat but each bite caused her to gag. Beth wrapped leftovers in tin foil while Angela washed dishes and Cindy dried them. Scraping the last of a Jell-O mold into a storage container, Beth took the dirty plate over to the sink to be washed. It slid out of her hands into the soapy water and splattered Angela.

Calmly, Angela scooped up some suds and flung them at Beth. In turn Beth flicked some icing from a cake back at her, but the frosting instead landed in the middle of Cassie's forehead. Cassie grabbed the spray bottle used for misting plants from under the sink and began furiously squirting everyone in the room with a feigned vengeance.

"I'll get you, my pretty!" she screeched, mimicking the witch from the Wizard of Oz. The playful battle released and relieved pent-up emotion. Laughing screams pierced the air as water and suds soaked the girls' hair and streaked whatever makeup tears had not washed away.

Slipping on the wet linoleum, Cindy landed with a thud. As the others reached to help her up, she pulled them down with her.

"God, you don't know how much I needed that," Cassie giggled. "I haven't had anything to laugh about in days. I really needed to get my mind on something else. I can't stand anymore funeral talk. Anything new happen back on campus since I left on Friday?"

Angela shrugged. "Oh, you know—same old stuff."

Cindy the social reporter chimed in. "Lucy Green broke up with Jason Butcher again. They'll probably be back together again by the time we get back. And Judy Florentina knocked over a whole stack of plates at Belmont Dining Hall. She nearly died of embarrassment. But I guess the biggest news is that the local Powerball winner still hasn't shown up to claim his prize. The couple in Arizona was on the national news Friday night. The man is a retired insurance salesman. I think his name was Goldman. He and his wife are planning a trip around the world. But can you imagine, the winner in our state hasn't even gone to the lottery office yet."

"That's smart, in my opinion," Angela affirmed. "Right now there are still reporters camped out trying to figure who the winner is. In a few weeks the frenzy to discover the lottery winner's identity will die down and they can claim their share of the prize anonymously."

Exasperated, Cindy said, "Angela, you and your secrecy all the time. I'd want to shout the fantastic news to the whole world if it were me that had won. What do you think, Cassie?"

Cassie teetered on the verge of divulging the truth. After all, these were pretty much the closest friends she had. She opened her mouth to speak, but a thought flashed into her head. The only people she had confided in were her parents and now they were dead. Perhaps sharing the news was a curse. "Sure, I guess I would want to tell if I had won. Why not? Maybe I'll have better luck next time." She paused. "Listen, I'm exhausted. I think I'll grab a shower and go to bed. You guys can stay up as long as you want. I'll see you in the morning."

The next few days Beth and Cindy ran to the supermarket, cooked meals, did laundry, and cleaned the house. Angela set the day's agenda and made it her personal responsibility to answer the unceasing telephone. The most persistent caller was Aunt Cecelia, who insisted on talking to her niece. Angela politely but firmly assured her and all the other well-wishers that she would relay their messages to her friend, but that Miss Delaine could not be disturbed.

This freed up Cassie to begin setting her parents' affairs in order. There was so much to be done. She visited the lawyer and the banks, and gathered all the necessary insurance documents. In a few days it became clear that settling her parents' estate was going to be a lengthy process. Cassie urged her friends to return to college. If they missed too much more they would not be able to catch up. She told them that she would take the rest of this semester off and then return to school, even though she knew she would not.

She watched Cindy's car disappear from view, taking with it her closest friends. Alone, she returned to the house and climbed the creaking stairs. Cassie had declined her aunt's offer to help, sensing her motives were not entirely altruistic. Though an extremely painful process, personal belongings needed to be sorted and boxed without intrusive suggestions. Clothing would be donated to charity, houseplants given to neighbors, unread magazines trashed, and a few requested mementos for relatives set aside.

Tentatively Cassie turned the knob of the door to her parents' bedroom. She hadn't been able to touch a thing in this room yet. Last week's issues of *Time* and *Newsweek* lay casually tossed on her father's nightstand. A romance novel opened to the third chapter cradled her mother's reading glasses on her side of the bed.

On the floor near the front window sat a large wrapped box with an enormous bow taped to the top. She had forgotten all about her birthday gift. Cassie knelt next to the present. Slowly she removed the wrappings. Inside were several thick scrapbook albums. Cassie settled to sit cross-legged and page through the first one. In addition to pictures of her were locks of hair and report cards. She smiled fondly, and giggling occasionally she examined the other books. They were stuffed with scout awards, soccer ribbons and team pictures, and programs from church plays she had been in. Larry Reed had been a full five inches shorter than her when she played Noah's wife in second grade. The last album had concert ticket stubs and pressed flowers from her prom corsage.

Each page was a work of art. Her mother must have spent hours getting ideas from scrapbooking magazines. Cassie particularly liked the photo of her with Mrs. Salerno decorated with bingo cards and chips. But her favorite album was the one filled with family holiday and vacation photos. The title page had a close-up of her mother and father at the beach. She kissed her fingers then touched them to the photograph.

Hours must have lapsed before pain in her lower back urged her to stand and stretch. Burt brushed by Cassie's legs then leapt onto the bed as if looking for the missing occupants. Cassie tiptoed over to the dresser; it seemed normal noise would be sacrilegious. An assortment of half-empty perfume bottles was neatly arranged on a mirrored tray. Amanda's favorite necklace and two pair of earrings were tossed in a ceramic dish waiting to be properly returned to the jewelry armoire. Cassie fastened her mother's locket around her own neck. The necklace from Greg lay about a half an inch below it on her chest. The next day she would pack up her sorrows and resolve to create her new life. But this day she could face no more. Cassie scooped Burt into her arms. She turned and walked out of the room, quietly closing the door on the past.

Bruiser

Chapter 5.

Once again Cassandra Delaine trudged up her driveway's steep incline after fetching the late afternoon mail. Midway up she paused briefly to catch her breath. *What a waste of energy,* she thought. It was mostly junk mail again. For the tenth time that day, Cassie wondered what had possessed her to buy this property. It had seemed like such a good idea at the time. Despite her financial advisor's reassurance that she could afford a much more expensive home, Cassie considered this one quite lavish enough. Obviously pregnant when she purchased this house, she wanted them both to live comfortably over an entire lifetime.

Besides, she had worried neighborhood children would be too distant for a young child to visit friends if they lived on an overly large estate. Fond memories of best friends sharing secrets in the backyard had prompted hopes of quality playmates for her child. Driving through this development she had noticed elaborate wooden playgrounds and children's playhouses resembling miniature versions of their homes. But now, three years after purchasing the lot, she was thankful her property was large enough to provide a little privacy from the others on Crestview Drive. Strange how what once drew her to this house and community was now a distant dream.

Originally Cassie had been impressed by how imposing her stone and brick two-story colonial looked as it sat high on the hill. But what once struck her as elegant now felt stifling. The English ivy elegantly cascading down the sloping front yard she now realized had been planted to avoid having to maneuver a lawn mower on such a steep incline. Throughout this community, carefully choreographed individuality marked the landscaping. Surgically snipped evergreen spirals stood sentry by front doors and mature trees and gumdrop-trimmed shrubs lined the walkways.

Loft Estates kept maintenance crews busy planting, pruning, mowing, and shoveling all year round. All that attention to spectacular curb appeal was impressive. However, the offending belching, clacking, and humming noises of those dreaded lawn service machines forced mother and child to evacuate the premises. Her child's screams routinely joined the clamor if Cassie was foolish enough to attempt to endure the racket. Unfortunately, there was no avoiding the roaring snow plows in winter. Protesting wails simply had to be endured when they were snowbound. This past winter, thankfully, had been relatively mild. Cassie hated backing her Mercedes down the slope in ice or snow.

Far too often, these practical matters intruded into her romanticized vision of what life should have become. She wistfully remembered herself as the pretty blond of not so very long ago. Now the woman who greeted her each morning in the mirror frightened her. Trips to the hairdresser were rare these days. Money most certainly was not the issue. Instead it was the chaos that ensued each time she brought her toddler to the beauty salon. Touching up dark roots at home rarely worked well, either; there never seemed to be a long enough stretch of time available.

And her hair was not the only negative part of this transformation. Cassie once had a stunning figure. But try as she might, over two and a half years after giving birth she still couldn't seem to take the weight off. That wasn't too horrible, she supposed, but those dark circles under her eyes from lack of sleep concerned her. Perhaps once back inside she could rest her eyes for a few minutes.

Somehow this was one of those extremely rare times when her child was peacefully in a light sleep. Cassie sat down on the overstuffed sofa in her family room. She kicked off her shoes and curled her legs beneath her. Burt leapt effortlessly onto the companion loveseat. Typical of most cats, he wanted to be close enough to keep her company but sufficiently distant to avoid unrequested petting.

Cassie absentmindedly flicked through the stack of advertisements for low interest credit cards as her mind wandered over events of the last few years. The enormity of the lottery win and her parents' deaths had barely begun to sink in when she realized she was pregnant. Her religious beliefs prohibited considering abortion and the prospect of raising a child promised a sense of purpose for her future. In the midst of liquidating the Delaine estate, the life growing within her provided something positive to focus on and simplified her decision to move from Amberville. The last thing she wanted was local wagging tongues speculating on who, why, when, and where.

The most difficult self-debate had been regarding Greg. A few times after she left college, he had asked Angela for her unlisted phone number. Cassie adamantly refused to give it to him until she knew how much she wanted to tell him. A thousand times she had changed her mind as to whether he should know. What would she say? If she told him she was pregnant would he feel obligated to marry her? Worse yet, would he shun her and demand an abortion? If he did choose to remain involved in their lives, would he grow resentful of her and the baby?

Most troubling was her lottery win. Would knowing about her windfall falsely encourage Greg to pursue a relationship with her? Would they truly have chosen a life together if none of this had happened? In reality, there had only been a handful of dates, and she'd had no intention to get physical so quickly. Somehow a drink or two too many and Greg's flowery praise had eroded her previously unbroken commitment to an abstinence pledge.

Cassie had so many unanswered questions. The more she anguished over what course to take, the more time elapsed. In the end, her inaction became the action. The passage of time made contacting Greg too uncomfortable to even consider. She never did call. She was too afraid of the potential answers. Worse yet, her failure to inform Greg caused her to have a fight with Angela, ending their friendship. With some sadness, she resolved her future would have to be bright without anyone from her past.

After the bouts of morning sickness had subsided, the rest of the pregnancy was rather uneventful. She ate healthily and took special vitamins prescribed by her obstetrician. The next months were busy with investment choices, purchasing her home, and equipping the nursery with the latest and best available. Determined to make mothering her career, Cassie read several books on parenting. Confused by experts' contradictory views on various issues, she was nonetheless enthusiastic that she would be the best mother ever.

Signing up for birthing classes at Sweetwater Hospital had been awkward at first without a partner. Then the instructor introduced her to a maternity nurse who volunteered to fill in. Pamela Brooks coached her to find a focal point and control her breathing. After childbirth classes they would go for coffee and dessert to Heaven's Delights pastry shop. Each week Pamela asked what the current answer was to her pressing question.

"Okay, Cassie what's the name going to be? You better decide soon!" she mockingly admonished.

Cassandra pondered long and hard for weeks as to what the name should be. For a girl it was no question, at least at first. She always was partial to the name Jennifer. But the more she thought about it, lots of other lovely names were under consideration. Lindsay, Samantha, Danielle, Alyssa, and Erin were all beautiful names. Marissa sounded so melodic, but then again so did Brianna—and Josie was such a friendly name. Hmm, the choice for a girl was not as easy as she had first thought.

Pamela asked Cassie how her own name had been chosen. The only thing she knew was that her mother had a fondness for movies and movie stars. Amanda always said if she had another girl it would have been either Scarlett or Sophia.

Unable to decide on a girl's name, she shifted her attention to boys'. She wanted a good strong name if her baby was a boy. Maybe Jeffery or Albert would do. Perhaps she should choose a biblical name like Matthew, John, or Benjamin. She like the sound of the names Ian and Jared but wasn't sure how well they fit with her last name. Many names reached the top of the list but she kept coming back to her grandfather's. He had died when she was only five years old. Even though she had been very young, she still had very fond memories of him. Brian. Yes, if it were a boy, it would be Brian Peter Delaine in memory of her paternal grandfather.

On the morning a taxi rushed Cassie to the hospital, contractions had begun at three a.m. Miraculously her labor was only five and a half hours long. Pamela held her hand and encouraged her until a pudgy, nine-pound-three-ounce boy burst into the world looking like he would tackle anything in his path.

Pamela took one look at the mini fullback and exclaimed, "Cassie might name him Brian but she should call him Bruiser."

Suddenly, Cassie's reminiscences ceased as her son set to wailing full force upstairs. *Why won't he sleep?* she worried. Not only were his naps virtually nonexistent, but he constantly awakened throughout the night as well. As soon as the sleeping child's cheek touched his cool sheets, he would jerk awake and threaten to rouse the entire neighborhood with his screeching wail.

Outings weren't much better; if one more stranger at the grocery store offered unsolicited advice on how to calm him, Cassie thought she would scream. Didn't they all realize she had tried the standard parenting book suggestions to no avail? Nevertheless, each experienced mother expected her advice was a novel approach Cassie had not heard before.

Cassie had even briefly tried a nanny. This supposed professional didn't have much luck with her son either and quit. In fact he seemed to cry even more gustily with any babysitter that she hired. Cassie felt like such a failure; women of all sorts of backgrounds and intelligence raised children. She should be quite capable; she was rather bright, in fact. Why did she have so much trouble?

At least Bruiser had calmed slightly when he started walking. Correction: when he started running. Still, he seemed a paradox. Content to flee through an unfamiliar mall, he was terrified when he was in one room and his mother left to retrieve something from another. What on earth was his problem now?

Slipping her feet into her loafers, she wearily climbed the stairs and pushed open the door of his circus-themed nursery. Cheerful clowns holding primary color balloons were boldly painted on the wall next to his dresser. Pale blue and white stripes topped a circus train border at chair rail height. A four-foot plush lion wrestled an equally large stuffed tiger on the floor. Painted on the wall next to the window was a juggler balancing on one foot.

True to the circus theme, hanging like a trapeze artist, Bruiser hovered above the floor dangling by a sleeve snagged on the crib's rail post. Cassie gasped like a crowd realizing there was no net below. With the skill of an acrobat, she darted across the room to catch the failed circus performer.

Instead of being grateful for the rescue, Bruiser arched his back, screeched, and struggled to free himself from his mother's arms. But before permitting his disappearing act to continue, she struggled to change his diaper and then released him to play with his toys.

While picking up his discarded socks, trousers, and stuffed animals flung from the crib, Cassie trembled, realizing how close he had come to injury. There was no time to gather her composure, however, for suddenly she heard a gurgling, sputtering whoosh. Bruiser had scampered down the hall to flush the toilet. From past experience she knew he never used it for its intended purpose. He merely liked to watch the water swirl away then reappear.

Exasperation rose as she viewed the scene through the bathroom doorway. Next to the toilet, Bruiser stood atop a step stool meant to assist with potty training. He plunked his toothbrush and a bar of soap into the bowl. Along with those items, five giant pop beads, three stacking cups, and a rubber ducky floated in the commode. She swept her son off the stool and plopped him into the tub, where he was quickly bathed against his will. Dried and dressed, Bruiser was deposited in his playpen.

Cassie returned to the bathroom to fish out the potpourri of floating toys, then thoroughly washed and dried them. Frustrated, she realized something had to be done; her son's energy level was beyond her ability to cope.

A quick peek assured her that Bruiser was contently playing with a pop-up box in the playpen. She determined it was safe to get an ever-so-brief shower. For added security, she latched the child safety gate across the top of the stairs. Too much time would elapse if she shaved her legs, so instead she just quickly shampooed her neglected hair. As if trying to beat a stopwatch she quickly pulled on a jersey top and a pair of blue jeans over her still damp body then wrapped a towel turban style around her head. Then she darted back to find an empty playpen. Frantically she dashed back through the hallway. Draped over the safety gate was his diaper. Suddenly aware of furious pounding, she dashed down the stairs and flung open the front door.

A prim and proper matron in pearls stood fuming in the doorway. Ester Bagley, Cassie's irate neighbor, was president of the local horticulture society. Her hair was disheveled with flecks of drying mud on her right cheek. Naked below the waist, Bruiser squirmed under her right arm while she clutched broken rhododendron buds in her left hand. Mud splatters from the toddler's hands and feet were smeared all along the skirt of her lavender Lord & Taylor suit.

Looking at Cassie's towel headdress Mrs. Bagley's face grew beet red. "Ms. Delaine, do you see this? While you were apparently luxuriating in a bubble bath, your little brat wrecked my garden again. Every last bud from my prized 'Trinidad' rhododendron has been plucked off. There won't be a single bloom this year! As if that weren't enough, while he plundered the bushes, he turned the spigot on and flooded out the 'Snowbird' daffodils and 'Ballade' tulips."

"I — I'm so sorry, Mrs. Bagley. I don't know how he managed to get outside," Cassie stammered.

"Really!" Ester Bagley snapped. "Maybe if you spent a little more time watching him instead of pampering yourself you wouldn't have such an uncontrollable child."

Cassie bit her tongue, determined not to show her irritation at the stinging accusation. "I'd be happy to pay for—" she began.

"You most certainly *will* get a bill from the landscaper to repair my front garden. But nothing can replace the fact that the rhododendron won't bloom. Don't think I've forgotten what he did to my hyacinths last week either."

Bruiser began to pee down her leg.

"*Oh my God!*" she shrieked. Releasing the toddler, who scurried past his mother toward the kitchen, she screamed "Good day!" before turning abruptly, throwing her head back, and storming away.

Cassie shut the door and sighed as she muttered to herself, "She must never have had kids. Or if she did, I bet they were perfect little robots." She walked to the kitchen to find what Bruiser was into. Somehow he had pushed a dinette chair next to the refrigerator and pulled himself up onto it. Now he was standing on tiptoes trying desperately to retrieve a bag of chocolate chip cookies safely out of reach on top of the fridge.

"Brian Peter Delaine! What am I to do with you?" Cassie scolded.

He ignored his mother's voice as if he had not heard her and continued to claw at the sides of the icebox. She grabbed him by the waist and toted him up the stairs for his third bath of the day. Despite the pointlessness of her efforts, Cassie casually tossed a few bath toys into the tub as she filled it. Bruiser ignored the playthings, instead clutching the bottle of baby shampoo and vigorously shaking it while his mother's angry hands soaped his body.

Bruiser was oblivious to his mother's fury as he repeated the process of shaking the shampoo then watching the bubbles slide down the side like an hourglass again and again. Muddy water from Mrs. Bagley's garden gurgled down the drain. All the while Cassie, the Powerball winner, wondered not if she had the money to try a nanny again, but if she could stand the disappointment of another one quitting.

Cassie carried her son back down to the kitchen. He pointed toward the cookies and screeched. It was now past dinnertime and she hadn't even started cooking the evening meal yet. After Bruiser was lifted into his high chair and firmly strapped in place, she eyed a box of Cheerios in the cupboard. Cassie promised herself that she would prepare a better meal the next evening. She just didn't have the energy to assemble ingredients while having to constantly glance over her shoulder. Her son must have studied under Houdini.

She poured the cereal into a green plastic bowl then set it on the high chair tray. He screamed with annoyance, sending the bowl to the floor. Little oat circles rolled under the stove and kitchen table. A few even landed in Burt's water dish. Too weary to care, Cassie returned to the cabinet where the bowls were kept. Silly mother, how could she forget? Cheerios belong in the blue dish. The green bowl was for Rice Krispies. The yellow bowl was reserved for Cinnamon Toast Crunch, and never put anything but Lucky Charms in the red bowl.

Once they were in their proper blue dish, Bruiser happily munched away on the Cheerios. Cassie popped a frozen entrée into the microwave. She should be eating steak and shrimp at Roberto's. Instead she ate something that tasted like cardboard and had far too much salt. What was it anyway? No matter, she thought, a bowl of rocky road ice cream would wash away dinner's aftertaste.

After vacuuming the last bit of cereal into his chubby face, the tornado broke free. A cartoonish Tasmanian devil spun his way into the family room. Though barely able to reach the button, he managed to turn the television on. With his back to the screen he dumped a container of brightly colored die-cast cars onto the floor. He scooped them back into the tub, and then dumped them out again. Next he picked the cars up individually and stacked them in a specific order in the bin. First a black Toyota Camry fell into place, then a blue Ford Explorer. Next the yellow school bus crashed into the bucket. Two blue

Chevy convertibles preceded the dump truck. A green Harley Davidson followed a red pickup truck. The Volkswagen beetle landed on the Mitsubishi and the Jeep. He didn't like the purple minivan; it was flung to his right under the loveseat, barely missing Burt. A white Cadillac topped the collection.

When he was finished, Bruiser raised the bucket over his head. With great gusto the overturned bin rained metal vehicles. Deftly finding the Camry, the process was repeated again and again until his eyes refused to stay open any longer.

Cassie carefully carted a sleeping Bruiser to the nursery. Fearing too much jostling would wake him, she laid him in his crib without changing him into pajamas. After all, he would awaken in a few hours anyway; she could change him then. Using her last ounce of her energy she cleaned up the kitchen. In the morning, Cassie vowed, she would find some help.

"Hello, Mrs. Clifton? This is Cassandra Delaine. I saw the sign on your property indicating that you have a childcare service in your home." Cassie struggled to keep the phone cradled between her left ear and shoulder while trying to diaper a moving target. Bruiser was desperately trying a new Houdini move, but with rodeo-like skill his mother managed the Pamper and a change of clothes. "I'm interested in a part-time situation to give me a little break. Do you have any openings?"

"As a matter of fact, I do. Normally I watch six preschoolers; two are my own," a cheerful voice informed her. "Recently the father of two of my regulars was transferred to Atlanta. I miss having a full house. It's good company for my own children. How old did you say your child is?"

"Bruiser, I mean Brian, is three years old. Well, almost three. He'll be three in a few months."

"Is he potty trained yet?" Sally Clifton asked.

"No, I'm afraid we haven't had much luck in that department." Cassie hated to admit that Bruiser wanted nothing at all to do with sitting still that long.

"I prefer potty trained children but I've gone through it with my three- and four-year-old. I'm sure we can work on that with your son. Sometimes being around other older children encourages toddlers to want to be a big kid, too. Before Molly was born I worked as a teaching assistant in a kindergarten; it's amazing what kids are willing to try in order to fit in." The voice on the other end of the line sounded confident and experienced. "Why don't you stop by and check us out. If you're comfortable with the situation you can leave you son for a few hours so we can get to know him. When would you like to come?"

"Is today too soon?" Cassie eagerly inquired.

"Well, I guess today is as good as any other day. Why not? Let's say around eleven o'clock. If there's no answer when you knock, come around back. It's such a lovely morning I'll probably have the kids playing outside for a little while before lunchtime. We have a new wooden playground set; the kids have been itching to play on it. I like them to get plenty of fresh air and exercise. So then, I'll see you in a little while."

Excitedly Cassie packed the diaper bag, hoping that Sally Clifton and a brood of children would be the answer for Bruiser. With keys in her right hand, she attempted to harness her cyclone.

Bruiser hated to be buckled in his car seat but loved to go for a trip in the car. He loved any kind of motion. Rides in the Mercedes or jaunts in a stroller were thoroughly enjoyed as long as you didn't stop. Cassie had become quite adept at finding back roads to avoid some of the traffic lights because red signals seemed an eternity with a screaming toddler. But once a pattern was set to a familiar place, the same route was required for subsequent trips to avoid tantrums. Fortunately the few signals en-route were green today.

Cassie pulled up in front of a tidy split-level home on Greenbrier Lane. A stockade fence enclosed the rear yard, protectively shielding the occupants from intrusion. Or better yet, Cassie hoped it would secure her son the mountain goat from escaping.

As she and Bruiser walked up the front path, voices rang out cheerfully playing behind the enclosure. She wandered around the side to find the gate secured. *That's a good sign*, she thought as she firmly rapped on the tall wooden fence.

"Mrs. Clifton? It's Cassandra Delaine."

The gate unlatched and a short, jovial brunette beckoned them to enter. Sally's round face beamed as she welcomed the Delaines. "Please come in. The children are anxious to meet you."

Four children bounded from across the back lawn, curious to check out the new kid. Sally tapped each one on their head as she introduced them.

"These are my two. The Shirley Temple ringlets belong to Molly. This is Robert—it's his turn to be the leader today. Isn't it, Bobby? This little sweetheart is Marie and over there is my helper of the day, Justin. Say hello, kids."

"Hi," they obediently responded.

Sally stooped to child's height to face Bruiser. "What's your name, young man?"

He looked past her to a sandbox in the rear of the yard. Ignoring Mrs. Clifton and the other children, Bruiser pushed past them and ran to the object of his focus. At once he began gathering sand in his hands and then releasing it through his fingers.

Sally laughed. "I guess he's just too anxious to begin playing. That's okay. Listen, why don't you take a look inside? I need to stay out here to keep an eye on the children, but you can go on in. See if you think the setup is satisfactory. Just go through the sliding glass doors there on the patio. I pretty much stay on the lower level the whole time the kids are here. It's safer that way for the little ones."

Cassie slid the door open to find everything arranged with the children in mind. The large bright recreation room had several beanbag chairs and a comfortable sofa facing built-in bookcases. Lower shelves were secured behind locked doors. In the middle was a television with VCR and DVD players hooked up. An ample supply of children's videos was visible to the right. On the left a brimming pile of games, coloring books, and crayons was stored. Sleeping mats and light blankets were stowed in the corner for naptime. Toys were sorted into large plastic bins. A kitchen table and child-size picnic tables were set on the far side of the room next to a small refrigerator and cupboard filled with nutritious snacks. Everything seemed in order.

Cassie returned to the backyard. Sally Clifton was seated on a bench under a large shade tree blowing bubbles. Four children wildly chased them with glee, but Bruiser remained engrossed by sand slipping through his fingers.

Sally continued to blow bubbles while she spoke. "He seems a bit shy for this rowdy, noisy bunch," she laughed. "Don't worry, I'm sure he'll warm up to them. Listen, the mall is just down the road a bit. Why don't you leave him here for an hour or two to get to know us? Before you know it he'll join right in."

Cassie hesitated. "I don't know. You don't understand; he is really a little whirl-wind and can be quite a handful when he gets going."

"Trust me, I know children," Sally Clifton reassured her. "He'll be fine, and you look like you could use a little break. We'll discuss payment details and the schedule of what days you want him to come after you get back."

Cassie scribbled on a slip of paper. "Okay, here's my cell phone number. Call if he's any problem and I'll come right back."

"Don't worry! Go. Relax and have some fun."

Driving alone felt like soaring through the clouds on brightly colored wings. She had not been in public for such a long time without Bruiser. What should she do with this freedom? Trying on a new outfit without a stroller stuffed in the fitting room would be so liberating. The last time she tried a dress on he had squirmed free of the stroller straps and crawled under the dressing room door into another stall. The half-clothed executive in the next cubicle did not find it at all funny having a toddler rummage around looking for keys in her purse. Then of course there was the time she dragged her tantruming son out of Van Beck's. His blood curdling screams sent security scrambling after them, perhaps thinking she was an abusive mother.

Savoring this unexpected liberation, she turned the Mercedes onto Lincoln Boulevard. One block before Sweetwater Mall was Laburnum Cafe. It was a little early for lunch, but it would be such a lovely treat to dine alone in peace and quiet unencumbered by motherly responsibilities. Yes, her delightful indulgence would be a meal that was not nuked in between dodging Cheerios and wiping sticky fingers. Had she planned this outing more thoughtfully she would have dressed up, but at this point Cassie really didn't care about her appearance. Her blue jeans and cream-colored sweater had not yet succumbed to Bruiser's artistry so she was fairly presentable.

A short stocky maitre d' with fringes of dark hair crowning his head like a laurel wreath ushered her to a booth by the front window. Cassie glanced outside. Near a bed of late spring flowers, several birds flitted back and forth searching for leftover supper crumbs.

Tearing herself away from the pleasant panorama, she studied the leather-bound menu. A handsome young waiter approached and artfully described the daily specials as he filled her water glass. Delighted by the sound of ice clinking against the glass, Cassie reveled in the simple pleasure of having someone wait on her for a change. What was all her fortune for if she couldn't be pampered once in a while?

Her mouth watered as she ordered French onion soup and a spinach salad. The waiter placed a basket of warm rolls on the linen tablecloth and then proceeded to repeat the specials to a group of businessmen newly seated near the bar. Rapidly the popular restaurant began to fill with hungry patrons. Again Cassie's attention was drawn by the view out the window as the siren of a hook and ladder truck screamed by, momentarily startling the birds.

In short order a steaming hot bowl of onion soup baked with a gooey cheese crust was set before her. Carefully cooling it slightly with a breath she savored the warmth. By the fourth spoonful, she nearly forgot her troubles.

Someone's annoying cell phone started to ring, disturbing the tranquility. All eyes in the now crowded establishment darted around the room attempting to locate the direction of the inconsiderate sound. Suddenly Cassie realized that she was the owner of the offending phone. Hurriedly she fished through her purse and finally retrieved it after the fifth ring.

A desperate and breathless voice urged, "Ms. Delaine, I'm sorry but I'm afraid you need to return immediately."

"Mrs. Clifton, what's the matter? Is Brian all right?"

"Yes, he's okay now, but you need to come back right away. Please hurry. Goodbye."

Confused and concerned, Cassie signaled the waiter over. She explained there was an emergency and needed to leave. He stood at the table rapidly dumping the remainder of her onion soup and as yet untouched spinach salad into Styrofoam containers while Cassie frantically searched her wallet for the correct cash to cover the bill and an appropriate tip for such a hasty retreat. Grabbing her leftovers, she darted through the parking lot to her Mercedes.

Cassie was even more alarmed to see the hook and ladder truck from before parked in front of Mrs. Clifton's home. Hurrying through the open gate, Cassie stopped dead in her tracks. Several firemen were milling about trying to help Mrs. Clifton calm crying children. A raincoat clad rescuer knelt in front of the pig-tailed blond, gently wiping tears from her face. Another fireman safely corralled two curious boys while a ladder was retracted from the roof of the house. Sally Clifton sat cradling a sobbing mop of brown ringlets seated on her lap. Back by the sandbox a husky fireman struggled to retain his firm grasp on her squirming Bruiser.

Fearful of what the response would be, Cassie tentatively inquired, "What happened?"

"Ms. Delaine! Thank God you're back. I'm sorry but I just don't think your child is going to fit in here. The other children tried to make him welcome but as soon as Justin sat next to him he threw sand in his eyes. I scolded Brian but he seemed not to hear me. While I was trying to help Justin, he bit Marie's arm. I sat Brian on the bench and said he had to stay there in time-out. I ran into the house for just a minute to get some peroxide and band-aids for Marie. But by the time I returned, your son had scaled the playground equipment and climbed into the tree. I yelled for him to come down and he ignored me. I tried to climb after him." Sally paused, trembling from the experience and trying to catch her breath. "The closer I got to him the higher he climbed until he jumped from a limb onto the roof of the back porch. All of the children called after him but he kept climbing higher. I had to call 911. Ms. Delaine, is your child deaf? Why didn't you tell me?"

"No, he isn't deaf," was all Cassie could manage.

"Well, why doesn't he speak at all? I couldn't get him to say a single word. That's very peculiar for a child his age. What does the doctor say?"

Cassie ignored the question, turned and sheepishly retrieved the troublemaker from the struggling fireman. "I'm so sorry he was such a problem. Please accept this donation for the firemen's fund," she said, handing him two large bills. Before returning her wallet to her purse, she paid Mrs. Clifton three times the normal daily fee for childcare.

"I did warn you he was quite a handful, but again, I am sorry for the catastrophe he caused." Cassandra lifted her son onto her hip to carry him to the car. He arched his back, not wanting to be in contact with his mother. Nevertheless, she grasped him tightly to her as she strode back to the Mercedes, muttering under her breath, "This was one hell of an expensive outing. What do you have planned for the rest of the day, buddy?"

The drive home passed in silence. She was too furious to utter another word. Dejected, Cassie parked the auto in her driveway then opened the rear door to unbuckle Bruiser. He bolted for the front door and hung on the locked handle trying to get in. Once inside, the whirling dervish made a beeline to the television. He turned it on and swooped up his bin of Matchbox cars. They rained down onto the floor. As if compelled to repeat his ritual, the child sat and selected cars. First a black Toyota

Camry fell into place. Then a blue Ford Explorer followed. Next the yellow school bus crashed into the bucket.

His mother wearily tossed the plastic bag with her partially eaten lunch onto the kitchen counter. The salad was already a wilted mess. Her stomach turned, not even wanting to see if the rest of the soup was salvageable. She scooped both containers up and heaved them into the trash. Slowly she proceeded to the family room and dropped into a sobbing heap on the sofa.

Two blue Chevy convertibles preceded the dump truck. A green Harley Davidson followed a red pickup truck. The Volkswagen beetle landed on the Mitsubishi and the Jeep.

An eternity later, Cassie dried her eyes, grabbed a granola bar as a substitute for her fine lunch, and resumed with resignation the typical chores she had dreamed she would never do again upon winning the lottery. Careful to always keep an eye on her son, she unloaded the dishwasher and proceeded to attack a basket full of clothes.

Her silent, self-pitying thoughts were suddenly interrupted. *Come, answer me*, the telephone insisted. Even if it were a telemarketer, the sound of a somewhat friendly adult voice would be welcome. Cassie stopped folding laundry and reached for the remote control to turn the television's volume down. Bruiser was contentedly dumping his fleet of vehicles in the middle of the family room seemingly oblivious to the ringing phone. The moment the din of the commercial began to soften, Bruiser jumped up and raced to the TV. He pressed a button until the volume resumed its previous level. Turning his back to the screen he darted back to his task of crashing metal toys into his bucket.

Grabbing the cordless phone from its perch, Cassie walked to the kitchen. She could still keep an eye on the collisions but maintain a more normal tone of voice from that distance.

"Cassie?" the voice on the other end of the line asked. "It's been a century since we talked."

Cassie could hardly believe her ears. "Angela, is that you? It's so great to hear your voice. What have you been up to?"

She could barely contain her excitement at hearing her old pal's voice. They hadn't spoken since before Bruiser was born. Angela had been adamant that Cassie should tell Greg about the baby. The ensuing argument resulted in hurt feelings and stubborn positions on both sides. A rift widened with each passing day, and stubbornness kept each of them from apologizing. Cassie had wanted to renew her friendship countless times in the intervening years, but fear of rejection forced her to replace the receiver every time before the first ring. How lovely it would have been to share the pains and pleasures of motherhood with her dear friend.

Angela spoke in a rush. "Cassie, I know we said a lot of hurtful things to each other the last time I saw you. Can we forgive and forget? I miss your friendship something awful."

"Of course," Cassie gushed. "I've wanted so much to talk to you again. There's so much to tell you and I can't wait to hear what's going on in your life. Do you have a boyfriend? How's work?"

Angela interrupted. "I'm afraid I don't have much time to go into things right now; I have to get back to a meeting. But, maybe we can get together and have a nice long visit? Perhaps you could get a sitter and we can go to that Italian restaurant we were supposed to go to the last time I was in your area. What was the name...Roberto's?"

Most of the local babysitters made excuses when Cassie called. Even if she could locate one, it would be disastrous to have her visit cut short by an emergency phone call; the experience at Laburnum Cafe was still fresh in her mind.

"Why don't you come here?" Cassie offered. "I haven't had a reason to use my mother's china since I moved here. It's a sin to have that beautiful Noritake just sitting in the china cabinet unused."

"That would be great if you're sure you don't mind. How about this Friday night? I have a business trip in your area. I'll be staying at the Rosewood Inn overnight."

"Don't be silly. I have plenty of room here for you to sleep in one the guest rooms. It will be like old times."

"I don't want to be an imposition." Angela argued. "I mean, I don't want you to go to all that trouble."

"Please, Angela, I would love the company of someone who doesn't listen to the songs of an obnoxiously happy, purple dinosaur!" When they hung up the phone, Cassie felt better than she had in months. Finally, something to look forward to.

Chapter 6.

Friday found Cassie frantically finishing up the last details of preparation for her reunion with Angela. She intended to splurge and hire a cleaning service, but unfortunately there were no openings on their schedule with such short notice— or at least that's what they told her. The previous attempts at retaining regular housekeepers had ended in disaster. Cassie felt sure that Rosa and Sophie from AAA Maids had informed their employer as to why they would not work at her house. Rosa had lasted a few months. But, the repetition of straightening up the family room only to have toys dumped in front of the vacuum before she could turn it on, wore the frustrated maid out. Bruiser screamed and covered his ears with his hands whenever the motor roared to life.

Sophie quit after less than a week. For some reason that Cassie never figured out, Bruiser hated Sophie. All the rotund housekeeper had to do was enter the room and he would begin to hurl whatever was at hand in her direction. She kept a wary eye on the toddler while gathering magazines he had scattered like stepping-stones on the carpet. After turning to find the last periodical wedged between the television and a stack of videos, Sophie straightened up. Before she had time to react, Bruiser's sipper cup sailed through the air and hit her squarely between the eyes. In the blink of an eye, Sophie filled a baggie with ice which she pressed to her forehead then swooped up her belongings and left.

AAA Maids was unable to find a permanent replacement to work at Crestview Drive after that. Inquiries left on the answering machine of Duchess Cleaning Service were not responded to either. Obviously word spread quickly that a little demon ruled this roost.

So, Cassie spent the next few days attempting to harness Bruiser's energy as she tried to make the house spotlessly clean for Angela's visit. But as soon as one room was straightened and almost clean, Bruiser had demolished two others. By some miracle the house was fairly presentable by Friday afternoon. Hopefully her friend would understand if things were not perfect; Angela knew she had a toddler. At least dinner would be special. Roberto's was going to deliver a sumptuous feast at five o'clock. All she needed to do before her friend arrived was to set the table.

Her dining room furniture was pristine; Cassie had purchased an entirely new suite upon moving to Crestview Drive. Considering her grief over her parents' deaths it had been emotionally easier for her to sell the house in Amberville fully furnished. The only possessions retained were Amanda's china and jewelry, Carl's coin collection and golf clubs, a few sentimental knick-knacks, and her birthday scrapbooks. Besides, it had been fun working with a decorator picking out an entire house full of furniture to match her own style without worrying about the cost. Whenever feelings of depression or grief threatened to overtake her, Cassie had forced herself to focus on decorating details and delivery schedules.

She particularly loved how the dining room turned out. Unfortunately there had been little opportunity to use it. Most days the French doors to the dining room were locked to protect its contents from the proverbial bull. From time to time when she was certain Bruiser was safely occupied or asleep, Cassie would lovingly dust the furniture's glassy surfaces. The table's highly polished finish shone like a mirror; it almost seemed a shame to hide it under the lace tablecloth. She carefully slid a soft cloth along the beautiful Queen Anne-styled cherry buffet and china cabinet while she admired how her mother's china sparkled in its display.

Cassie tugged on the handle of the cabinet door. It was stiff and unyielding at first, probably from lack of use. A second yank proved more successful.

After removing a delicate saucer from the shelf, she ran her finger around the rim, admiring this pattern she had at one time disliked. Her eyes welled up at childhood memories of these dishes filled with favorite family recipes. Every Thanksgiving and Christmas, her mother prepared for a house full of relatives by carefully setting the dinning room table with her prized Noritake china. Not so subtly, Aunt Cecelia hinted every so often that she would dearly love to have the bone china bequeathed to her and after the funeral Cassie had spotted her examining the collection while other mourners focused on the food.

One Christmas when Cassie was about twelve years old she was allowed to help carefully place the delicate dishes at each place. With great pride Amanda handed Cassie a cup and saucer. "Careful, dear," she had admonished. "Someday you will inherit my precious china." From that time on, Cassandra Delaine harbored an embarrassing secret: she didn't want this prized possession. Oh, sure, the china was pretty; petite roses and leaves graced the wide band of the plates in subtle tones of pink, yellow, and green. But she had longed to pick out her own things, what she wanted. The Shenandoah pattern looked almost antique to a young Cassie's eyes; at that age she preferred more modern designs. But Cassie felt that to admit she didn't feel the honor of the inheritance would prove her to be an ungrateful, disloyal daughter. So she kept her silence.

Now the passage of time and events had altered her sense of what was valuable and beautiful. The aroma of freshly brewed coffee and spiced pumpkin pie filled her nostrils though the cups and plates were empty. More than anything else possibly could, the Noritake brought her comfort when she longed for her mother's spirit.

After the last bread plate was carefully set on the table, she shut the breakfront door just as the phone began to ring.

"Hello? Mrs. C. Delaine? How are you this evening?" The unfamiliar voice oozed the sincerity of a three-dollar bill.

"I'm fine, thank you. Who is this?" she responded.

"My name is Cheryl Wolfe and I have some exciting news. You have been pre-approved by Sprigmore Bank for a generous line of credit on a low interest loan. Just think of the possibilities that an extra five thousand dollars would do for you. Maybe you have some home improvements that need doing. You could even use it for a down payment on a new car."

Cassie tapped her foot. Impatient to ensure the rest of the house was still presentable, she attempted a curt end to the sales pitch. "Thank you but I'm not interested."

"Mrs. Delaine, who couldn't use a little extra cash? Our interest rates are the lowest they have been for six months. The application process is really very simple. We'll issue a check along with a new credit card linked to your account. Just pay the minimum balance due on your monthly statement and you're in business."

"No thank you. I don't want the money or the credit card."

"But Mrs. Delaine, you haven't heard all the details. You see..."

Cassie sternly interrupted "I said no! Goodbye!" She slammed the receiver down with a thud. A crash echoed in response. Spinning around abruptly, Cassie noticed she had left the dining room doors open in her haste to answer the telephone. Her heart sank as a second shattering crash resounded. Standing on a dining room chair, Bruiser grasped a shard from a smashed Shenandoah plate. Holding it as a child grasps a crayon, he began to scribble through the tablecloth with the jagged piece of china. Gashes now scarred the mirrored finish beneath.

Blood trickled onto the lace cloth from the offending hand, but Bruiser seemed to not notice his cut. Had his horrified mother not snatched him up, he would have continued his artistry. She pried the china from his grasp and rushed him to apply first aid in the bathroom. A little pressure stopped the bleeding, as the cut was not too deep. Indignantly the child squirmed, unaware of the reason for this intrusive fussing with his hand. Once the bandaging was finally completed, he bolted for the family room and his bucket of cars.

The doorbell rang and a distraught Cassie rushed to the door. A longhaired waiter from Roberto's stood under the portico loaded down with Styrofoam containers. A perfunctory "Good evening, ma'am" attempted to conceal his annoyance at having to make a delivery.

Cassie dashed up the stairs to fetch her wallet. Passing a mirror she noted that her hair was disheveled and her clothes were smeared with blood. What a sight!

Fearing gossip about the state she was in, she included a more than generous tip in her payment. Then she sought the location of her mischievous child. A hasty glance into the family room found Bruiser dropping the yellow school bus onto the Ford Explorer with his bandaged hand. He should be punished, but time was running short. For a few minutes, perhaps, he was occupied enough for her to clean up the dining room.

An overwhelming sense of loss enveloped her as she viewed the scene. Anger, depression, and frustration simultaneously raged within. At first it was impossible to move as her emotions caused a paralyzing numbness. Then robotically she began to pick up pieces of her memories and throw them into the trash. Deep wounds in the table mirrored the scars in her soul. Hiding the damage beneath a new linen cloth, she reset the table.

The doorbell rang again, and a most welcome sight greeted her. Angela stood there impeccably dressed in a navy business suit. The collar of a pale blue blouse was turned up at her neck in a fashionable flair. Cheerfully she thrust a bottle of wine into her hands. "Cassie it's so good to see...Oh my God, Cassie, what's wrong? Have you been crying?"

"Have I?" Instinctively Cassie touched wet streaks on her cheek. "I guess I have. Oh Angela, it's been so long since we've seen each other. I wanted everything to be perfect but somehow it has been one disaster after another. Nothing is the way it's supposed to be." Cassie caught herself rambling. "Here I am going on and on and not even inviting you in. Please come on in."

As Angela entered the foyer, she got a better look at her old roommate. She was obviously startled to see how much Cassie had changed in a few short years. Then noticing red stains on her old chum's clothing, Angela exclaimed, "Cassie, what the hell happened here? Are you bleeding?"

Still somewhat disoriented, Cassie responded, "Oh...no, I'm okay. It's just that Bruiser cut his hand and got it all over me. Good heavens, I must look like something the cat dragged in. Give me about five minutes to freshen up and I'll fill you in on the saga. Can you do a super huge favor for me and watch Bruiser while I go change? I don't think it's possible for him to get into any more mischief than he's already been in today."

Cassie led Angela into the family room. The toddler appeared to take no notice of the new intruder into his world. He sat with his back to the television crashing toy vehicles into a large container. Two blue Chevy convertibles and a dump truck were flung in.

Cassie chose to ignore her friend's puzzled expression. A more detailed explanation would have to wait until she changed. Motioning for Angela to sit on the sofa, she swiftly disappeared.

While climbing the stairs, she faintly heard Angela ask, "Hi, Bruiser. What are you doing?"

Cassie knew her child would ignore the question and continue to toss cars into the bucket. Blaring music from the TV could still be heard as she reached the landing. But before Cassie turned into the master bedroom, the familiar refrain that always accompanied the local weather forecast was interrupted. Even from this distance, she recognized the deep melodic voice, "This is CNN."

In the next moment, Angela uttered a loud painful yelp. No doubt her son had flung the purple minivan in protest of the channel being changed.

Cassie debated whether to forgo freshening up upon hearing Bruiser bang repeatedly on the TV. However, in a matter of a second or two, the familiar Weather Channel music resumed.

Her son most certainly would continue his vehicle routine now that things were again as they should be.

Somewhat fresher, Cassie reentered the family room lugging a folded playpen. She was still frazzled but looked a slight bit less stressed in clean clothes and with her hair brushed.

Angela's own impeccable appearance was now marred by a new run in her pantyhose.

"I hope he wasn't too much trouble," Cassie politely inquired despite knowing full well what she had heard. Without waiting for a response she continued, "I'll set up the playpen in the dining room with some of his favorite things. Hopefully that will allow us to eat in relative peace."

As far as possible out of reach from anything breakable, Cassie unfolded the portable corral into a corner of the room and filled it with some of her son's treasures. There was a half-chewed picture book, two superhero action figures, and an unsharpened blue pencil. To that she added a laundry basket and a plastic ice cream dish in the shape of a baseball helmet. The final "toy" was a liquid minute-timer filled with green and blue oils. She poured Cheerios into the blue dish and placed it in the center of the pen along with a sipper cup of apple juice. She then returned to the family room to fetch her child.

"Angela, could you please carry the bucket of cars into the dining room for me while I get Bruiser?"

Game for anything, Angela complied. "Sure. Anything else?"

"No, I think that will do. Leave the TV on. The sound of the Weather Channel is comforting to him; that may keep him from fussing too much so we can talk over dinner."

Bruiser squirmed, arching his back as his mother picked him up. He desperately tried to free himself but she firmly grasped him about the waist and held him close.

Angela laughed when she saw the playpen. "Cassie, there won't be any room for the baby if I put these cars in! What is the laundry basket doing in there?"

"Trust me. I know what he wants." Cassie set Bruiser in the pen. He grabbed the blue pencil with his left hand and climbed into the laundry basket. With his free hand he pulled the blue dish of Cheerios into the basket as well. Never releasing the pencil, he began to eat his cereal.

"Please have a seat; I'll be right back." Cassie carried several serving bowls and plates to the kitchen. She was determined not to have this gourmet meal ruined by serving it straight out of Styrofoam. Quickly she spooned mussels into a serving bowl and placed freshly baked bread into a napkin lined silver basket. Returning to the dining room she caught Angela sizing up the obviously expensive furnishings. Cassie felt she ought to preemptively offer an explanation.

"I didn't realize my parents had such a large nest egg. My mother was so fanatical about saving money; put it in the bank, she always said every time I got a dime. She spent so little on herself that they left quite an estate for me."

Angela smiled. "Your home is lovely. I'm really impressed. I'm sure they would have been happy to see you enjoy what they put away for you. It's just a shame they never got to see their grandson."

Both young women turned their attention to the playpen. Bruiser remained nested in the laundry basket. Pencil still tightly clenched in his left hand, now he clutched the liquid timer in his right just inches from his face. Within the plastic hourglass, colored oil droplets trickled slowly through the clear water. The toddler sat totally engrossed. When the last of the blue oil reached the bottom, he turned it over to watch again without releasing his grasp on his pencil.

Angela spooned some mussels onto her plate. They swam in a light broth flavored with garlic and olive oil. "These are delicious. Are they from Roberto's?"

"Yes, they are," Cassie said as proudly as if she had cooked them herself. "I'm glad you like them. Roberto's doesn't usually deliver but I promised a really big tip if they would do it just this once for me. I don't seem to have time to cook the way I'd like to and I wanted our reunion dinner to be special."

Angela grasped her hand across the table. "You went to a lot of trouble for tonight's dinner, Cassie. Thank you, I really appreciate it. We let too much time pass us by being angry with each other. I desperately want us to be friends again." Angela hesitated uncomfortably; then, in true form, the words tumbled freely. "I came here with so much to tell you but now—please don't be angry, but what is wrong here? Why were you so upset when you answered the door?"

Cassie lowered her eyes and stared at the dish in front of her. She didn't want to look at her friend, fearing she would be unable to contain her tears. "Nothing is the way it was supposed to be," she began. "I mean, I've got enough money to be comfortable, but I miss my parents something awful. I've been so alone. Everyone from college has gone their own way; I've lost touch with just about all my old friends. Partly I guess it's my fault; since I moved here it has been a bit far for anyone to visit.

"Still, I thought being a mother and raising a child would be enough. I remember how I loved to baby-sit kids when I was a teenager. I thought I knew just what to do. But Bruiser is more difficult than you could possibly imagine. I'm at my wit's end trying to figure out how to control him. No one will watch him anymore, even when I offer to pay double their normal rate. I can't even hire housekeepers to help me clean because he terrorizes them."

Angela rubbed her shin under the table but said nothing about the incident to Cassie. "Have you tried day care? Maybe he needs to be around other children."

"He got kicked out before we could even give it a decent try. He bites the neighbor children if they get too close. Now none of the other mothers will let their kids anywhere near him. They won't speak to me either other than to tell me what I'm doing wrong." Tears burned just under the surface. "I don't know what to do."

Timidly Angela inquired, "What does his pediatrician say?"

"I haven't taken Bruiser lately. It's such an ordeal going anywhere with him. It's exhausting trying to control him while waiting for an hour in the office for our turn. Besides, the last time I was there Dr. Friedman told me I was an overanxious mother just before Bruiser slugged him."

Angela paused with her fork in midair. "Bruiser slugged him?"

"Yeah. The doctor had just finished saying that boys are slower to develop than girls. I shouldn't compare him to other children in the neighborhood. Each child develops at his own pace. When I asked about why he hit the other kids he said boys will be boys. Then he turned to Bruiser and said, 'Isn't that right, young fellow?' And that's when Bruiser slugged him. We haven't been back to that doctor since. I was too embarrassed."

Angela dropped the fork and burst out laughing. "I'm sorry, Cassie. I know it must have been very traumatic. But you've got to admit that if you saw a scene like that in a movie you would be hysterical seeing a smug doctor getting sucker punched." Imitating a boxer's pose, she playfully punched the air. "Was it a left cross or a right upper cut? Do you think he should be entered as a bantamweight or a featherweight in the next Olympics?"

With that remark even Cassie began to chuckle. It felt good to laugh. "Maybe the heavyweight division," she replied. "He's such a little terror I think he would even give those guys a run for their money." She stood, clearing the appetizer plates away.

"Let me help you," Angela offered, reaching for a dish.

"No, please sit," Cassie said firmly. "For once I have things under control, I think. It's help enough just having you here. I'll be back in a minute with the rest of dinner."

She quickly returned with a salad of mixed greens, sliced cherry tomatoes, crumbled blue cheese, and chopped walnuts. A delicate china sauceboat held raspberry vinaigrette. Next she brought in a platter of veal scaloppini piled over angel hair pasta. The aroma of its marsala wine sauce promised a treat for the taste buds.

Cassie resumed her place at the table, and the two friends filled their plates. As they ate, noises from the toddler drew their attention to the playpen. Bruiser held the baseball helmet bowl on his head trying to make it fit. It was only five inches long so it just slid off. After several attempts to make it stay he gave up and grabbed the blue pencil again. Clutching it in his fist he held it inches away from the side of his face in a vertical position and scrutinized the object out of the corner of his eye, rotating it slightly to view a somewhat different angle. After a few minutes he poured the bucket of metal vehicles over his head then started to toss them back into the container. First a black Toyota Camry fell into place. Then a blue Ford Explorer followed. Next the yellow school bus crashed into the bucket.

Cassie recognized a familiar expression on her friend's face. Angela always had that look of self-debate whenever she considered keeping her opinion to herself. But despite the fear of damaging their friendship again, it was not in her nature to keep quiet.

"In all seriousness, Cassie, the last thing in the world I want is to offend you. But Bruiser doesn't seem to act like other children I've known. I mean, in some ways he does, but in others he doesn't. Like, well, I haven't heard him talk at all since I've been here. Doesn't he say anything yet?"

"No, he hasn't used any words." Somewhat defensively, Cassie continued, "He does kind of grunt pleadingly when he wants something out of reach. And it's not quite baby talk, but he makes a sort of singsong noise when he's playing sometimes, sort of like he was just doing. I know he can hear, though. Just yesterday I was opening a bag of chocolate chips to put in the cookie jar. Bruiser couldn't see what I was doing from the family room, but he came tearing into the kitchen when he heard the cookies tumble into the container. He clawed at my pant leg desperate for one."

Angela frowned. "It's not just his not talking that's strange though; what about the way he holds things up to the side of his face and stares at them out of the corner of his eye?"

"Oh, that's just the way he likes to check things out sometimes."

"Cassie, I know your last doctor appointment didn't go well, but don't you think you better try again? You said yourself that you don't know how to control him. Something is just not right here. If you don't like Dr. Friedman, pick another doctor, get another opinion. You can't live your life cooped up here even if you do have a gorgeous house. You need to find out what to do with Bruiser and you need some life apart from being a mom. You're too young to become a hermit."

Sarcastically Cassie said, "Gee, Angela, don't be so shy; tell me what you really think."

Angela leaned forward. "Cassie, you know me. I've just got to say what's on my mind. I wouldn't be me if I didn't. Besides, I'm saying this because I'm concerned about you."

Cassie sighed. "Don't worry. I'm not really mad. I guess I'm a bit defensive because of comments from neighbors and even strangers. You do have a point, though; I think I've put it off long enough. I just wasn't sure where to turn or what to do. First thing Monday morning I'm going to make an appointment with a new doctor. I promise."

The resolution to tackle the Bruiser dilemma visibly lifted her spirits. She looked over at her toddler, who was beginning to fall asleep in the laundry basket. "I'd better take a second and carry him up to his crib. If he falls asleep here and I go to move him later he'll wake up and I won't be able to get him to fall asleep again for hours. I'll be right back."

Cassie carefully lifted the child trying not to disturb him. Even though he was nearly asleep, he still had a firm grasp of the unsharpened pencil. She returned to the dining room a few minutes later with the pencil in her hand.

"I know I shouldn't let him play with a pencil but if I didn't give him that one, he would find a sharpened one somewhere else. He seems to always need to be holding something in his left hand for security. Half of the time it's not even a typical toy.

She sighed. "Oh, well. He's asleep now so I can really relax and enjoy our visit. It's so good to have you here. I needed your honesty and fresh view of the situation. I'm so glad you're going to spend the night, Angela. There's so much I need to catch up on. How is your career going? Have you heard from Beth or Cindy lately?" Cassie sat and twirled some pasta around her fork. It had cooled somewhat during her absence but it still tasted delicious.

Angela smiled. "Let's see, where do I start? I've got a lot of news about me but I'll begin with the latest reports from our old gang. Beth and Cindy both went to work for Majestic Cruise Line after graduation. Beth is working hard but loving to be around food twenty-four hours a day. The hustle and bustle of a busy kitchen is exciting to her and she said she's learning lots of food presentation techniques from the other chefs. She's in seventh heaven and not just because of her job either. She has a pretty serious relationship going with one of the pastry chefs. I wouldn't be surprised if one of their cruises turned into a working honeymoon someday. At least that's what Cindy seems to think.

"Speaking of Cindy, she worked with the activities director for about a year. You know her. She's a great people person; all the clients onboard thought she was fantastic. Then through some of the entertainers on one of the cruises she made connections with some Hollywood types. They convinced our star-struck friend to pursue her dreams. So, Cindy moved out to L.A. Before I knew it, she landed a job working for a small movie studio as an assistant to an assistant producer. He has her running all around town fetching obscure items for the film they're working on. Cindy knows she's at the bottom rung working her way up, but she couldn't be happier. I get e-mails from her all the time about her latest celebrity sighting. Last week she literally bumped into Martin Travers from—what's the name of that soap? Cranston something?"

"*Cranston Point?*"

"Yeah, that's right, *Cranston Point*. Cindy was at the market weighing some grapes. While lifting them out of the scale, she turned around so quickly to put them in her cart that she walked right into him. Cindy was so shocked at seeing a star in her supermarket that she was speechless. That really is a first for our Cindy, isn't it? Anyway, she said he had sunglasses on but you could definitely tell it was him. He made a little joke saying it was okay, his lines have been so few on the show lately that he's been feeling kind of invisible." Running a finger pensively around her glass, Angela mused, "You never know about show biz people. It's kind of nice to hear when one of them has a good sense of humor."

"I would have thought that a big star like that would have someone do the marketing and cooking for him."

"Who knows, maybe he wanted to rub elbows with the little people," Angela mocked. "Anyway, Cindy seems to have developed a knack for running into people. Two weeks ago she saw Ryan Colton from the show *Warefield Street* eating at Willows Restaurant." Angela took a sip of wine.

Cassie was thrilled to be hearing news of old friends. For a moment she nearly forgot the troubling last few years. She pictured herself back in college palling around with the girls. It was great to know that Cindy and Beth were living out their dreams.

"Cassie, you have a computer don't you?" Angela asked.

"Yes, of course."

"Don't let me forget. After dinner I'll get my laptop out and look up Beth and Cindy's e-mail addresses for you. I know they both would love to hear from you."

"That's great; I'd love to hear from them. I totally blocked out everybody and everything for a while after my parents died. Then I got so involved with the new house and the baby that I lost track of how much time had passed. I never should have let my friendships slip away. Don't forget to give me your e-mail address, too. Are you still living on Walnut Street?"

Angela wiped her mouth with a napkin. "Yes, well sort of, but not for long. That's one of the reasons I wanted to see you. I wanted to patch up our differences and see you again before I move."

"Oh, no! We just got back together again and now you're moving? Where to?"

"Chicago. The main headquarters for my company is in Chicago. I just got a big promotion but it means a move. I'm really excited but a little nervous too. My folks are devastated that I'm going to be so far away. You know how Italian parents are. They think I should stay in the same neighborhood, get married, and have some kids. Only then would they see me as grown up."

Like a balloon pricked by a pin, Cassie felt her newfound optimism dissipate. Her elation at having her friend back in her life vaporized. Hopes of a comforting shoulder to lean on escaped into the air, scattering emotions wildly about until they landed in a heap by her feet on the floor.

Seeing her old roommate's despair, Angela reached out for Cassie's hand. "Please be happy for me, Cass. I'll only be a phone call or a mouse click away. I promise I'm going to keep in constant contact with you, and I'll come back for visits whenever I can. I've missed your friendship too much not to."

"Of course I'm happy for you. It's just I'm sad that your good fortune will take you so far away."

"Maybe when Bruiser gets a bit easier to handle you can fly out and visit me. Think positive, Cassie. You'll go to the doctor and get some answers. Eventually things will be better."

Cassie stood to clear the dishes from the table. Determined to enjoy the remainder of Angela's visit, she said, "I know what will make me feel better. I got some macadamia nut ice cream for dessert. How about a huge scoop of that? When in doubt, eat ice cream, I say. Right?"

"You're going to make me waddle all the way to Chicago!" Angela teasingly complained as she helped carry the serving bowl and platter into the kitchen. "Do you have a container for these leftovers? There's probably enough of this veal to reheat for a lunch. It definitely was too good just to toss out."

"You'll find one in the second cabinet to the right," Cassie responded as she shoved scraps from her plate into the garbage disposal. "I'll just let these soak while we have our ice cream."

She retrieved two Noritake bowls and filled each with a large scoop of the rich dessert. Roberto's had included a small Styrofoam container of hot fudge that she drizzled over each. Carrying them back to the dining room, she noticed that a tiny chip was broken off one of the dishes. It must have happened during the move to Crestview Drive. Instantly she was reminded of the shattered plates from earlier in the evening. Tears crept to her eyes but she quickly shook herself back to present company. There would be time to mourn broken relics later.

"Leave those dishes, Angela. We'll get to them later. Come enjoy this scrumptious desert."

Angela returned to her dining room chair and sat back down. "Okay. Since you twisted my arm I guess I'll just have to force myself to eat this." She rolled her eyes and licked her lips at the first bite. "Mmm. Oh my God, this is fabulous. It's a good thing I'm moving to Chicago or I'd be eating at Roberto's every chance I got. I'd weigh three hundred pounds if I stayed within driving distance of that place."

Cassie smiled. "I'm so glad you enjoyed the meal. It was so much better and a lot easier than if I had tried to cook something. Funny, I never really appreciated how hard it must have been for my mom when I was a baby to take care of me, clean house, and cook delicious meals every night. Having a child sure changes your perspective on things."

Cassie paused, sensing that if she kept following her train of thought, eventually her path would lead to sad longings for her departed parents. Best course of action when faced with self-pity was to turn the focus of attention to someone else, her mother used to say. "Angela, speaking of moving, are you leaving anyone special behind? It's been so long since we talked that I don't know if you've been seeing anyone."

A mischievous smile crept onto Angela's face. "As a matter of fact there is someone. His name is Sam Copperstone. We've been going out for about eight months; we were talking about moving in together before this promotion came up. Can you believe it? He's actually quitting his job and moving to Chicago with me."

"That's great, Angela. I don't think that many guys would do something like that. It's funny but when a man has to relocate for his job he either dumps his girlfriend or just naturally expects her to pick up stakes and move with him. It's a rare guy who is willing to do the same thing for the woman. Where did you meet him? What kind of work does he do that he can just pick up and move like that?"

"Well, like I said, it happened about eight months ago. I was in the market for a new car and a colleague at work suggested I check out Price Motors on Market Street. So I stopped in on my way home from work. Let's just say I was sold on more than just a car by the time I left. Oh, Cassie, Sam is so handsome... wait a minute, I've got a picture of him in my purse."

After producing a photo of a dark-haired Adonis, Angela remarked, "Now tell me you could walk out of a showroom turning down a sales pitch from someone who looks like that! But it's not just his good looks that hooked me; he's kind, considerate, and he's so smart, too. He knows everything there is to know about cars, which is lucky for me. I can barely remember to fill it up with gas when I'm down to just fumes, let alone keep tabs on when routine maintenance should be done. He knows all that stuff, and at work when a customer comes in he can rattle off all the details on all the features of every car along with the reliability ratings and so much more. Sam said his boss is going to write a glowing letter of recommendation for him; he should be able to get a job at another dealership no problem in Chicago. Hey, speaking of cars, you don't still have that old beat-up Civic, do you?"

"No. I traded that in a long time ago." Wanting to evade the next obvious question as to what she was driving now, she quickly changed the subject. "Well, with this visit, you certainly came armed with head spinning news. So tell me, how soon do you move? Will we get a chance to paint the town red before you go?"

"I'm afraid not. They want me there by the beginning of next month. I've got so much to do in a short period of time." Angela hesitated a moment and then ventured into a touchy area. "Cassie, I know it must be tough with the baby and all, but um, how is your love life? Do you have anybody at all?"

Cassie scraped up the last of her ice cream and swallowed hard before responding. "No, not really. I guess somewhere in the back of my mind I was hoping...I mean, I thought someday I might look up Greg and see if he still remembers me at all.

But so much time has passed. I haven't even had the courage to call."

"I don't know how to break this to you gently, Cassie, so I'll just blurt it right out. I heard through the grapevine that Greg got married last fall."

"Oh." Somehow cocooned away from everybody in her past she expected that time had frozen and everything would be the same when she was ready to revive those relationships. What a huge mistake. Now it was too late. Her silent pause ached to be broken. But neither friend could formulate the words to keep emotions from tumbling over the edge. The best course was to finally come face to face with the reality of the situation. Fighting to control her composure, Cassie spoke first.

"Is it anyone I knew?"

"I'm not sure. Did you know Sue Snyder?"

"She was one of the cheerleaders. Wasn't she? I guess you were right about Greg and his trophy girlfriends," she tendered with a heavy dose of sarcasm.

"Come on, Cassie," Angela said gently. "Be fair. I admit that I initially thought he was a superficial jock. But Greg did ask about you; he wanted to get in touch with you. I still don't know why you refused to let me give him your address or phone number or tell him anything about the pregnancy. Listen, Cassie, it was only natural that he would eventually move on to someone else. Be realistic here. I mean, you disappeared off the face of the earth as far as he was concerned. What did you expect him to do?"

"Gee, thanks for being so supportive!" Cassie snapped. "Anything else you want to tell me about what I've done wrong in my life?"

Angela held up her hands. "Wait a minute. I didn't want to get in another argument with you. I've tried to be your friend and you even kept away from me. I thought you should know the truth about him getting married. Would you have preferred me keeping it a secret from you?"

Cassie calmed down. "No, of course not. I guess I'm just feeling really vulnerable right now. It's been really tough lately.

I guess I was hoping, I mean...Oh, I don't know what I was hoping. It was just really hard to hear about that right now."

"Please don't be mad at me, Cassie. Don't shoot the messenger because the news was bad."

"I'm not mad at you. I'm just really frustrated with the whole situation. I'm sorry that I snapped at you. Still friends, right?" Cassie rose and reached to hug her friend while silently bundling all her exasperation into one giant boulder, which she pushed back up the precipice she teetered on daily. She was determined not to allow it to tumble again for the duration of Angela's visit.

Forcing a lighthearted tone she teased, "It's a good thing I didn't order Chinese food tonight. With my luck I'm afraid the fortune cookie would be blank." Cassie turned and gathered the dessert dishes. "Back when we were in college, plates used to pile up like the leaning tower of Pisa. I know washing dishes was never your favorite thing, but if you don't mind, your old roommate could use a little help."

Visibly relieved by Cassie's brushing aside of uncomfortable news with a feeble joke, Angela smiled as she agreed. Cassie was grateful she refrained from inquiring about her financial ability. Instead Angela chatted about more of her moving plans and her career's rapid rise.

For the rest of the weekend they ignored the several years' absence their friendship had endured and instead cherished its rekindling. Cheerful laughter rang out often as the two young women reminisced about dormitory life and gossiped about their mutual acquaintances. All the while, Bruiser continued to be Bruiser, but with an extra set of hands he was somewhat easier to corral. The young women did not speak any further about investigating a possible cause for his unusual behaviors. It was understood that nothing could be done until Monday at the earliest.

Chapter 7.

Three weeks from Angela's visit was the soonest Dr. Stevenson could squeeze a new patient into his overcrowded schedule. He was, according to Cassie's neighbor Karen Taylor, the best pediatrician in the county. Now that she finally had decided to take action, all she could do was to wait. Bruiser's mischief continued to burrow under her skin, undermining any semblance of patience. How could one small toddler have so much energy? How could he devise so many ways to wreak havoc? More than ever, she anxiously hoped for an explanation to her son's peculiar behaviors.

When the appointment day arrived, Bruiser snuck outside minutes before they were due to leave the house. Frantic, Cassie searched high and low until something caught her attention. In the corner of her yard behind the blue spruce, a quiet sneeze accompanied a shower of dust particles.

Her filthy toddler sat mesmerized by specks of dust mingled with pine needles as gravity pulled the mixture back to earth. Before she was able to stop him, he again gleefully swooped handfuls of dry dirt and bits of pine into the air. Insufficient time remained to bathe him and still arrive anywhere close to his appointment time. So, grabbing him under the armpit, she hoisted the squirming child to his feet. Quick swats at his clothing with her free hand beat off as much dust as possible. Then she dragged him to the car and buckled his somewhat presentable body into his car seat.

Congested streets ticked precious minutes off the clock. The parking lot closest to Dr. Stevenson's office was full. She had to park four blocks away at the Green Street garage on the fifth level. Hurriedly she popped open her vehicle's trunk only to find it empty. In her haste, Cassie had forgotten to put the stroller back into the Mercedes. Cassie was reduced to half dragging her son along firmly with her right hand while she struggled to keep her purse and the diaper bag clutched tightly with her left. Crowded sidewalks continued to slow her progress.

Most pedestrians would have considered this to be a fairly clean city street, but it was a treasure trove of distractions to the toddler. Bruiser wrenched his wrist free from his mother by dropping his weight onto the sidewalk. Wedged into a pavement crack was a drinking straw from a local fast food establishment. In one swift motion, Bruiser pried it free then shoved it into his mouth.

"No, Bruiser, get that out of your mouth! Don't put things from the ground in your mouth; it's dirty." No sooner had she plucked the germ-laden straw away from her child than he spotted a crumpled cigarette wrapper on the ground. Again his weight slid his wrist from her grasp.

"No, it's dirty, Bruiser. Get up!" she yelled. Again she hoisted him to his feet. She wanted to be angry with the anonymous litter bugs. But if she were honest with herself, a few years earlier, she would have casually tossed gum wrappers on the ground and not given it a second thought.

At the corner she hurried across the street just as the traffic light began to turn. Unfortunately Bruiser spied a new prize. Ignoring blaring car horns, he plunked down in the gutter, snatching up a carelessly discarded beer bottle.

"No, Bruiser! God damn it, why the fuck don't you listen to me?" she screamed. "How many times do I have to tell you not to pick things up off the ground and put them in your mouth?" Suddenly aware of glares from passersby, she cut short further reprimands. Disapproving scowls from a perfectly coiffed businesswoman compelled Cassie to offer an explanation. She stammered, "I'm sorry. I swear I don't usually um...well...swear at my child. It's just that...Oh, hell! I don't have time for this."

Embarrassed by his squalling protest, she yanked Bruiser to his feet again. When they were still two blocks away from the doctor's office, a brown sedan slowed and pulled up next to her. Bruiser turned his head toward the whirring noise as the power window lowered.

"Excuse me, miss, do you need a lift?" the driver politely offered.

"Um, no thank you," she nervously replied. "No offense intended, but I don't know you from Adam."

She didn't dare trust this stranger. It was possible that he was a very sweet, honestly helpful man; but you never could tell. So, mother and child just had to plod on in their race against the clock.

The ancient elevator groaned as it ascended. Passengers glared as Bruiser began jumping up and down. Suddenly the elevator jolted to a stop at the second floor. When the doors creaked open to admit additional riders, Bruiser darted out. Embarrassed, Cassie pretended this was her intended stop and got off as well. He kicked his legs as she carried him on her hip up the additional flight of stairs.

"You're over fifteen minutes late. All new patients are supposed to be early to fill out necessary paperwork," she was informed at Dr. Stevenson's reception desk. The stern woman thrust a clipboard at Cassie. Bruiser scrambled down off his mother's hip and ran toward a pile of scattered toys in the corner of the waiting room. Stealing a tattered children's book right out of the hands of another little boy, he climbed into the half-empty toy box. The startled youngster began to cry.

"I'm so sorry," Cassie apologized to his mother. "I try but he doesn't seem to understand when I correct him."

The other mother launched a brief glare in Cassie's direction then lifted her child onto her lap.

Across the waiting room a hefty mother with short brown hair closed the magazine she was reading and tossed it onto the table beside her. Two little girls played with dolls at her feet.

"I don't know why she gave you such a hard time about being late," the woman mumbled under her breath. "They always run late; I don't think we've ever been seen on time." Her voice started getting louder. "I've already been waiting thirty-five minutes myself today. Maybe they would do a better job of scheduling if we started billing the doctor for our waiting time!"

Uninterested in acknowledgement of her complaint from anyone other than the receptionist, the robust matron turned her attention to one of her daughters. She rummaged in her purse for a tissue and helped the child blow her nose.

Cassie turned her attention to filling out the lengthy forms. All sorts of standard questions filled the first page. Name, address, phone number, insurance plan, employer...Cassie just wrote "self-employed." If questioned she would state that she took care of investments and omit the fact that she was her only client. Next the questionnaire asked about her pregnancy. Was it normal with no complications? Yes. Except for typical morning sickness there had been nothing out of the ordinary. Was the baby full term? Yes. In fact he had been a week and a half overdue. Every day past the due date had seemed endless.

The next set of questions was about Bruiser. He had received his vaccinations according to the recommended schedule. Thankfully she had remembered to bring along her record of the dates and dutifully copied them onto the form. Following the record of shots was a series of questions about his development. When did he turn over? When did he crawl? At what age did he sit up?

She had not brought any of that information with her. Some of it was written down at home in a cloth-covered baby book, but she had lapsed in her efforts to record every detail. Funny, at the time she could not imagine ever forgetting the exact day he did any of those things; each event had been eagerly anticipated. But now the date he first pulled himself into a standing position seemed unimportant. When did he first walk? Oh, that was an easy one. Bruiser was running by ten and a half months old. He could not wait to get into mischief.

When did baby say his first word? That question stopped her dead. There should be an answer, some date to fill in, but there was not. He made lots of noises. He cried. He screamed.

He made a singsong attempt at a simple syllable or two. But there were no words.

"Mrs. Delaine, please come with me." A slender nurse not much older than Cassie beckoned for her to follow.

"It's *Ms.* Delaine," Cassie corrected. "I'm not finished filling out the form yet. I'm afraid I don't remember when some of the 'milestones' were reached."

"That's okay. You can go over it with Dr. Stevenson when he comes in. Bring your son back to the hallway scale and let's see how much he weighs."

Cassandra handed her son a favorite toy then dug through the toy box for his discarded sneakers. Intently he stared at colored oil floating down through his liquid timer. He held it so close to his eyes that it nearly touched his nose. He seemed not to notice his mother propel him down the corridor, barely letting his feet touch the floor. He was so engrossed in the movement of colored droplets that the nurse was easily able to weigh and measure him for her chart.

Oh, great, Cassie thought to herself. *Now he is going to act like a perfect angel for this doctor and make a liar out of me. They will never believe he is such a terror.*

With an air of efficiency, the nurse promised the doctor would be with them shortly and dropped her forms into an acrylic container outside the door.

Checking her watch repeatedly did not make the wait in the small examining room go any faster. Cassie paced for a while then sat back down. Bruiser had long since given up his complacent demeanor. It was fortunate that his liquid timer was constructed out of heavy duty plastic and did not break when he repeatedly cast it to the floor. Tearing the paper that lined the table he sat on and tormenting his mother became a new game. At first Cassie scolded him, discarded the shredded paper into the trash, and roughly imprisoned him on her lap. But Houdini repeatedly struggled free, scaled the office furnishings, and persistently created confetti.

"Good morning, or I guess I should say good afternoon, now," boomed a voice as the door opened. Dr. Stevenson's jaw dropped at his first sight of the room. The impeccably dressed pediatrician was used to active children leaving his offices somewhat disheveled, but this was Armageddon.

"Well, well, what have we here, young man?" he forced himself to good-naturedly joke. "What is your name? Are you a patient or my new interior decorator?"

Bruiser ignored the man and focused on the stethoscope loosely dangling from his neck. He reached out to grab it, pulling it free from the dapper physician. Prying the instrument from the child's tiny fingers caused a deafening wail to be heard three rooms away.

"Well, at least he's not going to make a liar out of me now," Cassandra meekly offered. "I was afraid he would behave abnormally well when you came in and you wouldn't believe me when I explain how difficult a child he is."

The doctor gave her an intently thoughtful look. "Why don't you try and tell me what's going on here, Mrs. Delaine, while I examine him." He opened the door and called, "Nurse Cooper, would you assist in here please."

Nurse Cooper pinned Bruiser down in something resembling a wrestling hold so the skilled pediatrician could manage the standard observations of ears, eyes, and throat. While Bruiser resisted relinquishment of his wrestling title, his frazzled mother illuminated the physician on what life was like with her son. Dr. Stevenson completed his examination of the child and scribbled notes furiously in the new patient's folder.

"Mrs. Delaine, your son appears to be in fine physical condition from what I can tell. But I would like for you to make an appointment with a colleague of mine."

"Why? What's wrong with him?"

"Frankly I hesitate to say, Mrs. Delaine. Any diagnosis on my part would be pure speculation at this point; this is not exactly my field. That's why I'm suggesting you see someone to confirm my suspicions." Seeing Cassie's exasperated expression, he finished, "But I'm thinking it may be one of the pervasive developmental delays."

Normally, Cassie would have corrected this man for calling her Mrs., but at that moment the incorrect title seemed insignificant. "Pervasive developmental delay—what's that?"

"Now, Mrs. Delaine, let's not get all upset about this. It may be something else entirely different. I would recommend you see Dr. Hart. He's a fine child psychiatrist. His office is in the Sweetwater Hospital's annex. I really think he would be the one who could tell you for sure. If you need a referral for your insurance, see Mrs. Simmons when you check out at the reception desk." He closed the folder, handed it to Cassandra, and walked out the door.

Cassie was stunned. What did this mean? She had come here for answers and now she had more questions. She opened the folder. Little of the scrawl was legible. At the very end in large letters was a notation she could read but made no sense to her. PDD/NOS. What was that? She put Bruiser's shoes back on for the hundredth time that day, gathered her things, and left more perplexed than ever.

The excursion in town had worn Bruiser out—an extremely rare event. Even more unusual was that he had fallen asleep on the ride home. His mother knew that if she lifted him out of his seat he would wake up, so she carried the car seat into the house with him still strapped inside. Immediately she telephoned Dr. Hart's office for an appointment. The earliest opening was in six weeks.

PDD/NOS. What did that mean? Could she wait six weeks for an answer? She hoped Bruiser would sleep long enough to give her time to do some investigation on the Internet. Rarely was it possible to sit at her computer during the day; she dared not divert her attention that long from Bruiser. Yet at night she was too exhausted. If she were going to do it, now was the time.

When she typed PDD/NOS into the search bar, only two possible matches appeared. One of them didn't seem to have anything to do with what she needed to know. The other one was about Asperger Syndrome, High Functioning Autism,

PDD/NOS, and related disorders. She clicked the link but it seemed like that site focused more on this Asperger Syndrome, whatever the hell that was, than PDD/NOS.

Back to square one. She typed *pervasive developmental delay* into the search line. The screen flashed to life with the first twenty out of over eighteen thousand potential links!

Oh my God, she thought. *Where to start?* It was overwhelming. Cassie picked one with information about autism, pervasive developmental delay, and attention deficit. The site was for some hospital or treatment center or something like that.

Autism? This couldn't be right. She remembered seeing a movie about some weird guy with autism. That wasn't Bruiser at all. And there had been a news segment a while back on some kids with attention deficit. They took some pills that helped to calm them down so they could concentrate. Maybe that was what he needed. But this PDD/NOS? She still didn't know a thing about it. The web site talked about testing for urinary peptides, liver detoxification profile, and on and on. What the hell were they talking about?

She tried another link. This one was specifically labeled pervasive developmental delay. Initially the article threw terms like *qualitative impairments* and *reciprocal social interaction* at her. Just as she determined to give up on this site, she noticed a comparison to autism at the bottom of the page. There was that word again. Bruiser was not that weird guy. Was he?

The author mentioned one of the first most common traits was a lack of language development. What had Sally Clifton asked her? Was he deaf? Why didn't he speak at all? Then there was Angela. She, too, asked why Bruiser didn't speak.

No! No! That can't be right. Her mind started working frantically. *He hears me open a candy wrapper in the kitchen when he's in the family room. He wants the Weather Channel on, even when he can't see if the TV is turned on or not. Bruiser makes sounds; he just isn't ready to talk yet. He hasn't been around enough other kids. It's too boring for him with just me here. He hasn't needed to talk. All he has to do is grunt and reach for something and I give it to him.*

Cassie shut the computer off. Panicked, she slammed the door behind her as she stormed out of her home office. Some fabulous pediatrician this Dr. Stevenson turned out to be. What the hell did he know? Obviously Dr. Stevenson didn't have a clue what was wrong with her son, but maybe Dr. Hart would. She would just have to wait. Six weeks. Six very long weeks was an eternity to worry and wait.

While she waited, Bruiser turned three years old. There was no big birthday party with dozens of friends. He would only wind up hitting or biting any other children if she were to invite them. Cassie's own friends were scattered across the country now. The few neighbors she had met were busy with their own families. Cassie and her son didn't seem to fit in; she had not bonded enough to invite anyone to a party.

Instead she ordered a cake and some helium balloons. Wrapped toys ordered from a web site went unopened in the corner. Bruiser was more interested in dropping the black Toyota Camry into his bucket. Then the blue Ford Explorer, the yellow school bus, two blue Chevy convertibles, the dump truck...

Stumbling into the kitchen to brew her morning coffee, Cassie nearly tripped over her orange cat yawning up at her. Insistent meows accompanied his darting around and through her legs. She freed herself and walked over to the pantry to retrieve his food.

"All right, Burt!" she said, ripping open a pull-top can of smelly brown gook. "Well, are we ready for another exciting day in the life of millionaire stay-at-home Mom? What's on the agenda for today? Are we jetting off to Paris, sunning on the French Riviera, or late night partying with movie and rock stars?"

Burt meowed back an urgent request to be fed. "No? Are you sure?" Cassie placed the dish with his food on the floor. "Okay, I guess we'll just have to settle for ten loads of laundry squeezed in between hundred yard dashes to snatch Bruiser away from one of his gazillion attempts to foil my plans for the perfect life."

Burt paused and looked quizzically up at her. His ears twitched at the mention of his nemesis' name, and he quickly surveyed his environment. Having ascertained that the child was not present, he resumed his meal.

"Oh, wait a minute; we do have plans, don't we? There's an eleven-thirty appointment with Dr. Hart. I'll have to fire my scheduling secretary for such inept planning," she haughtily mocked as if speaking to a human friend. "Without a doubt, this will be a lengthy evaluation. The young prince will not be happy when he gets hungry for lunch. We'd better inform the chef to pack an extra bag of Cheerios in his highness' diaper bag and have the butler fetch an extra change of clothes for his lordship."

Burt ignored her soliloquy and wandered off to nap in a patch of sunshine. Left to eat breakfast in solitude, Cassie again wondered about really hiring some help. Nothing as grandiose as her prior ranting to the cat was needed, but surely there were some cleaning services in the area that had not yet heard of her little tyrant. Still her own mother's admonition not to squander her fortunes haunted her. It's frivolous to spend money having someone else clean your house, she would have thought. After all, Amanda had managed to raise her, keep a clean house, and work part-time.

Still, her mother didn't have to deal with a tyrant like Bruiser. Something definitely was not quite right with this child, but Dr. Stevenson's suggestion of PDD/NOS couldn't possibly be correct. Perhaps today Dr. Hart would have some answers for her.

Conveniently located on the first floor of Sweetwater Hospital's outpatient annex, Dr. Hart's office was clearly designed with young children in mind. Painted at child's eye level on the wall were bright, cheerful cartoon characters. Several larger-than-life stuffed animals invited children to wrestle with them. Just beyond this mini zoo, a toy box overflowed with toys donated by the local benevolent society. Child-size chairs were arranged in a semi-circle near a small bookcase lined with assorted picture books.

In the far corner of the waiting room, light reflecting off a wavy mirror caught Bruiser's attention. He bounded over to examine it closer. Distorted on purpose, the fun house mirror surely elicited giggles from most children, but Bruiser stood sideways, skeptically eyeing the strange view of himself. He clutched two die-cast vehicles in his left hand.

Cassie approached the reception desk. A grandmotherly woman smiled back at her, the wide grin making her face even rounder. Pinned to her uniform, slightly askew, was a nametag that read Ellen Sanders.

"You must be Mrs. Delaine," she said.

"No, that's Ms. Delaine," Cassie replied.

"I'm sorry, my mistake. Anyway you're lucky; the patient scheduled before you canceled due to a stomach virus. Dr. Hart hasn't had a chance to fall too far behind in his schedule yet. He's just in the middle of returning a phone call and then he'll be right with you. You should have just enough time to fill these out while you're waiting."

A pudgy hand held a clipboard with a pen securely attached by a dangling cord. Cassie hated pens tied to strings. The string was never long enough. She pulled a pen out of her purse with a sigh. Another doctor meant another complete set of forms to fill out.

The first page was pretty much standard. Next was the dreaded developmental milestones section. There were those questions again. *At what age did baby say his first word? What was baby's first word?*

Pondering her response, she bumped her leg on the waiting room's coffee table as she uncrossed her legs. A stack of magazines was neatly fanned out. Despite part of his face being obscured by another cover, Cassie recognized Ryan Colton on a fan magazine. Funny, when Angela recently visited, she mentioned Cindy's excitement over sighting this handsome Hollywood hunk. What was Cindy doing right now? she wondered. Somehow the lives of her college chums seemed preferable to the situation in which Cassie found herself. Who would have thought after winning a huge lottery windfall that she could be jealous of someone else's life? If only her parents were still alive. If only she had not become pregnant and then a single parent. If only Brian was not...well, whatever he was.

"Ms. Delaine, Dr. Hart will be ready to see you in just a few moments. We'll never get lunch today if we don't get started now. Just bring the clipboard along and follow me; the doctor will go over the rest of those questions with you."

After attempting to weigh and measure the squirming toddler, Mrs. Sanders led mother and son down a short corridor to yet another small examination room. She added the clipboard's form to a manila folder and deposited it into a clear acrylic pocket mounted to the outside of the door as she left.

Déjà vu all over again, Cassie thought. But unlike the pediatrician's office, this room had no table covered with crinkly tissue paper. Instead the room had a plain upholstered sofa set beneath a window that overlooked the street. Across from the couch sat a chair obviously meant for the doctor. In the corner was a child's table and chair with an assortment of toys and puzzles.

Cassie sat down on the sofa's edge, yanking at her skirt to keep it from riding up. Not letting go of the vehicles in his left hand, Bruiser dug with his free hand in the crevice of the sofa where the cushion met its arm.

A few moments later the door opened. Dr. Hart was a rumpled man in his late forties or early fifties. He had a ruddy complexion and enough weight in tow that he seemed perpetually out of breath. His sandy hair straggled over his ears begging for a trim. Nevertheless his warm smile and soft-spoken, tender voice aimed to ease her evident apprehension.

"Good morning, Ms. Delaine," he said. Squatting down to the child's eye level, the doctor directed his next greeting to Bruiser. "And this must be Brian. Hello, Brian."

Before the kindly psychiatrist knew what was happening, Bruiser swung around and punched the rotund man squarely between the eyes with all the force his three-year-old frame could muster. The startled physician rocked backwards over his heels, wobbling like an inflatable child's punching bag before landing with a thud on the floor. The file folder's contents scattered next to him.

Mortified that once again Bruiser was living up to his nickname, Cassandra leapt to her feet to restrain her child. Tears began to force their way to the surface as she apologized. "I'm so sorry, Dr. Hart. You see, that's one of his problems. He can't stand to have strangers look at him, much less talk to him. I'm afraid this is not the first time he has hit an adult. It's not even the first time he has hit a doctor. I've tried scolding him but he doesn't seem to understand."

"Well, this isn't the first time a patient has demonstrated he didn't want to be here, but I must admit I don't think a toddler has ever knocked me flat on my..." He paused, professionally censoring himself, "um, rear." The doctor chuckled as he gathered his papers then pulled himself to his feet. "Don't worry, I won't hold it against him. Have a seat again, Ms. Delaine. Let's try and begin again, shall we?"

Dr. Hart eased himself into his chair and began skimming through the file. After a few moments he spoke again.

"My notes here say that you made this appointment today because you're concerned about your son's unusual behaviors. We'll get to that in a moment but first I want to start out by asking some questions about Brian's development. I see from your responses on our form that most of his milestones were right on target." Dr. Hart appeared to be engrossed with the contents of his file. To Cassie's untrained eye he seemed not to notice Bruiser. The toddler darted over to the corner of the room and stood staring at his own fingers as he wiggled them to the side of his right eye.

"Yes, yes," the physician continued quietly. "He rolled over, crawled, and walked all well within the ranges for normal. How about his first words, Ms. Delaine? I don't see any response here."

"He doesn't say anything yet." She hesitated, then added, "He doesn't have anyone much to talk to if he did. I guess that's why he hasn't been interested in trying to talk. I know he will, though; he makes plenty of noises. Some people have asked me if he is deaf, but I know he hears me."

"How do you know that, Ms. Delaine?"

"Well," she said pausing for just a moment to think. "He can be three rooms away and he will hear me change the channel on the television and come in screaming for me to change it back. And when he isn't looking in my direction, he hears me open a bag of cookies then races over and claws at my leg until I give him one."

"Is that so? Hmm, you said when he isn't...well, let me rephrase that. When you talk to him, does he look you in the eye?"

"Well no, not exactly. He kind of watches me out of the corner of his eye."

"Like he's doing right now?"

Cassandra was surprised that the doctor had noticed. "Yes, he does that a lot."

"Okay, let's move on. How does he interact with other children?"

"If he notices them at all, it's usually to hit them."

"Well that certainly can be quite a problem. Hmm, all right, so he doesn't play alongside other children. Tell me about how he does play. What does he like to do?"

Cassie looked over at her son. His toys were still firmly grasped in tight fists. "He loves to play with his toy cars."

Hopefully, the doctor asked, "Does he pretend to race them?"

"Well no, he drops them into a bucket one by one in a certain order and then dumps them out again and again."

"What would happen if you tried to change the order by, well, let's say, maybe by removing one of the cars?"

Her eyes widened as she shook her head. "I wouldn't dare do that. He would have a tantrum that would go on forever!"

Dr. Hart thoughtfully paused again and appeared to grow more solemn before continuing with his questions. "How about other types of play?" he asked. "Does he ever imitate characters in stories or on TV, or try and pretend to do some of the household chores he sees you do?"

Cassie thought for a moment. "I don't know. I can't remember seeing him do that, but maybe I just don't remember."

The doctor was clearly going somewhere with this line of questioning but Cassie was unsure where. "Ms. Delaine, I'd like to try some testing to see what Brian can do. Come over here, Brian."

No response from Bruiser. Dr. Hart made a quick notation on a legal pad. "Ms. Delaine, perhaps we'll have a little more luck if you call him over."

"Bruiser, come here Bruiser."

The child made no response to his mother's call. Cassie got up to retrieve her son. As she picked him up, he arched his back and began to kick and scream.

"I'm terribly sorry, Dr. Hart, he just won't cooperate." The flailing child wriggled free and climbed up the back of the sofa to stare out the window. Something had definitely caught his attention. "Oh, I see what he's looking at," Cassie continued. "Down on the right-hand side of the street a landscaping crew is mowing the grass in front of—what's it called, the Compton Center?"

Dr. Hart rose from his chair and briefly glanced outside. "Yes, that's right." He pulled a small table from the corner over to the sofa and then rolled some colored bins next to it. "Let's see if we can get Brian calmed down somewhat and try some simple tests."

Cassie coaxed her child onto her lap with some Cheerios. Then Dr. Hart attempted to encourage her son to copy patterns of multi-shaped and colored blocks with a duplicate set. The purpose of this exercise eluded Bruiser. Blocks held no interest except as potential projectiles. After heaving numerous shapes at the red bin, this test was abandoned. Making more notations on his pad, Doctor Hart next tried to engage Bruiser with some picture cards of scenes with purposely drawn flaws on them.

Bruiser failed to indicate any interest in finding what was wrong with the illustrations.

Again more notations were rapidly jotted down. A few other tests were administered with minimal success. Last, some photos were spread on the table. Attempts were made to have the toddler point out the correct response to a question by touching his finger to a photo. Instead of interest in the colorful pictures, the child was transfixed by a pulled thread in the sofa's woven fabric.

Scribbling furiously and mumbling quietly to himself, Dr. Hart finally put down his pen. He looked down at the floor, mentally composing his choice of words. Then he straightened up and took a deep breath before speaking. He looked Cassie straight in the eye. Honest compassion was his goal. But like an ancient pine to the woodcutter's ax, he felled any remaining delusional hopes.

"Ms. Delaine. I need to further evaluate the results from these tests before I write up a formal report, but I'm afraid you are not going to be happy with my findings. My preliminary diagnosis is that of autism." Dr. Hart paused a moment for those words to register. "I'm not sure how much you know about this disorder. My secretary, Mrs. Sanders, can give you a list of some good books and recommend a few web sites to check out. We'll set up a schedule of visits to help monitor Brian's progress and discuss treatment options. Also, there is a local chapter of the Autism Society of America. They meet at St. Vincent's Church over on Fourth Street. I'm not sure if they meet over the summer months or not but I would advise you to contact them. The information and support they'll give you will be invaluable in the coming years." The physician paused a moment to allow his information to register. "Do you have any questions I can help you with right now?"

The diagnosis hit Cassie like a ton of bricks. The last time she felt this desolate was when Jordan had informed her of her parents' deaths. Queasiness washed over her more violently than the time she rode Devil's Mountain roller coaster three times in a row on a dare. She knew next to nothing about autism but what little she thought she knew frightened her.

"Years? How long is this?"

"I'm afraid this is a lifelong disorder, Ms. Delaine."

Cassie's face conveyed her emotions. The doctor sought to put some sort of positive spin on his devastating news.

"Fortunately we have come a long way in the treatment of individuals with autism. Years ago, before science understood that this is a neurological disorder, parents used to be blamed for their child's condition. People with autism were locked up in institutions for life. But we have come a very, very long way from there.

"Today, with government guarantees of free education for all individuals with disabilities, the outlook is much brighter. Children with special needs can access government programs pretty much once they are diagnosed. It will still be difficult, but with highly structured education you will be surprised at the improvements Brian will make. I can't make you any promises but he may even have a job someday."

Cassie stammered, "*May* have a job someday? Just how disabled is he?"

"That's difficult to say, Ms. Delaine. Testing individuals with autism is a challenge. Brian's unwillingness to cooperate makes accurate assessment problematic. Combined with the fact that autism is diagnosed primarily by evaluating behaviors that may change somewhat over time, the severity of his disability is uncertain."

"You mean you might be wrong? He might not have this autism?" she asked hopefully.

"No, that's not what I'm saying at all. I am fairly confident of the diagnosis. What I meant to say is, well...in my experience many young children have certain behaviors consistent with autism but not others, and then six months to a year later they may have dropped one aspect only to pick up two others. The degree of the disability is unclear, but from what I've been able to observe, I believe there may be some mental retardation accompanying his autism as well."

Disbelief battled a dawning realization that the physician's words rang true. Despite a resolve to retain her composure, salty tears distorted Cassie's vision. Her lower lip quivered as she asked, "Will he ever talk or am I just..." She brought a trembling hand up, covering her mouth in an attempt to conceal her anguish.

The doctor's voice was gentle. "I don't know for sure. It's possible he may not, but then again he may. Even if he does talk, though, he will probably need a great deal of speech therapy to help him understand the proper way to use language, to communicate.

"But listen, Ms. Delaine: this has been an awful lot for you to take in for one day. Why don't you dry your tears and forget about everything for the rest of the day. Take Brian and go do something special just for fun. There will plenty of time to work this all out. Just push everything out of your mind for now. Be Scarlett O'Hara: worry about it tomorrow. I'll have my secretary call you and schedule a follow-up appointment where I'll lay out my recommendations. Now don't forget, get Ms. Sanders to give you that list of books and the phone number for the contact person over at the Autism Society."

Chapter 8.

A glass of chardonnay perched precariously on the sill. Blankly, Cassie stared out the nursery window. She glanced at the rumpled blanket in the crib then back out to the blackness of night. Dried mud spatters covered her clothes, and dirt was caked deep under her fingernails. Who was this monster that had overtaken her? It was nearly midnight; she had been standing at this window for hours asking that question. A framed photo of her parents dangled in her right hand. Before setting it back on her child's dresser, she whispered, "What would you have done at the river?" Loving smiles of Carl and Amanda Delaine gave no hint that they would have even come close to what had happened that day. No, they had always been patient with her, even during rebellious teen years. Cassie turned the photo facedown; looking at them was too painful.

Returning to the window, she lifted her glass and took a large gulp of wine. Outside, her neighborhood didn't look any different than it had in the morning, but Cassie's world had changed dramatically.

Burt wandered into the room and sniffed at her legs. She had not showered yet so these smells were intriguing to him. After several nudges failed to elicit a response, he wandered over and curled up under the crib. Cassie could not bring herself to look inside—not just yet. Once more she needed to mentally review events that led her to the river. She wondered, *Is it possible that anyone is capable of committing acts of evil if pushed to the edge?*

It was hard to imagine that anything could be worse than hearing the words: Your son has autism. Somehow, though, the afternoon had gone from bad to worse.

Cassie was barely conscious of exiting the office, or of walking back to her car for that matter. Forgetting about everything was easier said than done. She thought about the movie she had seen. A spoiled young man kidnapped his autistic brother from an institution and held him ransom for his father's inheritance. In the end he grew to have affection for his brother but still took him back to the institution. Was that in store for her son? This most definitely was not the way her life was supposed to work out.

She buckled Bruiser into his car seat. "Damn it!" she muttered to herself through her tears. "I win the lottery and my life turns to shit! I should be happily living a life of luxury. Instead, my parents are dead, I'm a single parent, and I have no prospect of ever even dating again. What happens when word gets out about this autism thing? I remember being scared as a kid when my friend Ruthie's cousin came for a visit. I felt sorry for her, but I didn't know how to act around someone with Down syndrome. Now this? Autism? This is a lifetime sentence! I can see it now. I'll be eighty years old trying to drag my adult son away from some embarrassing situation in public. How will it be when he's twenty, forty, sixty?"

Despite her emotional state, growling stomach noises reminded her to satisfy their physical needs. Eating inside a fast food restaurant was out of the question; too much energy would be expended trying to corral the wild one. So she ordered at the drive-thru on Chestnut Street. A teenager thrust two soft drinks and a paper sack containing burgers and fries through her car window. Cassie pulled the car into the parking lot. As they ate in the Mercedes, she tuned the radio to a classic rock station just in time to catch the last few bars of her favorite tune.

It figures, she thought, *just in time for a commercial.*

The twang of a hokey jingle began:

"Leave troubles behind, when your cares come to call.
For delights you'll treasure, come to Sweetwater Mall.
Find everything you're looking for, we've got it all.

The sweetest pleasures are always found at Sweetwater Mall."

"Shopping," Cassie said aloud. "That's what I need, something totally frivolous." She reached behind her to help Bruiser with his fries. "God, it's been so long since I've gone to the mall with you, Bruiser. Do I dare chance it? You won't embarrass me with another screaming tantrum like last time, will you? I really need this, Bruiser. Please be good."

Flipping the visor down, she checked her makeup in the mirror. Mascara had run into black rivulets all over her face. Just throwing a pair of sunglasses on to conceal she had been crying wouldn't cut it. Perhaps if this was L.A, but not here in Sweetwater; it would be considered too pretentious to prance through shops wearing shades indoors.

Suddenly she remembered someone on a talk show saying they use unscented baby wipes to remove eye makeup. Cassie fished through the diaper bag and wiped the black streaks off her face. If no one looked too closely perhaps they wouldn't notice her eyes were still red and a little puffy. In between bites of her burger, she dug her cosmetic bag from her purse and applied a little fresh makeup. Maybe while at the mall she would stop in Well Spring to pick up some hair dye; those damn roots needed touching up again. If only she could find someone to watch Bruiser, it would be so much easier to go to a beauty parlor.

"All done?" she asked her son.

"Ehhh! Ehhh!" Bruiser whined as he swatted the air toward the soda, which was just out of reach in the cup holder.

"Here you go. Take a sip then let's go shopping."

Full bellies had brightened both their spirits. Cassie turned on the ignition and headed the Mercedes to Sweetwater Mall. Once the destination was in sight, she nearly felt giddy at the prospect of finding some tangible object to shift her emotions to. Before Bruiser had been born, she had spent many hours wandering through the upscale boutiques and high-end department stores as she accumulated furnishings and accessories for her new home.

Like a giant movie marquee, the sign outside the behemoth shopping center announced some of the prime draws for bulging purses craving to be lightened. At once she realized just what she wanted to buy. There had not been an opportunity to replace her shattered Noritake china since Angela's visit. Also, while dinning with her friend, Cassie realized her mother had never purchased any stemware to go with the china. Amanda may have chosen the Noritake but Cassie could choose the complementing goblets. Haughtley & Bristol's fine china department was the most likely place to find her Shenandoah pattern.

While attempting to find a parking space close to a mall entrance, Cassie was tempted to pull into a handicapped parking space. Technically, now she was qualified to park there, but other patrons would glare at seeing a young woman pull into a spot reserved for someone with a disability. No one would suspect that this beautiful child was indeed disabled; he looked perfectly healthy.

Determined not to repeat her mistake from Dr. Stevenson's, prior to her appointment with Dr. Hart, she had stowed the stroller in the trunk. As long as she was swift as a hawk in transferring Bruiser from car seat to stroller, she should be able to prevent his escape across the blacktop. Bruiser relaxed as she rolled him into Haughtley & Bristol's. Motion generally kept him happy. The trick was to keep him content when she stopped to browse.

Thoughts of sparkling china and crystal goblets helped to temporarily push the troubling diagnosis aside. Proceeding past the latest fashions, Cassie was now on a mission. She took the elevator to the second floor, where just beyond the luggage department, crystal and silver shimmered under showcase lighting. A quick glance showed that the motion of the stroller and the elevator had temporarily relaxed her son; perhaps he might even fall asleep. It was best not to take chances, though. She parked the stroller carefully clear of anything breakable. Bruiser seemed to be dozing.

Seated at the wedding registry desk, a sales clerk continued typing while avoiding eye contact with her. "Ms. Crane—

Gold Member Sales Associate" was etched on the satin finish nameplate affixed to the lapel of her perfectly tailored suit.

Cassie cleared her throat in an effort to gain some assistance.

After pushing glasses back up her nose, the haughty woman glanced up from the computer screen. Hardened hairspray kept her coiffure frozen in place as she tilted her head up to respond. "Can I help you, ma'am?"

"Yes, I'm interested in some crystal goblets to complement the Shenandoah pattern by Noritake...perhaps something by Waterford?" Cassie replied.

While still seated, the clerk ran her thumb and forefinger lazily along her pearl necklace. In monotone she replied "How lovely. Is this a gift for some lucky bride?"

"Actually, no it's for me. I feel the need to treat myself to something special."

Not budging from her chair, Ms. Crane sized up the woman in front of her. Ketchup stains from eating in the car, disheveled hair with dark exposed roots, and swollen eyes made the young mother's financial status seem doubtful. "Well, we can set up a convenient payment plan once we establish your credit; just fill this out," she replied handing over an application.

Indignant, Cassie snapped, "That won't be necessary. I'll be paying in full by check. Could you show me which goblets would go best with my pattern?"

Ms. Crane reluctantly stood, taking Cassie over to the Waterford display. Still skeptical, she lifted a delicate glass off the shelf. "I think this pattern would be a lovely choice. Did you want a pair?"

"No, I need a dozen. Also I need to replace two plates for my china pattern. Can you have these items shipped to my house?"

"Well, yes; come over to the register and fill out a delivery slip while I process your order. It may take a few minutes; I'll have to confirm your account with the bank for such a large order." Ms. Crane cradled the phone against her left ear while she began ringing up the sale, and Cassie devoted her attention to supplying her name and address for delivery.

Crash!

Smash!

Houdini had struck again. Despite straightjacket knots, the escape artist had freed himself and, in an effort to retrieve a cut glass bowl from the third shelf, had slipped in mid-climb. Scattered across the floor were shards of lead crystal that moments ago had been a rather large, elegant Waterford bowl. Commencing another climb, the toddler appeared not to have minded his tumble to the ground.

Cassie and the clerk scrambled to prevent further destruction, and Bruiser began screeching at the top his lungs in protest against being restrained. With both arms, his mother squeezed him close to her while he vigorously kicked and flailed his arms. The siren of his wail drew every customer in the vicinity to surreptitiously watch the show.

Ms. Crane seemed to be gasping with outrage. "You realize, of course, you will have to pay for that. What on earth possessed you to bring an uncontrollable child into a china department?" she demanded.

Too embarrassed to provide an explanation, Cassie rummaged through her purse while attempting to contain the erupting volcano. She sensed the eyes of every customer in the store piercing through her from behind; she just wanted to pay for the damages and flee. The approval process for her check was too time-consuming; at last she found her debit card for the purchase, and then dashed away from the scene.

Her feet couldn't move fast enough as she raced to the elevator. Pounding on the down arrow didn't make it come any quicker. Stares from women half hiding behind displays of coffee makers and blenders made her wish the ground would just swallow her up. She heard one concerned whisper debate whether security should be called as perhaps the screaming child was being abused.

Humiliation forced tears to stream down Cassie's face.

She drove as if in a trance, barely aware of which direction the vehicle headed. Mechanically her foot pressed the brake stopping for red traffic lights. Only by instinct green propelled her further. Distances grew longer between crossroads. Few cars ventured this far out of town at this hour. Houses gave way to meadows, which in turn disappeared into forest. Branches hovering over the winding road reminded her of those accusing fingers pointed by anonymous customers.

How could they understand? He doesn't look like there is a damn thing wrong with him. He just looks like a spoiled child with a mother that hasn't a clue how to discipline.

The Mercedes turned down a road that was only slightly better than a dirt path. Cassie stopped the car by the river's edge where clumps of grass grew thick and green interrupted by patches of pebbles poking their heads through the mud. A battalion of trees stood guard along the bank, witness to decades of weekend family picnics and late night lovers' rendezvous. Recent rain had swollen the river's flow to higher than normal levels. It gurgled and sputtered around arched limbs that dipped their fingers into the bubbling broth. Angry water tumbled over submerged boulders, frothing and foaming as it raced forward to destinations unknown.

Bruiser recognized this location from previous daytime outings on calmer days. He screeched with glee as his mother lifted him from his car seat, then wriggled free of her grasp and scampered down to the water's edge, scooping up as many pebbles as he could hold in his tiny fists. The cause of her misery flung his missiles full force into the mysterious dark liquid. He squealed with delight. Rapidly his fingers dug at the earth, and again projectiles violated the churning water. He repeated this process over and over.

A catatonic version of Cassie blankly stared in the direction of the fierce activity. Had she been a proud mother, the sight of her child happily playing would have been delightful. However, this shell of a woman found no comfort or tenderness after such a devastating day.

Shifting her glance to the right she noticed the old

abandoned boat dock less than fifty yards away. Three weeks ago they had visited this secluded spot. Brian had raced ahead, and before his horrified mother had been able to stop him, he had catapulted himself off the pier and into the river. Just seconds behind him, she dove in and rescued him. When she returned home after that misadventure, a neighbor had seen her dripping wet while unloading the child in the driveway. Cassie had explained how panicky she had felt trying to save him. And now, here she was in the same location.

Beneath a shroud of trees, her soul cried out in silence, begging release from the outcome of this life's lottery. She had not chosen to play this game. Getting pregnant on her twenty-first birthday was certainly not her intention. Even if she had wanted a baby someday, most certainly she never would have chosen to have a child with a disability, much less this one. Autism! Despite the resources of her fortune, the inescapable lot was cast before her. This was not some disease modern medicine could cure if you threw enough money at it.

Deep within her mind, a twisted thought process wormed its way to the surface. *Neighbors know how uncontrollable he is,* she thought. *This creature is a demon; my life is hopeless as long as he is in it. He sucks the very life out of me. My secret lottery winnings are worthless; I don't have any freedom at all to enjoy all this money.*

Crouching down next to the Mercedes she was barely aware of her own actions. As she clawed some rocks from the dirt, mud imbedded itself deeply under her fingernails. She rose to stand beneath the shadowy giants that hovered over the swirling water. Her tortured soul ticked off a checklist of torments and punctuated each with a violent splash.

"I have no family to help me. My parents are dead, damn it!"

Plunk!

Sobs mixed with her screams. "I don't have any friends to help, either. Beth is on some goddamned cruise ship! Cindy is in freaking L.A.! Angela moved to Chicago!"

Splash!

"I'm alone." Her shoulders felt the pressure of the universe crushing air from her lungs, and she gasped for breath. "I haven't got a soul to share the torture of raising this kid. Greg's married now. There's no chance of even going out on a date again let alone falling in love while I have this monster in tow."

Thud, splash!

She hit the trunk of a tree near the water, and the rock tumbled into the frothy torrent.

"There's no family or friends to help me tame this wretched beast. I'll never have any hope of happiness."

Whiz, splat!

The last rock she flung with all her might came perilously close to the child before angrily splashing into the churning water.

Hatred clouded her eyes as she stared hard at his tiny figure. With deadly calm she addressed him.

"You... You've betrayed me. I was supposed to have a happy life filled with luxuries and good times. Look at what you've done to me." The boy ignored his mother as he kept flinging stones into the river. Cassie rambled on. "You're not a loving child. You're just an it. You betrayed me. Betrayed...Judas... hmm...I wonder what Judas' mother would have done if she had known what he would grow up to do? She probably was a loving mother. I'll bet she did her best to raise him right; but no, he was evil. He betrayed Christ and he betrayed his loving mother's trust."

Dark clouds from an approaching storm descended like a heavy blanket. A horrific plan grew like a cancer in her semi-conscious state. Consumed by irrational thoughts, Cassie robotically scooped tiny pebbles into her empty soda cup from the afternoon's fast food stop. Her free hand reached out and grabbed the devil by his arm. At first he resisted and squealed. Then he saw she was leading him to the dock. When he attempted to wiggle free to run ahead, she released her grasp. The malevolent spirit propelled himself to the end of the pier and flopped onto his stomach, fascinated by sparkles in the dark water caused by glimpses of sun straining to break through the growing cloud cover. Cassie heard the rhythmic pounding of waves smashing against the piling.

Rational and irrational thoughts commingled as she placed her cup of stones on the plank next to the tyrannical creature. *Mothers have killed their children before*, she thought. *Must be careful, though. The ones that get caught are too sloppy with their stories.*

She remembered reading about a woman who strapped her sons into their car seats and then rolled her car into a lake. The whole made-up story about a carjacker stealing her children fell apart; it was too complicated a lie. Another mother drowned all her children in the family bathtub. Not only was there too much evidence, the stupid woman even admitted doing it to the police.

There was another case, somewhere in Texas she thought, about a mother whose two little boys were slain with a kitchen knife. The woman had her own throat slashed as well and claimed some stranger had attacked them in the family room where they were sleeping. But that would be too much pain, and there was a chance of dying herself. Authorities had become suspicious a few days later when she held a birthday party for one of her murdered sons on his grave. She didn't show enough grief. Yes, that definitely was something to remember. A mother should be grief stricken when her child was murdered...or in the case about to happen, accidentally drowned.

A chill shivered down Cassie's spine. She could get away with it. There was very little light cast on the river by the new moon. A failed rescue attempt was plausible. There was so much to remember, though. It would have to be carefully staged. Cassie stood only a foot or so behind Bruiser. A gentle kick of her toe would knock the half empty container of stones into the water. The boy would instinctively reach out and jump in after it. Cassie could wait until she was sure he was dead.

Later, police would investigate the scene; she would have to carefully construct the scenario. While the toddler was swept away to float in the river, she would calmly walk back to the rock-encrusted shoreline and gather more stones as if for the child. Then she would race out to the pier's end, dropping them midway as if in a panic. She'd pretend the boy had just jumped in while she collected rocks for him. Her muddy footprints in a racing stride would prove to police that she desperately had wanted to save her son. Of course she'd need to jump in the river and flail about just to have evidence on her clothes that this "loving" mother had attempted a rescue. Yes, that seemed like a plan that just might work. She would need to cling to the pier for her own safety, though; the current could sweep her away as well if she was not careful.

Was there anything she was forgetting? Motive! People would say she had a motive. Everyone knew this was a horrific child. Would they suspect she had indeed caused his death willingly?

What to say, what to say? She began to pace slowly back and forth contemplating an alibi. Surely it was evident she had been a concerned mother. Just today she had taken him to the doctor trying to figure out what his problem was. But then someone would say she was distraught over the diagnosis. And what about the incident in the department store? After all, there were plenty of witnesses to testify about how upset she was. Perhaps it would be best to admit: yes, she had been upset, but had cooled down. She'd say she realized it had been foolish of her to take him into the china department and had planned to get a sitter for future outings.

To further disperse suspicion, she would admit she was financially so well off the broken crystal could easily be afforded. Use the truth about the money since they'd probably find out anyway. In fact, she could embellish, saying that after the diagnosis she had planned to research the best possible treatments available. The drive to the river was just so he could burn off some of his energy. Her neighbor knew she previously had brought him here for just that purpose. Yes that's it. The plan could work! She would be free of this tormentor that sucked all joy from her life.

Looking down, she stared at the object of her misery.

Still sprawled on its belly, the creature dangled its paws in an attempt to catch the rushing torrent flowing less than a foot out of reach. Then it scrambled up into a crouching position and peered into the paper cup. The tormented mother lifted her right foot drawing it back in preparation to swing forward. She noticed the cup held one final pebble. She would need to refill it first if her plan was to work.

The little demon picked out the last stone and hurled it. The pebble plunked, briefly sending ripples in concentric circles across the water, until a new wave buried the pattern in its wake. The creature jumped up and down while uttering a familiar high-pitched screech. "Eeee eeee eeee." It turned.

For the briefest flick of a second, those eyes locked onto Cassie's. Quickly the glance was averted; eyes meeting eyes somehow appeared to be painful. Nonetheless, the cup was lifted toward her. For a fraction of a second, its eyes darted back to her again, long curly brown tendrils nearly concealing the event. With grinning, rosy checks its voice garbled, "More."

He spoke. He said his first word.

Clouds of dementia began to part as Cassandra realized the significance of the event. Three years old and at the moment before his potential execution, Bruiser had uttered his first word. The doctor had said some people with autism never learned to speak at all. But was it possible? Did he actually speak? Did she really hear it?

Cassie dropped to her knees and squeezed her son close to her, crumbling in horror at the monster that moments ago possessed her. How was it possible to have even allowed the thought of murdering her own son enter her head, let alone to actually plan it out? Surely she was the worst mother in the entire universe.

Unaware of the reason for his mother's hug, her son struggled to free himself from her embrace. "Hey, Bruiser," she whispered as she choked back tears. Trying to eradicate the concept that she was capable of such evil, she calmly asked, "Are you hungry? Let's go get some French fries."

Now even more urgent for his freedom, he pushed loose and raced back to the car.

Cassie smoothed back strands of hair from her face and wiped tears away with her sleeve. The barest trace of light somehow managed to cast a spotlight on her as she shamefully shuffled back to the Mercedes. She paused. Something was in her shoe but she pressed on because Bruiser was frantically trying to get in.

The enormity of what almost happened shocked her. Never had she been abused. There was no history of violence in her family; quite the opposite was true. Carl and Amanda Delaine had raised their daughter to be kind, loving, and respectful of life. How was it possible that she could even consider the idea of taking her own child's life? Sure, he was a difficult child. No, that was wrong; he was impossible. But still he was her baby, her little boy!

Tears continued to well up in the corner of her eyes as she buckled her son into his car seat. Double-checking the latch, she made sure he was safely and securely fastened in. Then, Cassie opened the driver side door and sat on the edge of the seat with her feet dangling outside the car. Magnified by the windshield, slivers of light illuminated her guilt. Sure, she knew the strain of caring for Bruiser had been getting to her and the announcement of his diagnosis was devastating. But murdering her own son? Was she actually capable of that? She had even considered the mistakes of others while plotting an elaborate scheme to cover it up.

Remorse and horror swirled through her while she removed her shoe. Gentle tapping released a small mottled stone into her hand. On impulse she examined the pebble. It was small and irregularly shaped. One part was smooth, but mostly it was rough, its tiny ridges imbedded with dirt. At first her intention was to toss the stone away. Just before releasing it, she stopped, reached for her purse and dropped the pebble into the coin section of her wallet. She promised herself to keep it forever, as a constant reminder of what had almost happened. This would always be a memento of what she almost did to her own son and where it nearly took place.

With forced cheerfulness in her voice she asked, "Ready, Bruiser?" Then she corrected herself. "Ready, Brian?"

Her son was deserving of her love and respect. He did not choose to come into this life with a disability anymore than she chose for it to happen to him. She needed to change the way she had been thinking about him, and she needed to start doing it right now. One way to do that was to change what she had been calling him. Not calling him Bruiser was going to be a hard habit to break. That was all she ever called him. *Brian. His name is Brian. Say it again,* she told herself. *His name is Brian.*

Cassie finished her wine and quietly approached the crib. Brian looked so peaceful now. Despite their disheveled appearance she had tried to ease her guilty conscience by letting him thoroughly enjoy their fast food trip. He swam in the pit of plastic balls and climbed over other children to tumble down the slides. Before bed, muddy splatters from the river expedition were washed down the drain, removing any evidence of the near fatal incident. Exhaustion kept him from resisting being toweled off. Then, pajama clad, he was snuggled under the covers in his crib.

Cassie stood over him listening as he breathed in and out. Merely hours ago, she had contemplated snuffing out the life force filling his lungs by submerging him in murky water. Now she shuddered at the thought of any harm coming to her precious child.

She studied every detail of his cherubic face. As he lay contentedly in the land of REM, he looked no different from any other typical three-year-old. There were no distinctive features to indicate his complex disorder. There was no characteristic flat face and downwardly curving mouth as would be typical in a child with Down syndrome. His upper lip was not thin and missing the Cupid's bow, nor were his eyes unusually narrow slits as was common in children with Fetal Alcohol Syndrome.

This perfectly beautiful child gave no hints in his slumber that anything at all was amiss. Were it not for his unusual behaviors and lack of typical toddler babbling, strangers would mistake him for being normal...whatever that was.

Careful not to creak any floorboards that would awaken this incredibly light sleeper, she tiptoed out of the room. Before showering the remnants of the last twenty-four hours away, she fetched the coin purse and pried open the clasp. Locating the pebble under the loose change, she ceremoniously placed it on the dresser next to her watch.

"Tomorrow and every day from now on I'll carry this with me," she uttered aloud. "I must never forget."

Kindred Spirits

Chapter 9.

A sign taped to St. Vincent's front door directed: *Autism Support Group: meet in the Fellowship Room, down the hall, first door on your left.* Tentatively Cassie followed the instructions with Brian in tow. Just inside the designated room stood a cheerful middle-aged woman whose shoulder length chestnut locks were casually tucked behind her ears.

"Hi, come on in. You must be Cassie and this must be Brian," she said, and then whispered, "Can he have a c-o-o-k-i-e-?"

"Yes, thank you," Cassie replied.

The woman stooped to Brian's height holding a chocolate chip cookie in front of her face. "Look at me, Brian," she said. For a fraction of a second his eyes met hers. "Good looking at me, Brian. Here...have a cookie."

He snatched the treat. While her son devoured it, Cassie sized up the figure before her. This woman was obviously accustomed to taking charge while simultaneously putting those around her at ease. She wore motherhood as comfortably as the fuchsia sweater casually unbuttoned over her simple black dress. Rosy cheeks and an easy smile seemed to have the power to disarm many a potential adversary. It was apparent she was a force to be reckoned with, though; after all, in a few moments she had breached the fortress Brian kept between him and the rest of the world.

Straightening up, the woman continued, "Hi, Cassie. We spoke on the phone the other day. I'm Virginia Troppus, but everybody just calls me Ginny. Why don't you take your son down the hall to the primary room? Some of the other moms bring their kids, too and pool their money to pay for childcare while we have our meetings. Maureen and Chris are wonderful; they're special education majors at Benton College and they've been watching some of our kids for a couple of years now. Vicky is new, just the last two meetings, but she catches on quick. Like I told you on the phone Cassie, you can relax; they'll take good care of Brian."

Hesitantly, Cassie led her son down a corridor lined with construction paper collages strung end to end. She couldn't help thinking about the incident at Sally Clifton's house. Sally had seemed confident and quite capable until she was confronted by the explosion of energy hidden behind Brian's angelic face. Could college girls who were a few years younger than she was really contain him?

In the childcare room, a tall redhead rose from her seat and slowly approached the new visitors. Cheerfully, but soft spoken so as not to startle the newcomer, she introduced herself.

"Hi. I'm Maureen. Ginny told me you were coming. Go on ahead to your meeting; Brian will be fine with us." Stooping to the child's height she said, "Do you like bubbles, Brian? Watch."

Maureen blew several bubbles close to Brian but away from him toward the center of the room. Brian reached out, trying to catch the iridescent globes. Slowly, Maureen blew a few more bubbles, leading him like a pied piper to an area with a drop cloth on the floor. She pointed to the television.

"Mom will be back when Peter Pan is all done," she assured him.

He appeared not to notice as his mother walked out of the room and back down the hall.

"Funny," Cassie mumbled to herself. "He didn't seem interested in bubbles at Sally Clifton's house." What was different? She decided to wonder about that later and instead focus her attention on what she had come here for.

In St. Vincent's fellowship room, approximately a dozen chairs were arranged in a circle. Refreshments were spread out on a small, cloth-covered table in the corner. Four ladies were already seated and two more took their seats as Cassie entered the room.

"We're just about to get started. Help yourself to some coffee and cake, and then grab a seat," Ginny instructed. She balanced a slice of apple cake on her knee, and then blew a cooling breath over the steaming liquid in the Styrofoam cup in her right hand.

"How do you like the cake, Maria?" a short, pudgy redhead inquired.

"It's delicious, Ellen. When do you find the time to bake?" inquired the woman next to her.

"Well, Danny is still getting up around three a.m. and staying awake for a few hours. By the time I get him to fall back asleep it's usually only an hour or so until Aaron has to get up for work. So, I figure I'm up and I may as well put the time to good use. I either bake or fill out another one of my contest entries. You know, with all that I've entered, I'm bound to win something sometime. I'm due to hit soon; I can just feel it. Anyway, back to the cake; I thought I'd give Elsie a break. Every month she always bakes the goodies and sets up our refreshments."

An elderly woman hovering near the table said, "Thank you, Ellen, I appreciate the thought, but really I don't mind the effort." Elsie tucked a loose strand back into the tight bun of gray hair piled on top of her head. Cassie thought she remembered her own grandmother wearing her hair that way several decades earlier.

Cassie helped herself to a piece of cake but passed on the coffee.

Turning to Cassie, Elsie said, "There's some soda and ice in the bucket if you prefer something cold."

Cassie thought it was strange to find such an old woman at a support group for parents of children with autism. Obviously this woman was way too old to have a little child; perhaps she had a grandchild with autism. But, judging from her age, perhaps she was even someone's great-grandmother. Then again, she thought, maybe she was just a church member there to help.

"Which reminds me," Elsie continued, "Ginny, it's really nice of St. Vincent's to let our support group meet here, but do you think maybe they would let us use one of the classrooms with a large table instead of this room? I seem to spill my coffee nearly every month. I'm not as agile as I once was and when I try to pick my cup off the floor, I have trouble seeing it right. I swear, if I live to be one hundred and three, I'll never get used to these damn bifocals."

"I see your point," Ellen the redhead chimed in. "But I kind of like the closeness of not having a table separating us when things get emotional."

A chocolate-skinned woman across the room suggested, "Why don't we get a set or two of tray tables for between the chairs? I'm sure St. Vincent's would let us keep them here."

Sitting next to the previous speaker, a young blond woman immediately bubbled, "I saw in the paper that Stubers department store has tray tables on sale this week. Maybe we could afford it if we all chipped in."

Eager at the prospects of possibly fitting in again with a tight-knit group of friends, Cassie interrupted. "I have two sets of tray tables," she lied. "Some friends gave them as housewarming gifts when I moved in. I really don't have any need for them. I'd be happy to donate them to the group."

Ginny looked surprised. "Are you sure? I mean, that's very generous of you. After all, this is only your first meeting."

"Yes, of course I'm sure. Besides, I don't think they would be safe to use at home. Bruiser, I mean, Brian would only pull them over along with anything I might try to put on them." Pleased that she could be of assistance, Cassie made a mental note to order two sets of tray tables over the Internet when she got home.

"That's really nice of you, Cassie. Thank you." Ginny motioned. "Have a seat over here next to me and let's get started with the introductions. You probably won't remember all our names right away but we'll be just like family after a while. I'll start." Ginny took a sip of coffee. "Well, as I told you before, I'm Ginny Troppus. My son James is fourteen. He's starting to get vocational training at Franklin Caresse School. I have another son, Nathan, who isn't autistic. He's twelve." Ginny turned to her left indicating for the plump redhead to begin.

"Hi, I'm Ellen Lavitsef. Danny is six years old and is in a self-contained classroom at Williams Elementary School. They do a lot of reverse mainstreaming with volunteers from Mrs. Jackson's fifth grade class."

"Tell her what you mean by self-contained and reverse mainstreaming," Ginny prodded.

"Oh, I'm sorry; I guess you don't know what that is." Ellen pushed her round glasses back up her nose. "You see, for lots of kids with autism, a full regular-size class is too intimidating. It's just too many people, too much noise, and too many distractions. So, my son is in a class with just four other children that all have autism; that's the self-contained part. Special needs kids separate from regular education kids. They do a wonderful job of teaching him personal skills like buttoning his own coat and brushing his teeth. Last year they worked with me to get him potty trained. They teach him school stuff, too, like using scissors and glue. But one of the most important things is they're helping him learn how to speak, to ask for things.

"Danny also needs to learn the social skills that come naturally to most kids. But like I said, if you put him in a full-size class, he would probably freak out. So, Mrs. Jackson has a small group of volunteers from her regular education class that come over to Danny's class during their recess or lunchtime. They teach them to take turns when they play games and one of them, Carolyn, eats lunch with Danny. She showed him how to use a napkin. That's the reverse mainstreaming part: when typically developing kids come over to the special education class to help out." Ellen finally slowed down enough to take a breath. "There. Did that make it any clearer?"

"Yes, I think so," Cassie hesitantly replied.

Seated beside Ellen, a Hispanic woman with lush, thick, shoulder-length curls prepared to speak. "I'm Maria Regna. I have two boys; Pablo is ten and Carlos is eight. My son Carlos is the autistic one. His school situation is not as good as Danny's. He's a runner and Claron School District doesn't have the foggiest idea of what to do with him."

"She doesn't mean he's athletic," Ellen interrupted. "She just means he's always trying to run away from people and from situations he doesn't want to be in."

Maria nodded. "Yeah, that's right, and like I said the school district doesn't know what to do with him. They put him in Morris Hill. It's a school for the severely disabled." Her voice intensified as she continued. "He doesn't belong there. They aren't helping him one bit. He runs away, so his teacher ties him to a chair. They deny it but I know they do it."

Ginny interrupted "Okay, Maria. We can get back to that in a minute, but first let's get the introductions out of the way so Cassie gets to know a little about each of us first."

"All right!" Maria grumbled, tossing back curly black hair.

Attempting to ignore Maria's agitation, the petite blond in a crisp white blouse bubbled her introduction. "My son Todd is four years old and has PDD/NOS. Oh, yeah, my name is Kari Lained. I'm friends with a teacher at the Montessori school so Todd goes there three days a week for a half-day. I drive him over to Bentfield Clinic the other two days for intensive speech therapy and then he goes for occupational and physical therapy. Todd is doing much better now; I've seen tremendous improvements. I think he is going to be just fine. We are going to start sensory integration therapy next week. That should help a lot, too."

After a brief pause, the black woman with tight natural ringlets spoke. "I'm Tamika Gray and my little girl is Monisha. She's seven years old. At first we were told she was autistic, but then the diagnosis changed to Rett Syndrome. She's over at Morris Hill, too. That school is for kids that can't make it in a regular school setting. She seems to be doing okay there, but it's hard to tell for sure. You know how it is when your kid can't tell you what's going on; it's so frustrating when they can't say how they feel."

The other women in the circle nodded. For the first time Cassie seemed to be in the presence of mothers accustomed to unusual behavior in their children, but so many of these terms were totally foreign to her.

Seated next to Tamika was the elderly woman that had been by the dessert table earlier. It was her turn to speak. "I'm Elsie. Elsie Eveirg. That's all. Next." She wiped a tear from the corner of her eye then abruptly stood and left the circle of women to refill her Styrofoam cup with more coffee even though it was still half full.

After a brief, uncomfortable pause, the elegant woman to Cassie's right smiled brightly as she turned to face this young newcomer to their group. "Hi. I'm Michelle Ammelid. My son Bradley is thirteen. He has Asperger Syndrome and he attends Jacob Fallows Middle School. He's mainstreamed into a regular education classroom that is team taught with a special education teacher. Full inclusion works quite well for his academics, but the other kids tease him unmercifully. I could go on forever about the benefits versus the problems of having a child with Asperger's but I want to hear what you have to say. So, now tell us a little about you."

Elsie returned to her seat. Now that her emotions were apparently once again in check, she appeared eager to display a warm welcome to the newcomer.

Cassie hesitated and then began. "I am in the right place, aren't I? I'm a little bit confused. I thought this was a support group for parents of children with autism."

Ginny gave a conciliatory gesture. "I'm sorry, Cassie. Some of us have been dealing with these issues so long that we forget how it was when our kids were first diagnosed. When people use the word autism, most of the time what they are referring to is Autism Spectrum Disorders. There wasn't even a name for what our kids have until 1943 when some doctor by the name of Leo Kanner called it early infantile autism. For decades very little about it was understood. As scientists have studied our kids more they realized there are a lot of disorders including Asperger's and PDD/NOS that kind of fall into the category of autism." She paused. "Let me think how better to explain this."

Puzzling for a moment, she continued, "When you go to the produce section of a supermarket to buy apples, at first you just spot the area next to the oranges and you see apples.

But when you get a closer look, you see that there are lots of different types. There are Red Delicious, McIntosh, Winesap, Cortland and Granny Smith just to name a few varieties."

Ellen teased, "Gee, I'm impressed. You sure know a lot about apples, Ginny."

"Thanks, Ellen," Ginny sarcastically replied. "Anyway, what I'm trying to say is that each variety of apple has its differences in texture and can vary drastically in taste, but they all fall under the broad category of apples."

"But there is a difference," Kari said. "My child doesn't have full-blown autism. His diagnosis is PDD/NOS: that means Pervasive Development Disorder/Not Otherwise Specified."

"Christ, Kari! Come on," Maria refuted. "That makes about as much difference as some rich white dude on the Titanic bragging that at least he's in first class and not in steerage. He's still on the same damn boat and he's going down with it just the same as the poor fool in the basement."

"I think of it more like as a rainbow," Ellen added with an attempt to lighten the tension between her friends. "After all, they do call it a spectrum disorder."

Summing up the analogies Ginny stated, "I'm not sure I'd equate our situation with the Titanic, but the idea of comparing it to a ship has some merit much the same as Ellen's idea of the rainbow. Your kid can be at one end and have Asperger's Syndrome and somewhere near the other end is Rett Syndrome, and somewhere else is low functioning autism and another place there is high functioning autism. Where your location is may alter what your particular experience is like, but in the long run we're all on a similar journey together. Some diagnoses are more well-defined but the distinction between autism and PDD can be rather murky."

"What difference does the terminology make?"

"Good question. In my opinion, not much. But sometimes the names we use in society change to be more accurate. You know I can remember a time when some children were referred to as mongoloid, but later that was more appropriately changed to Down syndrome." Ginny paused briefly, giving a pensive little giggle. "I can also remember a time when if someone said he was gay that meant he was happy; now it means he's a homosexual."

"We all know you're starting to get older, Ginny," Michelle interrupted to gently tease. "But do you suppose you could get your mind back on track? Get to your point."

"Well, it's like Shakespeare said, a rose by any other name would smell as sweet," Ginny replied.

"Or in this case, Autism, PDD, doesn't matter; it still sucks!"

"Maria!" Kari gently rebuked.

Ginny continued, "I guess what I'm trying to say is that it all depends on your point of view, your experience with your child's disability. Behaviors they use to determine which category to put your child in change sometimes. Several months after my son's diagnosis, certain behaviors kind of disappeared but then he picked up a few new ones. It can be very confusing trying to figure out which label is correct. So, my advice is don't worry about that; just make sure he gets good special education geared to his own unique needs."

"I'll tell you one thing for sure," Tamika added. "Autism is the great equalizer. It don't matter if you're rich or poor, if you're smart or dumb, if you're black, white, or any other color for that matter. Anybody can have a kid with autism. All I can say is at least nowadays they are finally starting to do some research. We need some answers for our kids and we need them now!"

Surprised Cassie asked, "You mean they haven't been doing any research until recently?"

"Oh, hon, of course they have." Ginny responded. "The pace has been somewhat slow until the last fifteen or twenty years, though. Research cost lots of money and, well, when you were a kid did you ever see a telethon for autism? And over the years there has been such an outcry demanding money for things like AIDS and cancer research that autism didn't have as much public attention to push for government funding."

Kari added excitedly, "There are a lot more fundraisers now that autism has been in the news more."

Ginny nodded. "That's true, but it's going to take a lot more money and time. Autism is a complex, confusing disorder even for professionals." She turned back to Cassie. "Listen, I can tell you've got lots of questions, but don't worry, there will be plenty of time for that. You can't expect to learn everything all at once. Why don't you go ahead and tell the others about yourself and your son?"

Glancing quickly around the circle, Cassie weighed just how candid to be. Her mother's cautionary attitude still held a dominant influence on her actions, so she chose to keep the sharing restricted to her son for now. "Okay. Like Ginny said, my name is Cassandra Delaine, but everybody calls me Cassie. My son's name is Brian. He turned three last month and I just got his diagnosis confirmed a week after that. The doctor said that I should have him evaluated by the school district so that he can get early intervention, whatever that is. I live in Sweetwater and I'm still waiting for an appointment with the school district."

"You're lucky," Michelle said. "Sweetwater has a pretty good program. I remember it took a while for them to do all their evaluations for us. But once my son Bradley started, they helped me set up a home program so I could be consistent with what they do at school. They have a wonderful speech pathologist there, too."

"In the meantime," Ginny interjected, "I have lots of books that will help you understand more about autism and the basics of applied behavior analysis. I think you'll find once you get in the habit of positive reinforcements..."

"In English, Ginny," Tamika reminded.

"I'm sorry. This terminology is second nature to me," Ginny apologized. "What I meant to say is small rewards for specific good behavior. That's really simplifying the whole thing, though. There's more to it: like trying to figure out why your child does something and then teaching a more appropriate behavior in its place."

She laughed. "Listen, I could go on for hours talking about autism and behavior analysis but I think it will make more sense if you borrow some of my books and then we can talk about how to use it. Why don't you stop by my house tomorrow afternoon? I'll loan you the books and give you a list of our names and phone numbers. We're all just a phone call away when you're at wit's end. Between the books, school, and all of us, there's so much more help than there used to be."

"I have to admit, we do have a lot to be thankful for," Maria added. "As bad as I think it is for Carlos at Morris Hill, at least now we have free public education for our kids. In the old days they would have been home with us 24/7 or shipped off to some institution. Thank God I never had to go through the Bettleheim era!"

"What was that?" Cassie asked.

The circle of women fidgeted as they exchanged nervous glances. An uncomfortable topic had inadvertently been brought up. Ellen elbowed Maria in silent admonishment, but before any of the others had a chance to formulate a tactful response, Elsie again rose from her seat. All eyes were riveted on the sad, frail woman. Awkward silence persisted while they waited for her response. With deliberation, Elsie took a small sip of her steaming coffee. She held the cup in both hands as if in prayer, begging for release from tortured memories.

"Bruno Bettleheim," she barely whispered. "Bruno Bettleheim was a fraud." Slipping from the corner of her eye, a tear followed a familiar path down her cheek, leaving behind a silvery trail.

Turning to Maria she continued, "You know he committed suicide, don't you? It was in 1990, I think. Lots of guilt...I had lots of guilt back then but somehow, I actually felt a sense of peace when I heard he'd died."

As Elsie took another sip, the slight slurp appeared decibels louder than it actually was. Were it not for the soundless vacuum, no one would have noticed the faint music coming from the children's video down the hall.

Turning again toward Cassie the old woman continued in a semi-trance-like state. "I may as well tell the story; if I don't, someone else will. Gossip later behind my back would only be natural. Better it comes from me." Seeking a source of inner strength, the old woman drew in a deep breath, holding it for a moment before allowing words and memories to gush forth. "He lied and a lot of people believed him. He wasn't a psychiatrist, but somehow he got famous and people believed him. Everybody believed him. He said it was my fault. He told lots of distraught mothers that. We came to him for help. He said our children were autistic because we were cold and unloving. *Refrigerator mothers* he called us. He took our children, our precious babies that we were desperate trying to figure out." More tears slowly streamed down her face as she relived heart-wrenching memories.

"I lived in Chicago then; that's where his school was. I was desperate. Back then it was unheard of for an unwed mother to keep her child, especially someone as young as I was. But I was determined—that is, until I realized there was something wrong with Roger. That man, that Bettleheim, had me go to therapy...said I didn't love my son enough. He said I made him autistic and then he took Roger away from me and put him in that school. That man wasn't even a psychologist, but when he misdiagnosed some children and then they got better, he claimed he had cured them. After he died, I read in the paper they found out one of the treatments he used on our children was physical abuse. He said *I* didn't love him enough." She cried it out again, "He said I didn't love him enough."

Elsie fought hard not to spill her coffee as she sobbed. "I'm sorry; I'm not much help this month. I have to go. I'll see you next time."

Tamika stood and wrapped her arms around the grieving old woman. "Your apartment is only a few minutes away, Elsie. I'll drive you home."

Silence hovered until they left the room.

Maria gushed an apology. "It just slipped out. I didn't mean to cause a scene. I've gotten so used to Elsie being here; I forget sometimes what she went through and how painful it still is for her. I mean...well, after all, we're supposed to be able to say anything here in this group. Aren't we? There aren't any forbidden topics. Right? For once I wasn't complaining about services for Carlos and I still managed to get myself in trouble."

"You're right, Maria," Ginny said. "We can talk about whatever is on our minds. It's just that it's awfully close to a painful anniversary for her. I'm sorry, Cassie. That was a lot of drama for your first meeting with us. Sometimes we do get a bit emotional, but lots of times we laugh, too. I hope you'll give our group a chance. We're a good source of information and we really do try to support each other when we're down."

Ellen added, "Usually there are a few others here as well. Sue and Rose couldn't make it today."

"Even if you can't come one month you can keep in touch by phone," Kari added. "There's always somebody to listen if you need some support. And of course there are also the chapter meetings you can attend with us."

Ginny explained, "The Autism Society of America is a national organization with lots of state and local chapters. We lobby for better services, promote community awareness of autism, and provide information to parents. This group here, though, is specifically for support. We don't have any agendas; we just get together, talk about our kids, share problems, and offer suggestions."

"Speaking of which," Kari eagerly asked, "does anybody have any idea how I can get Todd to leave the playground without having a major temper tantrum? There is always a scene with lots of kicking and screaming ever time we have to leave."

"Who's doing the kicking and screaming, Kari? You or him?" Ellen teased.

"Very funny, I'm serious. It's embarrassing. I feel like every other mother there is staring at me. I worry they're wondering if I'm abusing my kid. Does anyone have any suggestions?"

"Well, I can remember Bradley having tantrums whenever we had to go out of the house when he was younger," Michelle offered. "He hated to leave his toys. But he knew how to count at an early age, so I would tell him two more down the marble maze slide and then we had to go. That worked pretty well for me."

Ginny agreed, "Our kids with autism have such a difficult time dealing with transitions from one activity to another." Then she asked Kari, "Todd doesn't know how to count yet, does he?"

"No. I've tried but he doesn't understand that yet."

"You might want to use a portable kitchen timer—the kind with a dial." Ginny gestured with her hands. "Try setting it for two or three minutes and tell him when the bell sounds that it's time to leave. That way the timer is the bad guy, not you. Also, he can see time tick down with the dial moving. Our kids respond so much better to visual prompts—that is, to things that they can see rather than being told what to do," she explained for Cassie's benefit.

"You know, that makes sense," Maria agreed. "I mean, I know how it feels to be in the middle of watching my favorite program on TV and then the phone rings. I guess we all like to be given a little advance warning when we have to stop doing something we enjoy."

Ginny said, "I just remembered I still have the old timer I used to use with James. He can tell time and wears a watch now so I haven't used it in ages. I'd be happy to let you have it." She looked around the room. "Anybody else have something to share?"

"I do," Maria said. "For the most part things have not been going very well this year at Morris Hill, but yesterday something amazing happened. Carlos finally learned to tie his shoes! I can't believe it. We've been working on that for so long. He finally got it!"

The group applauded in unison.

"You must be so happy," Ellen said as she hugged Maria.

Cassie was puzzled and a little dismayed that all these women were so excited because an eight-year-old had learned to tie his shoes. Something most children of that age wouldn't give a second thought to was cause for celebration here. She wondered just how disabled Brian was. Slipping her hand into her pocket to touch her pebble from the river, she pressed it hard between her fingers, and her mind began to wander as the ladies continued discussing their children. On the one hand, it was reassuring to be in the midst of others who were struggling to raise special children. On the other hand, it was depressing that common milestones most children sailed through were hard fought battles for these kids. Did that make the victory all the more sweet or the struggle all the more devastating? As she worried and pondered, slowly she became aware her tiny stone had cut her fingers.

Kari noticed Cassie retrieve a tissue from her purse. "Oh my God, Cassie. You're bleeding! Are you okay?"

"Yes, I'm fine. I just cut myself a little."

"Good heavens, is there a sharp spot on your chair?" Ginny asked.

Cassie searched awkwardly for what to say. "Oh, no, I'm afraid it was, well you see, um...I kind of carry this pebble as sort of a good luck charm. I kind of fidget with it sometimes and I guess I cut myself on a rough spot."

Maria rose and offered her hand. "It must not be a very good lucky charm if you cut yourself on it; maybe you need a rabbit's foot instead. Come with me. I'll show you where the church kitchen is. They keep a first aid kit in there."

As Maria led Cassie out of the room, she heard the other women continue chatting about what should be mundane events in their children's lives but were not. Cassie dabbed at her bleeding finger as they walked down the hall and into the kitchen.

Opening an upper cabinet, Maria unhooked a first aid kit mounted inside the door. Nonchalantly, she began tending to the cut as a matter of routine. "Carlos is always getting scrapes and cuts. I should have been a nurse for all the times I've bandaged him up. He never cries though; he acts as if he doesn't even feel the pain when he gets hurt. One time when he came home from school, there was dried blood on his arms and wrists, and fingernail marks, but he acted like nothing had happened. Of course he couldn't tell me what happened 'cause he doesn't speak at all.

"I was frantic—his teacher had already left school for the day. I went in to see the principal first thing the next morning. Of course he had no idea anything had happened. After questioning the staff, it seems Carlos had been trying to run away again while they were loading the buses for home. One of the teacher aids had grabbed onto him. He tried to bite and kick her to get away. She held on so tight that her inch and a half designer nails dug into him. He didn't cry so nobody knew he was hurt."

Cassie gasped, half from the alcohol wipe Maria had just applied and half at her disturbing story. "Oh God! That's awful."

Maria deftly slipped a band-aid over the cut. "I'm used to it. Just another day in the life at that shitty school." She returned the first aid kit to its proper place. "All done. Let's go back and join the others."

Cassie hesitated. "Sure, um...you said Carlos doesn't talk at all and he's how old?"

"Eight. How about your kid, does he talk at all?"

"Only two words. A couple of weeks ago he said his first word. He said *more*. And yesterday he said *cookie*."

"That's fantastic! That's a great sign." Maria seemed genuinely happy for her. "He may never recite the Gettysburg Address, but at least he'll have some language."

"Just how much? How can I tell how limited he will be?"

Maria sighed but gave her a sympathetic smile. "You're so new to this, sweetie. You'll drive yourself crazy if you focus on twenty years down the road. Take it one day at a time." Seeing Cassie's face, she added, "Listen, I'm not saying don't plan for the future. You need to set goals and fight with the schools to make sure he gets all the services that he needs—things like speech therapy. But don't be always worried about the future or you'll miss today, the joys in the little things. Oh, I know I complain a lot. Hell, I'm mad at the world that my son is autistic. But let me tell you, I was in tears the first time Carlos chose to sit on the sofa next to me and leaned up against me. He never liked me to touch him before that. Even my husband couldn't fight back a tear when he saw what happened."

As the two women returned to the fellowship room, Maria asked, "How about your husband? How did he react when he found out your kid is autistic?"

"I don't have a husband. I'm a single parent," Cassie replied, fearing there would be a follow up question.

Tamika had returned at the same time and overheard them. "You're not alone, honey. As soon as Rose's husband found out their kid was autistic, he up and left her. So much for until death do us part. Men seem to have a tough time dealing with the idea that they fathered a child that isn't perfect—some macho thing, I think."

Maria shook her head. "I don't know, but I think it may be the way so many men are raised to be tough and not show their emotions. That may have something to do with it. Here in this group, we've shed many a tear. But most men aren't comfortable talking about their feelings. I think they hurt just as deeply as we do, but they're too scared to show it."

Tamika continued, "So much for us being the weaker sex. We are a lot stronger—well, maybe I should just talk for myself. I'm a lot stronger than I ever thought I could be. I never would have imagined I could deal with all I've gone through."

"I think it's changing with some men, though," Ginny offered as the women resumed their seats. "I noticed at the last chapter meeting there were lots more fathers than there used to be. And did you notice Carl Wilson and Steven Hill were elected officers? They've become very active participants in the organization."

"Yeah, and what about Dante Washington?" Michelle injected. "He organized a group of parents to go speak with some local legislators," she explained for Cassie. "They went to lobby for increased funding for group homes and vocational training. It took a long time, but they were pretty successful as I recall."

Tamika relented slightly. "I suppose some men are getting a little better at accepting their disabled kids. But still, even when they do get involved, it's like they have to find some major project. When it comes to everyday care, most of the time it's still up to us moms. For some moms, often it's a day in, day out heartache of managing their kid's tantrums—because they don't have any other way to communicate."

Before anyone else had a chance to respond, Maureen appeared at the door with a tearful four-year-old Todd Lained in tow clutching three chewed up action figures and a handful of rubber bands.

"I'm sorry, Kari," Maureen began. "But I think Todd is tired and wants to go home now. He started rocking and crying in a corner of the room. I knew it was almost time for your meeting to be over, so I brought him down to you. I hope you don't mind."

Kari immediately fetched her child, chattering away as she gathered up her purse and diaper bag. "It's okay, Maureen. It's time for me to go anyway." Turning toward Cassie she continued, "It was nice to meet you. I look forward to getting to know you better. Ginny will give you the list of all our phone numbers. Give me a call and maybe we can get together. Our kids are sort of close in age so we can swap stories and helpful hints. I'm free Wednesday; maybe we could take the kids to the McDonald's playground on Pine Street. It will give me a chance to try out the timer idea from Ginny. Let me know if you'd like to go."

"It is getting late," Ginny confirmed. "We better close up shop for the night. Don't forget to pick up your kids, ladies. As good as the girls are I'm sure they don't want unintended overnight guests. Maureen, here's your check and will you take these checks down to Chris and Vicky for me?"

"Sure, no problem."

The mothers rose, each instinctively knowing what needed to be done next. Michelle and Tamika folded chairs and stacked them neatly in the corner against a wall. Maria carted the soda and paper goods back to the kitchen while Ellen wrapped foil around the leftover cake.

"Is there anything I can do?" Cassie inquired.

"Do you think you can find your way back to the kitchen again? You could carry the coffeemaker back there; Maria can show you where it goes," Ginny responded as she bagged the leftover cookies.

Cassie happily complied, content that this extremely diverse group had instantly recognized her as one of their own. These women all had one common bond: a child with autism.

They did not look at her as a stupid, inept mother. Yet mingled with the exhilaration of being accepted in this sorority of mothers was confusion and concern for the future. The extent of Brian's disability was beginning to sink in.

Cassie walked toward the primary room half expecting to find Brian hanging from the ceiling surrounded by frazzled caretakers. Instead, her child was contentedly squishing his hands through a bin of uncooked rice grains. Surprisingly, neither Maureen, Vicky, nor Chris acted like Brian was some bizarre child. In fact, they seemed to take his odd noises in stride.

"Brian, look, Mom is back," Vicky said as she led the boy to his mother. "He was really pretty good for his first time with us, Ms. Delaine. He got fussy at one point when we wouldn't let him climb up on the table, but Chris redirected him over to the play area. Then we rewarded him with some M&Ms when he sat down to play nicely with the box of Matchbox cars from the toy shelf. I watched what he did with the cars and then I did the same thing with him. After awhile I took two cars and showed him how to race them on the floor. He's a bundle of energy, but really quite a cutie pie. I hope you come back again next month. I had a good time with the little guy."

"You did?" Cassie remarked incredulously then composed herself. "Oh, that's great. Thank you and, well, yes, I think we will be coming back next month. Time to go home now, Brian."

"Eeeyahh. Eeeyahh," the toddler wailed as he scurried into the corner of the room trying to escape his mother.

"What does he like to do when he first gets home after being out?" Chris asked.

After thinking about it for a moment, Cassie said, "He usually just dashes over to the television and bangs on it until I put the Weather Channel on for him to watch while he plays with the toy cars he has at home."

"Brian," Chris called. "Weather Channel. It's time to go home and watch the Weather Channel."

Brian ran to the TV that had played the Peter Pan video and began banging on it.

"No, Brian," Chris continued. "Weather Channel at Brian's house. Look at me, Brian. Weather Channel at Brian's house. Weather Channel home."

The toddler seemed to make the connection and bolted toward the door.

"Bye, Brian. Bye, Ms. Delaine. Now don't forget to put it on for him for at least a few minutes when you get home before you get him ready for bed."

"Okay. I won't," Cassie promised. "Bye." As she drove home, she replayed every aspect of the meeting in her head. Many questions were answered but many more took their place. Still, a sense of peaceful excitement overwhelmed her. Finally she had discovered some people to help her understand her puzzling son.

Chapter 10.

Cassie and Brian anxiously waited by the front door of a cozy ranch-style home half-hidden from the street by mature maples and oaks. "Ginny, I hope you don't mind me stopping by so early without calling first, but Brian was actually being pretty good this morning. I thought I'd better take advantage of it by running some errands."

"No, it's no problem, come on in. Please don't mind the mess, though; I haven't had time to straighten up yet. After James gets on the bus for school in the mornings, I usually fix myself a second cup of coffee and read the newspaper. If I don't schedule that 'me time' for myself in the morning, I never seem to do it later in the day."

Ginny led Cassie and Brian through a narrow foyer into the kitchen. Breakfast dishes were still piled by the sink waiting to be washed. Ginny hastily gathered up newspaper sections that had been spread across the table and stashed them into a recycle bin. "Would you like a cup of coffee, Cassie? I made a fresh pot of some hazelnut blend about ten minutes ago."

"Yes, thank you; that would be wonderful."

"We can sit at the table here, but oh, let's see...what shall we do about Brian? I don't have a high chair anymore." Quickly thinking, she answered herself. "Wait a minute, I know." Ginny rummaged through her pantry and a junk drawer for some supplies. She snugly wrapped the ends of a paper shopping bag around two thick phone books, securing the makeshift booster with duct tape.

"Would Brian like some Cheerios and a glass of apple juice?"

"Thanks, but I packed some snack containers in his diaper bag. He's very particular about what he eats off of."

"Ah yes, insistence on routine; been there, done that, I totally understand. Have a seat, Cassie."

Once Brian was settled, Ginny served her guest, then poured another cup for herself. "I love flavored coffees but my husband hates them. So as a treat, every so often I brew a whole pot for myself and just refrigerate what's leftover. When I want a cup the next day, all I have to do is put some into a mug and microwave it."

"It tastes great, Ginny! It must be nice to have some time for yourself on a regular basis. It's just so hard to do with Brian; he seems to get into trouble every time I turn my back for even a second."

Ginny leaned forward. "Cassie, it's not just nice to take time for yourself, it's vital. Taking care of a child with autism can be exhausting and stressful. I'm serious, if you don't schedule the time for yourself, you'll burn out and then you won't be any good to you or your son." She sat back and took a sip of coffee. "I can remember when James was young I would feel guilty if I was cleaning the house that I wasn't spending time with him. And when I was spending time working or playing with James, I would feel guilty that I wasn't spending time with my other son. When I spent time with Nathan, I felt guilty that I was neglecting the housework. My marriage started to suffer because of all the stresses and strains, and then I felt guilty about that. Lord, there was never any time for me and I became unglued."

Cassie was shocked. "You're kidding. I mean you seem to have it all together. It's so hard for me to imagine you at wit's end."

Brian dumped his cereal dish over, scattering bits all over the table.

Ginny gave a little laugh but seemed not to take notice of her own actions as she casually cleaned the mess up and refilled his bowl while she spoke. "Trust me. It takes a lot of work to look this calm. I learned years ago that if I didn't fill my own pitcher first, I'd have nothing to pour out to the people important in my life. It was hard to let go, though. I had this idealized vision of how life should be. My children would go to the best private schools, our home would be spotless, and I'd prepare gourmet meals the whole family would enjoy every night.

"Then James came along. Nothing prepares you for that punch in your gut we all go through when we realize we have a disabled child. I had to reevaluate my priorities. At some point, I realized that the people in my life, especially my family, are more important than things. So, I try to only focus on what is most important. And in order to have the energy and enthusiasm I need to accomplish that, I have to take care of me first."

Pausing to allow what she had said to sink in a little, Ginny took a long, slow sip of her coffee. "You mentioned last night that you're a single parent. When's the last time you went out on a date?"

Cassie shifted uncomfortably in her seat, reminded of the disastrous results the last time she left Brian with a sitter. "I'm afraid it's been a long time. There isn't exactly a long line of guys beating down my door. Every time I'm out and see a cute guy, I have Brian with me. His odd behaviors don't exactly encourage anyone to want to get acquainted."

Ginny rose from the table and began leafing through some folders she had stashed in a kitchen cabinet. "Here it is. This is the list I told you about last night of all the phone numbers of the group. At the bottom you'll find the phone numbers for Maureen, Vicky, and Chris as well. Pick a night, and then call them up until you find which one is available so you can go out. But whatever you do, don't put it off, because if you do, you'll never go anywhere. You need a break: something, anything, anywhere—just go."

Ginny leaned over the table to refill Cassie's mug. Habitually preoccupied by Brian's actions, Cassie had consumed her coffee faster than she intended. *This treat for the taste buds should be savored,* she mused. While Ginny topped off her own mug, Cassie reflected on how easily this woman had immediately befriended her. In many ways she was as authoritative yet disarming as both Angela and her mother.

Sighing, she realized how much she missed their counsel. "I suppose you're right," Cassie agreed. "The chance to get out by myself sounds wonderful. Last night Chris was apparently able to handle Brian pretty well, and Vicky actually seemed to enjoy being with him. But I'll worry about trying to meet someone later. I know it's been a long time, but I still haven't gotten over Brian's father."

Ginny gently prodded. "Is there any chance you'll get back together with him?"

"No. He's married to someone else now."

"Oh. Is he at all involved in Brian's life?"

At first Cassie was hesitant to reveal too much, but somehow Ginny's motherly gaze was reassuring. Besides, she needed someone to confide in. "No. Don't tell the others, but he doesn't even know that Brian exists."

Ginny raised her eyebrows. "Well, I guess that answers my next question as to whether he helps out financially. And you've said you haven't been able to go out without Brian up to this point. Do your parents send some money?"

Cassie fought back tears. "My parents died before Brian was born," she sniffled.

Ginny gently grasped her hand from across the table. "I'm so sorry for you. How on earth are you able to manage all by yourself?"

"Well, it's really hard being on my own but I'm doing okay I guess. I mean, financially everything is fine. I got a bit of an inheritance from my parents and um...well, I privately handle investments from my home."

Ginny skeptically raised an eyebrow. "You must be pretty good at it if you can pay the bills that way. Ellen will probably seek out your advice. Besides her obsession with entering contests, she is always looking for ways to get rich. If I know her, she'll definitely try and get some investment advice out of you."

"Oh, no I can't do that," Cassie hastily covered. "I mean, well, you see, my company has this policy not to give any investment advice to friends. It's one thing if a stock loses money for a client. Sure, they get upset, but you could lose a friend over a bad stock deal; I wouldn't risk that. I don't invest for friends."

Ginny nodded in agreement. "I see your point. Don't worry; I'll keep it to myself."

Brian finished his snack and squirmed down off the makeshift booster, making a mad dash out of the kitchen into Ginny's family room. Cassie jumped out of her chair in pursuit of her son. Within a matter of moments, he had picked up the remote control and figured out how to access the Weather Channel.

"I'm sorry, Ginny. He's just so quick." Turning to the toddler she hollered "Brian, no!"

"Don't worry about it," Ginny said, waving a hand dismissively. "Remember, I have a child with autism, too. I understand. Besides, since he made himself so at home it will give us a little more time to talk."

The kindred mothers settled comfortably onto the sofa with their mugs of java, carefully eyeing the toddler's kinetic activities. In the corner of the room, Brian discovered a treasure stashed in a large crate. Hundreds of assorted action figures and Matchbox and Hot Wheel cars were stowed inside; Brian rooted through the pile in a frenzy.

"I see Brian likes toy cars, too," Ginny said, laughing. "I swear I can't go to the mall without James wanting to buy another car. It doesn't even matter to him if they are plastic or cheap ones from the dollar store. Even though he's fourteen, he still wants more. Nate, my other son, used to get so annoyed when they were younger because James wouldn't play cars with him the way most little boys do. Nate wanted to race and crash them together, but not James. No, James would carefully make one huge long line of cars from one end of the room to the other. I would have thought he would have outgrown his obsession with them by now."

Ginny smiled pensively to herself and then she rattled off names and quirks of other children she knew with autism. "Michelle's son Bradley is obsessed with maps. He has a bookshelf full of them. If you ever meet him he'll want to know your address.

Last month he went up to someone he had only met once two years ago and told him how many turns there were from his house to theirs. Then there's Sue's son; you didn't meet her yet. Her son is as calm and compliant as can be, but he can talk your head off about *Jeopardy*. He can tell you on which date and what day of the week which contestant won how much money.

"Then there is Sammy; I know him from the chapter meetings. I don't know of any special memory talent he has— maybe he doesn't have one; after all, not all kids with autism are savants. Anyway, he walks around with glasses on. He doesn't need them to see, in fact, the glasses don't have any lenses, but he has to wear them everywhere or else he gets very upset. And there is Danny, Ellen's son; he's always chewing on a plastic straw." Briefly, Ginny glanced out the window, paused, and then pensively answered as if she had asked herself a question. "Yes, our kids with autism are each one so different from each other. Yet they all seem to have little obsessions or quirks that make it difficult for them to fit in socially."

Ginny paused again, as if considering how to phrase what she wanted to say. Then she tentatively continued, "Cassie, it's not really my business what you do, but I'll say this once and then not mention it again."

Puzzled the young mother asked, "What's on your mind?"

"No one really knows for sure what causes autism yet, but most researchers agree there is probably a genetic component. I think you ought to consider informing Brian's father about him. Even if you two never get back together, I think he ought to know about his son so he can make an informed choice before deciding to have any other children. There—I've said it. Now don't even bother answering me; I won't bring it up again. Let me change the topic. What did you think of our little group last night? I hope we didn't scare you off."

Cassie was glad Ginny didn't press her further. Uncomfortable thoughts of confronting Greg were shelved in the recesses of her mind to be dealt with later.

"Ah, well no. In fact I look forward to the next meeting already. I was a bit confused at first, but it was nice to be with other mothers who've gone through similar experiences. Everyone made me feel welcomed. I must admit, though, I felt really sad for poor Elsie. I can't imagine how horrible it must have been for her." She couldn't imagine how Elsie had been able to cope with a lifetime of blame. Simply being thought incompetent by the unsuspecting, unaware public was hard enough for Cassie; being considered cold and unloving by an "authority" must have been ten times worse.

Ginny shook her head with regret. "Unfortunately Elsie is not the only mother who went through the experience of being blamed for her child's autism. That was a very painful time for parents to be so wrongly accused."

Cassie timidly asked, "Where's her son Roger? What happened to him?"

"Lots of kids with autism get seizures." Ginny answered. "In fact if my memory serves me I think that one in four children with autism develop seizures by the time they reach puberty. My son James takes medicine to control his. Anyway, Roger had seizures, too—pretty bad ones. I think I remember Elsie saying he was twenty-six when that last one happened. I don't remember which institution he was living at then. I just know those places always seem to be so horribly understaffed by workers who make little more than minimum wage.

"Anyway, it seems that staff was busy trying to contain someone else who was having an aggressive tantrum. Roger wasn't being supervised well and while he was having a seizure he fell down some steps. There was a huge investigation. Everyone at the institution was devastated, but it was just ruled a horrible accident. Elsie's never been able to forgive herself for not being there to prevent his death. We keep trying to tell her it wasn't her fault, but she had that jerk drum into her head so much guilt that she hasn't been able to let it go. Years later when Elsie found out about our support group, she just showed up to see what she could do for us. I think it has helped alleviate some of the pain she felt in not being there for her son by doing what she can for us in our meetings. She shares in our trials and triumphs...and makes the best damn coffeecake I've ever eaten!"

Cassie smiled wistfully. "Somehow there's just something about her that reminds me of my own grandmother. She died when I was young, about six or seven, I think. I still remember the way she was always giving me fresh, home-baked goodies. My mother was afraid I'd get too fat if she gave me too much, but Granny said I'd run it off at my age. I miss her and my mother, too." Shaking her head to return thoughts to present day she continued, "I feel so bad for Elsie. She's obviously experienced a lot of pain in her life. Do you suppose there's anything I could do for her? I wish I could help in some way."

Ginny looked down into her coffee mug for a moment. "I think she's comforted by feeling like she's involved with our lives. Just open up and let her hear some of your stories. She's so very lonely. Her husband died several years ago, shortly after her daughter Claire moved to Florida. Elsie would love to be near her grandchildren, but I don't think Claire has the money to add an in-law suite to her home. She still has two kids living at home while they commute to the local college."

Chimes from the mantel clock drew Cassie's attention to the length of her stay. "Oh my goodness, I'm sorry," she said, standing up. "I didn't realize how late it had gotten. I only intended to stay a few minutes. Thank you so much for your hospitality. I hope I didn't keep you from anything..."

Ginny stood up to embrace her. "Don't be silly, of course not. I'm here for you anytime. I enjoyed your company. Housework won't run away; it will always be there, but the opportunity to commune with a friend should never be ignored. Let it pass and it may never come again."

Chapter 11.

High-pitched, delighted squeals from the McDonald's playground nearly drowned out the din of the Pine Street traffic. Safely fenced in, half-a-dozen preschoolers bounded from one activity to another. Tossing and tumbling among primary colored balls in the netted pit was the main attraction here. For most parents, dragging their children past the playground to eat lunch first was always a contest of wills.

Once inside, Cassie immediately guided her son over to a table where she spotted both Kari and Ellen. Their children sat jamming down fistfuls of fries and chicken nuggets, oblivious to the greetings their mothers called out.

"Cassie! I'm so glad you could make it. We just got here a few minutes ago but Todd couldn't wait to get started," Kari chirped. "Slow down, Todd! One! One at a time, like this." She demonstrated.

"Hi, Cassie," Ellen greeted. "I decided to join you guys. I hope you don't mind. Danny had another of his mid-morning doctor appointments. By the time it was over, I figured it was too late to go into work."

"No, of course I don't mind; it's great to see you. But, is Danny sick?"

"No, well yes—but not really. You see, he has lots of gastro-intestinal issues that aren't exactly the best topics for lunchtime conversation. Anyway, the doctor has done tons of tests on him and can't find anything wrong with him, but he said it's not that uncommon for kids like Danny."

"You mean that's something kids with autism get?"

"Not necessarily. It's just that it seems to be a lot more common for kids with autism to have problems like these than it is for the quote 'normal kids.'" Ellen gestured quotation marks in the air with her fingers.

While Cassie had been distracted by their conversation, Brian slipped his hand from his mother's.

"Little boy, what are you doing?" Increasing in volume and anger as she spoke, an old woman at the table behind Cassie demanded again, "Little boy, what do you think you're doing? Those are my French fries. What's your name?"

Brian's greasy hands again tried to swipe more, but the woman pulled her tray out of the hungry child's reach. "Is he with you?" the matron confronted Cassie. "Why doesn't he answer me? Is he deaf or just plain rude?"

Seeing a fry dangling partially out of Brian's mouth as he chewed, Cassie felt a wave of embarrassment flood over her. "I'm so sorry. I wasn't aware..." She paused slightly considering how best to explain his non-responsiveness. "Well, no, he's not deaf."

Impatient for quick explanation for his offensive behavior, the old woman again demanded, "Then why won't he answer me?"

"He's autistic," Cassie stammered.

Still defiant over the intrusive disruption of her lunch, the woman shot back, "What does that mean? Does it mean he can't talk? Oh, I think I've heard of that before. It means he can't talk, right?"

Ellen attempted to inject an explanation. "Actually it's a little more complicated than that. He doesn't understand social..."

The woman cut her off. "Whatever! That's no excuse. At least in my day we taught our children good manners." Abruptly she swept up her belongings and carted her tray clear across to the other side of the dining area, audibly muttering as she left, "I don't care how young; he needs to be taught a lesson. There is no discipline anymore! Parents today just let their kids do whatever they please. These parents have no clue..."

Still flabbergasted by the tirade, Cassie stood stunned by the stranger's animosity.

"Just forget about it," Ellen suggested gently. "Trust me, our children land us in lots of embarrassing situations. I used to be afraid to take Danny out, but then I realized he'd never learn how to behave in public if I didn't. Listen, why don't you leave Brian with us. We'll watch him while you order your food. I'll give him some of Danny's fries to keep him busy till you get back."

After Cassie returned to the table with her tray, Kari resumed the conversation.

"It's so hard for kids on the autism spectrum to understand social situations. For them everything is black or white; they can't comprehend gray areas, like the food. It was wrong for Brian to take from that lady, but nobody got upset when Ellen gave some of Danny's fries for him to eat. Another example is how Todd loves to splash around naked in the bathtub, but he can't understand why I get upset when he strips his clothes off to run through the neighbor's slip n' slide."

Ellen nodded. "I remember Michelle telling me that it took years to teach her son Bradley to share, not to take things away from other kids. Then when he started Special Olympics basketball, he couldn't quite get the idea of playing offensively. A teammate's father yelled for him to take the ball away from the other team. At first he wouldn't do it because he thought it was wrong. But when he was assured it was okay, he tackled the other kid to get the ball."

Danny tugged on his mother's sleeve and said, "You want soda." Ellen absentmindedly picked up a straw, put it in his cup, and handed it to him.

"Oh, and remember Steven Hill telling us about his son last year?" Kari asked Ellen.

"Yeah, poor guy. His neighbors were up in arms about the situation. His boy is a teenager," Ellen replied.

"Past puberty if you get my meaning," Kari coyly added.

"Anyway," Ellen continued, "hysterical neighbors saw his son masturbating half-naked on his back deck. They threatened to call the cops. Poor boy, he didn't intend public indecency; he just didn't understand the need for privacy. I remember after we heard about it, Ginny suggested while our kids are still young, we should start teaching them about appropriate private and public behavior—and to use those terms. Someday our kids will grow up and have sexual feelings just like anybody else. Having autism doesn't change that."

"Do people with autism date and marry?" Cassie asked. It was a whole area of Brian's growth that she hadn't even considered.

Ellen took a quick bite of her burger. "Ginny said she read about some that do. Perhaps it happens more often with some who have Asperger's. But for the most part, understanding complex social rules in relationships is too difficult. Many just have to be satisfied with well, you know, taking care of themselves."

Cassie wasn't sure what to think. "Brian is so young; I don't even want to think about that yet. I'm having enough trouble just getting by with today's problems let alone ones that will rise up ten years from now."

"Literally rise up," Kari giggled.

Struggling to get out of his seat, Danny whined, "You want play balls. You want play balls."

"Is he asking if you want to play?" Cassie asked.

"No. Danny is coming along really well with his speech, but one area that's difficult for kids like ours is called pronominal reversal: he says you when he means to say I." Turning to her son Ellen said, "Look at me Danny. I, I..." She paused, allowing time for her son to respond.

"I want play balls," he complied, completing the sentence.

"Good talking," she responded to her son. With that, Ellen helped him down and held the door to the play area open for him to enter. Todd and Brian both scrambled down to follow. The mothers gathered their trays and chose a table in the play area to finish eating their lunches while they watched their children.

Ellen continued her explanation. "Danny also does a lot of echolalia, too."

"Now you've really lost me," Cassie complained.

"Well, with 'typical' kids when you ask a question they say yes, no or give a complete response. With Danny, he'll just repeat back the question. I asked him, 'What do you want for lunch today?' Then he answered back, 'You want for lunch today.' Earlier in the car he was laughing for no apparent reason. I said, 'You're really happy today, huh?' While still giggling he said, 'Happy today.'"

Ellen paused for a sip of soda, gesturing with her other hand. "If I want to avoid feeling like I'm living in an echo chamber, I have to remember to speak in open-ended sentences with him. 'Today Danny wants to eat...' and then I wait for him to fill in the answer. If I know what he wants, I make the beginning sound of the word then try to have him to say the rest. Sometimes it helps to show him two or three pictures and have him point to what he wants."

She sighed good-naturedly. "You know, I swear, it's a constant guessing game trying to figure out what he's thinking. When I explained echolalia and pronominal reversal to my neighbor, she told me that was normal; all kids do that. He'll grow out of it, she said. I tried to tell her that autistic kids do lots of things that seem like normal stages, but they do them in more unusual ways for much longer periods of time than other kids. I don't think she understood, or if she did, maybe she thought she was being kind holding out hope that he won't be disabled some day. I know Danny will always be autistic, but that's okay; I'm fine with that."

Kari bristled, appearing uncomfortable with the finality of Ellen's last statement. "How's your salad?" she asked abruptly.

"Actually it's pretty good," Cassie responded. "I'm kind of surprised."

"I tell myself I'm going to order one each time I come here," Ellen lamented. "But somehow the smell of cheeseburgers gets to me every time. I'll diet tomorrow, I say, but tomorrow never comes. Oh well, there's just that much more of me to love."

"I like to come here after I pick Todd up from therapy on Tuesdays," Kari added. "It's nice to relax at a table while he's in the play area."

The mothers returned their gaze to their sons. Each of their children had isolated themselves within the ball pit. Danny amused himself by picking out all the red ones and piling them together. Todd stood in a corner walking his fingers up and down the ladder of netting. Brian repeatedly bent at the waist to bury his hands in the sea of orbs, retrieved a ball in each hand from by his feet, and then flung them at the netted walls.

Cassie noticed one of the other preschool boys sitting backwards atop the slide. The daredevil in training called out to a table across from where they were seated. "Mom, look at me. Mom! Mom, look what I can do. Mom! Mom!"

The woman he had called out to stopped talking to her friend and turned to respond in annoyance. "Tommy! Turn around and slide down the right way."

"But Mom!" the child whined. "Why can't I? I can do it! Just watch me. Bobby Krause slides down backwards. His mom thinks it's cool. Can I, Mom? Please? I won't get hurt. I promise."

"I said no!" the woman responded. "And next time, don't interrupt." Turning to her friend the mother said, "He drives me crazy! He constantly wants my attention, talk, talk, talk all day long. Sometimes I just wish he would shut up; he gives me such a headache!"

Cassie shifted her attention back to the netted pit. Crawling through the mountain of balls toward Brian was a cherub with blond ringlets gathered near the top of her head. She surfaced and thrust forward a stuffed animal clutched in her right hand.

"Hi! My name is Tammy. This is my teddy. His name is Teddy. What's your name?"

Brian ignored the questions as he tossed two more balls at the netting.

The little girl tried again. "I know how to count to ten. Wanna hear me? One, two, three, four, five, umm...six, seven, eight...nine, *ten*!"

No reaction came from Cassie's son.

The little girl persisted. "Is that your mommy over there? My mommy put my hair in a ponytail today. See how it swishes when I shake my head? She put a white ribbon with pink hearts in my hair. Pink is my favorite color. What's your favorite color?"

Again, Brian said nothing. He only dug down deeper, grabbed more balls and heaved them at the netting.

"Hey, why don't you answer me? Can't you talk?"

Turning his back on the intruder Brian continued his ritual. The blond gave up and joined two other girls as they climbed out and ran toward the corkscrew slide.

Kari barely whispered, "That is so typical; it breaks my heart to see other little girls and boys playing together. Either Todd doesn't want to or he doesn't know how." Shaking her melancholy off much the same as a dog would dry himself after coming in out of the rain, she brightened saying, "I'm taking Todd to play therapy with Dr. Newsome next week. That will help for sure. By the way, Cassie, have you heard from the school district yet?"

"Dr. Talbot called yesterday afternoon. He's in charge of the IEP team that's going to evaluate Brian. We have an appointment next Tuesday."

"Oh, you'll like him," Kari bubbled. "I remember Michelle talking about her meetings with him when she moved here. You do know what an IEP is, don't you?"

"No."

Proud to be able to shepherd someone else through the confusing maze, Kari explained. "That means *Individualized Education Program*. Every child in special education has to have one by law. When your child needs special-ed services, they are supposed to figure out what his strengths and weaknesses are. Then they work together with parents to develop a plan to help him learn. From what I hear, though, some districts don't do a very good job of individualizing their programs. You know, like a one size fits all approach."

"Don't worry," Ellen added. "Michelle said Dr. Talbot was really helpful. Are they going to do it all in one meeting? That's unusual."

"It would be so much easier if they would," Cassie replied. "Tuesday the psychologist, Dr. Silverman, tests Brian, then Friday we have an appointment with, umm, Mrs. Collins, I think her name is; she's the speech...speech..."

"Speech pathologist?" Ellen offered.

"Yeah that's it, and I think there is one or two more evaluations scheduled for that day. Then on Wednesday the twenty-third I meet with Dr. Talbot. Good heavens, it certainly is a long, involved process."

"Get used to it," Ellen advised. "Meetings become a way of life. Between school meetings and doctor visits, I've had to take so much time off I'm surprised I still have a job. Well, I'll solve that when I win a lottery."

"Somehow I don't think money would solve all those problems," Cassie timidly offered.

"Maybe not, but it sure would help!" Ellen peeked at her wristwatch. "Oh God, look at the time. I better get home and do some housework. I sure can't afford a maid and the vacuum definitely won't run by itself."

"At least you can run it when Danny is home," Kari complained. "The noise of the vacuum bothers Todd something awful. I have to remember to run it while he's at school. But speaking of the time, it is getting late. I've got to get Todd over to vision therapy. See you at the next group meeting." Kari retrieved Ginny's timer from her purse and set it for two minutes. "I've used this at home a several times already when it's time to get ready for bed. I think Todd's getting the idea."

Cassie watched Kari show her son the timer. Shortly after the sound of a faint ding, the boy followed his mother to their car.

Meanwhile, Brian scampered back to refuel with the remnants of his half-eaten lunch. As he reached with greasy fingers for his white Cadillac, the child's profile suddenly reminded her of Greg. Curly brown hair framed his face exactly the same way and the arch of his eyebrow was unmistakable.

Jabbing a forkful of salad then pausing midway to her mouth, Cassie let her mind wander back to the night of her twenty-first birthday. It had been a night full of promise and hope. In the euphoria of the moment, she had even fantasized a happy life as Mrs. Greg Robertson. But so much had happened since that night. Fear of being swindled had kept her from sharing the news of her fortune with anyone. Grief over losing her parents left her isolated on an island of loneliness. Yet the source of the greatest devastation was her son. Compounding the heartache of raising a child alone was the trauma of discovering he had a disturbing, confusing disorder.

At least now, contact with these other mothers offered companionship with kindred spirits. Cassie's self-inflicted segregation from society had been a mistake. Perhaps keeping her pregnancy and Brian's birth a secret from Greg had been a mistake as well. It might be a further mistake to keep this information from him any longer. Maybe Ginny was right; she owed Greg the opportunity to be aware of his son's existence. So much time had passed, though. How would she begin the story of the last few years? Showing up with her son in tow was probably not a good idea. She'd have to get someone to watch Brian so as not to shock Greg all at once.

Still unsure as to when or how to approach him, she pushed thoughts of him into the back corner of her mind while she finished her meal.

Chapter 12.

Dr. Arthur Talbot stopped writing in his leather day planner and rose to greet Cassie as she entered. Her tension dissipated slightly as he warmly shook her hand while offering a chair opposite his desk. Briefly, her imagination conjured the image of some artist heavy handedly sculpting his face in clay. Gouged furrows were etched across his wide brow and deep folds separated his cheeks from his mouth, yet crinkles at the corners of his eyes suggested a kindly nature. A full head of sandy hair suggested he might be younger than what his wrinkles portrayed.

"I'm sorry I was unable to greet you upon your arrival," he began. "I'm afraid my previous meeting ran longer than expected. I trust Mrs. Shultz gave you a thorough tour of our facilities and made arrangements for Brian to be in Miss Williams' class while we meet."

"Yes, thank you. She showed me the classes in the regular elementary school for the nursery school; then she showed me this wing of special education classrooms. I'm a little confused, though. Where will Brian be attending school—here?"

"That will need to formally be decided at the IEP meeting. However, judging from the evaluations before me, it is likely he would start in a small self-contained class; four other students with autism ideally would be a good start."

"Will he ever go to regular classes?"

"A lot depends on what the team decides is appropriate for Brian. For many of our special kids, the playground and circle time are very good opportunities for inclusion with preschool children. Sometimes during the younger grades, recess, gym, music, and art classes can be good venues to integrate into general education classes."

Pausing to scrutinize a file on the desk before him he added, "Perhaps even some basic math or reading readiness. Some students with autism are quite capable of progressing along traditional academic tracks with supports, but I'm getting way ahead of myself here. You see, in the early grades the gaps in understanding are not as great as, say, when youngsters are studying academic subjects in the higher grades. So, in my opinion, the best opportunities for successful inclusion occur with elementary age students."

"What about Brian?" Cassie asked anxiously. "What are his chances of being included in regular education classes?" She hated to obsess, but she was so tired of not knowing what she could realistically expect. Despite Ginny's cautions, she couldn't help but hope for some evidence that Brian would be able to participate in "normal" activities.

Dr. Talbot hesitated. "Ms. Delaine, legally we really need to wait to discuss this at the IEP meeting when the full team can review the results of his evaluations with you. Then after individualized goals are developed, we discuss appropriate placement choices."

Cassie leaned forward. "Please, Dr. Talbot, I'm tired of waiting and guessing what is going to happen with my son. I don't care about what is legal; I just want some sort of idea where Brian will be. Will he be in a regular class?"

Dr. Talbot shifted in his chair. "As I said, this is not definite until we agree at the IEP meeting...but based on our testing of Brian, it's not likely."

Cassie's face revealed her disappointment. The doctor quickly added, "I don't want to totally dash your hopes here, but given Brian's degree of accompanying mental retardation and behavioral issues that need to be addressed, I think it would be a far greater disservice to hold out false expectations for you."

"But the doctor said that IQ tests were unreliable with autistic children because it requires an understanding of language," Cassie protested. "And it's hard to keep their attention during testing."

Dr. Talbot scanned pages in Brian's folder as he responded. "Yes, that's true to an extent, but if you'll recall I'm sure our psychologist explained several of the tests we administer here utilize pictures and matching patterns. Over the years, we will regularly reevaluate through further testing, but frankly, I feel we have a fair representation of his educational abilities. As is typical with other children with autism, Brian exhibits splinter skills. Unlike children with Down syndrome whose level of disability is more or less consistent across all areas, children like Brian exhibit peaks and valleys. His education will have to be carefully tailored to help him capitalize on his strengths and do his best in areas of weakness."

Disappointed, Cassie tentatively objected, "From what I've been hearing from other parents, I was counting on his being mainstreamed into a regular education class."

Dr. Talbot's voice was reassuring. "He still may to a certain extent; it's too early to project that far into the future. But please remember, success for Brian will not be measured by whether he can someday sit still in an algebra class but by how much he can do independently.

"Ms. Delaine, I'd like you to consider this: since special education students receive services until age twenty-one, Brian will spend approximately eighteen years in school. Individuals with autism can have a normal life expectancy; that means he will spend less than one fourth of his life in school. I suggest that success in a typical classroom should not be the ultimate goal; rather, success in adult life. Of what benefit to Brian would it be for him to learn what happened in ancient Greece if he can't order his own fast food meal or have the skills needed to keep a job?"

He had a point, Cassie had to admit.

"But," the doctor continued, "it is still way too early to begin thinking about those matters. What we need to focus on now is more immediate skills. We can teach him things like the importance of wanting to communicate and then work on skills he needs to do that. Many children like your son are anxious and confused without a very structured learning environment. We can help Brian make sense of his world by providing order through the use of picture schedules and understanding the passage of time with clocks and calendars."

Dr. Talbot retrieved a blue, yellow, and pink triplicate form. "Legally we need to give you ten days notice of a proposed meeting, but if you agree to it, we can waive the ten days and meet next Tuesday."

Eager to finally get some help for her son, Cassie agreed. Dr Talbot finished scribbling information on his form. As he handed the document over for her signature he added, "As his parent, you are always an important part of the IEP team, your input is vital. However, sometimes meetings discussing your child can be very emotional; it can be helpful to have another family member or friend also attend." Dr. Talbot gave her the pink copy. "Fine, we're all set. We'll see you Tuesday."

Pondering whom should she invite as she left, Cassie fished her keys out of her purse before retrieving Brian. She thought Ginny would be a good choice. She seemed to know so much and seemed like she would be willing. After all, there were no family members other than—well, perhaps it was time to notify the boy's father.

Wilson's Corner attempted to replicate authentic English pub décor with dark paneling and intricately etched glass windows. Dim lighting meant to enhance its cozy atmosphere also helped customers to preserve anonymity. Cassie had chosen this neutral location for just that very reason. She drummed her fingers nervously on the table as she waited in a corner booth for Greg to arrive.

Finally, reflected in the mirror behind the bar, Cassie saw him surreptitiously scan the bar for familiar faces as he entered.

"Greg, over here," she quietly called out. She noted his quick look of surprise when he first caught sight of her. Her extra pounds and weariness from mothering were not disguised by the low lighting.

Quickly recovering from shock he lied, "Cassie, you look great." He kissed her cheek, motioned for a beer from the bartender, and then sat across from her. "I heard about your parents, but when you didn't come back to school I didn't know how to get in touch with you. I'm sorry for your loss."

"Thank you," she replied.

A few moments of silence stretched uncomfortably long as neither knew how to proceed. Finally Greg said, "It's been a long time. I must say, I was surprised when my secretary gave me your note saying you *needed* to meet with me."

"Yes, I guess it would come as a surprise after not hearing from me for several years, but before we get into all that, tell me how you're doing."

Cautiously, Greg began to disclose events from his personal history. "Where to start after nearly four years? Well, let's see, remember how I left school after your birthday? My dad had a heart attack. I went home to help my mother out for a few weeks. After my father got out of the hospital, he had me work with him at his company. I never thought I wanted to go into the family business, but I got hooked. I went back to college and changed to a business major. I've got a great job now at my father's company. He's got me on the fast track to take it over entirely someday, so the old man has me working lots of long hours." Greg paused, awkwardly fumbling for words. "And well, I don't know if you heard or not but I got married. I'm not sure if you knew her or not. Do you remember Sue Snyder?"

"Yes, I remember her." Cassie admitted. "Several months ago I had dinner with my old roommate. She told me you got married."

"Oh," Greg sighed with relief. "Well anyway, we have a nice starter home in the suburbs. Sue is a manager at the local Lauren Frey Boutique. Her mother has worked for that chain for years. You know, it helps having relatives in the company to get a leg up on the competition." He smirked and took a swig of his beer. Then his cautious demeanor returned. "Cassie, what did you want to see me about?"

A hard swallow of her margarita provided a temporary stall but failed to ease her apprehension. "How do I put this? I guess maybe I should back up to when it all began." Again she took another sip of her drink, and then drew in a deep breath before proceeding. "The night of my twenty-first birthday was the most special night of my life. I still treasure the gift you gave me. I've worn this necklace ever since." She ran her fingers down the chain to the heart pendant. "And, umm, well, you gave me something else too. I don't know quite how to tell you, but I got pregnant that night. We have a son. His name is Brian."

Greg's face turned ashen as the shock registered. Then anger overtook his initial reaction. Jumping up from his seat, he backed away from the table as if to physically remove himself from the situation. "Jesus Christ, Cassie! Are you sure he's mine? Why the hell didn't you tell me sooner? If you needed money to take care of it, all you had to do was ask. I could have scraped together enough for an abortion. Christ! I can't believe it!"

Cassie could feel tears welling in her eyes, but she pushed them down determinedly. "Greg, you must be kidding. I didn't want an abortion. I didn't know I was pregnant at first, and then when I did I was already dealing with my parents' funerals and settling their estates and all."

Assumptions and anger punctuated his next remarks. "Wait a minute. Why did you wait all this time to tell me? That was some bullshit innocent act a few minutes ago! You knew all about me getting married and my position in my father's company, didn't you? This is some kind of trap. Yeah, it's an attempt to blackmail me, isn't it?"

Cassie felt her heart sink. "God no, Greg, it isn't like that at all!" It wasn't going at all the way she planned. The whole scenario was worse, much worse than she imagined. "Greg, please sit down," she pleaded.

"No thanks. I think I've heard all I want to. If you think I'm going to pay up for a kid I didn't know I had..."

"Greg, please listen. There's more I need to tell you."

"What more could you possibly have to say?" he demanded.

With no further delay, she forthrightly announced, "Brian has a disability. He's autistic."

"What? What the hell is that?" Temporarily stunned, he steadied himself by holding onto the back of the cushioned booth. But quickly recovering he spewed venomous accusations. "You think I'm about to fork over my inheritance because you didn't take care of yourself when you were pregnant? Did you do drugs or something?"

Angrily she spat back, "It's not like that at all. I don't want any money at all from you. I took care of myself just fine: I ate right; I took vitamins; I saw the doctor regularly the whole time I was pregnant. Greg, nobody knows for sure what causes autism, but it's probably got something to do with genetics." More calmly she continued, "I just thought you should know. I mean if you and your wife decided to have a family I thought you should be aware that the possibility exists that..."

Despite the growing awareness that the few bar patrons were firmly fixated on the commotion they were causing, Greg yelled, "No! There is no goddamn way it's got anything to do with me. There're no damn retards in my family!"

Despite the anger and hurt she felt, Cassie's voice was surprisingly calm. "Greg, please calm down and listen. Lots of times genetic disorders are passed down through the mother's line, but they just don't know about this. It could be in your genetics or maybe it's a combination of the two of us that—"

Greg slammed his fist on the table "No, God damn it! There's no way! You're lying; I don't believe this kid is mine. Christ, we only had a couple of dates. I thought you were pretty hot—but then you disappeared. You got knocked up by somebody else and now you're trying to pin it on me looking for a gravy train. Did the other guy ditch you? I've heard stories like this before about women falsely accusing guys—gold diggers." He glared and pointed his finger at her. "Listen to me—I won't be blackmailed or have my family name slandered. Now leave me alone and don't ever call me again or you'll hear from my attorney. "

He tossed some bills at the bartender for his beer and then stormed out of the bar. Fellow patrons averted their eyes as Cassie grabbed a cocktail napkin to dab at makeup mingled with tears streaming down her face. Quietly, she pulled cash out of her purse to pay for her own drink then desperately tried to slide away into the shadows of early evening.

Dreams, of at least an amicable relationship with the man she once thought she could love, were smothered by disillusioned sobs. With great difficulty, Cassie pulled herself together before driving back to Sweetwater.

Once home, Vicky's report on Brian's activities during his mother's absence were cut short by the telephone.

"Cassie? It's Angela. You'll never believe where I'll be tomorrow! Just guess."

"Angela! It's so good to hear your voice. Hang on a second let me say good-bye to the babysitter. I'll be right back."

"No! Wait, Cassie! Ask if she'll be available tomorrow night."

Guessing that Angela was indeed coming for a visit, Cassie was relieved Vicky could accommodate her with such short notice. Her college roommate was just what she needed right now.

"You're not going to believe it," the voice on the other end continued. "All the stars of the Zodiac must be in perfect alignment. Beth's cruise ship is docked for a few days and Cindy is back on the East Coast for a meeting and then visiting family. But, Miss L.A. has to fly back to work the day after tomorrow. Since you're available too, the four of us can get together just like old times."

The agreed upon a restaurant that was a forty-five minute drive from Cassie's house. Despite all four friends being in relatively the same geographic region, they were distant enough from each other that a central location needed to be chosen. Beth's culinary contacts had suggested this upscale seafood establishment adjacent to Bay Breeze Yacht Club for their meeting.

The hostess led Cassie through a narrow corridor to a large, nautical themed dining room. Seated amongst a bank of tables along a wall of expansive picture windows, Angela and Beth were already deep in conversation. Beyond her old comrades was an exquisite starlit view of the Chesapeake dotted by yachts adorned with lights like so many strings of pearls.

Beth caught sight of her first. "Oh my God, Cassie," she squealed as she jumped up to hug her old friend. "It's so great to see you. I can't believe how long it's been. How are you?"

"Just fine, Beth," Cassie lied, returning the hug. Pushing aside the unpleasantness of the previous evening, she happily inquired, "What have you been up to? Angela said you've been working for a cruise line."

Angela chimed in quickly with her own hug before Beth had a chance to reply.

"Hi, Cassie, glad you could make it."

Cassie set her purse beside a chair and took her seat. Beth settled down her own sizeable frame again. "That's right, Majestic Cruises. As the ad says: 'We pamper our guests with sumptuous meals.'" Patting her stomach she continued, "I guess you can tell I really enjoy my work in the galley. I keep saying I'm going to start a diet, but it's so hard being around all that tempting rich food 24/7. Speaking of which, isn't this place great? It would be a fabulous setting for a small, intimate reception, don't you think? There's a private room over there to the right of the hostess stand."

Surprised looks from Angela and Cassie prompted a hasty explanation. "No, not for me, at least not yet. I just can't seem to get Jeff to commit. We've been living together for nearly two years and dated for over a year before that. What is it with men that they can't commit? My mother keeps bugging me all the time, asking when we're going to get married. If I hear the 'I told you so speech' one more time I think I'll die. I've tried to convince her that I'm the one holding off, but she knows the truth, I can tell."

Angela countered with, "If you think your mother is bad, you should just hear mine; Italian mothers can lay on as good a guilt trip as any Jewish mother can. She's convinced I'm living in sin and that Sam will never want to 'buy the cow if he can get the milk for free.' Jeez, what archaic thinking. Still I must admit I'm having second thoughts myself. I'm getting pretty tired of picking up socks three feet from the hamper and throwing out the newspaper he leaves lying around. I get the feeling he thinks I'm a live-in maid sometimes."

"How about your love life, Cassie?" Beth asked.

Cassie had already decided an up-front approach was best. "Well, dating hasn't exactly been easy with a baby; now that Brian's been diagnosed with autism, I've had an even tougher time."

"Oh yeah, Angela mentioned something about that. What's the problem there?"

"Well, his behavior made it nearly impossible to find babysitters until recently and I've been busy taking him to school evaluations and worried about his IEP and..."

Beth explosively interrupted as the final member of the quartet arrived. "Cindy! Look at you girl; you look fantastic!"

Cindy did her best model's strut wearing a form fitting Dolce & Gabbana suit. Replacing her simple long tresses was a chin-length style carefully moussed in place.

"Hi, guys. The four musketeers ride again." Cindy giggled as she kissed the air next to both cheeks of each friend.

"Well, well, Miss Hollywood. Look at those shoes," Angela admired.

"Aren't they to die for?" Cindy bragged, casually setting down her Chanel bag as she took her place at the table. "You won't believe what I had to do to get these."

"Do tell," Angela urged with mock indignation.

"Oh God, no! Nothing like that. What I meant was, Baron-Smythe had a huge sale: buy one pair, get fifty percent off another. Of course they didn't have my size in this style but the sales clerk promised to FedEx a pair to my home address. Well, I waited and waited and they never came. I was about to call and give them a piece of my mind when I found the idiot clerk had my address wrong; they were sent to my neighbor, Courtney, three doors down. I ripped open the box only to discover that the left shoe was a size six and the right, a size five and a half. I had to make an emergency detour to their shop to exchange them on the way to the airport. I needed these for an important meeting in New York. I nearly missed my plane. Honestly, the incompetence of some salespeople today!"

"Well at least you made it here all in one piece and you look stunning," Angela complimented.

Cassie felt herself fade farther and farther into the background as her friends chatted with seriousness about the mundane. Shoes, discarded newspapers, and scattered socks paled in comparison to the lifelong worries she faced with a severely handicapped child. Conversations ebbed and flowed over various meaningless topics for the rest of the evening.

Distantly Cassie participated from the sidelines. Autism was carefully avoided as an uncomfortable topic, yet it was clear that her concerns and those of her friends were worlds apart. Hours later she crawled in bed wondering if she had anything in common anymore with these women who were once her closest friends.

Years of her mother's penny-pinching advice was hard programming to break, but the next morning Cassie again contemplated hiring a housekeeper. Initially she had been reticent to spend money on something she could do for herself, but there were millions of dollars in Cassie's portfolio now. She mulled over recent events while she carted a load of laundry upstairs. Everyone from her past was busy pursuing their dreams, but they didn't have a disabled child. Even Ginny admitted that she couldn't do it all. Finding time for herself when she could trust Brian to not get into mischief was nearly impossible. Idealistic old TV shows of families were just that—idealistic.

Whoosh, gurgle, gurgle, swirl!

The sound came from the bathroom in her master bedroom suite. When she had gone to the laundry room, Brian had been in his bedroom playing contently with his toy cars. She had only been gone a few minutes; he couldn't possibly have done too much damage that quickly. Could he?

She dashed into the bathroom just in time to see her naked child flush the toilet again. He stood by the bowl clinging to her now empty twenty-first birthday jewelry box. Before she could retrieve them, her mother's locket and the necklace from Greg interlocked in a swirling dance—away to a watery grave.

"Brian!" she screamed through her tears. "How could you? No, no, no! It's not possible!"

Blood boiled beet red into her cheeks as her face transformed, anger and anguish overtaking any remaining sense of reason. A flurry of swift loud smacks rang out, leaving red handprints on the toddler's bare buttocks and thighs.

Soon the intensity of Brian's screams matched the volume of his mother's. Then, ever so slowly, the sound of his wails penetrated her insane fury. Cassie became aware that even her own hand throbbed with stinging pain. She trembled, realizing that this was more than just a little spanking; those few forceful swats had crossed the line.

Brian struggled to free himself as Cassie carried him to his room. Mother and child sobbed as she redressed the boy. "Oh my God, Brian, I'm sorry, I'm so sorry. Mommy won't hurt you like that again, I promise." She carted the toddler back to her room along with his treasured bucket of cars and trucks. His whimpers quieted as she turned the television in her room on to the Weather Channel. He would be in her line of sight now when she resumed folding the laundry, but first she needed to clean up the bathroom.

She gathered the clothes he had stripped off and tossed them into her hamper. Then the soggy diaper was disposed of. Bending over to reach behind the toilet, she retrieved the discarded jewelry box. As she straightened up, she closed the lid of her precious birthday present. Her fingers gently caressed the grooved carvings. Then, with her forefinger, she traced the painted word on the center of the lid: D-R-E-A-M-S. The box was empty now. She would call a plumber, but she doubted anything could be rescued. Why had she neglected to wear her necklaces today? Every day she religiously wore those mementos around her neck, but this day she had left them carefully nestled in her jewelry box.

Trembling with awareness of the monster that had so easily resurfaced, Cassie carried the empty jewelry box back to her room. With great ceremony, she gently set the box back in its place of honor on her bureau. Reaching into her pants pocket, she squeezed the pebble tightly. Earlier she had remembered to stow the talisman in her pocket, but in her anger had forgotten its importance. Just daily keeping it tucked into her clothing was insufficient to keep the demon at bay. Realization of just how swiftly she crossed the line from anger and frustration to violence terrified her. How could she? After all, he had a disability; he didn't understand the significance of his actions.

Neglecting the unfolded laundry, she hung her head in shame and then sat on the floor across from her son. Sobbing, she whimpered, "I must be the worst mother in the entire world. I don't know how I could have let myself hurt you like that. I'm so sorry honey. I'll never let that happen again. Never."

Reaching over to tenderly ruffle his hair, Cassie sighed as Brian flinched and pulled back from her touch. Ignoring his mother, he turned and dropped the yellow school bus into his bucket. He looked past Cassie to see the weather map on the television screen. Then he resumed dropping vehicles into the container.

The first plumber she called refused immediate action since it was not an emergency; he'd be unavailable until Monday morning. In hopes that someone else could come sooner, she called two others from the phone book. One complained he was already three jobs behind, but the last gave assurances he would to try to fit her in later that day.

Hearing the robotic drone of the current weather conditions announced for the hundredth time that morning, she stifled a scream. Was it possible to regain her sanity? How could one small child cause such turmoil? Her child looked so angelic, as if nothing at all had happened. No evidence of throbbing pain showed on his face as he pelted his matchbox Jeep with the VW

Beetle and then the Mitsubishi. Perhaps counsel from the one person she had instantly trusted would help.

Cassie knelt down in front of her son. "Brian, look at me." After gaining his attention she continued, "Put the cars back in the bucket. When the big weather map comes back on the screen, we are going bye-bye. You can bring two cars with you. See? One in each hand."

A few minutes later, she flung the diaper bag over her shoulder, bundled Brian into his car seat, and drove across town. In desperation, she stood on the front step and prayed her knock would be answered.

"Ginny, I'm so glad you're home. I know it isn't time for another support group day yet, but I just needed to talk to somebody."

Her friend pushed the screen door open wide. "Of course, Cassie, come on in. Please know that you are welcome anytime. Just excuse the mess; I was in the middle of trying to organize my files. I've got piles of papers everywhere."

As if sensing Cassie's turmoil, Ginny kept her voice calm and placed a gentle, steadying hand on her back. "Oh, I know, let's go out on the deck; it's such an unusually warm autumn day. Brian can play on James' old swing set while we talk. There's a bunch of soccer balls and other toys in the big bin over by the fence. Why don't you get Brian situated. I'll make us some coffee and be out in a minute."

Ignoring the swing set, Brian twirled in circles around a discarded softball mitt half buried in the mulch. Most other children would have collapsed in dizziness, but somehow he continued spinning around and around.

A few minutes later Ginny returned carrying two steaming mugs. After handing one to Cassie, she sat on the cushioned glider. Patting the seat beside her, she motioned for her to sit. "Okay. Why don't you tell me what's troubling you, Cassie?"

Unleashed tears, emotions, and words tumbled freely. "I don't know how to begin. It's nothing special, but then again it's everything. The anger and frustration keep building and building up inside me. I feel like if I don't talk to someone I'll explode."

Again Ginny placed her hand on Cassie's back. "Relax, sweetie, take a deep breath, and then just take things one at a time. You've caught me on a very good day. I don't have anywhere I have to be; we've got the whole day until James gets home from visiting his grandparents with my husband. And if that's not long enough we can keep on talking once I get his Saturday afternoon routine started. Breathe, Cassie."

Quelling her sobs long enough to take a sip of coffee, Cassie stole a glance at Brian. He tumbled down the slide then happily raced to the top again.

"He's fine, Cassie. I'll keep an eye on him out of the corner of my eye while we talk. He's not going anywhere. Remember, I James-proofed this yard years ago. Even he can't scale that stockade fence. Just focus on what you want to tell me."

Cassie let out a heavy sigh. "My life was supposed to be perfect, but it's all turned to shit somehow. Things kind of came to a head after a get-together with my college friends. They were whining about tough bosses and inattentive boyfriends. Earlier that day, I had run into my neighbor at the supermarket. She kept going on and on about how she had no time to get her nails done this week, and she had to shuttle her daughter Ashley back and forth to soccer practice and piano lessons, and she couldn't find the perfect birthday present for her eight-year-old nephew. Before that, on TV, I saw some ladies bellyaching on a talk show. They grumbled about how features on their faces or their thighs depressed them so much that they needed plastic surgery. God, all of that seems so trivial in comparison. If only they knew what it is like. I mean...well you know; the daily trials of raising a child with autism are unbearable sometimes."

Ginny nodded. "I know. Sometimes I have the 'Why oh why, pity poor me' days, too. It's okay to acknowledge life is hard and wallow in self pity for a little bit—but just for a little bit, mind you. Then, as difficult as it is, you have to shake it off and move on. Find what is good and then keeping going."

"But even you don't know everything, Ginny." Feeling the need to have someone she could totally confide in, Cassie continued, "You see, I lied to you about my job. I don't do private investing. Well, in a sense maybe I do, but my only client is me. Right after my twenty-first birthday I won the lottery: the Powerball." She paused, feeling the weight of the secret she had kept for years lift from her shoulders. "I won millions of dollars! Life was supposed to be a dream after that. But right after I told my parents, they got killed by a drunk driver. While I was still dealing with my grief over their loss, I found out I was pregnant. As bad as that was, still, I thought life could be great raising a child with a fortune to help me—but life has been hell."

Cassie took a quick breath and Ginny kept silent allowing her litany to continue. "At first, I thought it was because I was inexperienced and alone. I thought he was just colicky. So, I hired help but they quit; he tormented every housekeeper I had. Then I found out he's autistic. That information terrified me. I...I...I almost did something horrible." Instinctively she reached her hand in her pocket, touching the familiar stone. Then with more defiance in her voice, she continued, "I didn't do it, but it's just too hard. I can't handle this. I lost it this morning. Life just isn't fair! When I found out Brian's father was married to somebody else it crushed me. I had hoped...well, that doesn't matter now.

"Anyway, I took your advice. I met with him to tell him about Brian and he got angry. He said I should have had an abortion. Then he blamed me for Brian being autistic. On top of all of that, there is the constant whirlwind: Brian. It's so hard! I can't imagine a lifetime of this. It's just not fair. Winning the lottery was supposed to make magical things happen. Where's my happily ever after?"

Planting her feet firmly on the deck Ginny stilled their movement. In apparent astonishment, she stared wide-eyed. "What do I respond to first? There certainly were quite a few bombshells there." After a brief pause to gather her thoughts, she continued. "Well, I must say, I never would have guessed the mysterious Powerball winner from a few years ago was you. I'd have to admit, though, I didn't totally buy your private investor story. Frankly, I thought you're a bit too young and relatively naïve to have a large enough client base to sufficiently support yourself with investment work from home."

Ginny resumed the glider's soothing motion. "Now, as to your 'happily ever after,' that's just in fairy tales and movies, Cassie. Nobody's life is that perfect in real life, not even the rich or powerful. For example, look at the Kennedy family; even with all their money, still they had one tragedy after another. And how about President Reagan? Surely his life was a dream come true. First he was an actor, then governor, then a two-term President of the United States. How tragic that he spent his final years, a decade no less, stricken with Alzheimer's. Even though you don't always see the trials and tribulations of the rich and powerful, it doesn't mean their lives are nothing but champagne and caviar. It's much the same with friends and neighbors. Despite the appearance that someone else's life is a bed of roses, don't forget that roses have thorns."

Cassie sniffled. "Yeah, but this is autism we're talking about here. When my neighbor droned on and on I wanted to shake her, tell her to stop complaining about such insignificant problems."

"True, some people make themselves so busy that they forget to be grateful for their 'normal' lives," Ginny said. "Still, I think that a little grumbling about minor issues helps some steam to escape from our pressure valves. If we let those little bits keep building and building, we might totally explode when something major happens, when we need the ability to keep it all together."

Ginny sat back in the swing thoughtfully. "You know, most everyone encounters some major trauma at some point in their lives; it's all part of *life's* lottery. Some go through painful divorces while some others suffer the heartbreak of infertility. Drug and alcohol addictions destroy the lives of countless individuals and their families. And there's a multitude of handicaps and illnesses besides autism that some parents have to grapple with. Personally, when I get depressed, I think about the torment that parents whose children are terminally ill or have been murdered go through. I can't imagine the crushing pain it must be to lose your child.

"Frankly Cassie, you're right; life isn't fair sometimes...for lots of people. The trick, I think, is not to look for a happy-ever-after life, but to be forever living as happily as possible. Make the most you can with the numbers that life's lottery shoots out at you each and every day; that's the secret. It might surprise you to know, in some ways I'm actually grateful for James' handicap. It helps remind me to appreciate all that my other son, Nate, can do. Before James was born I had a tendency to take for granted his everyday normal accomplishments. But with James, every gain is a major victory. I was thrilled when he learned to button his own coat and my heart melted in joy the first time he asked a question. Life with autism is a trial, but in the process I've learned to see the treasure my James is."

Cassie hung her head, too embarrassed to look her friend in the eye as she spoke. "You are such a hero, Ginny; it's apparent you're such an inspiration to everyone you come into contact with. But me, sometimes I don't even know if I love my own child."

Ginny set her mug in the cup holder. Gently, she placed her hand on Cassie's chin and tilted it up to meet her gaze. "Hero? Love? People confuse those words. They think those are things or feelings. They're neither. They're actions. You watch any reporter interview somebody the press is calling a hero and nine times out of ten that person will say that they don't consider themselves a hero; they just did what needed to be done in a moment of crisis. And what about great figures in history? Were they great to begin with, or at critical junctures in time, events forced them to choose the correct difficult decision?" She shook her head. "I'm no hero; I just do what events in my life have compelled me to do."

Ginny placed her hand reassuringly on Cassie's knee. "Now then, let's talk about love. You say you don't know if you love your child. Love is not just a mushy-squishy feeling. It's something you do. It's a mother bear protecting her cubs from the wolves in life. It's guiding your child in the direction he needs to go and helping him to get there. Emotions come and go, but love is a series of committed actions. It's making crucial choices in favor of another when sometimes you would rather your life was headed in another direction."

Squeals of delight from the yard drew Ginny's attention. "Look, Cassie."

Brian sat on a soccer ball and rolled off. Thick layers of mulch cushioned his tumble. Giggling, he got up and repeated the attempt to balance his body on the wobbly orb. Again and again he performed this fascinating joke on himself.

"Look past the autism and see your son. Give yourself time and patience. I know you love him. You wouldn't be here if you didn't."

Ginny continued the glider's lulling motion for a few minutes as both women watched in silence. The child endlessly toppled off the ball only to scamper back to his feet, straddling it again.

Ginny cupped her mug in both hands, took a gulp, and then spoke again. "I'm sorry your meeting with Brian's father went so badly. I hope you're not angry with me for suggesting it."

Cassie shook her head. "Oh no, of course not. I knew it was over; he's married. Still, somehow his words stung in a way I didn't imagine they could. I guess my heart still held out some hope of...well, at least some kindness. At one time I thought I might be in love with him."

"Like I said, I'm sorry. If I'd have thought it through, I should have realized and warned you about the possibility of such a response. Most parents' first reaction to such news is anger and denial: it's not my child; it can't be happening to me; this diagnosis must be wrong. Generally, the next stage for many parents is grief: they mourn for the child they thought they were going to have. Over time, other stages swirl together in an emotional rollercoaster of feelings. Hopefully, eventually parents progress to acceptance of the situation and find ways to appreciate and love the child that they do have. But some get stuck in one stage or another. Take Kari, for example."

"Kari?"

"I love her dearly but the poor girl is definitely stuck in denial. She seems to think if she takes Todd to enough different therapies that someone somewhere is going to cure him and he won't be autistic anymore. She doesn't say it, but you can tell by her actions."

"How about you, Ginny," Cassie wondered. "Where are you in all this?"

"Well, I like to think that I've reached the acceptance stage. It's sort of like...well, right now you can't cure autism anymore than someone born without arms can miraculously grow new ones. A person without limbs can be taught ways to cope and function more successfully, but that doesn't change the fact that they still would be minus their arms. The same goes for autism. It's still there, but we can limit the negative impact of their disability through education and training."

"I get what you are saying, but that's a very detached, cerebral explanation," Cassie sighed. "How about you personally, emotionally?"

Ginny furrowed her brow slightly. "I guess I would still say acceptance describes the stage I'm in. James is the way he is and I've learned to love him as he is. Oh, I'm human. Sometimes I slip back into self-pity or anger stages and of course I worry about the future. But if you or I want any happily ever after, as you put it, we have to work hard at staying in the moment, finding all the ways our children can bring joy to our lives."

Soothed and supported, the two women gently rocked back and forth enjoying the child's mirth as he played his unusual game.

Several minutes later Ginny asked, "Just tell me to mind my own business if you want to, but I'm curious; what did you do with all that money?"

Still watching Brian fall off the ball, Cassie casually responded, "Not all that much really. Oh, at first I went on a spending spree. I bought the Mercedes, my house, and all the furnishings for it. But the novelty wore off pretty quick. I was still coping with the loss of my parents and the knowledge that

I would be a single parent. Spending money isn't as much fun when you have no one to share it with. Besides, after a while, words from my childhood haunted me. Every time I got a dime my mother cautioned me to put it in the bank. 'Save it for a rainy day, you never know when you'll need it,' she would say."

"Hmm...autism...if that's not a rainy day, I don't know what is," Ginny sighed. "Of course you want to be sure you and your son are set for life, but have you considered all the good you could do with your fortune?"

"Are you looking for a handout, Ginny?" Cassie teasingly giggled.

Returning her friend's laugh, Ginny stopped urging the glider's motion and turned to her. "I'd be lying if I said the idea of gobs of money didn't sound enticing," she said wistfully. "Who hasn't dreamed of a lottery win making their life cushy? Somehow, though, every time I get extra money it seems to disappear and I'm not sure what I have to show for it. Things are never quite as satisfying once you acquire them. Wanting the elusive gold merry-go-round ring is more exhilarating than actually getting it.

"No, what I meant is, there are lots ways to help others affected by autism. Charitable organizations like the Autism Society of America and Autism Speaks provide all kinds of information and resources to families. Then there are research groups like the National Alliance for Autism Research and Cure Autism Now: they fund scientists looking for answers to help our kids. In addition to autism specific charities, you might consider a donation to The Arc."

"Who, what?"

"The Arc of the United States. It's a non-profit organization that provides services to individuals with developmental disabilities and their families. There are so many needs, Cassie, not just for those with autism. And once they grow up...well, the list could go on and on. Think about it."

Ginny gently pushed on the deck with her big toe and the glider resumed its motion. Changing the topic she said, "Don't be too hard on your friends or neighbors. Right now you are so wrapped up in the world of autism you can't see much else. Sometimes it may feel like you're living on a different planet from them. Be patient. In time you'll learn to balance your passion for Brian's needs with appreciation for everyday, normal life."

She hesitated and then added. "You really do need to find a social outlet besides our support group, though. There's more to life than just concerns about autism. Maybe you could join some sort of a group in your neighborhood."

Cassie shrugged her shoulders. "I don't know, Ginny. I'm a little intimidated. Gossiping is like an Olympic sport with the barracudas in my neighborhood. Lord only knows what all they say about Brian and me."

Ginny smiled. "I know the feeling. I can remember the sideways glances I used to get from some of my neighbors. That's because they didn't know me. So one day I sent invitations out for a get-acquainted party. Now a number of those curious women are some of my best friends. We get together at least once a month. I find the best way to keep someone from gossiping about you behind your back is to meet them face-to-face. It's a little hard to talk about someone when they're in the same room with you!"

Cassie gave a sigh of released tension. "You've given me a lot to think about today. I really appreciate this, Ginny."

"Anytime, Cassie. Anytime."

Chapter 13.

Looking up from her morning paper, Cassie glanced at her son. Suddenly Brian had stopped munching his cereal. His gaze was firmly fixed on her coffee cup and the teaspoon poised above it. A mound of dry creamer imploded as the granules slowly sank into the liquid. Swirling her teaspoon, the mixture gradually changed to an even golden brown. Cassie hadn't noticed before, but this metamorphosis fascinated her son. Lately she was becoming more aware of how often his attention focused on tiny details.

After further testing, Dr. Hart had confirmed the autism diagnosis, and puzzling behaviors like this were beginning to make sense. When Cassie expressed confusion as to how he determined Brian's diagnosis, he showed her the massive *Diagnostic and Statistical Manual of Mental Disorders, Fourth Edition.* Evidently, her reaction revealed her intimidation by the technical jargon.

Dr. Hart shoved the book aside and reached for his legal pad. Swiftly he drew lines marking three columns. In each he made a series of descending lowercase letters.

"Ms. Delaine," he had said. "I'm sure you remember I told you that currently no medical tests can diagnose most forms of autism. Unfortunately we have to rely on observations of behaviors as outlined in this manual." Pointing to the lined tablet he continued. "Behaviors associated with this disorder are divided into categories — social interaction, communication, and repetitive stereotypical behaviors. An autism diagnosis occurs when at least six items are noted from these columns."

He circled some letters on the page in demonstration then set his pen down. "If the patient's behaviors don't quite fit the formula," he continued, "that individual may have one of the other associated disorders."

Further detailed explanation eluded her comprehension, so he sent some literature home with her.

Cassandra examined a sheet of paper the doctor had given her. Simple stick-figure illustrations filled the page. Beneath each was a brief caption. *Sustained odd play* read one; another said *preoccupation with parts of objects*. The more she studied this chart, the more she recognized her son in these pictures.

With both hands, Brian gripped the tray of his high chair and tried to push it away. In one motion, Cassie released his lap restraint and Brian scurried into the family room on his tiptoes. He flapped his arms as he moved. These were more of the strange behaviors the doctor had told her were common in children with this disorder. Cassie smiled at the oxymoron: *typical unusual behaviors*.

The phone rang. "Cassie? Hi, it's Michelle—Michelle Ammelid from support group. I was talking to Ginny earlier and she said you seemed a bit down the other day. I could use some company myself today and I thought you might be interested. School is off for a teacher in-service meeting. I was planning to do a little shopping to give my son something to do. Would you two like to join us?"

"Oh, I don't know," Cassie said hesitantly. "I really appreciate the offer, but it seems like every time I go shopping with Brian, it's such a disaster. He's a little terror when he gets in stores."

Michelle's voice was sympathetic. "Listen, Cassie, I'm sure every mother on the block has given you advice on how to raise your son; I know all the women in my neighborhood have with me. But I hope you won't mind if I give you a suggestion. Brian will never learn how to behave in public if you don't take him out. Just keep trips short at first so he doesn't get bored and every few minutes give him some positive reinforcement. You might want to try a few M&M's along with some praise."

"Positive reinforcement seems like a fancy term for a bribe," Cassie said dubiously.

"I guess you could think of it that way, but when you come to think of it most of us respond to positive reinforcement whether we call it that or not. My paycheck certainly prompts me to go to work, and as a kid I ate my vegetables so I could have dessert. Honestly, sometimes you've just got to use whatever works, especially if the long-term effects are positive."

Before Cassie could respond, Michelle continued, "Oh, that reminds me of another helpful hint. Call it the fine art of saying no while telling him yes. The other day Bradley refused to stop drawing a map of Chile when I called him for dinner—maps are one of his obsessions. I told him that yes, he could work on it again just as soon as he finished eating. Another time he wouldn't go to school. I promised he would watch his video about the former Soviet Union countries the minute he came home."

"It sounds like you have to play psychologist all the time."

Michelle sighed. "It's not easy, Cassie, but I think the more time we parents spend together, we learn ways to make parenting less difficult. Why don't you give it a try? I'll be in the movie department of Value Mart at eleven o'clock."

"What the hell!" Cassie muttered to herself, hanging up the phone. It would do her good to get out of the house, and a short trip probably wouldn't hurt Brian either.

As promised, at eleven o'clock Michelle was scanning a row of preschool videos. Initially, Cassie didn't recognize her friend so simply attired. At support group, Michelle had come from work still in her business suit. Her long hair had been down, elegantly draping a long neck adorned by a simple strand of pearls. Today she was dressed in a designer jogging suit and her blond hair was pulled back in a ponytail. Nearby, her teenage son nervously paced approximately five feet back and forth.

Michelle looked up from the row of children's videos as she heard Brian's familiar singsong moaning. "Hi, Cassie, I'm glad you came. My nephew's birthday is Friday and I was just trying to decide which *Blues Clues* video he doesn't already have."

Looking at the tape while he spoke Bradley said, "You should buy a DVD instead of a VHS tape. The sound quality is much better. The picture resolution is much clearer. Video recorders are obsolete. Aunt Sara has a DVD player. It is a Panasonic model no. DVPNS35S. They should have gotten a Sony model no. RDRGX7. It has more features. You can record with the RDRGX7; you can't with the DVPNS35S."

"Aunt Sara doesn't want Chris to use their good DVD player," Michelle said, sounding as though she'd explained this before. "He's too young and she's afraid he'll break it."

"VHS tapes can break. You have to rewind tapes. You don't have to rewind DVD. Video recorders don't produce as good a picture resolution. Video recorders are obsolete. Aunt Sara should let him use DVD."

"That's your opinion," Michelle said gently but firmly. "Aunt Sara has her opinion and she wants a VHS tape for Chris." Directing her son's attention to Cassie she said, "Bradley, this is Ms. Delaine. Do you remember seeing her at St. Vincent's?"

"Where do you live?" he abruptly asked. "How many streets did you have to cross to get here from your house? I can tell you if you took the right route."

"Bradley!" Michelle said with mild scolding in her voice.

Robotically he held out his hand to be shaken and responded with slight pauses between rehearsed sentences, "Hello. How are you? It's nice to meet you." He paused again and then before Cassie had a chance to say anything, he again asked, "Where do you live? If you need a DVD player you should buy a no. RDRGX7 at Electric Connection on Fourth Street. I could show you on a map how to get there from your house if you—"

"Bradley, that's enough now. Why don't you go see if Value Mart has any new maps in yet?" Her son immediately turned and left the video aisle, not waiting for a response from Cassandra.

"Sorry about that. Like I've said before, he's got this thing for maps and directions," Michelle explained.

Somewhat stunned at the abruptness of his retreat and the strange conversation, Cassie remarked, "He talks so much and seems so smart. It's hard to imagine Bradley and Brian have the same disorder."

"No, it's not the same; it's similar, on the same spectrum of disorders," Michelle corrected. "Individuals with Asperger's Syndrome tend to function at a higher level but you'd be surprised how much they have in common. Bradley can talk a lot more than your son, but in a conversation he doesn't recognize when other people are bored with a topic that fascinates him. Social situations are difficult, too, just like with autism and PDD. These guys take everything so literally and don't understand sarcasm or exaggeration. The kids at school make fun of him."

Michelle stopped to look at Brian who was seated in the shopping cart basket, contentedly clutching a matchbox car. "Hi, Brian, I like how nicely you are sitting. Good quiet sitting, Brian."

Cassie took the cue and placed two M&Ms in her son's hand. He devoured them and reached for more. Not seeing an available timer, Michelle took off her digital watch and set the alarm for two minutes. "Do more good sitting Brian. When this rings, you get more M&Ms." She handed him the watch. Brian began to fuss, but Michelle reminded him again, "More good sitting, more M&Ms."

"At the rate of two M&Ms every few minutes, I am going to have the fattest toddler on the block with a constant sugar high," Cassie complained.

Michelle laughed. "This may take a little getting used to, but once he gets the idea, you gradually increase the time between rewards. Eventually you will give just one special treat, a small toy, or a favorite activity at the end of a shopping trip. The point is to catch him being good and show him the benefits. They used this method with Bradley at school when he was little."

The women pushed their carts over to the toy section. Michelle added a bath time version of the blue dog to her chosen video. She asked, "Speaking of school, did Brian start yet?"

"Not yet. He starts next week in Ms. Mangione's class." Cassie scanned the row of plush animals. Since Brian did not show any interest in the teddy she picked, it was replaced on the shelf.

"I've heard she's a good teacher. Ms. Mangione's class can be helpful if he's behind in lots of his life skills. She can help you learn how to do task analysis so you can teach him things at home like brushing his teeth and tying his shoes."

"Task what?" Cassie asked, perplexed by another strange term.

"Task analysis: It's a way of breaking a job down into very small steps, then teaching the small steps to..."

Their conversation was interrupted by the sound of a shrill woman's voice screaming over the store's intercom "Security to checkout aisle five! Security: Checkout number five!"

Michelle went pale. "Oh God no, I hope it's not Bradley," she said as she rushed toward the front of the store.

Rounding a super hero display at the end of the aisle, Cassie saw Bradley struggling to free himself from a flustered security guard near the checkouts. Frantically she pushed Brian in her cart, trying to keep up with Michelle. Beep-beep, beep-beep went the timer in Brian's hand. Cassie fumbled to fish out two more pieces of candy for her son as she steered the shopping cart toward the checkout area, nearly knocking over a precarious stack of toilet paper.

Racing through the store while getting candy was most amusing for the toddler, so he continued to sit nicely while chomping on his treat. A small crowd of shoppers began to hover nearby. In spite of Cassie's concern over what might be happening, she stifled a laugh.

Prominent in the scene was a uniformed guard whose pants were belted below his belly. *If he were a woman, I'd bet he was eight months pregnant*, she thought. Perspiration dripped down the guard's forehead and his meager comb-over flopped forward as he struggled to maintain his grip on the teenager's shoulders.

"Settle down, son," he commanded.

"Let go of me and give me my free ride," Bradley responded, staring at the caterpillar like moustache above the guard's upper lip.

"What on earth is he talking about?" questioned the shrill voiced cashier to no one in particular.

Michelle dashed forward to intercede. "Please let him go; he's my son. He hates to be touched and might fight back if you hold onto him. He won't run away, I promise you. Please tell me what has happened here and we will deal with it."

Warily the guard relaxed his grip and the boy stopped struggling. Eagerly the middle-aged cashier spoke first. "I saw the whole thing," she proudly boasted throwing her shoulders back in an air of superiority. "Your son walked right up to the rack of maps, took one, walked right through the checkout, and announced he was taking it and not going to pay. Then he made that silly statement about wanting a ride."

"Is this true, son?" the guard asked.

"Yes," Bradley responded.

Michelle appeared puzzled. "There must be some mistake," she protested. "Bradley is so rule driven he would never break a law. I know he understands what shoplifting is; we've had this conversation many times before."

"You do know what shoplifting is, don't you?" the guard asked.

"Yes," Bradley responded matter-of-factly. "Shoplifting is when you take something from a store and don't pay for it. Rules are meant to be followed. But Mother says sometimes there are exceptions to rules; this must be one of them. Most stores think shoplifting is wrong, but this is a strange store. Can I get my free ride now? Do you suppose we could ride by Electric Connection on Fourth Street?"

"What the hell is this crazy kid talking about?" the cashier sneered.

Cassie watched as Michelle struggled to make eye contact with her son. "Bradley, you know shoplifting is wrong. Why did you do this?"

"This is a very strange store. They want you to shoplift. They give away free rides if you do. I want my free ride now."

"Where on earth did you ever get the silly idea that our store encourages shoplifting?" the cashier accused.

"It says so right on the sign in the window," Bradley replied.

An elderly gentleman in a business suit gently pushed through the crowd of shoppers. He began to chuckle rather loudly as a nearby woman pointed to a large poster prominently displayed near the exit. Pictured on the cardboard sign was a stern policeman standing beside a patrol car. One hand of the officer dangled handcuffs while the other pointed accusingly. Bold lettering on the sign read, *FREE RIDE IN A POLICE CAR IF YOU SHOPLIFT!*

The man's laughter drew the attention of the security guard. "Mr. Stemple," the guard stammered. "I'm sorry for the disturbance, Mr. Stemple. You see, this boy…"

The business-attired man interrupted him. "That's quite all right, Harry. I'll take it from here." He looked over at Cassie struggling to shush Brian's loud *eeee, eeee* noises while she fiddled with the beeping watch. Then he turned to face the confused teenager and his mother. "I think I understand what the problem is here. Ms…?"

"Ammelid, Michelle Ammelid."

"Yes, um, well then, Ms. Ammelid. I've got a grandson that, well, how shall we put this discreetly in front of your son? He— he has a diagnosis. Anyway, I guess I have an idea about the confusion here." Mr. Stemple called over his shoulder, "Harry, take that sign down and put the old one back up. You know, the one that says *Shoplifters will be prosecuted to the full extent of the law.*"

Next the man addressed the boy in front of him. "What's your name, young man?"

"Bradley Ammelid."

"Well, Bradley Ammelid, I know what the sign said, but what it meant was that if you shoplift, a police officer will arrest you because shoplifting is stealing. Then the policeman will take you to jail in his police car."

Bradley furrowed his brow. "Why didn't the sign say that? Mother says shoplifting is wrong, but I wanted a ride in a police car."

Michelle let out a sigh and rolled her eyes.

Thoughtfully, Mr. Stemple cupped his chin in his hand. "I'll tell you what I'll do," he said. "I have a son-in-law that works for the sheriff's department. If you promise never to shoplift again, I'll make arrangements for him to give you a little ride in his car this weekend. Okay?"

"That would be a sheriff's car, not a police car."

"Bradley, please!" Michelle insisted.

"Okay," he responded. "Make sure he takes Conner Avenue and turns left on Whitley Street when he comes to pick me up."

After Michelle gave Mr. Stemple her address, the mothers left the store and headed for their cars.

"I'm sorry to cut our outing short, Cassie. I think Bradley and I need to go home to have a long talk about what to do if he's confused about breaking rules. We need to have another talk about sarcasm and exaggeration. He has so much trouble understanding that not everything is meant to be taken literally."

Bradley got into the car and closed the door. Michelle turned her back so her son could not see her face. Cassie noticed her shoulders heaving up and down and assumed her friend was sobbing. "Oh God, Michelle, you must be so embarrassed. I'm so sorry."

Michelle turned slightly so that Cassie was able to see that the opposite was true. Instead of crying, she was hysterically laughing.

"Michelle?" Cassie whispered. "How can you laugh at this?"

"Listen, you'll go crazy if you don't at times like this." Michelle spoke softly so her son wouldn't hear. "Come on, you have to admit that if this whole incident had happened in a movie or to somebody else even, you'd see the humor in it. Can you believe it? He thought the sign was advertising a way to get a ride in a police car." Michelle shrugged her shoulders, shook her head, and let out a long sigh. Then she pensively added, "Sure, I could be mortified, I suppose. But long ago I learned not to let his odd behaviors embarrass me in public. He can't help that he doesn't understand when things aren't always exactly literal."

"But that cashier and all those people standing around," Cassie protested.

Michelle briefly placed a comforting hand on Cassie's shoulder. "Sometimes when I start to get embarrassed, I remind myself that the people observing the situation don't know us and I'll probably never see them again so it doesn't matter."

Cassie thought for a moment then, remembering some incidents with a few of her neighbors, Esther Bagley in particular, asked, "What if he does bizarre behavior in front of people you do know?"

"Well, if they know us, they usually understand the way he is and they are our friends. If they don't, that's their problem, not mine. I mean we still try and make sure that Bradley behaves appropriately, but if he gets confused our friends usually make allowances."

"Well that certainly *was* a short outing," Cassie mumbled to herself as Michelle drove away. "Great, kiddo, we're all just characters in some cosmic comedy." She snickered, recalling the guard's comb-over as it flopped in front of his sweaty face. "I wonder which actor Cindy would suggest casting for the role of Harry?" she laughed, searching for her keys. Then she remembered she had shoved them into her pocket prior to unbuckling Brian's car seat. As she jammed her fist into snug jeans, the elusive keys caught her river stone, causing it to tumble out of her pocket.

Quickly she retrieved it and lightly rubbed the pebble between her fingers. Somehow that action elicited a soothing sensation. After fastening Brian back into his car seat, Cassie carefully reexamined her talisman, noting every detail. Strange, she thought, its appearance seemed changed from that pivotal night. The little smooth part looked larger to her. Even so, it was mostly very rough. Most of the caked dirt from the tiny ridges had been washed away, yet imbedded deep within were permanent imperfections. Slowly she tilted her pebble back and forth. Sunlight made it sparkle as if flecked with glitter. Just beneath the surface she observed a few veins of color that were only evident upon close inspection.

With her other hand, she absent-mindedly touched the empty space where her favorite necklaces had formerly hung. Suddenly inspired, Cassie said, "Brian lets go to the mall. Mommy is going to get a necklace made with this stone. Then we'll get something to eat and then buy you a new toy car."

Before pushing the stroller into the gleaming jewelry shop filled with velvet-lined cases, Cassie knelt to make eye contact with her son. Most definitely there must not be a repeat of the incident in Haughtley & Bristol's china department.

"Remember, Brian: do good sitting and when the buzzer sounds you get more M&Ms." In the confusion at Value Mart she had forgotten to give the watch timer back to Michelle. She hated the idea of using candy so close to lunchtime. Yet perhaps just a few might help accomplish her mission.

Without explaining why, Cassie described to the saleswoman just what she wanted done. The clerk was unable to hide her quizzical expression while she examined the common river stone. Reluctantly the woman attempted to follow "the customer is always right" motto.

"Our jeweler has designed some rather unique pieces before. Maybe one of his former designs could be adapted for what you want." She pushed a large binder across the glass counter for Cassie to peruse. Tucked in the plastic pages were photos of unusual jewelry settings. "I'm certain you'll be satisfied with his work. He's very talented." She beamed with pride as if she were directly responsible for the magnificent pieces. "Mostly his designs are with precious and semi-precious stones. He has worked with other...material before but I must say this is a rather unusual request. Are you quite sure you don't want this polished up before it is set?"

Cassie considered. "Well, you can clean it up a little bit more but I want it in its natural state, not smoothed out. You see it has special meaning for me the way it is with all of the imperfections."

Apparently not convinced, the clerk continued, "I can understand, but there are some very rough edges that could be rather irritating on your neck."

"That's quite all right. As I said, I want it to be in its natural state," Cassie insisted.

"Well, as long as we are clear about it. I mean we wouldn't want you to be unhappy with the result after it's set." Pointing to the close-up of a pendant in the book the clerk asked, "How about something like this one? You'll notice the way the varying widths of gold bands swirl together to encase the gem in a teardrop. It's rather lovely, don't you think? "

"It's perfect," Cassie enthusiastically replied. "It's just what I would have designed myself if only I had the imagination for it! I—"

"Frr frr, frr frr!" Brian insisted as he reached from the stroller, yanking on his mother's pant leg.

Quickly Cassie reached for the bag of candy realizing it was time for the reward. Instead, her son pushed the hand containing the treats away while repeating the mysterious garble.

"What? What do you want, Brian?" his mother asked.

Struggling frantically, Houdini freed himself from his constraints. As he attempted to drag his mother out of the store by her pant's leg, she looked across the corridor to see a burger joint in the food court.

More urgently he repeated, "Frr frr, frr frr!"

"French fries! Oh, my God, I understand! You want the French fries that I promised, don't you?" Turning to the clerk again, she said excitedly, "He wants French fries!"

Confusion was evident on the clerk's face. "I guess it is a bit past lunch time. The little tyke is hungry, huh?"

"I'm sorry, you don't understand. You see, French fries— that's a new word for him."

Still puzzled, the clerk murmured, "That's nice."

"Listen," Cassie hastily explained. "I've got to reward this right away. Write up the paperwork for my setting. I'll be back to sign for it and put down a deposit when we're done with lunch."

To Brian she excitedly gushed, "French fries, we're going to get French fries!"

So overjoyed at hearing new words from her son, Cassie chose not to be bothered by the clerk's covert eye rolling and her barely audible mutter of "wacko." It was clear the saleswoman was unable to understand what all the fuss was about. Her son was clearly old enough to be babbling beyond the point most parents would wish for silence. Yet Cassie rushed to the food court, thrilled by the addition of this common request to his vocabulary.

Once they were seated at a little round table, she allowed herself to feel contented. Proudly she watched Brian jam a fistful of fries into his mouth. Somehow at that moment her son looked like any other toddler happily munching away. For once he seemed to fit in among the other patrons in the sunny courtyard of this upscale mall.

Chapter 14.

Scared. For a long time she had looked forward to his first day of school, but now Cassie wondered if she had done the right thing. She walked down the corridor looking for the entrance of the tiny room she had been shown earlier. So many things, including people, were distractions for these special children. So when the school was designed, a few of the classrooms had been built with small observation rooms. What would she find when she peered through the one-way window?

She squeezed into a space only large enough for three people to stand closely together. At first she was startled by one of Brian's classmates. Tommy intently stared at what should appear to be a mirror to the child. Once Cassie recovered from feeling that she was the one being watched, she scanned the room for her son. This was not the scene she expected to find when she dropped him off in the morning.

Brian had entered the school unaware that his mother would be leaving him in the care of the olive-skinned woman with wavy black hair. At first he had run to the child's height sink near the craft area. While Cassie spoke with Ms. Mangione, her son tried desperately to catch running water from the faucet.

"This section has a variety of activities to teach color concepts." The teacher pointed to several bins on low shelves. "And here we have toys that focus on the alphabet."

"What about talking?" Cassie asked. "He only has a few words."

Ms. Mangione smiled reassuringly. "Practically everything I do in this classroom will focus on language. See how there are pictures with words labeling everything in the room?" She touched a cardboard sign with the word *table* securely taped to the area where a small puzzle was spread out. "I place a lot of emphasis on the beginning sound of words initially and always try to get my students to attempt to use words."

The teaching assistant began guiding the children to sit cross-legged on the floor near the clock and calendar. Brian screamed and kicked as she led him away from the sink.

Ms. Mangione stopped Cassie before she could intervene. "Most in my class are returning students from last year. They know the routine and will help him adjust." She responded to Cassie's look of concern. "Brian has to get used to others in his life besides you. He will probably cry for a little while after you leave but then he'll be fine. Come back about a half-hour before the end of the day, and you can watch from the observation room."

Reluctantly, Cassie left. She wandered for hours through a bookstore. Unfocused, she flipped through romance novels and thrillers. A police siren screamed by the shop's window. Startled, she retrieved her cell phone and waited for it to ring.

Several minutes later when it was apparent no urgent call would come, she dropped it back into her purse. At China Dragon Buffet she filled a plate only to poke the uneaten lunch with her fork. For so many years she had waited for hours of freedom, yet she could not relax when given the opportunity. Brian's crying face filled her thoughts. She checked her watch repeatedly before it was time to return.

Now at the observation window, she regretted all the time spent worrying. Kneeling beside Brian, the teaching assistant helped him place colored magnets on a large white board mounted low on the wall. Under each they placed a paper square that matched the magnet's color. The four other children, with the exception of little Tommy, were equally occupied.

Thirty minutes passed quickly. Entering the classroom, Cassie helped Brian put his coat on. "I can't believe how well-behaved my child was for you," she said.

Ms. Mangione smiled but said, "Don't be surprised if he cries when you drop him off tomorrow. When he realizes we're to be part of a new daily routine he may resist. Despite what you saw, we don't perform instantaneous miracles. He will have lots of good and bad times ahead."

She slipped a marble composition book into a tote bag and handed it to Cassie. "This will be our lifeline," she said. "Every night before you go to bed, jot down a few sentences about what Brian does at home. I'll keep you informed about progress here at school as well." She chuckled and added, "This way we will literally be on the same page when it comes to teaching your son."

The rest of that week Cassie stood behind the one-way mirror each day before picking Brian up. Sequestered in this tiny booth she sensed more knowledge relevant to their lives would be gained here throughout the coming year than from all her college lectures.

Despite previously attending only one official meeting, the gathering of women in St. Vincent's fellowship room already felt as familiar to Cassie as hometown friends. Their phone calls and informal visits during the intervening weeks had made her instantly feel welcomed. With eager anticipation, Cassie left Brian with Chris and walked down the hall to join them.

All of the women from the last meeting were already chatting in the same seats as when she had first met them, with two exceptions. On this day, the only variation was the addition of two other women. These ladies were comfortably chatting away in chairs positioned between Ginny and a seat left vacant for Cassie.

A mild unsettling feeling overcame her. Despite the inclination to balk against assigned seating, most people tended to assume their same places at reoccurring gatherings. At the last meeting Cassie had been seated next to Ginny. Suddenly a childhood memory came to mind. One Sunday a new couple sat in the Delaine family's customary pew at church; her parents had been very uncomfortable. The next Sunday, Amanda and Carl made sure to arrive extra early to reclaim their traditional position. When Tim and Janice Moore (the new couple) arrived, they found an alternative pew to the right of the Delaines. In the following years the Delaines and the Moore family became steadfast friends, each carefully sitting in their self-imposed assigned seats.

Now, as Cassie observed the familiarity with which these ladies conversed with others in the group, she realized these women had not infringed on her location. Cassie was the newcomer. She took the chair reserved for her and offered an introductory "Hi."

The thirtyish brunette with chin-length hair beside her eagerly reached out her hand in greeting. "Hi, I'm Rose. Ginny said we had a new addition to the group. Did you meet Sue yet?" She indicated the woman with streaks of golden highlights in her hair seated next to Ginny. Sue's eyes crinkled as she smiled a welcome.

Before Cassie could respond further, Michelle addressed the group, "Ladies, have I got some stories for you this month!"

Cassie smiled, expecting her to relate the incident from several weeks ago at Value Mart. Instead she was surprised to discover a more recent event took precedence.

"Remember I told you I've been teaching Bradley how to make better choices when picking out his outfits?" Turning to Cassie she explained, "During the week if he puts together a strange combination, I tell him to choose either the shirt or the pants. Then I show him two things that go with what he picks. That way he still has control over his choices but it helps him learn what looks better."

Michelle returned her attention to the full group. "On Saturday I took him with me to run some errands. I was just about to gently explain why his orange and yellow striped t-shirt didn't go with his purple sweatpants when a woman entering the store caught my eye. She was wearing a long, lightweight cotton skirt, a winter weight sweater and brown leather sandals buckled over heavy socks. While I thought to myself what a crazy getup, I looked out the front window near the cash register. Coming out of Farley's Sporting Goods was a man wearing a racing jacket that looked like a roll of rainbow Lifesavers. He had it paired up with camouflage pants."

Michelle glanced around the group for a reaction. "As he headed for the parking lot I noticed three rows over there was a woman loading groceries into her car. She had skintight lavender sweats that were virtually painted on her. It might not have been so bad except that she must have weighed nearly three hundred pounds! Before I could say anything, the pharmacist handed our prescription to the cashier. I couldn't believe my eyes. Clowns at the circus wear less makeup than that girl at the register had on! Finally, I turned to leave and saw a teenager with the crotch of his jeans nearly to his knees, and he had piercings in his nose and through his tongue."

"So what did you say to Bradley?" Ginny asked, chuckling.

"Well, later on when we were home I explained what I thought would have been a better choice and why, but the whole incident made me stop and think. I decided not to be quite so uptight about what Bradley wears. After all, if so many 'normal' people can have no clue as to what looks good, I shouldn't let what Bradley chooses to wear bother me."

"I'm glad to hear that," Tamika said. "You always look like you stepped out of a fashion magazine. Maybe if you're not so concerned about Bradley's getup, you won't judge what I wear."

Michelle offered a quick apology. "Oh, please don't think that I've been at all judgmental about anyone here. It's just that I feel better about myself when I keep up a good appearance. I must admit though, I guess I am a little bit of a perfectionist, especially when it comes to clothes."

Maria added, "A little bit of a perfectionist? That's putting it mildly!"

Amused by private memories, Ginny laughed. "A man on a fast horse riding by would never notice."

Maria glared at her friend. "Okay, Ginny, you've come up with some crazy analogies and weird sayings before, but this time you've really lost me!"

Ginny looked mischievous as she began. "Well, before I had my kids I used to be a perfectionist about everything, including my clothes. One day when James was about two, I was loading him into his car seat to head out for church. He kicked his muddy shoes against my new white coat. I started to really lose it, and then old Mrs. Thompson who lived next door yelled over, 'A man on a fast horse riding by would never notice.' When I asked her what that meant, she said whenever she'd stress out about some minor detail, she'd ask herself, if someone was going by really quickly would they even notice that something was amiss? If the answer was no, it wasn't worth getting upset about. Somehow that phrase has helped me keep things in perspective over the years."

Rose added, "Well, there are times when even a man speeding by on a racehorse would notice how un-perfect my life is. I can hardly find time to grocery shop sometimes let alone spend time browsing the mall for the latest fashions."

"I'll admit I spend too much time at Sweetwater Mall," Michelle confessed. "But some of my outfits I get from GG's web site."

"I can never order anything online," Ellen complained. "I have to try things on. Clothes always look so stunning on those twig thin models in pictures, but they sure look different on my body!" She laughed.

Tamika retrieved a plate of cookies from the snack table and returned to her seat, taking one and passing them around. "Cassie, I'm glad to see we didn't scare you off last month. What's new with you? Did your son start school?"

"Oh yes!" Cassie brightened at the opportunity to join the mutual storytelling. "I've gotten several ideas from watching his teacher. I'm using Brian's fascination with Matchbox cars to work on color recognition. Together we sort his collection into piles by their color and then race them on the kitchen floor. Of course he still likes dropping them in his bucket but this gives us a new way to play together with something he already likes." She took a cookie for herself then passed the plate to Rose. "But what I really want to tell you about is what happened last Sunday—we had a power outage."

"Really? So did we," Kari exclaimed. "It was out for about two hours in our area. How did Brian react?"

"Well as usual, he had the Weather Channel on when the electricity cut out. He grabbed the remote control and started banging it on the table. I tried to explain to him what was happening, but he didn't understand. He pulled me over to the television and pushed my hand on the power button. Then... well, next came such a tantrum as you wouldn't believe."

Ginny nodded. "Of course we'd believe."

"It was lunchtime, and earlier I had promised to make chicken tenders, but I couldn't cook because we didn't have any electricity. I started to make him a peanut butter and jelly sandwich, but he kept screaming and tried to yank the freezer open. Finally, I couldn't take it any more so we drove to McDonald's, but they didn't have any power, either."

All eyes were focused on Cassie as she relayed the drama. "At first, Brian had settled down when I had told him we were going to McDonald's, but when he couldn't get his nuggets he started screaming again. The manager said the Oakgrove McDonald's had power. I never thought it made much sense to have another one only fifteen minutes away by car, but let me tell you I was never so happy that it was there."

"Oakgrove doesn't have a play area, do they?" Sue asked.

"No," Cassie replied. "But Brian had been in such a state that I wouldn't have wanted to stay even if they did. We just went through the drive-up window and took our lunch home to eat."

Rose leaned forward and asked, "What did you do to keep him calm during the blackout after you ate?"

"Well, I was at my wit's end trying to think up something."

Kari interjected, "So was I. After lunch Todd usually watches a little TV before his nap."

"Your son still takes a nap?" Maria exclaimed. "My son hardly ever slept at night, let alone take a nap at that age."

"How's Carlos's sleeping now?" Ginny asked.

"Wait a minute," Ellen interrupted. "I want to hear what happened next with Brian."

"Actually there wasn't too much more to the tale," Cassie replied. "I told Brian we would take a walk around the neighborhood and then have story time. He enjoyed the walk but started banging on the TV as soon as we got back in the house again. I told him to stop hitting the television; Mommy can't fix it and hitting it won't help. With that, all of a sudden the screen flickered on. Now Brian is going to think that I'm wrong and hitting the TV does make it work."

"Don't worry, Cassie," Ellen teased. "Banging on something to make it work is typical male behavior anyway, isn't it?"

"Yeah, I guess you're right." Cassie laughed.

Kari added, "Thankfully Todd was content to listen to his portable CD player before his nap. But now back to you, Maria, how is your son sleeping?"

"Well, I used to wonder how he could survive on so little sleep," Maria responded. "He's a lot better than he used to be, but every now and then he still wakes up around two or three in the morning and doesn't go back to sleep. I can never figure out what causes it. Once he's awake the rest of the house is, too. Thank God it doesn't happen that much anymore."

Cassie asked, "Ellen, do I remember you said your son has trouble sleeping? Brian does, too. Is that something all kids with autism have?"

"Not all do, but sleep problems are fairly common for kids with autism. Unfortunately Danny is one of the ones that does have trouble sleeping. At least I'm happy to say things were better this month."

Ginny pensively stirred her coffee. "You know, I nearly forgot, we had a power outage several years ago, back when the boys were little. It was a really bad storm; the thunder woke us all up. I had just put on some soothing music and turned on a light to try to comfort them when all of a sudden everything cut off. James was terrified; he kept flicking the light switch trying to make it come on. Little Nate was my savior that night." A peaceful smile settled on Ginny's face. "As young as he was, somehow he figured out to get a flashlight and showed James how to make shadow puppets on their bedroom wall. Nate has been such a help to me over the years. Oh, sometimes he does get mad at his brother, but most of the time he watches over him as if he were the big brother. I'm so proud of my Nathan. Still, at times I feel bad he's had to deal with having a brother with autism. But being the trooper that he is, he says he doesn't know any different; James is his brother and he is fine with that."

"He's such a good kid," Maria agreed. "And so is my Pablo. He used to be so embarrassed when I would bring Carlos to his baseball games, but he got over it. In fact, if some kid from the opposing team makes fun of him, Pablo sticks up for his brother."

"Is he going to play for the same team again next spring?" Sue asked.

"Of course, they won the county championship this year." She beamed. "Pablo is going to practice in the batting cages over at Fit n' Fun all winter to keep his game up. He's going to be a Major League player someday; you wait and see!"

Rose asked, "Tamika, your brother plays on a Triple A team, doesn't he? Maybe he could give Pablo some pointers."

"I'll be seeing him next month at Thanksgiving; I'll have to remember to ask."

"Thanks," Maria said. "I know Pablo would be thrilled. By the way, Tamika, how is your daughter doing?"

Tamika's brow was furrowed. "I'm afraid Monisha hasn't been doin' too good lately."

"I'm sorry to interrupt," Cassie said. "But I don't remember what you said your daughter has."

"At first the doctors though it was autism, but what Monisha has is Rett Syndrome."

Ginny explained, "There are a few other disorders including Rett syndrome and Angelman Syndrome that initially are diagnosed as autism because of some similarities. The lack or loss of language skills, unusual behaviors, and hand flapping or wringing are some of them."

"That's right," Tamika continued. "Rett's is a bit different, but because there are some things that are the same, I keep coming here to be among friends that understand what I'm going through." She took a sip of coffee. "Like I said, it's been a rough month. She had some pretty bad seizures and lots of trouble breathing. On top of that, the way she grinds her teeth drives me crazy.

"But I do have something good to tell. Last Wednesday, I was bathing her. She hates that. Then I took to washing her hair. I don't know if for some reason it felt good to her just then or if she just caught sight of herself in the mirror with all those suds. But all a sudden she busted out a giggling and a laughing. I started laughing, too. For a little while I forgot all about her Retts and her seizures and stuff. We just splashed and laughed. We were just a momma and her child."

Ginny smiled. "That's so nice to hear, Tamika. I'm really glad for you. Moments like that are what we live for. There is definitely nothing sweeter than when one of our kids connects with us."

"Speaking of shampooing," Ellen asked, "does anybody have any suggestions for me? I'm trying to get Danny to be a little more independent with washing himself, but every time he gets the shampoo, he pours half the bottle into his hands."

"Maybe what I did with Bradley years ago when he was little would work for you," Michelle offered. "I got a small pump bottle. While I showed him how to put two squirts in his hands, I made up a little song to go with it: One, two, squirts of shampoo." She motioned with her hands as she explained. "I held his hands together to rub them back and forth to lather it up. Bradley caught on pretty quickly. I think teaching to a tune helped it stick in his mind. We did that the same way night after night. Before I knew it, he was doing it all on his own."

"That's really clever, Michelle," Elsie said, complimenting the much younger woman seated next to her. "I'm certainly going to miss all of you. I'm not really sure how much I've been able to help anyone here, but it's been comforting for me to listen to all your stories. I think I've come to realize that even though I lost my Roger a long time ago, that I was still the best mother I could have been given the times I lived in back then."

Tamika asked, "Elsie, what are you saying? Aren't you coming to anymore meetings?"

"No. My daughter Claire—remember, I told you about her? Well, she wants me to come live in Florida. She doesn't think it's safe for me to live by myself anymore. Snow and ice are too dangerous for a woman my age, she says. She's afraid I'll have a fall and no one will know. I must admit I have a hard time getting warm enough in the winter around here anymore."

Surprise registered on all the women's faces.

"I thought you told us that her house was too tiny and there wasn't enough room for you to stay there," Tamika said. "What's changed?"

"I'm not really sure. It seems a local contractor was looking for a way to showcase their ability to build additions on older homes and have it look as if it was always part of the original house design. They're going to film the whole process to use in future advertising. Some private investment firm gave the contractor Claire's name as someone who might be interested. This Amana Coral Corp., or something that sounded like that, is paying for the whole thing. Claire insisted I should get ready to move as soon as possible."

Maria raised an eyebrow. "I don't know, Elsie. It sounds pretty fishy to me. Are you sure it's not some kind of scam?"

"Claire's brother-in-law is a lawyer. He went over all the paperwork and assured her it's legit. They even started work already!"

Ginny dabbed the corners of her mouth with a napkin. "Elsie, I'm going to miss you. You've so faithfully attended every meeting. But maybe now I'll be able to stick to my diet; your homemade goodies at every meeting are just too hard to resist. When are you leaving?"

"In two weeks. Apparently this Anda Carl Corp., or whatever it's called, is even paying for my lodging while the house is being renovated. They're going to put me up at one of those residence inn type places until the house is ready. It's all happening a little fast for my liking, but I'm so looking forward to being close to my daughter again. I've missed her so much."

"Do you need any help packing?"

"No, Claire hired a moving company. Besides, I don't have that much left. I got rid of most of my things when I moved into my apartment." She turned to Cassie and said, "I'm sorry I didn't get to know you that well, sweetie. I've been watching you and you still seem a little bit lost and confused by the situation you find yourself in. Don't worry. These are good women—good friends. They'll help you through this. They will be your rock when you need solid land and a pillow when you need a cry."

For a moment there was silence as the women took in Elsie's news. Then Ginny took a sip of her coffee and asked, "Sue, you've been unusually quiet; you don't quite seem to be yourself this month. What's up?"

Tears began to well up in Sue's eyes. After a few moments of nervously pulling at a crumpled napkin, she blurted out, "I'm pregnant."

"How wonderful!" Ellen exclaimed.

"No, it's not. I'm scared. Tim is such a handful. He's going to need special care for the rest of his life. What if I have another autistic child? I don't think I could handle another."

"You don't know that will happen," Kari attempted to reassure her. "I'm sure it won't. Look at Ginny. She had James and then she had Nathan. Nate isn't autistic."

"The first part of what Kari said is true. You just don't know," Tamika added. "But statistics do show a greater chance of having a child with autism if you already have one. Sue, if you're that scared...I mean, well...did you talk with your husband about maybe an abortion?"

"I don't think I could bring myself to that. It's against our beliefs. And Kevin had so looked forward to being a dad. He was crushed when we found out Timmy was autistic. Kevin tries to do all the normal father and son things with him, but it's just not the same. I know he desperately wants to have a child he can do those things with, but there's just no way to be sure. I don't know what I'm going to do."

Wiping her eyes she let out a mournful sigh. "Before Timmy was born, all my friends asked if we wanted a girl or a boy. I just gave the same glib answer most expectant parents do: 'I don't care, just as long as it is healthy.' I never really considered any other possibility."

"I think that's true about lots of things," Ginny replied. "When you watch the news, do you ever actually think about being the victim of a crime or losing your home in a fire or flood? We assume that happens to somebody else. Most us just go along with our lives until something dramatic smacks us head on.

Ginny leaned forward. "Sue, whatever you and Kevin decide, you know that we're family and we'll support you in any way we can."

"Of course we will," Michelle added.

"Absolutely," Ellen said.

The remaining women echoed those sentiments by enveloping their friend in a soothing verbal hug.

A few more tears trickled down Sue's face before she whispered in appreciation, "Thanks, guys. I honestly don't know what I'd do without you."

Chapter 15.

There was so much information and emotion to take in after this second support meeting. Drained and deep in thought, Cassie had not bothered to turn the car radio on as she drove home. Yet, upon hearing the protesting "Eeee" from her son at the silence, instinct propelled her to pop a CD into the player. This kept him content until he bounded through the door and made a beeline to the television.

Immediately a familiar voice droned on, "...major storm system in the Midwest resulting in isolated flooding in low lying areas. Now for a look at your local forecast. Currently the temperature is..."

Knowing that at least for a few minutes Brian would be safely occupied with his routine, Cassie headed for the kitchen. She decided a glass of wine would make watching the Weather Channel for fifteen minutes much more palatable.

The phone rang just as she dropped her keys on the kitchen counter. Resigned that some telemarketer would be on the other end, she reluctantly lifted the receiver. Instead, a welcome familiar voice bubbled away, barely taking a pause to catch her breath.

"Cassie? It's Cindy. I can't believe I'm back on the East Coast again so soon. My boss needed me to cover some meetings for him in the Big Apple again. I finished up early and I've got two more days before I have to be back in L.A.; I'd love to get together for lunch before I leave. Are you available?"

Cassie was thrilled. "Cindy! I'm so glad to hear your voice. Actually, tomorrow would be just fine with me. Brian started school and I haven't got any other plans in particular. Are Beth and Angela in town too?"

Cindy's voice was hesitant. "Um, I'm not sure, but if you don't mind I'd prefer it just be the two of us."

Surprised by the request, Cassie responded, "Sure, no problem. Why don't we meet at eleven-thirty so we'll have plenty of time for a nice leisurely lunch. How about Sandy Hill Tavern?"

"Great, I'll see you there."

With the exception of get-togethers with Angela, it had always been rare for Cassie to see one of the foursome without the rest of the quartet. While they were in college, some of her closest and best confidences had been shared by the whole close-knit group. But the evening at the Bay Breeze Yacht Club a few weeks earlier had not been as pleasant as Cassie had hoped. In retrospect, though, she realized it probably was not her friends' fault. A cascade of emotional events had eroded her ability to appreciate ordinary dilemmas of other people. Yet Cassie longed for those bonds that were at one time so strong.

So, the next day Cassie arrived fifteen minutes early. After being seated in a booth by the window, she let her mind wander as early customers trickled in. Strange, she thought, how some eateries have names that don't seem to fit at all. Sandy Hill Tavern was located in the middle of a bustling shopping center nowhere near sand or a hill. Perhaps Sandy Hill was a person's name. And while there was a small oak bar near the entrance, the place looked nothing like what most people would imagine a tavern to be. The décor was very light and bright, more on the order of a luncheonette. Several small tables were shoved together in the center of the dining area, apparently set for a business luncheon.

"Over here, Cindy," she called out upon seeing her friend approach the hostess.

Cindy hurried over. "I hope I didn't keep you waiting."

"No, not long; I just got here a few minutes ago myself. Wow! You look stunning again, and quite Hollywood with those shades, I might add."

With ease Cindy slid her slender frame into the booth across from her friend. She popped the sunglasses into a pouch that matched her designer handbag. "You know me, Cassie. I always did enjoy keeping up with the latest styles. I must admit, though, it can be intimidating living and working in L.A. You never know if someone is going to spot you on an off day and next thing you know, your picture is in some rag with a caption: 'What not to wear.'" She gestured quotation marks in the air. With the briefest scan of the menu she asked, "So, what's good here?"

"They make a killer Reuben sandwich but I guess after New York you probably had the best there. The French Dip is pretty good here too."

"Sounds tempting, but I've eaten a little too well this trip. I won't be able to zip these slacks if I keep eating the way I have." To the approaching waitress she said, "I'll have a small chef salad with light Italian dressing on the side and an Evian water."

"Same for me," Cassie ordered, now self-conscious of her own need to lose weight. "I'm glad you called, Cindy. We've always had good times together but I must admit I was a bit surprised that you wanted to meet without the others."

"Well, when we got together at Bay Breeze, you seemed a little left out of the conversations. The rest of us...well, somehow our lives have all gone in various career directions. With you being a stay at home mom, things are a bit different. Cassie, we're still friends; I want to know what's going on with you. But..." After a hesitant pause, she said, "Angela said we shouldn't ask you about Brian. If you don't want to talk about it, that's okay, but quite frankly if you don't mind, I do have questions."

Confused, Cassie replied, "I don't mind at all. Why would Angela tell you not to ask about Brian?"

"Well, maybe because of the autism thing and everything. She thought you might not want to talk about it."

Annoyance at Angela's false assumptions was evident as Cassie responded. "For heaven's sake, we're not talking about leprosy here! It's not catching and there's nothing to be embarrassed about. Like you said, we're friends. If I can't talk to you guys, who can I talk to?"

She paused as the waitress returned with their bottled waters and ice-filled glasses. After the waitress departed, Cassie resumed her train of thought. "You know, it's kind of like when my parents died. After the funeral, all their neighbors were afraid to talk about my mom and dad in front of me. Maybe they were afraid that the memory of how they died would be too painful. But to tell you the truth, what I wanted most was to have people reminisce about all the pleasant memories. I needed to talk about them and to deal with the circumstances of the tragedy. I'm beginning to learn that ignoring reality only postpones eventually facing it. It's kind of the same with Brian. Yes, I am a single mother; yes, Brian is autistic; and yes, it is difficult to deal with sometimes. At times, it seems like more than I can bear, but that's when I most need to talk about him with someone. Of course I want to talk to you about Brian, he's my son. He is my life now, and so is autism, whether I want it to be or not. So, fire away; what do you want to know?"

Cindy cautiously glanced about the room as if still uncertain the topic was permissible. "Well, what do the doctors say? How did he get his autism and what is it?"

Cassie's mind flicked back to her most recent conversation with Dr. Hart. "No one really knows for sure, but they think through genetics there's a problem with how the brain develops in people with this disorder. Somehow that affects their ability to communicate and understand social situations. Also, there can be problems with how the brain understands information coming from the senses. You know, like what you see, hear, smell, taste or touch. It's like the volume control on the senses is broken; information comes in too strong or too weak." Cassie smiled to herself, aware that Ginny's propensity for analogies was beginning to wear off onto her.

Cindy appeared genuinely interested. "How does that affect Brian?"

"Sometimes he seems to be in a world all of his own. At his school they told me maybe that's when he's having trouble dealing with all the information coming in through his senses. So he focuses on a routine. He's so intent on what he is doing that you think he's not aware of what's going on around him, but he knows. Just try and change the channel on the TV while he drops toy cars in his bucket. He'll run in and change it back. That's just one example, though. Sometimes his rituals and self-imposed rules run our lives." Pleased to be reconnecting on more than a superficial level, Cassie sat back and let her friend absorb what she had said.

Cindy looked sympathetic. "That must be so frustrating."

"Oh, you have no idea! But I'm starting to learn how to turn this love of routines to my advantage. Brian was an absolute tyrant about bedtime until his teacher helped me develop a consistent schedule for it. First I help him put his toys away, then he gets his bath and we brush his teeth. I tuck him in bed, read *one* book to him, and then leave the room."

"Isn't that what you do with most children anyway?"

"Yes and no. With other kids it may not be as important if you change the order of what you do as long as you do each thing. But now I understand the calming effect routines have for him; everything has a specific order in his schedule. Even though he still resists having his teeth brushed, he knows what comes next. Somehow it helps his world make sense to him if he knows what's going to happen and when. Like last night, after we finished with his teeth, he ran to get a book off the shelf on his own."

Cassie smiled remembering this small victory. "You have no idea what a big step that was. I know it seems like such a trivial, minor thing to be thrilled about, but with Brian every little step is a major accomplishment."

After Cindy thought for a moment, she said, "Cass, I'm not sure I really understand, but I'm trying. Won't he eventually grow out of some of these problems or learn on his own? Maybe now that he's around other kids at school he'll pick up stuff from them."

"I wish it were the case, but no; most of what comes naturally to most kids has to be taught to kids with autism. They tell me just putting Brian with other kids doesn't help. He has to be taught how to play; he has to be taught every little thing."

"Most little kids need help in learning how to share and take turns, don't they?"

"It's more than that. Brian doesn't even seem to get the whole notion of make pretend or imitating what someone else is doing. It's like he doesn't understand the purpose behind it."

"It all sounds so sad for you."

A sympathetic frown appeared on Cindy's face but Cassie just gave a nonchalant shrug of her shoulders. "It's not all gloom and doom, Cindy. There are times when what he does cracks me up."

"Still, well, I'm sorry I haven't been in touch with you that much over the last few years. I guess I just didn't know what to say and didn't want to say the wrong thing."

Cassie hesitated. "Not talking to you at all was worse. It felt like nobody cared at all."

"Cassie, don't ever think that." Cindy leaned forward across the table. "I know I can get pretty busy with my career but anytime you need me, just call or e-mail me. I don't want to lose touch again." She paused as the waitress returned with two plates overflowing with lettuce, shredded cheese, luncheon meats, and hard-cooked eggs. "My God! Look at these enormous salads. How on earth could anyone eat that much? Restaurants put enough food for three people on plates nowadays. Look at the size of this!"

Cassie chuckled. "You know, that reminds me of something Brian did the other day. He obviously doesn't understand proportion either. We were in the preschool room of the church where my support group meets. One of the helpers was trying to get him to play with a dollhouse. Brian took out one of the little wooden chairs and was trying to figure out how he could sit on it. It was so comical."

"That must have been quite a sight," Cindy agreed. She stabbed a piece of lettuce minus the dressing and held it up. "I could name a few stars in L.A. that must be trying to fit into chairs that size. This forkful would be a whole day's worth of calories for them."

"Oh, do tell. Fill me in on all the dirt!"

Conversation slipped away from autism to Tinsel Town for the remainder of lunch. But both friends were now aware that topic could comfortably be raised between the two of them many times in the future.

Chapter 16.

One final tap and the nail was in place. Cassie set her hammer down. There was a small ding in the drywall but the frame would cover it. The latest addition to be hung was the best picture she had taken of Brian yet. He smiled, giggled, and laughed frequently, but he often seemed somber when she reached for her camera. It was hard to find pictures suitable for display because his expression in posed shots made him look like he was lost.

She stepped back from the desk to admire a gallery of photos on the opposite wall. Hung above the bookcase was a matted series of eight by tens.

The first brought back vivid recollections each time she viewed it. Constant rain had prevented mowers from tending to the overgrown lawn. Brian was crouched low to the ground examining miniature flowers in the grass. His gaze was transfixed by yellow petals, smaller than his fingertips. Cassie had watched for a while before deciding to snap his picture. She dashed into the house. Several minutes elapsed before she was able to locate her camera. Returning to the yard out of breath, she was amazed he had remained motionless. Before pressing the shutter, Cassie noticed a wild rabbit under a bush five feet away from her child. Hoping to capture them both, she pushed a button activating its zoom lens. The whirring noise startled the bunny. He scampered away but her normally active child continued poking the tiny patch of yellow. Even without the rabbit this was an endearing picture.

Next to that was a beach scene taken before Brian's diagnosis. Despite the long drive it had been an unusually good day for him. He had giggled as waves attacked his ankles. Cool water was refreshing on that ninety-six degree day. Under a rented umbrella she had watched him play near a group of children digging in the sand. Brian patted at a puddle the outgoing tide left in an abandoned hole. She snapped this shot just as he shoved a handful of sand into his mouth.

Pictured further on the wall was a mountain of leaves. Brian had actually joined some neighboring children as they plopped into the huge mound. After they raced off to seek a new diversion, Brian continued crawling through the crunching leaves. Alone in the picture he seemed not to care the others had left, but perhaps he just didn't show it.

The seasonal theme was completed by an ornament laden Christmas tree with hundreds of lights. Fragrant branches had enticed Burt to curl up beneath them. Scattered to the left was a pile of newly opened toys. But in the right foreground, a large cardboard box was tilted so the opening faced forward. Sound asleep inside, her son tightly held a new Matchbox car.

A new memory prepared to take its place on a blank wall. Cassie picked the framed photo off the floor and placed it on the nail above her desk. This one made her laugh in spite of how that day began. A registered letter had arrived from Crawfield, Stone and Limbley on behalf of their client—Mr. Greg Robertson. If there was any lingering question as to his stance, it was clarified by this carefully worded warning. Threats to defame his character would not be tolerated; blackmail would not be paid. Any further attempts would promptly be reported to the police.

Cassie's heart sank. In spite of her best efforts he had totally misinterpreted her intent. All her follow-up letters after their meeting had been returned unopened. Genetic testing could prove her veracity, but what was the point? Clearly Greg did not want to believe her. Either Angela had been right years ago, or his prospects of inherited wealth had altered the person she thought he was.

The UPS truck had drawn her attention away from what might have been. A large crystal vase ordered over the Internet had been packaged in a box four times its size. Protecting it as it traveled were hundreds of Styrofoam peanuts. Cassie returned to the kitchen after carefully placing the new treasure in the dining room. Handfuls of the white packing material were tossed up before floating down again. Brian giggled uncontrollably as he repeated the process, completely covering the floor around him. Cassie was reminded of the day they were late for Dr. Stevenson. Brian had tossed needles from the spruce tree in much the same manner. She wasn't angry this day, though. Her son's mirth was contagious. She scooped up as much as she could hold and, standing over Brian, released a white waterfall. He squealed with delight. Once more she pelted him with nuggets lighter than air.

Cassie was grateful the camera had been nearby; this sliver of time was more precious than any item she could purchase.

Bit-by-bit, Brian made gains in school. His teacher wrote daily notes in the communication book and each evening Cassie wrote back. Taped to Cassie's refrigerator was a picture schedule of his routines. Throughout their home, items were labeled in words and pictures identifying what the object was.

Brian learned to express his desires by taking a Velcro attached picture off the poster in the kitchen and trying to say the word. In this manner he added the words *book*, *cars*, and *TV* to his spoken vocabulary.

Fall had turned to a bitter cold winter. Cassie had been so busy teaching her son, the time between group meetings seemed to race by. Eagerly each month she anticipated seeing her friends to share what was happening and catch up with what occurred in their lives. Brian had begun the new year with marked improvement in taking turns with classmates.

Brushing snow off her coat before hanging it up, Cassie joined the circle in the fellowship room.

"I saw the most wonderful story on the news this morning about a family with autism," Ellen bubbled as Cassie took her seat. "The parents were so frustrated by their son's lack of progress, one of them moved clear across the country so he could go to a big name school. After a few years, their family being separated was too much. So they joined with another family, raised tons of money, and opened their own school. Now, their son is doing just wonderfully!"

"I hate stories like that," Maria grumbled as she perched her coffee on the tray table between herself and Ellen.

Shocked at her critical response, Kari objected, "What? How can you say that? It sounds like such an inspiring story."

Maria crossed her arms, turned to face Kari, and defiantly continued. "Stories like that always make me feel so inadequate, like if I don't perform miracles for my child, it must be because I don't try hard enough. They seem to imply that if only I climbed a mountain or swam an ocean, my child would be perfectly normal."

"I know how you feel," Michelle agreed. "I remember reading years ago about a woman who took her son to France for a therapy called auditory training and he was 'cured.' Lots of parents spent thousands of dollars getting the same treatment for their kids. Some swear their kids made dramatic improvement, but I don't think there were any other miraculous cures."

Rose asked, "Do you remember the furor over the hormone Secretin? There was a rush of parents clamoring for injections. As far as I know, though, scientific studies have been unable to prove any of the dramatic claims."

Tamika added, "How about swimming with dolphins? I heard some parents believed that therapy would work for their kids."

"Yes, there have been lots of therapies du jour over the years." Ginny responded. "Some help a little."

"It sounds a little crazy. Why do parents do that?" Cassie asked.

"Because they're desperate to reach their child," Maria answered. "They're desperate just like I am, but I don't have the strength to climb a mountain or swim an ocean. I'm stronger than I ever knew I could be, but I'm not that strong."

"It's not just about strength," Ginny advised. "Sometimes it's wise to be patient, to see if a therapy truly works. If you run from therapy to therapy you'll wear yourself out."

Kari refuted, "If you wait, too much time passes by. I might miss an opportunity to help my son!"

"Therein lies the dilemma—and the frustration, I might add," Ginny pointed out. "We are back to that old guilt thing again. If you don't climb that mountain, you're not trying hard enough to make a miracle for your child. But my theory is that if I constantly try to 'cure' my son, I miss out on loving him for who he is. He's autistic. I wish he wasn't, but he is."

"I can't just sit by and do nothing," Kari complained.

"I'm not saying you should give up. But don't push so hard expecting a miracle cure. Just try to help him be the best he can be within his disability."

Ellen shifted uncomfortably in her chair. "Well, I thought it was an inspiring story. I mean, maybe I can't start my own school, but if I'm patient and work hard with Danny, who knows how far he'll progress."

"You know another thing that bothers me about stories like that?" Maria complained.

"What?" Ellen snipped, annoyed at being interrupted with Maria's attitude.

"Well, most of the time, you only see stories of superhuman parents. You never see the everyday, painfully slow struggles we go through. You don't see the countless stories that are not miracles. Sometimes I think because of stories like that, people who are not in the same boat as us think we're supposed to be these divine saints or something."

Ginny added, "I have to admit, I'd like to stick a fork in the eye of the next person that comes up to me and says, 'You must be such a wonderful person. God only gives as much as you can handle.' I know most people mean to say that in kindness but it makes me want to scream at them, 'Thanks a lot for a God that loves me so much that he dumps this shit on me!'"

Kari's jaw dropped. "Oh my God, Ginny, not you! You're so strong, you're so..."

Ginny rolled her eyes. "Come on, Kari, I'm human just like you. I get tired of being the strong one all the time. Sometimes I feel like locking myself in my room and crying or walking out the door and not coming back. Lately, I just don't know how I feel about God or the people at church anymore."

"I can't believe it!" a shocked Ellen replied. "I never would have guessed you ever felt that way. I guess I'm so surprised because my church has been so supportive. They have extra helpers in Sunday school class and during church to help with Danny."

Sue piped up. "I kind of know what Ginny means. I remember the nursery teacher at church asked me to tell her what autism is and how to work with Tim. I was about two sentences into my explanation when she started to get a glazed look in her eyes. I got the message; I just stopped talking and took Timmy home."

Tamika added, "I used to volunteer for every committee at church before Monisha was born. It was hard for them to see me as needing to be on the receiving end of charity. Some church members have an easier time reaching out to someone they don't already know, like a far-away mission or a new neighbor. They've come around, though. Somebody is always volunteering to help out with my daughter." Tamika paused. "Still, it's such a shame you feel so angry at God, Ginny."

Added moisture was evident in their leader's eyes. "Oh, don't get me wrong, ladies," Ginny reassured them, dabbing her face with a tissue. "Most of the time I'm secure in how much I love my boys. It's just that last week was particularly tough. For some reason James started pounding on Nathan's door trying to get at him. I tried to intervene but he was in such a state that he turned on me. I'm still black and blue. See these bruises?"

Ginny showed her arms. Impressions from her child's fingers were nearly tattooed up and down her forearms.

"Oh God!" Cassie exclaimed. "What did you do to calm him down?"

A hush fell on the room. All eyes were riveted on Ginny waiting for her response. "Nate came to my rescue when he heard me screaming. James kicked and tried to bite us but we managed to stay out of his reach. I locked him in his room and called his pediatric psychiatrist. He wasn't in so they had to page him. Eventually James got tired and calmed down. When it was clear the episode was over I made sure he understood there would be consequences for his actions. He had to pick up the mess he created during his tantrum and vacuum his room and the hallway—he hates vacuuming. Even though we weren't bleeding, I had him help put a band-aid on Nate and one on me so he would get the idea that he hurt us. Two hours later when everything was all over, the doctor called back."

"What did he say?" Tamika asked.

"Well, we discussed my concerns that James has been showing signs of being more and more on edge lately. He's already on some medication that helps to keep his mood more stable. Dr. Peterson told me to increase his afternoon dose, watch to see if there is improvement for a few weeks, and then come in for an appointment."

"It feels like we live in doctor's offices sometimes, doesn't it?" Tamika offered.

Michelle reached across Cassie to grasp the group leader's hand. "Ginny, I'm so sorry for you. I can't imagine how horrible that must have been for you. I've been fortunate; Bradley has never been aggressive, but lately he's been going through bouts of depression. With Asperger's he's been able to communicate more than your son is able, but still he realizes he's different from other kids. I don't know what is worse, not knowing what's going on inside your kid's head or knowing what they're thinking and finding out how bad they feel."

Frightened, Cassie asked, "Is that what I have to look forward to with Brian? Do all kids with autism have aggressions or bouts of depression?"

Tenderly Ginny returned Cassie's anxious gaze with a Mona Lisa countenance. "Not all do, but I'm afraid it's not uncommon either, particularly around puberty. Heck, puberty is a rough time for typical kids without disabilities. Now just imagine for a minute that you are suddenly taken to a foreign country..."

"What the hell are you talking about? Where are you going with this analogy?" Maria interrupted.

"Just go with me for a second," Ginny urged. "Like I said, imagine you're in a place where you don't speak the language. Let's go a step further: neither of you understand each other's gestures either. How do you think you would feel? What would you do? Maybe you'd be frightened and withdraw, or perhaps in your confusion you would get angry and strike out. It's kind of like that for our kids; they have so much trouble figuring out this whole communication thing."

"I think I get your point," Cassie admitted.

"One more thing," Ginny continued. "Think about how you feel when you've had a little too much to drink."

"Ginny!" Kari interrupted indignantly. "That's awful to suggest that kids with autism are like drunken bums."

"Easy, don't get offended. I'm not suggesting our kids are like drunks, but when people have too much to drink their senses are impaired. Our loved ones with autism often have problems understanding or tolerating sensory information, too. On top of that they have thrown at them the added confusion of new hormonal sensations that all teenagers go through. So, again picture yourself in that same scenario, only now you're tipsy from three or four drinks in a place where you can't make sense of what's going on around you."

"Oh God, that's horrible. Isn't there any hope?" Cassie asked.

"Well, the most obvious solutions are to help your child improve his communication skills. Demonstrate behaviors you want him to use, and give positive reinforcement when he does what you want."

Kari objected, "But, Ginny, you know all that stuff and still James attacked you!"

"Sometimes even with the best education, the best therapies and so on, there is still something going on inside our kids that all the behavior management in the world won't help ease their internal turmoil. That's where we are with James: he needs medication to help smooth out his mood swings. Probably just readjusting his meds—"

"Oh, I don't think I could ever drug my child!" Kari smugly interrupted.

Ginny sounded slightly irritated. "Listen, if Todd were diagnosed with diabetes, wouldn't you give him insulin?"

"Well, yes, but that's different."

"Not in my opinion. My son doesn't need insulin but he does need something to help regulate his erratic emotions."

Cassie mumbled, "I'm still reeling from Brian's diagnosis; now I have to worry about what happens when he reaches puberty?"

Ginny smiled wearily at her. "No, Cassie, don't worry about it; just be prepared to deal with what happens when it comes. It will probably be rough going for a while, but then again the teenage years can be tough for most parents. You know, I'm reminded of when I went through child birthing classes before my first was born."

"Here we go again: another analogy," Maria teasingly groaned.

In response Ginny waved a hand with mild annoyance at her friend. "Oh hush. Anyway, I remember being scared when I heard about the pain of the transition phase. When I actually went through it, it was less scary knowing that period of labor was the shortest: at most it would be twenty minutes. Sometimes advance knowledge helps you prepare for what may come so you're not as stressed out when it happens."

Looking around the room, Cassie noticed she wasn't the only one troubled by the disturbing conversation. It was time to lighten the mood. "Speaking of giving birth, how are you doing, Sue?"

"Well, pretty good, I guess, now that the morning sickness has subsided. I don't know why they call it that; it was all day sickness." She reached for her water bottle and took a swig.

"Do you still worry about your decision to keep it?" Tamika asked.

"I was thinking about it last night again while I was up," Sue admitted.

"You can't let worrying keep you from sleeping," Kari advised.

Sue laughed. "That's not what woke me up; it was my husband. Kevin snores like a broken machine gun. I think even the windows were rattling last night. It gets so loud that sometimes he startles himself awake wondering what the noise was."

Laughter from the other women joined Sue's. "I'm still concerned, but I decided worrying won't change anything. Kevin and I want this child so I'm just going to think positive thoughts." Smiling and looking down at her stomach as she rubbed it, she said, "You're going to be just fine, aren't you?"

"Did you think about any names yet?" Ellen asked

"I kind of like Travis, Brennan or Cole for a boy and if Timmy had been a girl I was going to name the baby Melissa. I think I'll stick with that if this is a girl."

"That's a pretty name." Maria agreed. "Hey, Cassie, I just noticed your necklace. Isn't that stone your lucky charm, the one you cut your finger on?"

"Um, well yes."

"I never would have thought of making it into jewelry but it looks really nice."

Ginny reached for the pendant to get a closer look. "May I?" she asked.

"Yes, of course," Cassie replied.

Ginny studied the swirls of gold encasing the simple pebble. "This is quite unique."

"Is that a polite way of saying you don't like it?" Michelle teased.

"No, not at all. It's quite nice actually. In fact looking at this jogged loose some childhood memories."

Maria quietly groaned at another impending story but Ginny ignored her. "I had this friend, Fran, who begged her parents for a rock polisher for her birthday one year. She was so excited when she got it. I remember helping her set it up the first time she used it. It was quite a lengthy, involved process. Fran added washed stones to a tumbler with grit and water. Several days later she rinsed them and put them back in the polisher with more grit and water for two more *weeks*. I watched Fran clean the rock tumbler then add polish to let them tumble for *another full week!* Despite weeks of tumbling there were tiny pockmarks or different colored ripples in each polished stone. Somehow the slight imperfections are what made them so interesting and beautiful. Each one was unique."

"Thanks for the science lesson, Ginny!" Ellen teased. "So, what's the point of this analogy?"

"Well, think about it, I mean our kids..."

Maria rolled her eyes. "Great, our kids were apples, drunks, and now you've got them being rocks!"

"They are each one very rough indeed," Ginny continued unperturbed. "They require a tremendous amount of effort to polish. That was certainly the case with James this past month. Anyway, even when polished, our guys still will have lots of imperfections and flaws. They may never be what our vision of perfect once was, but they will always be unique and beautiful. With a lot of hard work we can help bring to the forefront the beauty within them."

"My old friend Ginny," Maria said fondly. "Were you a philosopher in a past life?"

Kari jabbed Maria. "Wait a minute, I thought you didn't believe in any of that stuff: past lives and all."

Maria shrugged. "Who knows, maybe I'm doing penance for something from a previous life. If I display enough patience, maybe next time around I'll be on easy street. Hey, that's it, all Ginny's stories are really meant as a test," she teased.

While the friendly jousting continued, Cassie's mind wandered. This fanciful analogy stemmed from a stone that got kicked up into her shoe, one she kept to remind herself of just how close she came to a monstrous action. But perhaps Ginny was right; Brian was like this pebble. Raising him was extremely difficult, but already she was finding a sense of accomplishment in the polishing.

Chapter 17.

Winter winds had whipped icy crystals into huge irresistible mounds. Before Brian left for school each morning and in the afternoon when he retuned, his mother fought a losing battle. From house to school bus and back again were insurmountable distances to keep her child dry, yet Cassie learned to take it in stride. A complete change of clothing was kept at school. Ms. Mangione would change him at school if needed and then send his wet things home to be laundered. Sometimes his outfits were damp from snow and other times from accidents. Potty training was progressing fairly well at school, but he still had occasional setbacks.

Cassie flipped through the afternoon's mail as she waited for Brian at the end of her driveway. When the mini school bus came in view, she jammed the advertisements and credit card offers into her deep coat pockets.

"Hi, Ms. Delaine," the bus assistant said as she helped Brian down the steps. Miss Stacie gently but firmly held his hand until releasing him to his mother. The fraction of a second that the transfer took was all he needed. The child swam across the white waves until his face was buried at the base of the largest mound.

"Oh, no. I'm so sorry. We actually had him in the same clothes you sent him to school in all day."

"Don't worry about it," Cassie replied. "I was going to let him play in the snow for a little while this afternoon anyway. How was he on the bus today?"

"Well, let me tell you."

"Oh God, what did he do?" Cassie asked, worried.

"Relax, it wasn't anything bad. It's just that he had a laughing spell, that's all. He was buckled into his seat by himself on the second row. We were stopped at a traffic light. Nothing special was happening; we were just waiting for the light to turn green. All of a sudden he started laughing hysterically. I looked all around, and I still can't figure out what started it. He kept laughing and laughing, harder and harder. It was kind of contagious. I couldn't help myself; the next thing I knew, I was laughing right along with him."

Cassie acknowledged his unexplained emotional demonstrations. "Last week Ms. Mangione said he started crying for no reason in the middle of lunch time."

"Yeah, these little guys do that sometimes, but at least today it was laughing. It sure was funny. Well, we better get the rest of these kids home. Goodbye, Brian," she called over her shoulder as she climbed the bus steps.

The child did not turn to face the women, but very quietly his mother heard "Bah."

As the bus sped away, Cassie praised her son. "Brian, that was good saying bye! That was good talking; good using words." She crouched next to him, scooped snow between her hands, and packed it into a hard snowball, which she gently rolled down the glittering mountain next to her son. He excitedly flapped his arms. To a stranger it may have looked like he was doing "the royal" wave with both hands in fast forward or like an attempt to frantically unscrew two light bulbs at once. But Cassie recognized he was just happily excited. From behind, she cupped his left hand in her left and his right in her right. They bent together at their waists to reach the cold surface. Pushing his hands together she helped him to make a crude, cold snowball, which he rapidly rolled down his mountain.

"Eeee!" he screamed excitedly while pogo sticking up and down in the snow. His mother repeated cupping her hands over his to make more, again and again until her fingers were raw. Brian would have willingly stayed outside, unaware he was cold, but at the mention of "Weather Channel" he scampered to the door.

After being clothed in clean warm clothes, Brian dumped out his fleet of cars on the family room rug. The sound of elevator music accompanied a view of the local radar on the television screen.

Cassie settled herself in front of another screen just a few feet from her son. Sometimes browsing the Internet for news was easier than wrestling the TV from her son. She scrolled down the page to scan the highlights. A fire...labor disputes...sports scores...more trouble in the Middle East. And then she noted a request from a local homeless shelter—the supplies in their pantry were running dangerously low. It had been an unusually harsh winter; Ginny had the flu and February's support group was canceled due to snow.

Donations...hmm. Quite some time ago Ginny had suggested some of her lottery wealth could be put to good use.

Cassie had not given much thought to her finances for a while. Once Brian had started school, she had arranged for automatic bill paying from her computer for most of her routine bills. Even the new *Maids for You* fee was billed directly to a charge account that in turn she deducted monthly from her checking account online.

Looking up from her computer's screen, she now scanned her environment. Exquisite furnishings filled her elegant home. She realized how fortunate she was in that regard; so very many people lived paycheck to paycheck, including some of her newest friends. After-school therapies were hard on their budgets; they would envy such a lack of financial worry.

Her friends...Was there some way she could help without them knowing it was her? The tray tables had been such a little thing to do, but it had given her such a boost in spirits. Even more rewarding had been the secretive plot with the Florida developer so Elsie could be with her daughter. Using her parents' names for the fictitious corporation sponsor made it doubly sweet. Poor Elsie couldn't quite get the name right, but that didn't really matter. What could she do for the others? Perhaps an opportunity would arise later; she would see them again soon. In the meantime, Cassie clicked on her bank's web site, logged onto her account and added the homeless shelter and food bank to the list of charities.

A few weeks later Cassie mentally checked off a list of accomplishments as she reclined in the awkward chair at her hair stylist's. More new words were being added to Brian's vocabulary at an ever-increasing pace, and his ability to brush his own teeth was improving. Following his schedule without a tantrum completed his list of big accomplishments. As Brandy sprayed warm water through her hair, Cassie hoped a new cause for celebration would be added by day's end.

Brandy's strong fingers massaged shampoo through Cassie's freshly tinted hair. Relaxing while someone else tended to this task was now a pleasurable routine while her son was at school. The brightly lit salon was full of energy. Hairdryers nearly drowned out the small talk clients shared as they were clipped and curled. After being toweled off, Cassie sat in front of a wall of mirrors. Perhaps someday Brian would tolerate the beauty parlor's stimulating sensations. In the meantime, they would keep visiting Charley—they had an appointment to see him after school.

Standing behind the chair, Brandy ran a comb through Cassie's hair. "Same cut as last time?"

"No, I thought I'd try some layers like the style in this magazine," Cassie replied, showing her stylist the page.

Brandy nodded. "Very trendy. I think that will look very nice with your face shape, and it will draw attention to your pretty eyes."

Cassie smiled at the compliment, admitting, "There's a special occasion this Saturday I want a new look for. A friend is having an engagement party."

Brandy's scissors began snipping away, lightening the weight of her previous length. "How nice," the hairdresser replied. "Have you known them for long?"

"I haven't met Jeff yet, but Beth and I went to college together." Cassie smiled pensively. "Funny, I hadn't seen my old friends for several years and now we seem to be getting together every couple of months."

Brandy agreed. "Yeah, it's like that with some of my friends, too. They drop out of sight and then when one gets engaged a chain reaction starts, one wedding after another."

Conversation casually slipped to ordinary current events but in the back of her mind Cassie wondered if marriage would ever be in the future for her. She continued pondering the likelihood while lunching at Roberto's. Several businessmen offered favorable smiles as she glanced about the restaurant. Pleased that her new hairstyle had been a wise choice, she timidly acknowledged them. Yet Cassie hesitated venturing into the dating world again. There was not time for flirting now anyway. Charley would be waiting for them.

After school Brian ran up the walk of an old Cape Cod-style house. They had come here every day for nearly two weeks. The gray-haired man held the door open with one hand while steadying himself on a cane with his other.

Brian stripped off his winter jacket letting it drop to the floor.

"Coat, Brian. Give me your coat." His mother held her hand out waiting for compliance. Promptly he exchanged it for the miniature Jeep she offered. "Good giving me your coat, Brian." To Charley she said, "I think today may be the day."

The old man smiled and placed a gentle hand on her shoulder before turning and following Brian, who was already tracing a familiar path down the hallway to the left. Charley opened the door to the addition which had been built a decade before Cassie was born. Though retired now, his tiny barbershop was still immaculate. On their first visit, Brian had cried just seeing the chair in the middle of the room. Charley had taken a container of lollypops off a shelf and placed a yellow candy from the jar on the chair. After Brian grabbed the treat they had left. The goal for the first day was just to get him into the room.

On following days, Charley got her son to briefly sit in the chair, then to hold a mirror and comb. His patience with her son was remarkable; Ginny's recommendation was definitely warranted.

Brain scampered onto the chair without hesitation, and Charley placed a candy within view on a nearby tray. "Haircut today, then lollypop," Charley said. The barber proceeded to skillfully trim the youngster's hair. At times Brian scrunched his shoulders up to his ears, and the old man calmly reassured him, reminding him of the prize for good sitting.

"See how nice you look." Charley held the mirror close. Brian just briefly looked at his reflection, more interested in the sweet treat his barber provided.

Cassie was pleasantly surprised how well it finally went. The old man had done a beautiful job despite Brian's occasional squirming. While driving home she longed to share this milestone with someone special. Amanda and Carl would have been so proud to see their grandson making progress. Cassie longed for encouraging words she'd never have the opportunity to hear, but took comfort in hopes that they hovered nearby.

As soon as they got home, she did the next best thing. Cradling the phone on her shoulder, Cassie filled Ginny in on all the details of Brian's first willing haircut.

Getting lost was just the beginning. A flat tire changed what should have been an early arrival to half an hour late. Beth's engagement party was in full swing when she opened the fire hall door. Beth's mother was the first to spot Cassie and raced to greet her. There was no mistaking Mrs. Franklin. Mother and daughter were but older and younger versions of each other.

Throwing hefty arms around her new guest, Maureen Franklin bubbled with excitement. "Cassie! It's so good to see you. I'm so glad you could make it, I hope the drive wasn't too long." Looking around she continued, "Where's your son? Beth said you have a little boy."

Recovering from the exuberant hug, Cassie smiled graciously. "Thank you so much for inviting me. The teaching assistant at Brian's school does respite so I left him with her."

Mrs. Franklin looked disappointed. "I'm sorry I don't get to meet him but at least this way you can relax and have fun. I can remember when my children were young; it was a rare treat to go out without them." Above the din she called across the room. "Beth! Beth, look who's here."

Mrs. Franklin swept away toward another arriving guest as Beth approached on the arm of what had to be Jeff, grinning from ear to ear. Cassie knew that many couples grew to resemble each other over time, but somehow these two already looked like they belonged together.

Beth hugged her friend then rolled her eyes as she gestured about the room. "Can you believe this? My mother went crazy decorating. I know we met and work on a cruise ship but I hope she doesn't think we are going to use this theme at the wedding, too!"

Balloons and streamers hung everywhere. Taped to the walls were giant cast posters from *The Love Boat* TV show. The official logo was lettered over a cruise ship picture strategically positioned above the buffet table.

No sooner had Beth introduced Jeff to Cassie then her mother beckoned the young couple to say hello to the minister. Unfamiliar with anyone else in sight Cassie prepared to fill a plate with food from the large spread. Behind the punch bowl a woman with obvious Down syndrome ladled drinks. Replacing empty salad bowls was a man with a noticeable twitch. A middle-age woman supervised these individuals plus two other employees.

Before finding a table to eat, Cassie approached the caterer. "It's so nice of you to let disabled people work for you," she said.

Glancing from side to side, the caterer seemed to note all her employees were out of earshot, then whispered back. "Nice? Nice has got nothing to do with it. Those two are my best workers. Caroline always has a smile on her face and Jamal asks for more work when he's finished what he's assigned. They're happy to be working for me and their performance far exceeds what I originally expected." Pointing to her other employees she continued. "But those guys, all I ever hear is complaints: their feet hurt, they'd rather be out partying with their friends."

Cassie was about to reply but her shoulder was jabbed from behind. Spinning around, instantly she was enveloped in a bear hug.

"Don't say hello or anything!" Angela playfully chided. "At least *you* came. Cindy is tied up in L.A. but promises she'll definitely make it to the wedding." Angela grabbed her by the elbow. "Bring your plate over. We've got a table in the other room."

Almost five years since they had been roommates and little had changed; Angela was still in charge. Cassie glanced back over her shoulder as her friend led. Already the caterer had resumed fussing over sterno-warmed trays as her employees went about their duties. Apparently this scene was nothing out of the ordinary, and that made Cassie smile.

Laughter and clinking glasses drew her attention to the small room where she was being led. Half a dozen tables were filled with couples eating, drinking, and socializing. As they entered a tall, dark-haired man rose from his seat. Angela kissed him then pulled Cassie to sit next to them.

"Finally you two get to meet," Angela said. "Cassie, this is Sam. Can you see why I had to drag him out to Chicago with me?"

Sam smiled affably. "It didn't take much to convince me. I wanted to check out the Windy City anyway. From the time I was little I always wanted to see a game at Wrigley Field. They've got the Bears for football and the Bulls for basketball." Angela nudged him. He winked then nonchalantly added, "Oh yeah, I guess being with Angela is okay, too."

She poked him again in response to his gentle teasing. "You should come visit us, Cassie," Angela added. "I could play tour guide, there's so much to do. You should see how beautiful the skyline looks at night on a moonlight cruise."

"It sounds wonderful." Cassie shrugged. "I don't know what I'd do about Brian, though. This is the first time I've left him and it's just overnight. I'm happy for the freedom but already I'm worried about how he's doing."

Angela hesitantly suggested, "Maybe you could bring him along." But quickly she changed the topic. "Well, Chicago is a great place but I must admit I'm jealous; Jeff picked a fabulous place to honeymoon."

Swallowing her mouthful of potato salad Cassie said, "Don't tell me they're taking a cruise!" She laughed, and Angela joined her.

"Believe it or not yes they are! They love life on the sea and when they're working there's not much time for sightseeing. Besides they've chosen ports of call they've never visited before." Angela nudged Sam and batted her eyes. "How romantic—Tahiti and Bora Bora!"

Cassie dreamily agreed. Pausing over a mouthful of honey baked ham, she recalled the aborted plans for a tropical vacation before her parents died. Such an adventure seemed doubtful now with her parenting responsibilities. Yet Ginny often cautioned her not to place limitations on the future.

Surveying the room while Angela babbled on, Cassie wistfully watched the many happy couples socializing. The empty chair beside her was cold, and no one would fill the seat unless she took some action. It was time to stop waiting on the sidelines for life to happen.

When Angela and Sam got up to dance, Cassie sought out one of the few obviously single men at the party. They danced and enjoyed the banter of casual small talk for the remainder of the evening. He lived nowhere near her, which meant she'd probably never see him again but at least she was back in the game.

"Ellen, you're here early," Ginny affably remarked while carrying the coffeemaker into the fellowship room. "What are you doing?"

The plump redhead was busy scribbling on some crumpled papers. With uncharacteristic curtness, she replied, "Filling out lottery and sweepstake entries."

Ginny filled the brewing reservoir and asked, "Cassie, would you set out the sugar and creamer for me?"

"Good God, what a waste of time," Maria snipped to Ellen while placing a plate of brownies next to the coffeemaker. "Lotteries! Gambling! I wonder how many people hoping to win some pie in the sky jackpot realize their chances of having an autistic child are a hell of a lot greater than the likelihood of them winning some damn lottery."

Ginny agreed as she arranged folding tray tables between chairs. "The estimate now is that one out of every one hundred and fifty children born today will be diagnosed on the autism spectrum."

Ellen curtly replied, "Well, I've got to do something to bring in some money." A tear slipped quietly down her cheek.

The rest of the women entered and began helping themselves to refreshments.

Softening her normal gruff demeanor, Maria sat beside her friend and with true concern asked, "What happened, Ellen? What's wrong?"

Barely above a whisper, Ellen whimpered, "I lost my job. I got fired."

"Why?" the women echoed in unison as they rushed to surround her.

Unable to retain her composure any longer Ellen sobbed uncontrollably while she answered. "My boss complained my performance was down; I've missed too may days lately. I couldn't help it. It seems like every time I turn around there's another doctor appointment or meeting at school over Danny. What could I do? I mean, my kid comes first, right?"

Ginny handed her a tissue. "What did Aaron say when he found out?"

Dabbing diluted mascara off her face, Ellen sniffled, "He thinks we'll manage all right on his salary if I clip more coupons and be a little more frugal. Aaron said not juggling work and Danny's care will be less stressful." Sighing heavily Ellen continued, "That all sounds well and good, but what am I going to do about the van? I don't know what I'll do if it breaks down again on I-95 on the way to the doctor. We'd planned on buying a new one next month."

"Try and cheer up," Cassie said as she put her arm around Ellen's shoulder. An idea was already forming in her mind. "You've always got such a sunny attitude; I just know things will work out for you. You'll see. Maybe one of those contest entries will pan out for you after all."

"I've filled out so many, I don't even remember the names of some the companies I've written to. I'm bound to win sometime," Ellen said as if trying to convince herself.

"Somehow, I'm sure you will," Cassie reassured. She made a mental note for Carlmanda Corp. to award a new minivan from their latest "contest."

"Listen, Ellen," Ginny offered. "If you're that worried about the van, let me know when the next doctor appointment is and I'll drive you."

"Yeah, I can help, too," Maria added. "You know you can count on all of us. Think positive; you'll get through this."

Ellen offered a watery smile. "Thanks. I really appreciate it."

"Come on, ladies," Ginny instructed in her customary take-charge voice. "Let's take our seats."

The sisterhood complied, but no one was sure of what to say next.

Finally Ellen let out a sigh. "I know I don't usually show it, but sometimes I feel so frustrated, like the world has taken a great big dump on me. I wish I could let it all out and just scream at somebody."

"Why don't you?" Maria asked.

"What?" Ellen stopped sniffling. Staring back at her friend, shock and confusion registered on her face.

Maria folded her arms and made a defiant suggestion. "Scream."

"At whom? Where?"

Calmly Maria insisted. "Here, now."

"You must be joking. I'd be so embarrassed."

Ginny prodded, "Go ahead; you're among friends. Maybe it will help to let it out."

"Yeah, go ahead," Tamika said. "We won't mind."

Timidly Ellen looked side to side at each of the ladies around her and then uttered a weak, "Ahhhhhh."

"That was pitiful," Maria complained. "You can do better than that."

"It just feels so weird with everybody looking at me."

"Why don't we join in?" Tamika suggested. "Haven't we all felt like yelling at the world from time to time?"

"Sure," Michelle replied, "but I'm not the sort of person to yell out loud. I don't know..."

Everyone turned to Ginny as she began to scream. Initially the volume was moderately loud, but then it ended with an operatic crescendo. Stunned silence greeted her outburst, followed by some giggles. Then each mother birthed emotions from deep within secret places, bursting free in acknowledgement of shared angst. The intensity of their screams masked the sounds of footsteps racing down the hall toward them. The door flew open to reveal Maureen's ashen face.

"What's wrong?" she exclaimed. "Is someone hurt?"

"No, no," Ginny stammered. She quickly recovered to reply, "We were just practicing some self-defense techniques I saw on a recent talk show. Sorry if we startled you. I guess I should have warned you. Everything is fine."

Relieved, Maureen retreated back down the hall to the classroom where the autistic youngsters were quieter and in more control than their mothers had seemed. After her departure, the group giggled.

"Well that was fun," Ginny said when the laughter had died down. "But something tells me it would be better to have tried this in a sound-proof room."

"Why don't we try it again," Sue suggested, "but this time do a silent scream."

Cassie exchanged a confused glance with Michelle. "What?"

"You know. Use all the emotion, but just not let any sound out. Or try to scream a whisper."

Once again they screamed out their frustrations. This time, however, it was barely audible. With the tension now released, the atmosphere of the rest of the meeting was much more relaxed.

"It's been a long time since we last got together," Michelle said. "How are things lately with James?"

"Much better, thanks for asking," Ginny replied. "The little bump up on his meds seems to have settled him back to normal." She laughed. "Normal—whatever the hell that is!"

"I'm so glad to hear he's doing better," Tamika affirmed. "Monisha has been doing pretty good too; she hasn't had any seizures. I think maybe we finally got the right med to keep that under control. My poor sweet girl, she is so pretty, such a good little child. It breaks my heart to see her muscles so tight and her spine twisted like an S. But she gives me the sweetest smiles."

Again Ginny took charge of the meeting. "Ladies, I hope you don't mind but I thought it would be a good idea if we shift the focus of the rest of this meeting to the fast approaching summer."

"Fast approaching summer?" Cassie incredulously asked. "You must be joking!"

"You'd be surprised," Michelle replied. "Without normal school routines, summer can be a trying time. The more advance planning you can do to minimize potential problems, the more enjoyable it can be for both you and your son."

The women talked about camps that catered to special needs children versus regular day camps with inclusion assistants. Then, they made plans for get-togethers with their children. A day trip to the seashore was carefully planned.

Ginny reviewed aloud notes she had prepared prior to their meeting. "We'll need to take turns supervising activities. Some kids will be playing in the sand while others want to wade in the water. We'll set up home base near the lifeguard stand at Third Avenue. James and Nate learned it was easy to spot the bike rentals on the boardwalk behind that stand from the water.

The beach is so wide open we don't want anyone getting lost, so make sure to point out those landmarks to your kids. And don't forget to bring plenty of sunscreen, everybody; we don't want them to get sunburned," Ginny warned.

"I don't know how I'm going to get any on Brian," Cassie complained. "He absolutely hates it. When I tried putting some on him last summer, he screamed at the top of his lungs."

"It's that damned 'tactile defensiveness' again isn't it?" Tamika asked. "Maybe you could start now getting him used to sunscreen before he really needs it on the beach day."

"How do you suggest I do that?" she asked.

Tamika advised, "Start with a small area like say, the backs of his hands or maybe just his forearms. Try every day at the same time—like when you're getting him dressed. Then, get him to tolerate a little more until eventually you get his whole body used to it."

Maria added, "Pablo hates to have me rub that oozy stuff on him, too. I squirt a little in the palm of his hand and then guide him to rub it on himself. Just don't expect miracles the first couple of times, but he'll get used to it. Do you think your son will tolerate the long drive to the beach?"

"Brian loves long rides in the car," Cassie replied, "but just to be sure, why don't we plan on a stop at Lighthouse Diner? It's a little more than halfway there. A quick coffee for us and some of their famous pastries will give the kids a break."

"Sounds good to me," Kari added. "But what'll we do if it rains that day? Todd will keep checking his calendar once I tell him about our trip. If we have to cancel for rain, he'll tantrum all day."

Michelle offered, "Why don't you just write 'outing' on the calendar? If it rains we can take the kids to the movies instead."

Rose said, "Let's plan another outing, too. That way if it rains the first date, we'll go to the shore on the second."

Cassie frowned. "I'm not sure Brian will sit for a movie; I've never taken him to one."

"Don't worry," Ginny said. "First of all, we'll pick a short kid movie. Just remember to take along plenty of reinforcers to keep him busy if he gets a little bored. And buy some snacks to eat during the movie. If he gets too fussy you can leave early. The next time you take him to a movie he may last a little longer."

"What about a trip to the zoo?" Cassie suggested hesitantly.

"Danny hates the zoo," Ellen said. "I think the smells get to him. He is pretty good about noises now but smells bother him: that's his sensory issue right now."

Tamika asked Sue, "Do you think Kevin would bring Timmy if we planned a trip to Longacre State Park? You're due in the summer and that would give you and the new baby a little time to yourselves. Longacre has a really nice kiddy pool."

"I'm sure he would." Sue smiled widely then looked down, gently rubbing her belly. "I'm starting to get excited about the new baby now. We've set up a changing table in the nursery and started having Timmy practice being a big brother."

"How have you done that?" Cassie asked.

"Well, we bought a lifelike doll. I take Timmy into the nursery and have him give me a baby wipe and then a paper diaper. He helps me dress the doll and then I hold the 'baby' for a while before putting it in the crib. I even turn on a tape recording of a baby crying sometimes to get him used to the sound. He is doing pretty well with our practice sessions so far. My neighbor three doors down had a new baby, and I asked if she would come over so he will get used to a real baby being in our house, too."

The conversation became more and more chaotic as each woman enthusiastically shared recent triumphs and ideas for summer plans. Confident that her viewpoint was valued, Cassie actively participated adding some ideas of her own. With a thrill of anticipation she hadn't felt in a long time, she had a feeling it was going to be a wonderful summer.

Chapter 18.

Those busy winter days spun into an equally busy spring. Cassie treasured every little success without allowing worries about the distant future to intrude. Instead, conscious of potential problem areas, she planned according to Brian's abilities. Life was improving in ways far beyond what her day at the river would have let her believe. Perhaps the friendships that had grown deeper with each passing month had inspired her bright outlook on life.

"Cassie! What a pretty outfit!" Ginny welcomed her friend, pushing her door open wide. "I'm so glad you could come over for lunch. It's so unusual to have such warm weather that I just had to set everything up outside. I hope you don't mind my selection of rabbit food."

Artfully displayed on Ginny's back deck was a beautiful feast intended for the two of them.

"It looks delicious," Cassie exclaimed. "You must have spent hours putting this spread together. I'm honored that you went to so much trouble. I wouldn't call it rabbit food, but what is it?"

Ginny pointed to one dish proudly. "That's a spinach and artichoke dip with low-fat yogurt. I absolutely love it on the raw carrots and cucumbers."

"I was hesitant to say anything at our last meeting, but I thought you looked like you've lost some weight. It's obvious now. When did you go on a diet? How are you doing it?"

Ginny pulled out a chair and gestured toward the table. "Come on and sit down, Cassie. Help yourself. We can eat while we talk. In fact, if I talk enough in between bites, maybe I won't have time to eat too much." She laughed. "It's not so much of a diet as it is a mindset, really. You see, I was getting my daily dose of Oprah about two months ago while I was folding laundry, and I heard something that clicked for me."

Cassie popped a tuna salad tea sandwich into her mouth then loaded her plate with fresh vegetables, dip, apple slices, and grapes.

Ginny poured iced tea into a large tumbler for her guest and water for herself, plunking a lemon slice in each. "When summer rolls around I put sprigs of mint in my water, anything to liven up the flavor of plain water. I grow the mint in a large planter by my kitchen door. You have to be careful, though, about planting mint in your garden; it'll take over an entire flower bed if you're not careful."

Handing Cassie her drink, she settled her self into a chair opposite her. "Anyway, as I was saying, I heard one of Oprah's guests saying something like 'most people would never think of continually breaking promises to their best friend but we do it all the time to ourselves; we do it every time we promise ourselves to lose weight and then don't.' That got me to thinking how right she was and of how in some bizarre way as a child I got fat trying to think of others and not myself."

"What do you mean?"

Ginny smiled ironically as her thoughts turned to her childhood. "I can remember my mother admonishing me for not finishing my dinner. She would say, 'Virginia! Don't you know there are starving children in India?' Of course, as an adult I realized that what she meant was that I should be grateful that I have plenty to eat; I shouldn't take more food than I can eat and then waste it. But as a child I thought that by inhaling every last morsel from my plate I was somehow helping a starving child in India to eat. Silly isn't it, but it's funny the way a child's mind works."

She paused long enough to crunch a carrot while Cassie slathered some dip onto a wedge of red pepper.

"I got fatter and fatter helping that poor Indian child. By the time my own kids were born, I had been on and off so many diets that I couldn't keep track of them all. Making matters worse, over the years I've gone through the pity poor me for what I have to deal with—with James' autism, that is. I would tell myself I deserved something nice for having to be so strong to handle the trauma of raising a child with autism. I'd reward myself, be good to myself, by eating things that would make me feel good. Chocolate cheesecake was my favorite."

Ginny grinned ruefully and took a sip of her ice water. "I'm always trying to help others like the women in our support group. But it finally dawned on me how important my own health is if I want to keep helping others. I need to keep that promise to myself of losing weight."

Cassie shook her head. "You're amazing."

Ginny waved her hand dismissively. "No, I'm not. I'm just a human being like anybody else. Sometimes in the midst of adversity I fall and there are other times I fly. The best any of us can hope for is that we fly more times than we fall. And if we do fall, we get right up and try to fly again."

"Okay, Ms. Human Being, so you're not superhuman. Still, you look great. Have you been following any specific diet to lose the weight?"

Ginny shook her head. "I'm old enough that I've heard endless suggestions over the years and I've just kind of incorporated all those tips into my own system. I don't count calories but I'm aware of portion sizes and making healthy choices. I drink lots of water and I try to avoid unconscious eating while watching television. Most of all I try to get away from the buffet syndrome."

Cassie gave her a puzzled look over a mouthful of tuna sandwich. "What?"

"Well, have you ever been to a buffet and piled your plate with a huge variety of things, only to discover that you really like one of those things a whole lot, in fact so much that you go back for seconds?"

"Yeah, I guess so."

"I would feel guilty about wasting food so I felt that I had to finish what was on my plate. Then I'd go and get more of what I was really enjoying. Sometimes I would be thinking about going back for more while I still had plenty of what I wanted on my plate. Now I remind myself to take reasonable portions and not go back for seconds at all. If there is something I really enjoy, I slowly savor every morsel because I know when it's done, that's it; there is no returning for seconds. Hmm, come to think of it, kind of like how we should go through life: savor every moment because when it's done we can't return to it."

"Ginny, you seem to have a life lesson in everything, don't you," Cassie laughed.

"I try," she giggled back. "You know, you're looking pretty good yourself; you look more rested. Are things better at home?"

"Yes, actually. Ever since having Brian at school, there's been so much more time for me during the day. Then I have more energy for him when he gets home. His teacher has been really good about giving me suggestions on ways to work with him. It took me a while in the beginning to discipline myself to daily write in the communication book, but it's been well worth it. Looking back it's amazing how far we both have come."

Ginny sat back in her chair and cocked her head to the side closely examining her. "I sense there is more to this, though. What else have you been up to?"

"Well, I finally took your advice about needing to focus on more than just Brian and autism. I joined a gym. I work out every morning after the school bus comes or just before lunch."

"Really? That's great. Which one did you join?"

"I thought about joining Dancing Divas but decided against it. On the one hand, it would be more comfortable getting back in shape among other women, but like you said, I need more of a social life. So I figured a coed gym like Sweetwater Athletic Club would be more conducive to meeting a few men."

Ginny nodded in agreement. "Smart thinking, cookie. How's it working out?"

Cassie modestly giggled, "I guess I'm not in as bad shape as I thought. Some guys that work out during their lunch hour have tried to pick me up and there is this one guy who works night shift that's been eyeing me."

"So, have you gone on a date with any of them yet?"

"I'm supposed to meet Ted Harrison for lunch tomorrow. I'm a bit hesitant, though."

Mumbling through a mouthful, Ginny asked, "Why? Is he all brawn and no brain?"

"No," Cassie laughed. "It's not that. I kind of like him."

"But?"

"I'm afraid that he'll bolt for the door when he finds out about Brian."

"There are lots of single women with children in the dating scene nowadays, Cassie," Ginny admonished.

"Ginny, you know it's more than that. Guys might be willing to pursue a relationship with a woman that has a kid, but an autistic child—that's another story."

Ginny sighed. "I know, Cass. I guess I'm lucky; Sam and I had a pretty strong relationship by the time James was born. It was tough on him, but he was committed to me already when James came along."

"I just don't know what to do," Cassie admitted. "I mean, I don't want to lie to him, but I don't want to scare him off either by announcing first thing on the date that I've got an autistic kid. What do I do?"

Shaking her head Ginny replied. "I don't know, sweetie. Last time I gave you advice in that area it didn't work out too well. I guess if it were me, I would wait until there was some way to naturally work it into the conversation."

"On the first date?"

"Cassie, only you are going to know when it's the right time to bring it up. I'm afraid I can't help you here. I wish I could."

Cassie sighed. "That's okay. Do me a favor, though, and don't mention this at support group. I appreciate talking this over with you, but I'm not sure if I'm ready for a whole brood of mother hens giving advice about my love life. Let me be the one to bring it up if I change my mind."

"Sure thing, hon." Ginny took another bite of cucumber as she slid a copy of the latest gossip magazine across the table toward Cassie. "Well on a totally different topic...Did you see what Rita Ventina wore to the award show?"

Primping for dates used to come so naturally for Cassie—before Brian was born, that is. Now, somehow she couldn't decide on the right outfit to wear for her luncheon date. The question was how to look stunning but appropriate for daytime, stylish yet not snooty, available but not desperate. Finally, after an hour of trying on practically everything in her closet and then discarding the outfits on her bed, she settled on a simple straight black skirt paired with a black and white striped satin blouse.

As she had chosen to err on the side of formality, the customers already seated by the massive bar could easily have mistaken her for a woman meeting a client for a business luncheon. She checked herself in the bar's mirror while she waited for the seating hostess to check if Ted was already at the table he reserved.

Cassie had heard the food at Stingers restaurant was popular with the business crowd, but the fact that it was situated on the first floor of a hotel gave Cassie an uneasy feeling. She feared Ted might attempt to rush her into something physical before any relationship existed. It had been so long since she was with a man that she wanted to take her time. In fact, on second thought, she had never been with a man; they had been boys—not mature at all. That much was clear to her now. Even she had to admit to her own immaturity back then. So easily, in the moonlight on that birthday, she had been swept away by idealistic romance. But like it or not, she had been forced to grow up fast. Determined not to repeat the mistake of letting emotions and hormones dictate her actions, she had an easy excuse to escape if needed: business.

Still, the proximity of hotel rooms made her nervous. At least she had been wise enough to request their first date be a luncheon.

The hostess ushered Cassandra to the table where Ted rose politely as she approached. "Cassie! You look fantastic," he said as he greeted her with a friendly kiss on the cheek. "What time do you have to be back at work?" he asked, making assumptions from her attire.

"Not until two, I have a meeting with a client," she lied. He pulled her chair out for her then sat across from her. "Where do you work? We never really had much of a chance to talk about work at the gym."

Cassie opened her menu so she could feign interest in food choices while reciting her rehearsed lie. "I work for Carlmanda Corporation. It's a small private investing firm."

"I've never heard of it before. Where about is it?"

Her eyes remained fixed on descriptions of the day's specials. "Oh, the main office is in New York and I have to commute several times a month, but mostly I make calls from home and visit local clients. It's a convenient arrangement really." Glancing up from the menu to assess his reaction to her fib, she noticed Ted sizing her up. Uncomfortable at having her measurements estimated by his eyes, she quickly returned her gaze to the menu.

"Investment firm, huh? You got any good tips for me?"

"I'm sorry, Ted, my boss is very strict about not sharing any information."

He flashed a confident smirk. "Come on, Cassie. What's the harm? How's he to know?"

She squirmed under the pressure from his gaze and his questions. "Gee, I'm really sorry, but this is a very firm rule. You know how nervous people are about accusations of insider trading and such. Even the most innocent remarks can be misconstrued."

Ted shrugged his shoulders. "Hey, lighten up; I'm not out to make you lose your job. Still, maybe once we get to know each other a little better, you can advise me where to stick my... money."

His lame attempt at humorous innuendo felt sleazy. Anxious to change the subject, yet pleased he apparently accepted her fabricated story, she asked, "What's good here?"

"You've never been here?"

"Can't say that I have."

Ted hadn't even opened his menu. "Oh, I come here all the time usually before heading in to work in the evening. It's pretty quiet Monday through Thursday nights but I avoid it like the plague on Friday and Saturday. Anyway, I really like their southwest chicken sandwich, but you might want to try the New York Reuben to see how it compares to the real thing."

"Huh?"

"You know. With all your trips to New York you must have had plenty of Reubens."

Cassie felt blood rush to her cheeks in response to a flaw in her cover story. Quickly recovering she said, "Oh, yeah right, well to tell you the truth I've been trying to watch my weight lately. How are their salads?"

Ted waved his hand in a dismissive gesture. "I don't know. I never much went in for them. You girls! You're always on some kind of diet."

"Well, I've been working really hard to get the last few pounds off."

With pen in hand the waitress interrupted, "Can I get you something to drink from the bar while you decide, or have you folks already made up your minds?"

"I'll have the New York Reuben," Ted responded. Then to Cassie he added, "That way you can try a bite of mine to compare with past experience."

Cassie seriously regretted mentioning New York. Hopefully, he would let it drop. What if he began asking questions about different places there? And his comment should have referred to food, but somehow his offer sounded lewd. What had seemed a playful jesting attitude in the gym now felt a bit lecherous.

Second thoughts about this man prompted Cassie's decision to work motherhood into the conversation sooner rather than later. "I'll have the chef salad with light Italian dressing on the side."

To the waitress Ted said, "Now look at her; does she look like she needs to diet?"

Seizing the opportunity, Cassie responded, "It's just that

I've never been able to lose those last ten pounds after the baby was born."

Before Ted could do more than raise his eyebrows in surprise, the waitress replied, "Tell me about it! I've got three kids; I've given up on ever wearing a size ten again. I stayed up a size after each one." She looked down at her order form. "You want anything to drink?"

"Just ice water, please," Cassie answered.

Ted ordered a J&B on the rocks. After the waitress left, he jumped right in. "You've got a kid?"

Anticipating that he would want to rush through lunch after this revelation, Cassie proceeded to tell him. "I have a little boy; his name is Brian. He..."

"I never would have guessed," Ted interrupted. "You don't look like...oh, hell what's someone who is a mother supposed to look like? But, well hey, that's no problem. I've got a boy, too. How old is yours?"

Stunned to think that she was not the only one with a past, Cassie stammered, "Umm three and a half, well no, I guess he's a little closer to four now."

"Matt is five," Ted offered. "Back in college I got my girlfriend knocked, um...I mean, pregnant. She wanted to keep it. We didn't get married or anything but I still try to do right by her. Her mom watches him mostly when he's not in preschool. With me being on the night shift at the hospital, I help out when I can. I take him on the weekends to Bennett Park and play catch. You should see the arm that little kid's got. Hey, I've got an idea. Why don't you bring Brian to the park on Saturday?"

Ted's image had vastly improved in the last few minutes. He beamed while talking about his son. Perhaps she should give him a chance. She may have misjudged some of his earlier comments, but if that were the case, meeting Brian so soon might be disastrous. "I don't know, Ted. I'm not so sure that's a good idea. You see..."

"Nonsense, I'm great with little kids," he interrupted.

"You'll see. Give me a chance. I won't take no for an answer. Ten o'clock, Bennett Park, behind left field near the swings."

Against her better judgment, Cassie agreed. Before she had a chance to explain any further, Ted insisted that they save any more talking about their kids until Saturday morning; now was time to get to know each other. The rest of the date was devoted to talk of how long each had lived in Sweetwater, where they grew up, and the typical, superficial, personal history that people are inclined to divulge on a first date.

Brilliant sunshine and a cloudless morning on Saturday negated any possible weather excuse. There was no way to avoid taking Brian to meet Ted. The rest of their date had gone rather well, but somehow Cassie had been unable to naturally work autism into their conversation. If a relationship was to progress, at some point she would have to let Ted know, but she wished she could have delayed the inevitable. It was going to be difficult to keep an eye on her speeding bullet while explaining the situation.

"Brian, we are going bye-bye after I finish packing this bag. Let's see, do we have everything?" Nervously she repacked the backpack checking to be certain she had enough of each item. Three juice boxes, a container of Cheerios, the colored liquid timer, M&Ms, and a change of clothes were jammed in with an assortment prepared for any contingency. "Have I forgotten anything? No? Okay, let's go."

Brian attempted to scoop all his toy cars into his arms, creating his version of a traveling security blanket.

"No, Brian. You may take just one—like this." Cassie demonstrated by placing all but one car back into his bucket.

Throwing himself and the car to the ground he began to tantrum, kicking his feet and flailing his arms.

"Brian, we are going," Cassie said firmly but calmly. It was a struggle to remain composed in the midst of tantrums, but his teacher stressed that sometimes bad behaviors increased if you gave a dramatic reaction. Also, giving in to him might be easier in the moment, but it was confusing if she was firm one time and gave in the next. In the future Brian might think the way to get what he wanted was to scream louder and longer.

"Take *one* car," Cassie said as she gently molded his hand around the Camry.

He threw it down again and clawed at his entire pile of vehicles. Once more Cassie gently pried his fingers free of the fleet. He struggled and grabbed the old yellow school bus. Since starting school, that was now his favorite vehicle. Before he had a chance to reach for more she took his other hand, grabbed the backpack, and led him to the kitchen.

"Good, Brian. Now you have one. One. That is good listening to Mommy. Here, have an animal cracker." Hoisting him onto her left hip while he munched, she thrust a handful of extra crackers into her pocket.

Brian's tantrum vanished as quickly as it had begun, and the ride to the park was surprisingly smooth. Near the swings, Cassie spotted Ted playing catch with a child who was obviously his son. Darting from the parking lot across the softball field to the playground beyond, Brian was oblivious to the fact that he had just scampered through a Little League practice. Skirting the edge of the playing field so as not to further disrupt game play, Cassie caught up to her son as he pushed past Ted to climb the sliding board.

Somewhat startled, with a laugh Ted asked, "That's Brian?"

Cassie was a little embarrassed. "Yes. I'm sorry for his rudeness. I try and teach him better manners but it takes lots of repetition before he understands certain concepts."

Ted continued tossing the ball back and forth to his son as he answered. "I know—Matt here is the same way. I get blue in the face correcting him sometimes, but that's the only way kids learn."

"No," Cassie countered. "It's not quite the same with Brian; he needs even more repetition than most kids. You see, he's autistic."

"Artistic?" Ted's brow wrinkled. "My best friend's kid is

pretty artistic too. They can be a little temperamental, but talented or not, you've still got to teach them manners." The softball whizzed back to Ted. He seemed not to notice Cassie's frustration.

"No, you heard me wrong. He's not artistic; he's autistic."

Keeping the volley going with his own son, Ted casually replied, "Autistic? Oh, I think I remember reading an article about that once. He sits in a corner and rocks back and forth all day?"

"No, Ted, I think you can see Brian is really active." Cassie directed Ted's attention to her son going down the sliding board for the fifth time since they began talking.

Ted frowned and stopped throwing the ball for a moment. "Hmm, he's not like the kid in the article I read. Are you sure the doctors got it right? Maybe he's not autistic."

"Yes, I'm sure." Cassie acknowledged. "There is more than one way that children with autism act. Some are very withdrawn while others like Brian are very active, but most have trouble understanding what is socially appropriate."

Matt stared as Brian slid down yet again. With confidence Ted took charge. "Well, Cassie, maybe he just needs a man around to show him what to do. I mean, you being a single mom and all. Bring him over here. Matt and I will play catch with him; I've got an extra glove with me."

"He doesn't know how to play catch," Cassie objected.

Ted sounded impatient. "Come on, Cassie. I told you I'm good with little kids. Easy as pie he'll be tossing the old ball around with us in no time." To his son, who was gesturing for his dad to resume throwing the ball, Ted said, "Hold up, Matt. Let me get Brian here to join us."

Reluctantly Cassie retrieved her son, and Ted positioned him about ten feet away from his own son. When he pried the yellow school bus from the child's hand and set it by his feet. Brian reached down to retrieve his security toy.

"No," Ted said, again prying the toy out of the boy's grip, "you need both hands free to catch."

Brian picked up the vehicle again. Once more the bus was freed then placed at his feet. "We'll make this easy for you, kid," Ted said as he backed up to form the third position of a triangle. "Okay, Matt, toss it over easy."

Gently sailing at Brian, the ball hit him in the chest.

Ted rushed over. "No, kid, like this; hold your hands like this." Ted positioned Brian's hands ready to catch then picked up the ball, backed up, and tossed it to Brian. Brian stood with his hands still open ready to receive the ball as it again hit him in the chest then dropped to the ground.

"Come on," Ted encouraged doggedly. "You've got to close your hands around the ball when it comes close to you." Again the ball hit Brian in the chest and rolled to the ground.

Ted was growing obviously impatient. "Brian, pay attention. Look at the ball and close your hands around it when it comes close to you."

Cassie had to interrupt. "He doesn't seem to understand, Ted," she objected. "The ball keeps hitting him. Why don't you just keep playing with your son and let Brian play on the slide?"

Ted didn't look at her. "Nonsense. He'll get the hang of it; he just needs to toughen up a little and pay attention." Turning again to the child he yelled, "Brian, watch the ball."

Brian did just that; he watched as the ball came at him and again hit his chest and rolled to the ground. This time, Brian bent over, picked up the ball in one hand, his yellow school bus in the other, and then he ran across the clearing behind the playground at top speed.

Sensing potential danger as her child headed toward the road, motherly adrenalin propelled Cassie with a velocity she hadn't known she possessed. Snatching her child out of danger a split second before he reached the road, she gulped for air. Difficult as it was to catch her breath, the cause of her trembling was emotional, not physical. Once more, she recognized, her son had been moments away from ceasing to exist. Not so long ago, brief insanity by the river's edge had welcomed the concept of such freedom. Not now, though. Thoughts of losing Brian terrified her.

Ted raced up behind her with Matt trailing behind. "Are you guys all right?" he asked.

"Yes, but I think I've had enough excitement for one morning. I better take him home. I'll see you at the gym on Monday." Without waiting for his reply, she turned and left.

But on Monday when Cassie waved hello to Ted, who was chatting with some of the other men that usually watched her every move, uncomfortable nervous smiles were her only acknowledgement before their eyes quickly darted away. Surmising that she and her son had been the topic of conversation, Cassie proceeded to the far side of the gymnasium to commence her workout.

Palpable tension stifled the air in the health club on her two subsequent visits. Every male shot glances in her direction but averted their eyes when she returned their gaze.

The following week Cassie canceled her membership and joined Dancing Divas.

Ellen bounded into the fellowship room of St. Vincent's. "Oh my God, girls, you are not going to believe it." She took one deep breath and then bubbled, "I had the absolute best month of my entire life. I never would have guessed there would be such a dramatic difference this month. You just never know; one minute you're down in the dumps and the next everything turns around. Out of the clear blue something totally unexpected occurs and—"

"All right already!" Tamika urged. "What gives, what happened?"

"Well, you know how I'm always entering all those contests and lotteries?"

Kari and Tamika both groaned. "Duh! Of course."

"Well one of them actually paid off and I can't even remember entering this one."

"So, what did you get? Don't keep us guessing," Kari insisted with excitement for her friend.

"Come on out to the parking lot and I'll show you."

Kari, Tamika, Ginny, and Cassie hustled to keep up with their excited friend. In the parking lot, they were joined by Sue and Rose who were just arriving.

"What's going on?" Rose asked.

"I won this!" Ellen beamed, pointing to a brand new minivan. "Look at all the features this thing has. There's a power lift gate and a power sunroof. It's got a GPS navigation system and best of all there's a DVD player to help keep Danny occupied while I'm driving. Wow! Isn't it great?"

"It sure is." Maria agreed as she helped Carlos out of her own car. "Where'd you get it?"

"Well, I think it was an orange juice coupon—the kind with an automatic contest entry when you redeem the coupon."

"You mean you don't even know for sure?" Ginny asked incredulously.

"Well, I think that's what it was. The letter arrived by special delivery from a Carlmanda Corporation. There was a lot of legal gobbledygook; I had a hard time making sense of it. But the letter said to go to Bright Star Motors to pick it up. When I got there the salesman said it was paid for free and clear; even the taxes on it were paid for! I still have to pinch myself. Look at this color; the salesman said it's called Inferno Red!"

Ellen demonstrated the vehicle's various features like a game show model. With admiration, the ladies examined her gleaming prize. They opened every nook and cranny as they oohed and ahhed.

Cassie couldn't help but notice that Ginny seemed distracted. "Carlmanda," her friend mumbled under her breath. "Now where do I recognize that name from?"

Cassie anxiously looked away. Perhaps she shouldn't overuse that name, but giving to others in her parents' names gave her such a peaceful feeling.

Finally Ginny convinced the group to go inside for coffee. Once seated, she opened up the discussion by asking if anyone else had something special to share.

"I do," Michelle offered. "I'm afraid my story is not as spectacular as winning a new car, but I saw an interesting story on the local news last night,"

"What was it?" Rose asked.

"Remember we met Gary Spenser's sister at the state chapter meeting last April?"

"Who's Gary Spenser?" Cassie asked.

"He's a Major League player with Atlanta—outfielder, I think," Ellen answered. "Anyway, his sister's little boy was on the local news last night. They were doing a story on the rise in diagnosis of autism and they showed Catherine's three-year-old. He's so cute; those big brown eyes just melt your heart."

Maria crossed her arms. "I wish they wouldn't do that," she grumbled.

"Who? What?" Kari asked.

"The news media," Maria answered. "They always focus on *celebrities* who have relatives with autism—like the rest of us don't matter."

"That doesn't bother me so much," Ginny countered. "I mean if famous people can raise autism awareness, so much the better. But what does bother me is that every time they do a story on autism, they show a toddler and talk about children with autism."

"What's your point?" Tamika asked.

"Well, it's just that children grow up and become adults. The media rarely focuses on them. You ask any passerby on the street; if they know anything at all about adults with autism, most likely they'll mention *Rain Man*. I don't want to complain too much, most people had never heard of autism before they saw that movie. But it was made nearly twenty years ago and ends with him returning to the institution. There are so many different possibilities for adults with autism now. Most can have a job and live in the community if they get special supports. But government services for adults aren't guaranteed and can be expensive with long waiting lists." Ginny sighed. "I don't think James will ever be able to live on his own and I just can't see him living with me when I'm eighty."

"Gee, Ginny," Ellen complained. "I was all upbeat about my new van and hearing about that news story until you brought me down."

"I'm sorry. It's just that James is turning fifteen and I'm starting to focus on the future. The more I look into it, the more the bureaucracy seems like a tangled, knotted web." Dismissing her look of concern, she replaced it with a pleasant smile. "Oh, enough about that, I really am very happy for your good fortune, Ellen." She glanced over at Cassie. "You've been awfully quiet today; did I bring you down, too?"

"No, it wasn't you," Cassie replied. "I've just been thinking that even though we have so many problems to face with our special children, our kids have brought us together; you're all my family now. I only wish...I wish...well, I thought by this point in my life I'd have a 'soul mate' and things just haven't..."

"Cassie," Ellen interrupted, "I've been waiting for an opportunity to tell you about my neighbor's brother! We'll have to arrange a chance opportunity for you to run into him."

Tamika shook her head. "Ellen, you're a lousy matchmaker," she chided. "Remember the jerk you tried to fix Rose up with after her husband left? Don't listen to her, Cassie, and don't worry; you'll meet someone. You'll see; it will be when you least expect it."

"She's right," Maria added. "Such a pretty girl like you, you'll meet the right guy; just give it time."

Cassie smiled, appreciative of her friends' optimism. "I hope you're right, but sometimes I just don't know. Brian does tend to put guys off once they see what he's like."

"Maybe that's actually good," Sue suggested. "He can help you weed out the losers that are too superficial to handle rough spots in a relationship. Sometimes I complain about my husband Kevin, but he is really being so supportive in all my ups and downs with this pregnancy. He's worried just like I am; still he reassures me everything will be all right. You'll find someone like that, too, Cassie, and so will you, Rose."

Ginny asked, "How are things in that department for you, Rose, if you don't mind my asking?"

"Oh, pretty good actually," Rose replied, blushing a little. "I met someone at a single parents' social in Sandalwood. We hit it off and went on a couple of dates before I met his five-year-old daughter. Then I introduced him to Dennis. We're taking both of the kids to the zoo on Saturday."

"Wait a minute," Tamika laughed. "He met your little whirlwind and he still wants to go out with you? Sounds like a keeper to me; hold on tight, girl! Hey, Cassie, why don't you try going to one of those socials? It sounds like it might be a nice place to meet a guy for you as well."

Kari objected, "The only problem with that is the only men there would be parents, too. I don't think if I were in Cassie's position I would want someone that has their own kids as well. If a relationship developed, well, I mean she's got Brian and then to take on other kids, too?"

"That's a double standard, don't you think?" Rose asked. "We want to have a relationship with someone willing to be accepting of our kids so it's not unreasonable for us to need to do the same." Rose turned to Cassie. "Would you like me to let you know when the next single parents social is?"

"Um, well, I guess maybe," Cassie replied. She was skeptical but at the same time hopeful she'd have more success there than at the gym.

"Okay, it's settled. I'll check my calendar when I get home and give you a call."

Rose followed through with information on the single parents socials. Alternating employment of Chris, Vicky, and Maureen allowed Cassie to date without too much fear Brian would demolish the house while she was out. She managed to connect with a few men that interested her. Still, no one lasted more than a few dates before information about her son's disability caused phone calls not to be returned. Disappointed

but not depressed, she planned to attend a few more socials —
determined to not give up.

Chapter 19.

Like overheated molecules confined in too small a space, six women frenetically bounced from one end of the fellowship room to the other. Instead of arranging chairs in the usual circle, they formed a semi-circle facing a large pink and blue decorated table laden with wrapped boxes in all shapes and sizes. Ellen wobbled as she perched atop a step stool trying to fasten more streamers from the ceiling to the table. Tamika placed a frilly lace umbrella next to the seat of honor while Kari arranged baby rubber duckies around a mama duck centered on the gift table. Helium balloons were anchored at varying heights to each chair by curly ribbon streamers. Whenever one of the ladies rushed by, they danced wildly in place.

Careful not to disturb Kari's arrangement, Rose artfully intertwined more curled ribbon through the pile of presents. Maria poured chips and pretzels into bowls as Ginny flitted back and forth, adjusting little details throughout the room.

Cassie and Michelle entered the room carrying a large sheet cake. They pushed aside other goodies on the dessert table to make room for it.

Michelle exclaimed, "What time will Sue be here?"

"In a half-hour," Maria answered. "What took you so long? We'd better hurry and finish. Her husband took her to his cousin's to borrow their bassinet and then they're coming straight here."

"Do me a favor and get the juice from the kitchen refrigerator, will you?" Ginny asked her. "And tell Vicky to give Sue five or ten minutes after she arrives to see how everything is decorated before they bring the kids down."

Cassie asked, "Does Sue have any family to help out after the baby is born?"

Ginny replied, "Her mother is going to fly in but she can only stay for two weeks."

"A new baby! It's so exciting," Ellen bubbled. "Still, it's going to be quite an adjustment for Timmy. Even with all their preparations, he'll probably act out demanding attention for himself."

"They're going to have their hands full," Tamika agreed. "Maybe we could chip in and offer to pay for a several hours of respite once Sue's mom goes home."

"I like that idea. I'll volunteer to be in charge of the finances for the group," Cassie offered. "Let me know what you want to chip in and I'll make the arrangements."

At the appointed time, Sue's arrival was greeted by cheerfully loud calls of "Surprise!" and handfuls of colorful confetti.

"Oh my goodness, I can't believe it!" Sue's shocked expression was genuine. "I certainly was not expecting another shower! Kevin's cousin Susan threw me a shower two weeks ago. We were just over there to pick up—"

"We know," Maria interrupted. "She called after you left to say you were on your way. And she called Ginny after the shower she gave you to let us know what you already got."

"You guys are so devious," Sue exclaimed, laughing.

Within a few minutes, the college girls marched eager children into the fellowship room and over to the dessert table. With full plates, they returned to enjoy their treats back in the primary room. Sue began daintily opening her presents.

"We'll be here all night if you keep unwrapping that way! Just tear into them," Maria urged. "Do we need to bring Timmy back here to show you how it's done? Come on, let loose!"

Sue happily complied. In rapid succession she revealed a car seat, diaper bag, and nursery monitor. Several boxes overflowed with crib sheets, hooded towels, and warm, cozy blankets. Packages with adorable outfits for the infant were greeted by oohs and ahhs.

After the last box had been opened and Sue had profusely thanked everyone, Cassie took her aside and nonchalantly whispered, "There's another box in the corner. It's just some things that Brian outgrew and I held onto for some reason. He grew so fast he didn't have time to wear them out. There are a few girl things that I'd been given and never took the time to return. Maybe if you have a girl you can use them. And if there's anything else you didn't get, before you go out and buy it, give me a call to see if I still have one packed up in my basement."

When Sue would eventually go through the box from Cassie, she would find hundreds of dollars worth of attire for sizes infant through twenty-four months. In secret, Cassie had gleefully spent hours picking out beautiful new baby clothes. With great care she had removed all stickers and price tags before washing each item once. That is, except for the irresistible, miniature dresses; they were left unwashed with the size stickers still attached. After all, she could not pretend they had been used.

On her way home from the shower, Cassie squeezed in a quick stop at the supermarket. Brian had eaten the last of his favorite cereal and if it were not replenished by morning, a full-blown tantrum was likely to erupt. Cassie hoped her son would be good for just a little while longer before heading home.

Preston Market had become a familiar location for outings since Brian started school. Initially grocery trips were short. Gradually as he became more accustomed to the routine, she had increased his time shopping while he usually played happily with his liquid timer. Eventually he would be taught to help locate items by using pictures from advertisements, coupons, and written lists.

Before venturing off to locate the few items on this evening's list, cravings for seafood salad sent Cassie to the deli counter. With care, she parked the cart out of arm's reach from the stacks of freshly baked bread and bagged rolls lining the lunchmeat counter. Deciding to further occupy her son while she shopped, Cassie gave Brian a store-baked doughnut with chocolate frosting. To remind herself to pay for the treat, she tossed an empty bakery bag into her cart.

Rubber-banded lobsters in the tank adjacent to the seafood counter caught the toddler's attention. More correctly, it was not the bobbing crustaceans he stared at but the bubbles floating to the surface from the filtration system. Brian strained to climb out of the shopping cart's restraint to gain a closer look. Content her son would be occupied, Cassie lifted him down while waiting for her salad. He pressed his face to the glass.

"Excuse me, ma'am." A hair-netted woman from the deli counter addressed Cassie. "I don't seem to see any...oh, wait here it is." She paused with a frown. "There's not much left in this bowl." She leaned closer to Cassie from behind the counter as if to impart some important secret. "Frankly, I don't think what's left of this lot is too fresh. I know Tom made up a new batch about a half-hour ago and stuck it in the fridge in the back. It'll take me just a few minutes to find where he put it."

Cassie glanced at her son as the woman retreated into the back room. Ignoring the sea creatures, he hardly blinked as the bubbles floated upward to burst. Enticing smells drew her attention to the prepared hot foods section at the far end of the deli counter. Mingled aromas of rotisserie chicken, barbeque beef, and pizza tempted further inspection. Before wandering down to choose what else to take home, Cassie again glanced at her son. He had not moved a muscle; it was safe to move fifteen feet away for a closer look.

"I'm sorry, ma'am," the returning woman said. "I thought Tom made up more seafood delight; he made shrimp salad. Would you like to try this instead? Let me give you a little sample."

She handed Cassie a tiny pink spoon with a dollop of salad to try. "So, what do you think? Do you like it?" the woman asked.

"It's quite good actually," Cassie acknowledged. "I'll take a small container of that and a small chicken from the hot foods to go."

A puzzled look crossed the deli woman's face. "Hey, didn't you come in with a little boy?"

"Yes, he's over by the..." Cassie turned and stopped short. There was no face smooshed against the glass tank. "Brian! Brian, where are you?" she called anxiously.

Leaving her cart, Cassie frantically scanned each aisle as she ran through Preston's searching and calling for her son. Five rows over, a mountain of cereal boxes littered the floor. Nestled in the midst of them, her son clawed the top of a bright yellow box, trying to open it. Kneeling beside Brian was a dark-haired man who seemed to be in his late twenties. Draped over the handle of his cart, which was parked just short of the cereal mountain, the young businessman's suit coat and silk tie were smeared with chocolate icing.

Dark eyes smiled at her as he laughed. "I've heard of a cookie monster before but this is the first time I've ever met a Cheerios monster. Is this little guy yours?" he asked, standing up. Despite slightly rumpled hair, it was apparent this handsome man took great care in his appearance. Just the top button of his tailored blue shirt was unbuttoned.

Cassie felt blood rushing to her cheeks. "Yes, I'm afraid he is. I'm so sorry about this mess, and oh, your coat! Please allow me to pay for the dry cleaning."

"Don't worry about it," he said, brushing it aside. "I've got three nephews; this isn't the first time I've had to take a suit in for cleaning from a little guy's handiwork."

Nervous embarrassment prodded Cassie to quickly kneel and begin to reshelve cereal boxes as she spoke. "I just took my eyes off him for a minute, I swear. I'm normally so careful to make sure he doesn't get away from me."

The young man knelt again to assist in the cleanup. "I'm sure you are," he said. "Like I said, my brother's got three kids; they're all under six years old. I know they can be fast."

Cassie reached for a box at the same time as the handsome stranger. She noticed his smile widen while he looked at her left hand. Self-conscious, she looked away back toward the jumbled pile.

"Perhaps I will take you up on that dry cleaning offer, though. That way I can get your address so I know where to bring the bill—or at the very least, maybe I can get your name." Tilting his head to the side and below hers, he looked up.

Shocked into meeting his eyes, she stammered, "Cassie. My name is Cassie Delaine."

"How about your son, what's his name? I tried to ask him but he wouldn't tell me."

Having ripped through the cardboard box, Brian held a fistful of Cheerios slightly above eye level, then stared at them as he let them drop. Before she could stop him, crunchy bits were scattered all over the aisle.

"Brian! Stop that!" she shouted removing the open box from his grasp. Then to the young man she said, "Oh, his name is Brian."

"So I gathered." Extending his hand for the youngster to shake, he said, "Hi Brian, my name is Jason Wright."

The child ignored the extended hand, scooped bits of cereal from the floor into his hands, and then let them rain on the floor once more.

"Well, I can see I didn't make much of an impression on him." Jason dropped his hand. "I hope I made a better one on you. Listen, I've really got to finish up and get home. But I'd like to give you a call sometime and maybe we could get to know each other in more amiable surroundings. Dinner, perhaps?"

"That'd be great," Cassie said, still in shock while she fished through her purse for a pen. Not finding any paper to write on, she ripped off the box top from the cereal and jotted down her phone number.

Box top in hand, Jason stood up again and chuckled. "This certainly has been one of the most unusual ways I've ever met someone." As he wheeled his cart away, he called out over his shoulder, "Thanks for the intro, Brian."

Thank God for Maureen. Both Chris and Vicky already had plans for Friday night, but Maureen was available to watch Brian. That first dinner date with Jason had gone remarkably well, so well that he had asked to see her for an outing with Brian on Sunday. Cassie stuffed the backpack with an assortment of small toys, snacks, and drinks to help occupy her son should he become bored while they were—well, wherever they were going. Despite pleas from Cassie to elaborate, a surprise outdoor adventure was all Jason would say. She explained that Brian was uncomfortable when he didn't know what was going to happen. So Jason had told her to bring along a ball and tell Brian they would play catch.

Memories of the fiasco with Ted concerned Cassie, yet somehow she was confident things would go more smoothly with Jason. Brian's diagnosis had not been fully explained to him, but hints she dropped about his peculiarities only seemed to entice her date to know more.

She paced while mentally ticking off a checklist. "Have I forgotten anything?" she said aloud. "Of course, how stupid of me: the ball!" She rummaged through a toy box and produced a small red rubber ball. Thinking twice, she tossed it back into the box and instead retrieved one made of bright yellow foam. Turning to her son she said, "It won't hurt so much if you miss catching this one." With that the doorbell rang.

"Hi Cassie. Hey, Brian, are you ready to go?" Jason asked. Dressed comfortably in a golf shirt paired with khakis, he looked as if he had just stepped out of a magazine ad.

"I hope Brian won't do too much damage to your clothes this time wherever we're going," Cassie remarked.

"The manufacturer assures these are stain resistant," James laughed. "Shall we go and see if they stand up to the Brian test?"

"Okay, but you've been forewarned about my little tornado. I'm not paying the cleaning costs this time," Cassie teased back. "I think I've got whatever I need for our mysterious outing, but if you don't mind can we take my car? It would be a pain transferring the car seat and Brian does so much better if he's in familiar surroundings."

"Sure, but only if I can drive. You're not getting the location out of me that easily."

She led Jason to the Mercedes parked in the garage, casually tossed her backpack on the floor of the backseat and buckled her son in.

"Nice set of wheels!" Jason whistled. "What exactly did you say you do for a living?"

"I didn't," she replied. "Besides, the car is, well, after both my parents died in a car accident I got a small inheritance."

"Small, huh? I only hope I get such a small inheritance someday." Seeing a frown creep onto Cassie's face, he thought better of his insensitive comment. "I'm sorry, Cassie. I shouldn't have said that. It must have been tough on you to lose both your parents at the same time."

"You have no idea how hard it's been," she admitted as she tossed the keys to him.

Jason transferred a small cooler, a blanket and a grocery bag from his own vehicle to the trunk of the Mercedes. After starting the ignition he asked, "How old was Brian when your folks..."

"They died before he was born. In fact I didn't even know I was pregnant when they were killed." Her eyes began to cloud with tears; she still missed them more than she wanted to admit.

Jason put a sympathetic hand on her arm. "I'm sorry, Cassie. I'm not doing such a good job of starting this fun adventure on a happy note, am I? Can we start again?" He cheerfully gave two quick light taps on the horn and said, "Let's see where the yellow brick road takes us, shall we?" And with that he effortlessly guided conversation and the Mercedes away from the everyday.

As they drove, his playful banter distracted Cassie from the uneasiness of not knowing their destination. Past Sweetwater Mall, Bennett Park, and every other potential destination she could have guessed, her auto sped happily onward. Blurs of fiery orange daylilies brightened the winding, tree-lined road. It had been quite some time since she had driven this far from town, but the road was not unfamiliar.

Vaguely she became aware that just beyond the dense trees, the river raced parallel to the road. Her pulse quickened and her palms began to sweat. It became difficult to focus on what Jason was saying, yet he babbled on with getting-to-know-you small talk.

"Have you ever been to a pro football game? Or do sports not interest you?" he asked.

Jason steered the Mercedes ever onward. At several points the river was visible from the road and then veered away from view, but Cassie knew it wasn't far beyond the veil of trees. Not wanting to focus on the view out her window, she turned toward Jason's profile. Neatly trimmed hair and clean-shaven face made him look refined even when dressed casually. His haunting dark eyes enchanted her. He stole a quick look at Cassie then back to the road.

Swallowing hard to calm herself she managed to reply, "We never went to a pro game, but occasionally my dad and I watched them on TV. And of course I cheered my friends on at high school games."

His melodic voice made her hang on every word as he recounted a childhood tale. "I couldn't get enough football when I was a kid. Somewhere in my parents' attic there's a shoebox full of trading cards, if my mother hasn't thrown them out. Anyway, my father took me to see the Eagles and Redskins once; it was for my twelfth birthday. Before we left for the game, my mother told me a dozen times to be on my best behavior because the tickets cost a small fortune. I'll never forget that day. We piled onto a bus loaded with guys yelling and screaming all the typical things loyal fans do. I felt so grown up; I was the only kid on the bus and they treated me like I was one of the guys." Jason chuckled, "I remembered to be on my best behavior like my mother told me, but...well, let's just say I learned a few new colorful words at the stadium."

Remembrances of her own father's passion for the sport temporarily distracted Cassie. Sitting on the sofa's edge, her father often yelled at the inanimate television as if somehow there would be a response. Carl Delaine emphatically explained why the ref needed new glasses. Despite not understanding the chess-like rules, she had enjoyed bonding with her father while watching those games.

Nostalgia quickly gave way to the present and her uneasy feelings returned as Jason turned her Mercedes into a small, stone-cluttered clearing. The tires crunched noisily over countless pebbles begging to be tossed into the river a short walk away. Cassie had not been back to this spot since that day she dared not forget. Fear that Jason had somehow read the chapters of her heart caused blood to rush to her cheeks. If that were the case, he feigned ignorance of her guilty recollections as he unbuckled his seat belt.

"Well, this is it, Cassie; this is the secret place my dad and I would go fishing," Jason confided. "After we eat the picnic lunch I brought, I think Brian will have fun down by the river. There is an old abandoned dock…"

"Ohnz! Ohnz!" Brian yelled excitedly.

"What's he saying?" Jason asked.

"Stones," Cassie replied quietly. "He is asking for stones to toss into the river."

"He's been here before? Aw, I was hoping—well, I guess it's silly to think no one else knows about this place."

Gathering her composure, Cassie realized she also was foolish to imagine he could know about her experience here. "It's been a long time since I brought him here. I know he's going to have a great time; it was so thoughtful of you to plan such a nice day with Brian in mind. I don't think he'll be able to wait until after we eat to play, though."

"No problem. Lunch will keep for a little bit. Why don't you grab your backpack and head over to the dock with Brian? I'll get the stuff out of the trunk and bring it over."

As soon as the child was loosened from car seat straps, his energy exploded, propelling him full speed toward the river. His mother dashed after him, now worried an event once wished for would occur.

Pausing only momentarily to gather stones, Brian stopped just inches shy of the dock's end before flinging pebbles into the flow. Close to one full year since they were last here, but it might as well have been just yesterday in her son's eyes. He dashed back, gathered more stones, then, exactly retracing his path to the dock's end, heaved a half-dozen at once, delighting at the ever-widening ripples.

Amused by her son's mirth, Cassie relaxed. She slipped her shoes off and dangled her legs over the edge of the dock. Her eyes slowly panned from left to right. So much had happened since that perilous day, yet the scene before them was virtually unchanged. Tall trees continued their silent watch over occasional human intrusions, their graceful limbs dipping leafy fingers in the passing cool water. The only difference seemed to be the pace of the flow. Perhaps, the last time had seemed more ominous due to the rain induced frantic rush. Now, it gently meandered from one bend to the next.

Brian showed no sign that this was at all different to him. Again he raced to gather more pebbles, returned to the edge, and then flung his treasures into the deep.

Sounds of the cooler and the bag being dropped on the ground drew her attention to Jason. He prepared to set up the feast a few feet from the base of the dock.

"Can I do anything?" Cassie asked.

"Just help me spread out the blanket if you don't mind. I can handle the rest."

Grabbing two corners while Jason held the others, Cassie shook the blanket open and crouched to place it neatly on the ground. Jason set the cooler and grocery sack in the center. Poking out of the bag was a familiar big yellow box.

Cassie laughed as she pulled it out. "You certainly thought of everything, didn't you?"

"I couldn't forget to bring the most important thing to our picnic! After all if it weren't for Cheerios, we might not have met."

A little more seriously, Cassie continued, "It really is sweet and I must say a bit surprising the way you've taken to Brian. You don't know what it means to me. Thanks."

Jason shrugged and continued unloading the bag. "No big deal. Like I told you before, I like kids. It seems I'm always around them. My brother has three and my next-door neighbor has five. When I don't get home too late, they're always pestering me to toss the football around with them." Jason smiled pensively. "When I was in junior high my aunt and her two toddlers lived with us during her divorce. I practically raised Blair and Christy. Even after Aunt Cheryl moved out, I still watched them after school while she was at work."

"Still, it's different with Brian," Cassie countered. "You must have noticed by now that he is not, well he's..."

"Special? Yes, of course I noticed. Do you mind my asking what his disability is?"

"Autism."

"I thought that might be it," Jason admitted. "One of the women at work has a son with autism. Sometimes she works from home. She has trouble arranging day care on their school's in-service days. From time to time I've dropped paperwork off at her house, and I met her son a few times."

Surprised Cassie said, "You knew and you still decided to go out with me? Most times when a guy finds out I never hear from him again."

"Your heart doesn't always give your head a choice in which direction it leads you. Even if it did, I probably would have chosen to go out with you. You're smart, pretty, and kind. And I get a kick out of Brian; he makes me laugh." Jason finished arranging the containers of food on the blanket then fished a final item out of the bag. Holding up a bottle of hand sanitizer he exclaimed, "See, I know what I'm doing; I come prepared. Why don't you see if Brian is ready to eat? We can clean his hands up with this."

"It will be tough to distract his attention from the river," she explained, still reeling from the compliments. "But maybe this will help." Noisily shaking the Cheerios box that Jason had brought, Cassie called out to her son. "Brian! Look, Brian, Cheerios!"

Apparently the child was hungry. He kicked up a cloud of dirt as he raced over to plop on the blanket. His mother squirted sanitizer into his grubby paws and rubbed them together.

Writhing in distress the child fought having his hands in contact with the goo. Moments later though, his clean hands shoveled mouthfuls of his favorite cereal into his eager mouth.

Content that her son was now occupied, Cassie surveyed the array of food before her. Melon cubes, grapes, strawberries, and pineapple had been artfully arranged on a tray from Preston's Market. Little chunks of cheeses and meats were surrounded by three kinds of crackers on another. A small basket contained slices of French bread.

Jason opened the cooler to retrieve a juice bottle for Brian. Next, he produced a chilled bottle of chardonnay and two plastic wine flutes. "I figured with Brian here it would be safer to use plastic," Jason explained.

"You certainly did think of everything," Cassie complimented.

Brian made happy moaning sounds in between mouthfuls of cereal. He rocked back and forth while eating. With a deathlike grip he clutched a Matchbox vehicle in his left fist. Jason and Cassie leisurely sipped their wine as they ate. Allowing herself to relax with this rather remarkable man was easier than she could have imagined. Not only was he attentive with her, but somehow he seemed in tune with Brian's needs and was unflustered by behaviors others may have seen as bizarre.

"It looks like your son is slowing down," Jason said. "If he's full, maybe I can get him to play ball before he takes off back to the river. Where's the ball?"

Cassie handed it to him. Instead of tossing the foam sphere at the child, Jason called Brian's name and gently rolled the ball along the blanket. Brian picked it up and squished it tightly.

Jason urged the child to roll it back, but the boy still clung to the toy. "Cassie, why don't you sit behind him and when he relaxes his grip guide his hand to roll it back to me?"

Surprised, she complied and asked, "How did you know about that? That's the kind of thing his teacher does with him."

"Well, I guess I have to admit this is not the first time I've been around a child like Brian." After calling Brian's name again to gain his wandering attention Jason rolled the ball back. "When I was about eight, a boy who acted a lot like your son moved next door. I don't know if he had autism or not, but he definitely had mental retardation. He was a few years older than me but acted a whole lot younger. My mother insisted I play with him for at least a half-hour every day that summer."

Briefly it seemed Jason's mind was lost in recollection. "I resented it at first. I wanted to play with my friends from school. Mike, that was his name, had trouble understanding how to play with me. His mother showed me how to roll the ball like we're doing now. Eventually, she stopped guiding his hand and in a few days she totally left us alone to play together. It started out being kind of a chore, but by the end of summer I looked forward to my time with him. "

After a few more volleys, Brian tired of the game and darted to the end of the dock with more stones. Jason refilled their wine glasses and handed Cassie's back to her.

Watching pebbles sail through the air, Jason thoughtfully continued. "I guess my time with Mike made me realize that just because someone has a mental disability doesn't mean they can't do anything. I remember a few weeks into the summer, as I was getting used to Mike, I told my mother that I felt sorry for him. She told me that people with challenges—that's what she said, challenges—don't need our pity. Pity doesn't do anybody any good. She said they need our understanding and when asked for, our help. She said it was okay to offer help but not to automatically jump in and do something for somebody without asking first. There's a sense of pride in being able to do something by yourself. Mike showed me lots of ways to help him learn to do things on his own over that summer."

Cassie sipped her wine, at first unsure if it was wise to press further explanation. Jason seemed willing to be candid so she asked, "Just that summer? Whatever happened to Mike?"

"My dad got a new job that October and we had to move. I lost touch with him after that. You know how kids are; I got busy myself trying to fit in at my new school. Besides, I knew Mike couldn't read if I wrote to him. I guess his mom could have read letters to him if I had written but, well, I just didn't. Anyway, I'll never forget Mike. Somehow I think I'm the one who gained the most from that experience."

Genuinely pleased at his insight, Cassie reached for his hand. "I guess I'm lucky that you met Mike. Maybe you wouldn't have bothered with Brian or me if you hadn't."

"I don't know, maybe, maybe not. It's hard to imagine how different you would be as a person if you didn't have certain experiences. I like to think that I would still be a kind person and sensitive to other's needs, but who knows?"

Jason drained the last drop of wine from his glass and surveyed the remnants of their picnic. He had bought far more than two people could comfortably eat in one meal; half-full trays needed to be rewrapped and returned to the cooler. Stray Cheerios were scattered on the blanket where Brian had been sitting. The hungry toddler had managed to spill nearly as much on the blanket as he had shoved into his mouth.

"Why don't you go keep an eye on your son; I'll clean up here," Jason offered.

Satiated by the gourmet picnic and serenely contented by the conversation, Cassie strolled over to where her son dug his grubby fingers into the dirt mining for more missiles to fling. Brian dashed to the end of the dock with his mother following close behind. Both his tiny hands heaved their contents into the water. Sparkles of reflected sunlight danced on the surface in response. But the little boy raced back down the dock for more without taking time to notice the results of plopping his treasures into the gentle water. A sense of purpose drove the child to repeat his motions again and again.

Despite her child's frantic mission, Cassie allowed herself to breathe contentedly. She didn't wonder tensely what her new companion thought of the strange singsong noises Brian made as he raced happily back and forth. Instead, she dared hope.

Hope: that was a word that hadn't seemed real for a long time. Was it possible? Could there be a happy relationship in her future? She stared up at the umbrella of trees lining the bank and resolved to banish thoughts about the future; instead, she concentrated on enjoying this moment now for what it held.

Turning her attention back to the car, she noticed Jason toss a handful of oat circles to some curious ducks that had waddled near his blanket. After he deposited the last picnic item into the Mercedes' trunk, Jason stooped to gather some stones and joined the pair at the end of the dock.

"Brian. Watch," he said as he took a flat stone and skillfully skimmed it across the water. Like a frog hastily leaping from one lily pad to another, the stone skipped several times before sinking.

Brian had appeared to be looking in another direction when Jason skimmed the stone; at least that is what a casual observer might have thought. But the child had carefully watched out of the corner of his eye.

Again Jason skimmed a stone across the river while Brian appeared not to see. Jason straightened up, stuck his hands in his pockets, and admired the view. The little boy heaved his pebbles into the water and watched them sink. Then he grabbed Jason's pant leg and pulled him back toward the pebble laden dirt patch. Once there, Brian pulled on Jason's hand attempting to make him gather stones. Jason complied, and all sense of time faded away as Cassie watched this kind man repeatedly gather flat smooth stones and skip them for her son.

Chapter 20.

Sunlight streaming through the family room window begged Saturday afternoon chores to be put on hold. After Cassie finished her lunch, she would take Brian to Bennett Park. He had loved it when two Saturdays ago, Jason pushed him on the playground swings, while Little League teams practiced on the adjacent ball field.

Now, wind-up timer in hand, Cassie walked over to where Brian was seated tossing a toy Cadillac onto a jeep. Stooping down to his level, she gently guided his chin upward to match her gaze. "Brian, when the timer goes off, Mommy's turn with the TV. And when the clock chimes, we're going bye-bye to the park."

Relinquishing the remote to his mother, the child dumped his vehicles into a big pile in front of him. Although he still did not like surrendering control of the screen, the use of a timer had made transitions from one activity to another easier.

Brian understood the passage of time much better now through a variety of methods. It had taken several months to get to the point that he was now; still the improvement was worth the hard work.

Even bedtime was a breeze now. Initially, enforcing the routine had been difficult. The first night had been the hardest. She'd had to repeatedly return him to his bed and actually had to sit in his doorway to prevent him from escaping downstairs to the family room. The second and third nights were a little easier. Progressively it got better until occasionally, Brian would bring the timer to his mother when he sensed it was close to bedtime.

Cassie sat on the sofa and propped her feet up on the coffee table. Taking a bite of her tuna sandwich, she changed the channel to catch the noon news. Anchorwoman Sandra Mayfield's trim frame caused Cassie to put down the potato chip she was about to munch.

It's a good thing Jason doesn't know I used to have a figure like that, she thought to herself. Somehow, it felt as if she had known him all her life; the sight of the skinny newswoman reminded Cassie that it had only been a few months. Such a short time really, but already she couldn't imagine life without him. Perhaps the trip to the park after lunch would help take her mind off his absence. Jason was away on a business trip; otherwise, she would have invited him to go with them.

Thoughts about business made her feel slightly guilty. Occasionally Jason had asked about her employment but she had managed to bluff her way through with stories of a considerate employer, flexible work at home hours, and her "small" inheritance to supplement her income. As much as she thought she might love this man, it was still too early in their relationship to 'fess up to her considerable wealth.

"We have breaking news coming to you this noon; an exclusive live report from WTSM's Janie Lou Hudson on the scene at Bennett Park."

Startled, Cassie sat forward in her chair. An unsettling feeling grew with the realization that their intended outing was the location of this news story. Attempting to dispel the odd sensation she joked aloud, "Breaking news! Gee, Brian, for once something is breaking and you're not the one doing it."

The reporter's nasally voice, heavily laced with an edge of drama, eagerly began her report. "Thank you, Sandra. Behind me you can see the peaceful scene, so familiar to many residents of Sweetwater, has been marred by an unimaginable tragedy. Earlier this morning, parents were cheering on Wakeland's Hawks as they took on Caulfield's Eagles. All eyes had been riveted on eleven-year-old Wesley Sutter as he slid in to home plate tying up the score. The cheering was suddenly interrupted by the screech of tires from a florist delivery truck. The vehicle struck a nine-year-old special needs child. I have with me Mrs.

Doris Boxwell, who was an eyewitness. Mrs. Boxwell, could you tell us what you saw?"

The reporter thrust her microphone toward a stout woman with a ruddy complexion. Barely able to catch her breath she stammered nervously. "We...we were all watching the game. The little boy—his family always comes to all the games because his brother plays for the Hawks. He, the little boy, that is, is always running; such a bundle of energy. His mother usually watches him climb the jungle gym while the game goes on. His brother had just smacked the ball way out into leftfield. Out of the corner of my eye, I noticed the boy's mother running after him, but I didn't think anything of it. I was yelling for Wesley to slide as he ran to home plate from third. The next thing I knew I—I heard the squeal of tires and then that awful sound as the little boy got hit."

While the woman spoke, the camera panned the familiar field of emerald green grass and then to the street on its north border. Police vehicles with flashing lights rimmed the perimeter of the accident scene. A distraught driver stood outside the delivery van being questioned by an officer.

The camera cut back to the reporter, who donned her most convincing serious façade. "The nine-year-old was transported by Med Evac to St. Christopher's. There is no word on his condition at this point. Police are withholding the name of the child until extended family members can be notified." With a look begging for network notice, she concluded with, "Reporting from Bennett Park, this is Janie Lou Hudson. Now back to you, Sandra."

"Thank you, Janie. We'll have a complete live update on this story tonight on the early news at five. Next, we turn to Ethan Stickels at the scene of an overnight fire at Hooper's Glen. Ethan..."

Cassie took another bite of sandwich. She thought how awful it must be for that poor family and wondered what kind of disability the unnamed child had. The telephone interrupted her thoughts. After a quick swig of her cola, Cassie answered.

"My God, did you hear, Cassie?" Ginny's panicked voice was filled with anguish. "Did you hear about Carlos?"

Instant realization washed over her. The poor faceless, nameless, "special" child was Maria's son. Cassie trembled. "I just saw it on the news but I didn't know it was him. Oh, Jesus, poor Maria! Have you talked to her yet? How's she doing?"

"She must still be at the hospital. She was awfully shaken up. I'm still shaking myself; I was there! My next-door neighbor's son plays for the Hawks. Oh, Cassie, it was horrible. Maria was trying to get Carlos to go over to the bleachers so she could sit and watch Pablo play, but Carlos ran into the street right in front of that van. He never understood the concept of danger from moving vehicles. Oh God, it was...there was blood everywhere."

Ginny paused for a second trying to compose herself. "Listen, Cassie. Do you think you could call Kari and Ellen for me? I'm trying to get the group together to figure out what we can do for her. Whoever can make it; we'll meet at the church at one o'clock. Chris and Maureen agreed to watch our kids. There's got to be something we can do for Maria."

After calling the other women, Cassie hastily threw together a tote bag with anything Brian might need for a several hours. Bottles of juice and bags of cookies were tossed into a grocery sack for all the children to snack on. Quickly checking her wallet, she pulled several large bills out and shoved them into an envelope. It would likely be a long day stretching past dinnertime. The girls could order pizza for the kids. Brian didn't like pizza but they had watched him often enough by now to know to get French fries for him. Momentarily, she smiled, pleased at how adept she had become at anticipating potential problems and preparing for solutions in advance. She had come a long way this last year.

Brian seemed to feel the sense of urgency as they rushed out the door. Once buckled in his car seat, he began fussing, and he began to cry, "Paag, paag, paag," when his mother did not make the customary left turn toward their promised outing.

"I'm sorry, Brian," she apologized. "We will go to the park some other time. We are going to St. Vincent's to see Chris and Maureen." Brian continued to whimper, but not as vociferously. St. Vincent's was no longer a strange place to him but a familiar retreat for all the mothers and their children.

Pulling into the parking lot, Cassie spotted Kari hastily carrying Todd through the church's side door. Spotting the Mercedes, Maureen continued holding the door open for the Delaines as they rushed in. More noise than usual greeted their entrance as the halls echoed with children's groans and whining.

"I'm afraid they sense the turmoil you moms are feeling," Maureen suggested. "Particularly Danny, he knows this is not the right day to be coming here. Funny, some of the kids react as if nothing unusual at all is happening when there's a major event. It's like they are totally unaware of what is going on around them. And the others seem hypersensitive to the emotions others around them display. Danny gets really upset when he hears babies crying. When I help Ellen with him at the supermarket, if he sees a mom hollering at her own kids, he starts crying."

"I have a feeling we all are going to be doing some crying today," Cassie replied. "I heard on the car radio on the way over here that Carlos didn't make it."

Ginny entered just behind the Delaines. She confirmed, "Maria is going to need all the strength we can loan her as she plans the funeral."

Why did every funeral parlor smell the same? An answer became obvious as Cassie made her way into the room designated for the Regna family viewing. Overpowering perfume from floral bouquets engulfed the young boy's casket. Vivid memories of Carl and Amanda Delaine's funeral fought to overtake Cassie's resolve to remain strong for her friend. The women, bonded as sisters from their meetings at St. Vincent's, took their places in a long line waiting to offer condolences. Grieving black-clad relatives and friends filled every spare corner of the parlor.

Strangers, who only knew the boy was a "special" child, came to empathize. Maria's tormented wails became more discernable as the group edged closer.

"*Por qué Dios? Por qué Dios?*" Maria sobbed. Her cries were punctuated with utterances Cassie couldn't understand.

"I don't remember very much of my high school Spanish," Cassie whispered.

Dabbing a handkerchief at the corner of his eyes, the man in front of Cassie stifled his own tears and said, "She is crying out to God. She asks why; what has she done that God should punish her by ripping out her heart and crushing it beneath his feet."

Wails continued alternating back and forth between English and Spanish. Ginny reached Maria first and embraced her sobbing friend.

"My reason for living... Why him, God, why? My poor sweet little boy," Maria wept. "I loved him so much."

Kari's face showed a silent questioning look.

"What?" Maria screamed. "You think I didn't love him just because I complained about the shitty lot we were dealt? I loved Carlos. I hated his autism. I hated how hard it was for him, the way people gave him disapproving looks when he made strange noises, the trouble he had learning simple things, the frustration he must have felt not being able to tell me all that was on his heart. Life was never going to be easy for him, but he tried, I know he did. He was making progress—little things, but still progress. Carlos inspired his brother; Pablo wants to be a special education teacher to help other kids like him."

Cassie grasped Maria's hands. With love in her voice, through her own tears, she spoke. "At my parent's funeral, I couldn't imagine ever feeling such grief for anyone else's passing, but from the deepest part of my heart, I cry for you, Maria. You and these other women have become the family I no longer have. I just wish there were some way that I could lift some of your pain. If only there was something I could do for you, I would. After my mom and dad died, I remember friends being there for me, wanting to help, but nothing really could. Surrounded by loved ones, I was alone. And now, here I am...

desperately wanting to help, but knowing nothing I can say or do can diminish your pain."

They embraced, each heart longing to alleviate shared pain.

Then Cassie found a seat next to Ginny and waited for the others to join them. Silently she stared at the coffin. Carlos appeared to be dreaming. What dreams did that child have? How had his mind seen the world? Cassie knew so much more about autism now, yet how and what they thought about was still a mystery to her. Had the child been happy? She had seen him laugh and play, but she had also seen him cry from some unknown cause. His sweet face seemed at peace now. His face...

Cassie shook her head to clear the vision that was before her. Instead of Carlos, she saw Brian. Instinctively, she grasped her stone pendant and ran it back and forth along its gold chain. That could have been Brian in there a year ago. She could have been the one standing beside a tiny casket.

Silent tears streamed down her cheeks. Looking over, she saw Kari was openly weeping as well. The others would assume Cassie was crying for Maria. But Cassie's revelation caused her own tears. More so now than at any other time, she realized how much she loved her son, how devastated she would have been had her plot at the river been successful. She loved her son— that was all, nothing more, nothing less. He was, well, where do you begin the ways to describe him? But none of that mattered; Brian was her son. He had grown and changed so much in the last year or so, but he was, and always would be, autistic.

Somehow, that was okay now. Perhaps it was not Brian that had made the dramatic change; it was her. Each day that passed she had begun to appreciate every little crumb of progress as if it were the scaling of Mount Everest. He had potential. His life mattered. Reflecting on past meetings of her group, she knew she had seen that in the eyes of each of the other mothers. Despite complaints and problems, each one desperately loved her children. All of their conversations had been born from a desire to be the best parent they could be for these precious souls.

Cassie was unable to quiet her mind as the preacher spoke. How anyone could grant Maria the peace she needed was beyond her, but he endeavored to calm her grief with scripture and prayer. Maria seemed calmer, or at least quieter as he continued. But Cassie barely could keep still. All she wanted was to get home to Brian and hope he would tolerate the hugs she desperately wanted to give him.

After the service, she drove home and greeted Jason, who had returned the day before, with a kiss. Brian allowed her a temporary hug before pushing his mother away in favor of retrieving a Volkswagen beetle.

"Thanks for watching him for me," she said. "Could you give me a few minutes more? There's something I need to do."

"Of course," Jason replied.

Cassandra walked down the hall closing the door of her home office behind her. Impatiently, she waited for her computer to hum to life. Scrolling down her list of favorite Internet sites, she located the one for her checking account. Several mouse clicks later, she was satisfied her favorite autism charities would be pleased by substantial donations in memory of Carlos Regna.

She wiped one last tear from her eyes and returned to her family room. Jason handed her a glass and motioned for her to sit beside him on the sofa. Cassie nuzzled up next to him and silently sipped her wine.

Beyond the picture window, swirls of florescent pink, orange, and yellow collided into deepening hues of blue. Across the sky, the colors briefly danced once more before the velvet cover of night chased them to sleep.

Suddenly, her enjoyment of the peaceful sunset was interrupted by the familiar clinking of tiny vehicles raining out of a bucket and onto the floor. In the background a meteorologist droned on about a forming weather system over Guam. Reality snuck back into the room.

Cassie allowed her thoughts to be heard. "I used to imagine my life was like a Hollywood movie and wondered what category they would label my story."

Jason stroked her hair. "Real life isn't like that, Cassie. Most of us experience a little of everything in our lives: comedy, tragedy, romance, suspense...some of us even experience horror...and of course everyone's life is filled with lots of drama."

"Oh, I guess you're right," Cassie sighed. "I was just thinking about my fantasies when I was a child. In the storybooks I read, the heroine was a princess who came through the other side of adversity and then lived happily ever after: the end. I used to wonder whatever happened to my happy ending."

"Ah, but you've missed the point, Cassie, my dear," Jason said, smiling. "Listen to what you just said: happy ending. That's just it; it's the end, final, all done, no more. You're a grown woman now; you know life isn't like a child's fairy tale or a movie." He retrieved the bottle of wine from the coffee table and refilled their glasses. "Well, wait a minute, then again maybe it is. There's a beginning, a middle, and an end; you're born, you live, and then you die. I doubt you remember being born and hopefully it will be a long time before you die." Returning his arm around her shoulders, he looked into her eyes. "It's the middle of our stories that are important; it's how we live that matters. Instead of wishing for that happy ending, we have to try and focus on happily *living* now."

Ginny had said something similar to her once before; there was obviously truth in needing to appreciate the present.

Another waterfall of metal toy cars crashed onto the floor. Both adults paused momentarily to watch the familiar repetition of the blue Explorer following the black Toyota.

Staring at her son's apparent oblivion to their presence, Cassie said, "Sometimes that just doesn't seem possible. When life should have started to be a dream, everything fell apart. I miss my parents terribly; they were killed far too young. Then, of course, there's Brian. I want what's best for him but I worry. What does his future hold? Will he ever hold a job or live on his own?" She faced Jason then continued, "And frankly, I wonder about you and me. I think I'm falling in love with you. You've been great with Brian; you're so patient and understanding. But I'm afraid, well, let's be honest here; you're not his father. Sometimes it's hard enough for me to weather his tantrums and do this behavior management stuff, and I'm his mother. I fear that I'll lose you because of my son."

Jason hesitated slightly before answering. "Cass, you're a very special woman; I may even love you. In fact, I think I do. But it's too soon to make promises about our future together. Please trust me when I say that what ever happens between the two of us will be about us. Nobody has any guarantees that their children will be free of disabilities. Brian is a tough little guy at times; he's also lots of fun. I get a kick out of watching him pour those cars out over and over; he seems fascinated by every detail on each one. And I love the way he laughs hysterically at his own private jokes." Jason paused, looked over at Brian then back at Cassie. "Brian is special—and I mean that in a good way. He kind of reminds me of that necklace you're always wearing."

Somewhat defensive, unsure if somehow its true meaning had been revealed, she asked, "Just what do you mean by that?"

Laughing as he touched the pendant, he answered, "Unique, it's totally unique. Sure, lots of women wear pearls or diamonds around their necks. But this...this isn't like anything else I've ever seen and it intrigues me. I like to examine every aspect of it when you don't think I'm looking; it seems to change as you move. I wonder about the story behind it, but I am satisfied just to marvel in its special qualities."

Cassie interrupted him with a loving kiss. Yes, this man was a keeper.

Full Circle

Chapter 21.

Standing on a peaceful residential street in the neighboring town of Forrest Hills, Cassie glanced at her watch. A crack in the crystal made it difficult to tell time. When or how it had broken she couldn't quite remember, and a trip to the jewelers for repair was difficult to fit it into her schedule; life was so busy anymore. Energized by the conference she attended the week before, ideas buzzed in her head. She was anxious to share information with their growing support group and implement new strategies to help with Brian's ever-improving speech and behavior.

Before driving to Forrest Hills she had dropped off a donation of books and teaching materials she had purchased for Brian's school. After her visit here, she needed to pick up groceries; otherwise there wouldn't be an opportunity until after the meeting of Special Olympics volunteers. Maybe the watch repair could be squeezed in on Thursday after the governor's commission on people with disabilities or before Brian's after-school speech therapy.

Taking a deep breath to clear her mind, she vowed to banish all thoughts of her busy schedule and focus solely on the occupants of the split-level in front of her. Through the half-open upper window, Cassie heard the doorbell sound as she pressed the button. Looking up she noticed child safety bars had been installed over the window to prevent a fall.

A minute later, a Hispanic woman in her late twenties opened the door. Cassie couldn't help but think about poor Maria. Time passed so quickly; it was hard to believe it was more than three years since Carlos' funeral.

"Hi," she greeted the woman. "I'm Cassandra Delaine-Wright, but you can just call me Cassie. My friend Ginny Troppus asked me to stop by and see you."

The woman's puffy eyes announced that recent gut wrenching tears had been shed. Pushing locks of disheveled hair back from her face, she held the screen door open for Cassie to enter. "Yes, of course. She told me you'd be coming by. I'm sorry to keep you waiting. I'm Rita, please come in."

Climbing the few stairs to the upper level, Cassie was led to a sparsely furnished living room. In the center of the room a mesh playpen held a little girl with thick, curly, black hair. Dense lashes framed coal black eyes that were intensely focused on the child's own wiggling fingers.

Crouching down to child's level next to the playpen, Cassie attempted to gain the toddler's attention. "Hi." Then she rose and spoke to the child's mother. "She is absolutely beautiful! How old is she?"

"Twenty-two months. Her name is Anna. Please, have a seat." Rita directed her guest to a worn beige sofa. "Can I get you something to drink? A nice cold iced tea?"

"Please don't go to any trouble."

"No, it is no trouble at all. What can I get for you?"

Sensing it would be rude not to accept her hospitality, Cassie accepted. "Thank you. Iced tea would be just fine."

Moments later, Rita returned with a tray containing two glasses, a pitcher, and a plate of cookies. Previously there had been no indications that the toddler was aware of her surroundings, but her mother's return with cookies prompted her to scamper to the railing of the playpen and reach out in desperation while grunting an incomprehensible plea. Cookie in hand, the child dropped her diapered bottom onto the play yard's floor with a thud.

Rita placed the tray on the coffee table and sat on a loveseat opposite her visitor.

"I guess Ginny told you all about me and Anna."

"Some," Cassie admitted. "She said you've been having a difficult time since the diagnosis. I've been there, too; I know how devastating it can be. I have a little boy with autism."

"I'm still not sure I believe it," Rita said. "I mean, just look at her; she's such a good baby, never gives me any trouble. Not that I know that much about autism, but what little I had heard well, I always thought it happened to boys and that they were hyperactive, difficult children. Anna is a dream; she hardly ever cries." Soft, almost happy moans came from the contented cherub wiggling her fingers to the side of her face.

"I know it's difficult," Cassie began, "I used to have one picture of what I thought autism was, too. Slowly I've come to understand that autism can present in many different ways."

"I don't know, I just don't know." Unwelcome tears slipped down the corners of Rita's eyes. Dabbing her face dry with a napkin, she confessed, "I feel so alone. My mother doesn't understand. She says Anna is just a little slow, that she'll come around. It's years away, but she has already stared sewing lace on a dress for her first communion. I don't know, will she be able to do that?"

"Like you said; that is still years away. Who knows? I mean lots of religious groups have gotten pretty good about finding ways to include children with disabilities into their ceremonies and rituals."

"Children with disabilities," Rita vacantly echoed. "It's hard to hear those words and think of my own child in the same breath."

Cassie rose from the sofa and sat next to this new mother, cradling Rita's hands in her own. Intently gazing into a new sister's eyes, she said, "Listen. There is one thing I want you to be absolutely clear on. You are not alone. Our support group is filled with mothers just like you. We've all felt the pain. None of our stories are exactly the same but they are so similar you'll feel an instant bond. And there is the local chapter of the Autism Society. I met lots of fathers there, too. When your husband is ready, he can meet some of them. And there are families all across the country, even all across the world, that are newly hearing the term *autism* associated with their children. You are not alone."

Drawing a jewelry box from her pocket, Cassie continued. "I almost forgot. I brought a present for you."

Rita opened the box and took out a lovely gold chain with a unique pendant suspended from it. Intricately twisted gold encased a tiny colored stone. Confused as to its meaning, Rita nonetheless graciously thanked her guest.

"I had this made for you," Cassie explained. "It's similar to one that I wear. It's not a diamond or an emerald. It's not a ruby, a sapphire or even a cubic zirconia; it's just a pebble. In fact, I'm not even sure what kind of stone it is. You see, when we give birth to a child, we have all these visions of what we think they will be. They are our precious jewels. Then mothers like you and like me find out that our children are not quite the way we thought they were. When you are hoping for a diamond and you get a plain rock, at first there is disappointment; you feel gypped. But look closely, it's rather pretty, don't you think? When I first found it, the stone was buried in mud. I cleaned it up as best I could; that helped a lot. I was able to see some potential: colors and some sparkle. Then I got some help; the jeweler polished it up nicely and created a special setting to highlight its special beauty."

Rita took the pendant, holding up to the light to admire it, and Cassie continued.

"In time perhaps you'll find that even though this is not a diamond, you will treasure this stone. Not everyone will recognize its value; they don't all slow down and take a close look."

Cassie paused and with a smile gently stroked the gold wedding-band on her left hand. "But others do. The pebble—its beauty is there; it's just different. It took me a little while to realize this, but your child and mine may not be what we originally hoped for, but they are their own kind of precious stones, to be cherished...to be loved...to be polished."

LaVergne, TN USA
22 February 2010
173895LV00007B/88/P